LAST WITNESS

ALSO BY STAN WILCZEK JR.

The Kept Secret

The Soma Man

Death's Revenge

LAST WITNESS

Stan Wilczek Jr.

Pyramid Publishing Inc.
Utica, New York

This book is a work of fiction. Certain real locations and public figures are mentioned, but all other names, characters, places, and incidences are either a product of the author's imagination or are used fictitiously. Any resemblance to actual persons, living or dead, businesses, companies, organizations, events, or locales is entirely coincidental.

Printed in the United States of America

First Printing: October 2013
10 9 8 7 6 5 4 3 2 1

ISBN 978-1-886166-38-7

Library of Congress Cataloging-in-Publication Data

Wilczek, Stan.
Last witness / By Stan Wilczek Jr.
pages cm
ISBN 978-1-886166-38-7 (alk. paper)
1. Kennedy, John F. (John Fitzgerald), 1917-1963--Assassination--Fiction. 2. Witnesses--Fiction. I. Title.
PS3623.I534L37 2013
813'.6--dc23
2013026071

Pyramid Publishing Inc.
PO Box 8339
Utica, New York 13505

www.pyramidpublishing.com

For Rose

Every time I think it can't get any better . . .
You prove me wrong!

ACKNOWLEDGMENTS

Although I am publishing this novel a year after *Death's Revenge*, it has been years in the making. My shelf is packed with books, and files are full of articles, on the JFK assassination. I have been obsessed with the topic since that fateful day on November 22, 1963 when my sixth grade teacher, Mr. Furgal, walked into our classroom, visibly shaken, and delivered the news.

Many thanks to those of you who answered my questions on topics from Alzheimer's, to the assassination, to . . . well, you'll find out as you read on. A special thanks to Frank Baran for your detailed editorial comments and suggestions

A very special thanks to the staff at Pyramid Publishing, specifically Zach Steffen. None of this would happen without you.

To those who think you see yourself or others described in this book (you know who you are), let me assure you that you do not. Also, because this novel is totally fictitious, nothing in it is true, except of course for the parts that are!

Finally, I want to thank all of you who took the time to read and then provide me with such great feedback on *The Kept Secret*, *The Soma Man*, and *Death's Revenge*. I hope you again find this book clutched in your hands when you know you should be doing something else.

As a final note, any and all mistakes contained herein are mine.

LAST WITNESS

Prologue

November 22, 1963

The black Lincoln Continental was about to change from a limo to a hearse right before the four-year-old's eyes.

"Papa . . . I gotta pee."

"Reece, here comes the president."

"Where?" Even though he wasn't sure what a president was he stood up, ignoring the pain in his over-filled bladder, and stared at the approaching parade. Reece knew for days of the president's visit through stories from his father. However the only thing he could remember was the president was like a king, only he didn't wear a crown. As he balanced on his tiptoes he was again reminded of the hour-long drive to Dallas earlier this morning from his home in the prairie – he had to pee.

"Wow . . . motorcycles!" Reece looked up at his father who was standing next to him and pulled on his arm.

"Reece, stop it. I can't hold the camera steady with you pulling on me."

"But Papa, motorcycles. Police are riding them."

"Stop hitting me!"

"Can I take a picture of the motorcycles?"

"Yes . . . but be careful with my camera it's . . . "

"I know, I know . . . it's not a toy."

Reece picked up the thirty-five millimeter Pentax camera from the leather bag and placed the cloth strap around his neck. He reached down and brought the camera to his eye, just as the motorcycle passed in front of him, adjusted the focus on the lens like his father had taught him, and snapped the picture. He reached with his thumb, flipped the lever on the top of the camera to advance the film, and took a second picture of the policeman on the motorcycle.

"Reece, here comes the president."

Just as he snapped the third picture of the motorcycle, Reece jumped as the loud cracking noise echoed across the plaza.

"Oh boy . . . firecrackers."

"Reece, there's the president. Take his picture."

Before he could get the camera up to his eye and aimed at the black limo a second loud cracking noise startled him and his finger snapped a picture. Without thinking he advanced the film and aimed the camera at the car now directly in front of him. As his finger pressed the button on the camera several more loud noises again caused him to jump. He stared through the viewfinder and saw something red spray out of the car.

"REECE, GET DOWN!"

Before Reece could look up he felt his father falling on him crushing him to the grassy ground.

"Papa, you're hurting me."

Reece tried to push his father away.

"Papa . . . there's blood on my hands."

1

"Professor . . . is it true that . . . " – the longer than normal pause told Reece exactly what was coming next – "you were in Dealey Plaza when . . . when they killed the president?"

Reece continued to write on the whiteboard as he glanced down at his wristwatch. Fourteen minutes. Another record broken. It was just over twenty minutes before the previous seminar participants got up the nerve to ask that question. This was a lot sooner than the seminars conducted years ago. He smiled. So much for the theory that today's youth only speak their mind when hidden behind the clicking of their invisible digital walls.

Dealey Plaza. Fifty years ago. He had been there. Along with 417 other people – although the exact number, like it seemed everything else about the JFK assassination, may never really be known – who watched the most famous, the most documented, and the most witnessed murder of the twentieth century.

Ask anyone who was four years of age or older on that day, "Where were you when JFK was shot?" and they would likely still be able to tell you exactly where they were and what they were doing. But how many can say they were there, within twenty feet of the president, as the shots rang out. And how many can say their entire life had been shaped by those brief six seconds in Dealey Plaza. From the first seconds following the gunshots, to almost fifty years later.

Reece glanced at his watch again as he turned and faced the thirty pairs of eyes bearing down on him from the elevated classroom. “Who asked that question?” A young, very good-looking, petit, short-haired, blonde sitting in the front row raised her hand without hesitation. Reece glanced at the name card in front of her. “Ms. Dexter?” She nodded. “Yes . . . I was in Dealey Plaza. But as to whether ‘They’ killed the president, that’s what you are here to try to determine, isn’t it?”

2

Reece stood in the doorway staring at his mother staring out the window. He would give anything to know what she was thinking. And he would give more than anything if what she was thinking was real.

"Hi Mama," Reece said in a quiet voice as he tapped on the heavy, light oak, wooden door with the tip of his fingers.

Without turning around Dora Landis responded in a not so quiet voice, "Would that be my favorite son coming to visit his favorite mama?"

"Favorite son?"

Dora turned around. "Even though you are my only son, you can still be my favorite one, can't you?"

"And favorite mama?"

"Favorite mama sounds better than only mama."

"So does favorite son."

They walked toward each other, clasped hands, and leaned in to kiss.

"You had me concerned there for a second."

"Thinking you had a long-lost brother?"

"Thinking you were going to tell me you were not my real mama."

"But I've told you many times before that you were not my real son, so that shouldn't be a surprise to you."

"Not today though."

"No . . . not today."

Reece looked into his mother's eyes. "How are you doing today?"

"Today is a good day. At least I think it is a good day. That's the thing about Alzheimer's. I could be having the best day of my life and not even know it. Of course, I could also be having the worst day of my life and not know it. The disease does have its side benefits. By the way, who are you again?"

"Funny."

Reece made it a point to visit his mother at Loretto, a senior residential community in Syracuse, New York, at least three times a week. He had moved her there less than two years ago, first into independent senior housing, which lasted only six months – or until the third time Dora had wandered off and came to not knowing where she was – and then to a facility with twenty-four hour care and supervision.

Dora started exhibiting signs of Alzheimer's in her late sixties, although no one, including her, would admit it. When she turned seventy, however, the disease seemed to progress exponentially. Now at seventy-three, she did have good days and bad days. Unfortunately it was becoming more and more difficult to know if it was Dora who you were speaking to, or the disease that had taken over her mind.

"Didn't you start your JFK seminar this morning?"

"Yes I did. You remembered."

"How many years have you been doing this?"

"It's my twentieth year."

"Oh my Lord. How time flies. Are they still impressed that you actually witnessed the assassination?"

"To some extent I think so, but it certainly has a lot more meaning to your generation and mine than it does to today's youth."

"That's because we lived through that terrible time."

"True. But today's generation doesn't seem to be as interested as others were years ago. I read somewhere that if you asked the question 'How did JFK die?' the baby boomer would say he was assassinated in

Dallas, Texas, the Generation Xer would say in a plane crash off Martha's Vineyard, and the Generation Yer would type into their smart phone 'Who is JFK?'. Most of the participants are made up of this last generation."

"Well, that's one of the challenges of teaching college now-a-days. You can end up with three or more generations of students in your class. If you would have taught kindergarten like me, you wouldn't have that problem. But being a law professor at Syracuse University . . . well I guess that's a little more challenging than my job ever was."

"I don't know about that. I don't think I could deal with twenty-five five-year-olds. Although sometimes I think that is exactly who I am dealing with. I remember last semester when a student explained that she didn't have her homework because her dog had eaten her flash-drive. Funny, when I was a kid dogs ate paper. I wonder what it is about dogs and homework?"

"So how are your participants in this year's seminar?"

"Based on this morning's meeting, I'd say this year's seminar may be one of the better ones. They all appear to be Type A personalities and very motivated. Most of them are in their mid-twenties. Naïve, but along with that comes a questioning attitude with no preconceived biases. There is one older woman, I mean in her maybe mid to late thirties, and she has already passed the Bar. But she also has degrees in computer science and art and photography of all things. She must be a professional student."

"How much longer do you think you will be conducting this seminar?"

"What do you mean?"

"It's been fifty years. Are people still interested in the JFK assassination?"

"I still have a waiting list every year of people trying to get into this seminar, taught in the summer I might add. So that's one indication. Of course it doesn't hurt that anyone who participates in this seminar is pretty much guaranteed a job with any one of a hundred law firms around the country."

"You should be proud . . . it's a tribute to who you pick and how you work them. You're pre-screening the applicants for these firms."

"True, but I don't want people to participate just for the guarantee of a job. It bothers me that none of these people have lived through the event. And after twenty years of these summer sessions, we've almost run out of conspiracy theories to study."

"And you've disproved them all."

"Actually, the seminar participants disproved them all. I just facilitated the discussion. And that's the premise of the seminar. Let a young fresh set of eyes look at the evidence and come to a conclusion."

"And you are still fully funded?"

"The Foundation that funds it – my salary and expenses, a generous stipend for all participants, along with the tuition and room and board expenses – still pays in advance, every January first, so we can advertise and fill the seminar well before the summer semester starts."

"And the only thing they want from you is a final report of what the students found?"

"That's it . . . and of course my commitment to do it all again next year. Obviously I'm one of their selling points for the program. Probably attracts a better cohort of students. Doesn't matter how good I am or how good the seminar is . . . I was there. Regardless, I have enjoyed doing every one of them."

"And . . . I'm sure you will enjoy this one."

"I'm sure I will too. Hey, look at the time. I should be going." Reece walked over to his mother who was again staring out the window and kissed her on the cheek. She didn't move. "See you on Wednesday."

Reece turned and walked toward the door. Just as he reached it Dora said, "I know I probably shouldn't tell you this . . . but your father was here today. He is very proud of you."

Reece stopped, turned, and stared at his mother. She finally turned and looked him in the eye. "He also loves you very much and wishes his life with you could have been different. His whole life has been about protecting you and me you know." She wiped a tear from her cheek. "He said someday you would understand." She again turned and stared out the window.

Reece walked out of the room and down the hall. His eyes went blurry with tears. It wasn't the first time his mother had claimed to have seen and talked to his father, and he was certain it wouldn't be the last. The disease would make sure of that. He was also now certain that this was not as good a day as he had thought for her. He assumed it never was whenever she claimed to have seen and spoken to his father, since he died on November 22, 1963 – six hours after the president was assassinated.

3

"Tia?" Tia, texting three people at once on her smart phone, looked up at the woman who had interrupted her concentration. "Hi Tia, I'm Kayla."

"Hi Kayla . . . Tia Diaz." The women clasped each other's right hands as Kayla slid into the curved chair surrounding the round tabled booth.

"Kayla Dexter."

"O M G! You're the one who asked the question this morning."

"Somebody had to . . . I just figured, why not me?"

"You know what that means, don't you?"

"That's just a rumor that's been passed down from year to year. It's almost like all those conspiracies we are trying to disprove."

"Or prove!"

"Okay, or prove. But in this case I can't find any factual basis behind it. As I said, it's just a rumor."

"If it's just a rumor, why were you so quick to be the one to speak up?"

"Well . . . in case it isn't just a rumor . . . a girl can never be too prepared."

"You watch, you're gonna be his favorite one. The person who asks that question, 'Were you in Dealey Plaza?', becomes his favorite. And you just happen to sit in the front row. I suppose that was a coincidence?"

"Like I said, a girl can never be too prepared. Besides, as my mother used to say, 'I wouldn't throw him out of bed for eating crackers'. Would you?"

"No. But I think the more modern version of that saying is I wouldn't throw him out of bed for texting."

"Crackers, texting, what's the difference? I know I wouldn't throw Dr. Landis out of bed for . . . I'm not sure if there's anything? Am I right?"

"Maybe . . . maybe not. It doesn't matter anyway. You've already claimed that spot."

"But you do admit he's hot?"

"For an older man."

"Older men are more experienced."

"And you know this how?"

"Rumor."

"By the way you are blushing, I don't think it's by rumor."

"Okay then. Way too much information for having met only three minutes ago."

"You're right. Way too much information. But by the way you are blushing I have a feeling I'm going to know every juicy detail before this month is out." Tia then winked.

"So . . . where's the third member of our team?"

This morning's seminar concluded with an assignment to divide up the group into three-person teams. Each team would spend the afternoon getting to know each other and to start to lay out the next month's plan. Team six decided to meet at Citrus on the Hill, the bar located off the lobby of the Sheraton Syracuse University Hotel, the same hotel all seminar participants would call home for the next month.

"Good question. Our third teammate is R. Stone. Male or female . . . do you know?"

"I have no idea. That's one of the problems when you text someone you don't know. Digital communications can be sexless."

"Excuse me. You wouldn't happen to be team six, would you?"

"We sure would. I'm Tia Diaz." Tia reached over the table and shook hands.

"And I'm Kayla Dexter." Kayla replaced Tia's hand. "Come sit." She patted the couch-like seat next to her.

"Hi, I'm Rose Stone. Sorry I'm late. Lost track of time."

"No problem. We were just talking about how Kayla here is going to have sex with Dr. Landis."

"Were you the one who asked about . . . "

"Yes, that would be me."

"See . . . you've already made an impression on all of us. You no doubt made an impression on him too."

"I'm sure that's just a rumor. Anyway, I think he has a lady friend."

Kayla and Tia turned to Rose with that 'how do you know' look on their faces.

"I have a friend who works at the college. She told me . . . what?"

"Why would you even be curious?" Kayla asked.

"Probably for the same reason as you and every other woman in that room is curious. He's not married, never has been. He's gorgeous, especially for a fifty-four-year-old, although he looks like he is no older than forty. And, he's hot. It's just too bad he's not my type."

"And if you don't mind me asking," Tia butted in, "how old are you?" Rose just stared back at her. "I mean, you have to have a bachelors degree and either be pursuing or completed a law degree to be accepted into the program. None of us has a full time job. But if we do well, and get a good recommendation from Landis, we will. Everyone else in the room this morning appeared to be in their mid-twenties, and certainly no one looked older than thirty . . . except for maybe you. Oh, and that guy in the front."

"I don't think you look older than thirty," Kayla now butted in.

"You're right. I'm probably not the typical person who applies or gets selected for this program. I completed my undergraduate degree almost twenty years ago in art with a minor in photography. I also have an undergraduate degree in computer science and just passed the Bar. I worked for about fifteen years, but now I don't need to. My father and mother were killed in an automobile accident five years ago. I was their only child. So now I can afford not to work. My father was a lawyer. After he died I decided to fulfill his dream and be a lawyer, or at least become a lawyer. So that's what brings me here. And as you've probably already figured out, I'm in my forties . . . early forties."

"Regardless of our ages, I'm not sure how we ended up with an all female team and worse yet an all blonde female team, although I don't think we are all real blondes."

"Yeah . . . how are we ever going to be taken seriously?"

"We are going to do it by working harder than any other team here. We've got to come up with our own theories that no one else has thought about. Why don't we share what we've already come up with?"

"Sounds like a great idea to me."

The three of them spent the next three hours sharing their own thoughts and ideas, ones that in some cases they had each thought about for years, about the JFK assassination. By the end of the afternoon it was as if the three had known each other forever.

"I still don't think you look older than thirty."

"It doesn't matter how old I look, does it Kayla? I don't think I will be in competition with you for Landis. First, I don't plan on making a pass at the gorgeous doctor. As I said, he's not my type. Second, you asked the question. You are probably going to be his favorite." Rose slid out from behind the round table, took a step, and then turned around. "But before I go, I should let you in on a little secret. Some men prefer older women. They are much more experienced, and take my word for it . . . I am."

4

"I'm in the mood for you tonight."

"And what kind of mood would that be?"

"Whatever you want, I'll do. The choice is yours."

"You're gonna bottom."

"Did you wanna think about it?"

"I've have been thinking about it. Ever since we talked."

"Bad day, huh?"

"Tough day . . . emotionally tough day . . . frustrating too. And we might as well add depressing." Reece picked up his drink – Single Barrel JD, straight up – from the bar he was leaning on and, after sniffing the aroma of the room-temperature liquid, took a long, slow sip.

"I had a feeling from our conversation that you might be in the mood for a session. I also had a feeling that you might want to take your frustrations out on me."

"Oh you did?" He sipped his drink again, only this time longer.

"Uh-huh . . . and I got wet thinking about what you might do to me." She somehow slid her hand down her belly and into the skin-tight waistband of her jeans. Her face was expressionless as her fingers found what they were looking for and lingered for more than a moment. She slowly removed her hand and placed her soaked fingers first on his lips, gently rubbing the top then bottom one, before forcing them into his mouth. He bit down, closed his lips tight, and slowly moved his tongue between her fingers. Seconds later he loosened his teeth and she slowly pulled her fingers out from between his still tightened lips.

She reached down and picked up her large glass of Grey Goose and pink lemonade. She stirred the ice around with the same fingers that were a second ago in his mouth and took several long sips from the glass, all the while her eyes never left his. "I'll be back in fifteen minutes." She turned and slowly walked across the room to the open metal circular stairway, and then even more slowly strutted up the stairs, her high heels clinging loudly against each metal step, as she disappeared through the opening to the floor above.

What started off as a great day for Reece – the beginning of his annual summer seminar on the Conspiracy Theories Surrounding the JFK Assassination, which has always been the highlight of his year for the past nineteen – turned depressing as he walked out of the doorway of his mother's room. Outwardly she was the picture of health looking ten years younger than her actual age of seventy-three. And if you didn't know she had Alzheimer's, you would think she was a specimen of health on the inside too. She could carry on an intelligent conversation for hours, recalling the most minute details of a past event. The trouble was, unless you were familiar with the event she was talking about, you didn't know if what she was saying really happened or was something invented by the disease invading her mind.

What was even more frightening was that the disease seemed to be speeding up its assault. Reece felt as if his mother was being kidnapped right before his eyes, one body part at a time, and there was nothing he could do to stop it. And to make matters worse, it appeared to Reece that the disease was purposefully taunting him. It started six months ago with a simple sentence that somehow made its way into the middle of a conversation he was having with his mother. "You know your father loves you very much."

At first he wrote it off as a simple mistake – "loved" not "loves". In fact, the more he thought about it later, the more he was certain she had said "loved". He forgot about it, until three months later, when she said out of the blue, "You just missed your father." Only that one statement. No mention of it again for the remaining hour he was with her. Then a month later, then two weeks later, and now weekly there is another comment about his father – always doing things in the present – as if he were alive. And now less disguised. Not just a single sentence buried in the conversation – one you might miss if you were not listening carefully. But several sentences – a much more complete thought. And for the first time today preceded by, "I know I probably shouldn't tell you this," as if the still healthy side of her brain knows she shouldn't be sharing a secret, but the diseased side has taken over and makes her reveal it.

As he stood in the doorway of the room earlier today watching his mother stare out the window he wanted to run over to her and scream in her ear, "My father is dead . . . he's been dead for almost fifty years!" Instead he bit his tongue, turned, and walked out of the room. His racing heart and heavy breathing quickly combined with tearful eyes.

"Why is she doing this to me?" he cried out in anger when he got to his car. Then he realized it wasn't her – it was the disease. Why was the disease attacking him then? Wasn't it enough that it was devouring his mother?

On his drive home to his townhouse in Fayetteville, a village in the town of Dewitt, just east of Syracuse, he decided he needed to de-stress. Happy hour at one of his favorite local establishments, Shifty's, a bar located on Burnet Ave in Syracuse, seemed like the best place to go. An hour into several glasses of Jack and diets he received a call from his companion, although Meeka considered herself his woman, or more precisely, his only woman. After all, she had her own drawer, several changes of clothes in his closet, makeup and toiletries in the bathroom, and spent most, but not all, nights in his bed. The call was short. It didn't take Meeka long to figure out her man needed cheering up. And she also knew what an hour or two of a happy hour would do to him. He would want something when he got home, and she would be ready. As she sat at the bar in the playroom – although most people would just call it a den – on the ground floor of the townhouse fantasizing, she could feel herself get wet.

Reece felt his heart pound in his chest as he heard, faintly at first, but then grow louder with each step, her seven inch stiletto platforms as they clanged against the metal steps. The sound suddenly stopped. Reece looked around the room one last time to make sure everything was in place. The room was dimly lit by dozens of scattered candles and a small spotlight that shined down from the ceiling casting a round, four foot circle of light on the middle of the floor. The faint sound of rapper music, the kind that contained more profanity than a men's room wall, could be heard in the background. On the bar were his instruments as he liked to call them. This evening he thought he would only go with a few – a twenty-six inch riding crop with a two inch leather tail, an eighteen inch rubber slapper, and a pair of silver Japanese clover clips lay neatly spaced along the right front edge of the bar. Draped over the edge of the bar was a well worn, but very effective, twenty-four inch black leather flogger, tails slightly hardened from dried juices, both male and female.

"May I enter, Master?" Meeka's voice, slightly trembling with combined excitement and fear, echoed down the round opening of the stairwell.

Reece reached for his drink and emptied the last of the Jack into his mouth. He put his hand on his bare chest. He could feel his heart pounding. He could also feel the pounding in his crotch as the tight black leather pants he was wearing, the only thing he was wearing, held his throbbing rod from going stiff. He took a deep breath to try to calm himself. He didn't want her to know how excited he was, although after three years of role-playing with her, BDSM being one of the things she had taught him and she enjoyed the most, he knew she knew he was probably throbbing so hard he couldn't walk, or talk in a normal relaxed voice.

He took another deep breath. "Take your place."

Within seconds the clanging started again and slowly Meeka circled down the round staircase exposing first her platforms, then long black seamed stocking covered legs, black leather garter belt, and nothing else which exposed her perky 36D breasts with their dark pointed silver dollar sized nipples. She kept her head down as she slowly strutted – knowing what effect she was having on what she knew was his throbbing pole – to the circle of light, turned to face him, then kneeled, back straight, arms to her side, and head still bowed.

Reece walked over and stood in front of her, just out of the circle of light, but close enough that he knew she could smell the heated leather of his pants. "Are you ready to please me?"

"Yes, Master. I am ready to please you."

Reece again took in a slow deep breath. "Anything I want?"

"Anything," Meeka answered without hesitating.

"Assume the position against the bar."

Meeka stood up, head still bowed, walked over and leaned against the bar with her arms and legs stretched out straight and spread apart. It was a position she was very familiar with. She glanced to her right at the top of the bar to see what her master had in store for her. Her heart, already racing, pounded even harder when she saw what was there. She turned her gaze forward and closed her eyes, contemplating what he might do next. Her wait was short.

"AHHHH!" Her scream echoed through the room. It felt as if the rubber slapper had just taken a bite out of the cheeks of her ass. "He's going right to the bad shit . . . must have been a real bad day," Meeka mumbled to herself.

"What did you say?"

"I said . . . you're a sick sadistic prick!" and then she braced herself for what she knew was going to happen next.

5

"Mama . . . why does blood start off red, then turn black? And how come it looks blue under my skin?"

"Reece, keep your hands under the water and scrub harder with the soap. Oh Lord . . . you've got blood all over your dungarees. Get them off so I can wash them with your father's clothes."

"But Mama . . . where did the blood come from?"

"Honey, your papa cut himself when he fell on top of you."

"Mama . . . after the president's parade everyone started to run. Me and Papa ran to the car. Some people were crying. Why were they crying? What happened?"

"Honey, it's nothing for you to worry about. Why don't you go upstairs and take a nap. You must be tired after all the excitement."

"Mama . . . "

"What is it . . . "

"I . . . I peed my pants too."

"Carl, we need to get you to a doctor."

"No! I told you Dora . . . no doctor."

"But I don't have anything to clean the wound except soap and water."

"I'll go into town and get something."

"I don't want you driving. You've lost a lot of blood. I'll go."

"No! I don't want you going into town. Is Sage around? Maybe he can go."

"He is still out hunting. And if we don't leave for town soon, the drug store will be closed."

"Yes officer, can I help you?"

"I'm sorry to bother you ma'am. Does a Carl Landis live here?"

"Yes . . . he's my husband. Is something wrong?"

"Do you know if he was in Dealey Plaza earlier today?"

"Yes he was, but . . . "

"We found this name tag in the grass along the road where the president was shot."

"This is from his leather bag. It must have broken off."

"Can we speak with your husband?"

"He's not home right now . . . he's gone into town."

"There has been an accident."

"Oh my Lord . . . is he alright?

"I'm sorry . . . "

"NOOOOO!"

"No . . . no . . . no . . . "

"Babe."

"No . . . "

"Babe, wake up."

"NO!" Reece bolted up in bed and stared around the room.

"Reece, it's alright. You were dreaming." Meeka reached up and ran her fingers through the hair on the back of his head. "You are dripping wet with sweat. Are you okay?"

"Wow . . . I haven't had that dream in a long time." Reece laid back down.

"Do you want to talk about it?" Meeka moved toward him and draped her naked body over his side, then placed her hand on his chest.

"Not much to talk about really . . . it was the day my father died. He was killed in a freak car accident. I was in my bedroom, taking a nap I think, when the police came to the house and told my mom. Fifty years later and I can still remember the screams. It's been years since I had that dream. It used to haunt me as a kid. Man . . . what brought that on?"

"Maybe it was me screaming last night?" Meeka pushed her body more tightly into his and started to run her finger nails lightly over his chest.

"Did I . . . did I go too far with you last night?"

"Did I ask you to stop?"

"No . . . but then again you have never asked me to stop anytime I played with you. You do remember the safeword, don't you?"

"What safeword?" Meeka could feel his head turn toward her. "Of course I remember – yellow. As I recall . . . you never ask me to stop anytime I play with you either." She continued to rub him but her fingers drifted closer to his stomach.

"Did you enjoy it?"

"Did you?"

"Answer the question!"

"I guess I'm still bottoming for you." Her fingers moved further down his stomach. "Of course I enjoyed it. I've told you before. You are definitely the best, or I should say the worst, I've ever had."

"And will you ever tell me the truth about how you learned about . . . "

"You'll have to beat it out of me."

"I've tried."

"Mmmm . . . I know you have. I'm getting excited."

"Why . . . why do you . . . "

"Enjoy it so much?"

"You must have had a very experienced Master at one time."

"Not as experienced as you."

"Well . . . I've had a very experienced teacher."

"It can be . . . you can be very nasty . . . but I love it." Her fingers drifted down until they brushed along the edge of his pubic hair. "And . . . I enjoyed last night."

"I did kind 'a get into it last night, didn't I?"

"I would say you did. You really got into it. I mean a lot! You were like an animal. Insatiable."

"Well . . . I didn't want to disappoint you."

"Believe me, you didn't."

"Whenever I touched you, you were . . . "

"Dripping?"

"That would be a good adjective. That's how I . . . how I know . . . "

"That I enjoy it?"

"That you really enjoy it."

Meeka's fingers brushed through his pubic hair to the base of his shaft. She gripped him, slowly slid her hand toward the tip, hesitated for a moment, then slid back toward the base, only to repeat the process over again. "This was . . . was everywhere last night." Her strokes were now a little firmer and faster.

"Mmmm . . . that feels good."

She squeezed harder, slid her hand toward the tip, and held it there. "Speaking of being wet, someone else is dripping. I guess I'll just have to take care of that." She edged up, sucked on his nipple, nibbled and bit it, then continued down his body flicking her tongue on his skin until she found his dripping hole.

6

"Good morning."

"Good morning." Only about half of the group responded and most of them were low whispers with no eye contact.

"I said . . . GOOD MORNING!"

"GOOD MORNING!" Every one of the thirty pairs of eyes were now staring at him.

"That's more like it." Reece glanced across the room and eyed every student. "I would have to say that most of you probably enjoyed last evening a little too much. Show of hands – how many of you have a hangover?" Half the hands went up. "Keep your hands up. How many of you have a hangover and don't want me to know you have one?" Almost all of their hands were now in the air, and several people in the front row raised both of their hands, which made the entire group erupt in laughter. "As you know I have had a lot of experience teaching this seminar. And if there is one thing I have learned, it's always good to bring a new bottle of these to the second day to share with everyone." He reached into his briefcase, pulled out a red box, and walked over to the young man in the front row on the right side of the classroom first making sure to glance at his name card. He then held up the box so everyone could see the white letters – Tylenol. "Take two, or in your case Paul, maybe three, and pass it on to the person next to you. Please notice it is a five hundred tablet container so it should last at least a week." He handed the box to Paul. "Or . . . maybe not." He turned and walked to the center of the room, just in front of the whiteboard.

"While we wait for the coffee and drugs to kick-in, let's review what we covered yesterday and then I want you to share your team's thoughts and ideas regarding the assignment for today. Does that sound reasonable?"

"Yes." Again mostly whispers came from the group.

Reece stared back at them and placed his cupped hand to his ear.

"YES! YES! YES!" The entire group was again responding and looking at Reece.

"As I said yesterday, this is going to be a highly participative seminar. If you thought you were going to spend four weeks listening to me share what I know about the JFK assassination, you are wrong. It would take years, not weeks, for me to even begin to tell you what I know, and probably even longer to tell you what I've forgotten. And what would be accomplished by that anyway? What new insights would we uncover?"

He hesitated and glanced around the room. All eyes were on him so he spoke more softly. "You are a generation who has grown up with more tools and technology to help analyze and scrutinize data and evidence. You can do in hours what it took a similar team on the Warren Commission months to do – and you can do it better. You also have the advantage of almost fifty years of studies, and theories, and analyses, and conjectures, and hypotheses, and new evidence, and new data to analyze. It has been said that more words have been written about that day in Dallas than any other single day in human history. But, you have access to more and better technology – technology that didn't even exist ten years ago, let alone fifty years ago. You are the fresh set of eyes that may see something that no one else has. You will be the ones to share what you find out about the assassination with me. You see, regardless of all that I might know about the assassination, none of it can prove without a shadow of a doubt who killed the president. Was it Oswald alone who killed Kennedy as indicated in the Warren Commission Report and supported by hundreds of studies since then? Or was it one of a hundred or more other theories out there that people have come up with to indicate it either wasn't Oswald, or a more credible scenario that it was Oswald not working alone, either knowingly or unknowingly. If you are able to come up with a definitive, undisputable, and evidence-based answer to those questions, then you will have accomplished something that no one else for almost fifty years has been able to do.

"My question to you is – are you up to the task?"

"YES!" This time their response was both loud and in unison.

"I guess the caffeine has kicked in."

"And don't forget the drugs."

Reece, who had been pacing back and forth in front of the room went back to the lectern and glanced at his PC.

"I see that you have submitted your team make-ups. How did you make sure you randomized the process as I requested?"

Several students turned and looked at one of the men sitting in the center of the room. "I guess that would be for me to answer. We assigned a number to each student. Then I used a random number generator to pick three student names at a time until all ten teams were filled."

"Math major, Ryan?"

"Actually, a minor in statistics."

"Good job, Ryan. And why do you think we have ten teams of three?"

"Because three goes into thirty ten times," Kayla shouted out. The group erupted in laughter. "I'm not a math or statistics major." More laughter. "Actually, I believe you picked an odd number of participants so it would force us to come to a majority conclusion in our final reports. And I believe you picked a small team size so it would force each of us to fully participate in the process. If there is a slacker, you lose one third of your team. You may never complete the project, or I should say produce a quality product."

"Anyone have a different answer?" Everyone gazed around the room at each other but no one spoke up. "Excellent answer, Kayla. You were right on both counts. I want a report that comes to definitive conclusions and is thorough. In order for you to do that, your entire team is going to have to work, as you have already seen over the past four weeks you spent preparing for this seminar, very, very hard to achieve the stated objectives."

Reece walked back over to the lectern. "The next thing I asked you to think about was all the reading you did in preparation for this seminar. You were given access to, and asked to read, all of the prior reports that have been generated from the previous nineteen seminars. One hundred and ninety reports comprised of almost three million words, which translates to over eleven thousand pages, or the equivalent of about thirty-five novels. Obviously, no one expects you to remember everything you read. The purpose of exposing you to this information is to use it as a primer, although no one would say this is a small introduction, for your own work. These reports gave you both an idea of what has been done before, so you do not duplicate it, and what is expected in your final product.

"Yesterday I asked you to think about those reports and share something you thought was outside-the-box regarding who may have been responsible for the JFK assassination. Who would like to go first?" A dozen hands shot into the air.

"Yes . . . Tia."

"I was surprised to find that there was so much circumstantial evidence, especially with respect to motive, regarding the potential role of the vice president, Lyndon Johnson, in the assassination."

"What things were you aware of before you read these reports?"

"I know Johnson, a senator from Texas, was asked to be on the ticket as a VP candidate because it would help Kennedy win the south. And it appeared that is exactly what occurred. So you would think that Kennedy would be grateful to Johnson. But that doesn't appear to be the case. There was no love-lost on either side between Kennedy and

Johnson. And you can also throw JFK's brother Bobby into the equation. Johnson was more or less ignored by Kennedy, rarely being brought into any of the important issues on their plate. In fact in 1963, Johnson spent almost no alone time with JFK. I mean, we are talking only a few hours. I thought it was just because that's how the role of the VP is structured. Ask anyone to name the last five presidents and they can probably do so. Ask them to name the last five vice-presidents and they go blank. Unless they become president, no one remembers them."

"So what other things did you come across regarding this issue with Johnson?" A hand shot up in the middle of the room. "Yes, Richard."

"Johnson was a powerful man before he became vice president. He was in the house and senate for almost twenty-five years. He was the senate majority leader. He was still powerful in his home state of Texas – someone to be reckoned with.

"So you have to ask yourself why did he accept the vice-president position on the ticket to begin with? He must have known he was going to lose his power base. Of course, I don't think even he realized it would develop into such a hate-hate relationship between him and the Kennedys. But I believe he accepted the position because of the potential it had to propel him into the presidency in eight years, assuming JFK won two terms."

"But . . . didn't he suspect he wasn't going to have to wait even the eight years?"

"So, Morgan . . . Morgan Cooper, are you saying, even before Johnson accepted the vice presidency, he knew of a conspiracy to kill JFK?"

"No . . . I mean, yes. I mean, not exactly."

"Spoken like a true lawyer. I'm listening."

"Johnson was a student of government. He knew how the government worked and how its leaders ascended to the presidency. Only one sitting senator had ever been elected President. And although at the time Kennedy would have been the second, the odds were still small. No southerner had been elected President since before the Civil War, and with the escalating civil rights movement the odds were even less favorable. Therefore, his only path to the presidency was by becoming vice-president."

"And that meant he would have to wait his eight years, doesn't it?"

"There is evidence to suggest he thought he might not have to wait a full eight years to become president. I do not believe he knew of a specific plot to assassinate JFK. But he knew the odds were much better that he could ascend to the presidency from the powerless vice-president position. Ten vice-presidents had succeeded to the presidency, and seven of those had made it because the president had died in office. Therefore his odds at becoming president, while he was vice-president, were about one out of five. And he knew his odds were even better if he looked at the past hundred year time frame, one that was probably more representative of current times. Then his odds were better than one out of four.

"He rarely mentioned these odds, but several of his close confidants have come forward indicating he was well aware of them. Although we can't know for sure, it was probably the single most important reason why he accepted the vice-presidency.

"Again, he did not know of a specific plot to assassinate JFK. But he did feel the odds were quite high that something would happen and propel him to the presidency."

"Yes, Richard?"

"Unfortunately, by the summer of 1963 a lot of things had changed. He had not only lost his power, but others were gaining it. His hopes of being nominated for president post JFK in 1968 were fading. A more likely candidate was emerging. In fact rumors were circulating that JFK might replace Johnson on the ticket for the 1964 election. His replacement? His nemesis, the president's brother, Bobby Kennedy. In fact there was even speculation of a Kennedy dynasty – JFK, Bobby Kennedy, and the newly elected senator from Massachusetts, Edward Kennedy – twenty-four years of Kennedy presidencies.

"Johnson had to be worried. If he were thrown off the ticket, he had lost far too much power and no hope of ever regaining it."

"But, is there enough evidence to indite the Vice President as a conspirator in the assassination? Yes, William."

"Bill . . . "

"Let's get that name card changed, along with anyone else who likes to go by a different name than what is shown. You were saying, Bill."

"Although there is other, I will call it not even circumstantial but peculiar evidence to suggest Johnson's involvement, such as rushing the Warren Commission to come to a conclusion that a lone assassin killed JFK, in fifty years nothing has been found to directly link Johnson to the assassination."

"And that is essentially what has been concluded regarding Johnson's involvement in the assassination – he had none. What other out-of-the-box hypotheses did you find in the reports?" Now almost everyone's hands were in the air.

"Yes . . . Joseph . . . or is it Joe?"

"No, it's Joseph. Joseph Whitmore."

"Alright, Joseph."

"I found intriguing the hypothesis that JFK was assassinated to keep secret the fact that a nuclear warhead was left behind in Cuba following the Cuban Missile Crisis."

All at once almost everyone in the room either nodded in agreement, or started talking.

"Alright . . . quiet down please. One at a time . . . Joseph."

"The hypothesis was based on a novel written post-911, *The Kept Secret*, that there was a secret agreement negotiated among the US, Cuba, and the Soviets to keep a nuclear warhead on the island, under Castro's control, as a deterrent against the US ever invading the island again. JFK, along with others, were assassinated to keep the secret safe."

"And?"

"The report concluded that there was no direct evidence to either support or refute the hypothesis. More data would need to be gathered from

Soviet cold-war files to try to track uranium and plutonium production, warhead production, warhead shipments, and even warhead destruction following the breakup of the Soviet Union. An almost impossible task, even if the records existed."

"It was an interesting hypothesis, but the fatal flaw in the reasoning was if everyone who knew about the secret agreement were killed, how could the weapon be used as a deterrent? That is, it wouldn't be useful as a deterrent if I as an attacker didn't know Cuba had it." Reece could almost see their brains working to try to solve that conundrum.

"I'm glad to see that you all read the past reports. As you have surmised, there are many conspiracy theories regarding the assassination. Castro upset with The Bay of Pigs invasion and the CIA's attempts to assassinate him. The Mafia upset with the Kennedy's crackdown on organized crime. The war in Vietnam and the Military Industrial Complex that wanted to see it escalate. The growing Civil Right's movement and the southern extremists who despised how JFK was handling it. The Cold War and Communism. Parts of our own government, like the CIA, had its motives. Extremists like Oswald, and at least two others that we know of who already tried to assassinate Kennedy during the previous three years. And even the sexual escapades by JFK himself create their own motives.

"And I can go on and on, but I won't. After almost fifty years of analyzing motives, it's time to put another set of fresh eyes to look at this issue. Your eyes . . . and brains. Was someone else involved in the assassination? Was there a conspiracy? Because, if there wasn't, why within the first seconds of the shots being fired in Dallas did so many people already believe there was?"

7

He knew the human mind was programmed to remember a face. Walk into a crowded room of strangers and as you gaze across it you will recognize a face not seen in twenty years. Of course the facial recognition part is easy, probably because that part of the brain developed eons before we could speak or assign names to things. It is the who, what, when, and where of the face that our brain usually fails us. "Damn evolution," Reece said as he walked down the hall to his mother's room. At least that's what he was blaming for not being able to place where he had seen the face before or who it even belonged to.

Just seconds ago, as he was heading down the curved, well landscaped concrete walkway leading from the parking lot to his mother's building at Loretto, his eyes locked onto the face of the man walking toward him. With his head tilted slightly forward and eyes focused on the sidewalk in front of him, Reece thought the stranger might be just that, a stranger. But as the two were almost side by side the man glanced up at Reece's face, and their eyes met for only a moment, before they passed. Reece's brain was spinning. He glanced back to see that the man was now walking more briskly toward the parking lot. Had he waited a moment longer before turning back, he would have seen the man glancing back at him too.

8

"At least we've made some progress." Tia finally broke the silence that had lasted far too long following the very heated discussion that just took place among them. "We've got it down to just three possible scenarios."

"We've been at this for six hours . . . I don't know about you guys but I'm beat." Kayla got up from the chair, walked over to the small refrigerator that was tucked under the built-in corner desk, opened it, and grabbed a cold can of diet Coke. "Anybody else want anything?"

"The same."

"Water please."

"Tia's right. Don't forget we started out with thirteen. We've got it down to three. I think the reason why we are having so much trouble trying to decide is they are all great topics. I'm sure with any one we picked, we'd be happy with it." Rose reached out as Kayla handed her the can of diet. "Thanks."

Kayla sat back down at the round table located near the window of the hotel room. Each of the thirty seminar participants had their own room in the Sheraton Syracuse University Hotel, which was located on the 'hill' of the Syracuse University campus. The rooms, each with a king-sized bed, had plenty of space for a round conference table and chairs where the second of what would normally be two queen beds would be located. The team decided they would rotate their meetings to each other's rooms on a weekly basis. The decision to do so was a good one, since just six hours into their very first meeting the walls of the room were already plastered with large poster paper covered with notes written in different colors and dozens of yellow Post-it notes of various sizes stuck on them. Rose had volunteered her room for the first week, but it was becoming clear to her that it might get extended since the posters could become a more permanent fixture, making it difficult to move to the next room without upsetting the thought process unfolding before them on the walls.

"Let's go over the three proposed topics one more time." Kayla glanced back and forth at the other two women.

"Let's do it."

"Go for it."

"Should we order a pizza?"

"No! If we get food, we'll be here all night. If we get hungry, we'll want to end sooner."

"I like your reasoning, Rose."

"Okay then. Let's look at the first one." Tia stood up and walked over to one of the posters hanging on the wall near the bed. "Can we implicate the government, in this case either the CIA or FBI, in the assassination? What do we know and what might be missing from the evidence we have?"

"We know that the FBI opened a file on Oswald in 1959 when he defected to the Soviet Union, which by the way, was very unusual for a U.S. Marine to do."

"You know who else opened a file on him in 1959 . . . the KGB. Rumor has it that they have a five foot thick, six volume file on all of his activities for the three years he was in the Soviet Union."

"Can we get access to it?"

"No way. It's never been released. The day JFK died and Oswald's name came up, the entire file was flown from Minsk, where Oswald lived, to Moscow. It's kept under lock and key. Eight declassified KGB documents were released to President Clinton during a G7 Summit in 1999. Obviously it was only a small fraction of what they supposedly have on him and nothing of importance. They have promised for years to release the documents. Except for the 1999 release nothing has ever happened. And my guess is it never will as long as Putin, an ex-KGB leader, is around.

"Anyway, in 1959 . . . "

"Actually, I think the FBI may have done a background check on him two years before that." They both now stared at Kayla. "When he was in the Marines he was stationed at the Atsugi Naval Air Base in Japan. He had access to highly classified flight plans for the Strategic Air Command and the U-2 spy plane. This was during the cold war and we had B-52 bombers flying around the clock loaded with nuclear bombs ready to attack the Soviet Union. I can't believe that the FBI didn't perform some kind of a background check on him then. But I have to admit I couldn't find anything in the record on it."

"Plus, if such a check was performed, you would think it would have come up when he defected to the Soviet Union?"

"The FBI also had a file on him when he returned to the US. They interviewed him several times. Let's see . . . he returned to the US on June 13, 1962. The FBI first interviewed him on June 26 in Dallas. Since he had just returned from the Soviet Union, the FBI labeled him as a security threat. The agent who interviewed him was not comfortable with Oswald's responses to his questions. He conducted a follow-up interview on August 16. After that meeting he concluded that Oswald was not a security threat and closed the file on him.

"They opened it back up again three weeks before JFK was assassinated."

"And that's what I don't get," Tia interrupted. "In September 1962 Oswald got a job working for a company called Jaggers-Chiles-Stovall in Dallas as a photographic trainee. This company had a contract with the US Army to develop photographs from U-2 spy planes.

"Think about it . . . October 1962 . . . U-2 spy planes."

"No way," exclaimed Rose.

"What?" Kayla was confused.

"The Cuban Missile Crisis," Rose responded. "Are you saying Oswald may have developed the pictures from the U-2 spy planes that flew over Cuba?"

"I'm not sure what he may have done. But don't you find it ironic that a man who defected to the Soviet Union, then defected back to the US, and had a file at the FBI, was allowed to work at a company that handled top secret U-2 spy plane photographs? Don't you think someone would have done a background check on him?"

"Are you saying the FBI?" asked Kayla.

"I am . . . but nothing exists to suggest any type of background check was done on him. The FBI didn't pay attention to him again until . . . "

"November 1, 1963 . . . three weeks before JFK was assassinated."

"Why did they open the file back up?"

"Actually, they had opened the file back up on him in March. He had been arrested in New Orleans when he got into a fight while he was spreading pamphlets about Cuba and communism. At the time the FBI was focused on anyone and anything having to do with communism. Then on November 1, the FBI actually went to try to interview Oswald. The visit was prompted by the CIA informing the FBI of Oswald's visit to the Cuban consulate and Soviet embassy in Mexico during the prior month. He wanted a visa to travel to Cuba. The FBI agent went to the apartment where he was living and spoke with his wife Marina. Based on that discussion, the agent concluded that Oswald was not a threat."

"Wow! Can you imagine what that agent felt like three weeks later?"

"There is one other thing buried in the agent's notes from the meeting. Marina also told him Oswald had gotten a job working at the Texas School Book Depository on Elm Street in Dallas."

"But," Rose interjected, "why two weeks later, when the Secret

Service visited Dallas to checkout the motorcade route, didn't the FBI inform them that a communist sympathizer worked in a building right on the route?"

"Now you know why the conspiracy theorists believe our own government was somehow involved in the assassination."

9

"We did it." Kayla raised her glass. Tia and Rose did the same and they clanged their glasses together.

"Is everyone happy with what we came up with?"

"Yes."

"Absolutely . . . it's a great hypothesis."

"It took us forever to agree on this. I hope its not an indication of what the rest of the month is going to be like."

"We needed to spend the time we did on this. If we aren't totally committed to this idea, in two weeks we are gonna wish we spent more time debating it and flushing it out."

"Now we just gotta sell it to Landis."

"That's gonna be easy. Don't forget we have a secret weapon." Tia and Rose just looked at Kayla. "Me!"

"We are definitely going to test that theory tomorrow."

"Make sure you wear something tomorrow that's . . . "

"Sexy?"

"Low-cut?"

"I was going to say provocative."

"How about all of the above?"

The three of them clanged their glasses again. They had spent the past eight hours trying to come up with a new hypothesis regarding the assassination. You would think after fifty years of studying the JFK assassination that there would be nothing left to analyze. But nothing could be further from the truth. From the first seconds of the bullets hitting the president's skull when Jackie Kennedy yelled "THEY killed my husband," to seconds later when the spectators in Dealey Plaza pointed to the Texas School Book Depository Building, grassy knoll, and other locations indicating where they were sure shots were fired, to police running to those same locations, to hours later when the FBI realized the arrested suspect, Lee Harvey Oswald, was someone they had just spoken with weeks before, to days later when Oswald, claiming he was just a patsy, was himself murdered, in a police station, on national TV, the words JFK assassination and conspiracy became synonymous.

Even fifty years later, most Americans do not believe Oswald was the assassin or if he was that he did not act alone. An ex-marine. A defector to the Soviet Union, who three years later is allowed to return to the US. He buys a $12 rifle designed specifically for killing humans. He happens to work in a building with a vacant sixth floor that is a perfect snipers nest overlooking the presidential motorcade at the exact point where it almost comes to a complete stop to negotiate a sharp turn. He fires three shots at the most powerful man in the world with the accuracy and speed of the best marksman. He calmly walks away from the scene and an hour later is arrested less than four miles away. Two days later he is killed in a police station on national TV by a person connected to the mob. It sounded incredible as it played out in the days after the assassination. It sounded incredible in the official government report published by the Warren Commission. Fifty years later it still sounds incredible.

As time passes, events seem to further support the public's skepticism. Watergate, documents released over the years showing the CIA and FBI tried to cover-up their involvement with Oswald, President Johnson's later doubts of the accuracy of the Warren Commission

Report, and President Clinton's questioning of the official government version of the assassination.

"Seriously, why do you think there is so much doubt and skepticism about the assassination, Tia?"

"I think a lot of it has to do with the fact that it all played out on TV right in front of the American public. Like the first televised presidential debates three years before, it makes a lasting impression on anyone old enough to remember.

"The assassination, the exact moment he was shot, was the most photographed crime in history. Think about it. We have a movie of a president being killed. Then two days later, millions of Americans watched his suspected assassin get gunned down himself on national television. In a way they all became eye witnesses, and you know eyewitness testimony is the most unreliable form of evidence."

"You know what I think," Rose was beginning to feel the effect of the alcohol in her empty stomach. "I think what it really comes down to is no one wants to believe an insignificant nothing like Oswald could change history the way he did."

"I think we need to get something to eat. Your words are slurring."

"What's this place called?"

"Phoebes."

"It looks like a great place. And within walking distance from the hotel too. I think we'll be coming here alot. You guys ready for another round?" Rose pushed her glass toward the back of the bar to get the bartender's attention.

"This place seems a little pricey to me."

"Tia, you're on an expense account. Remember what Landis said, don't get too unreasonable and you'll be okay."

"Regardless, I don't like eating a meal that costs more than my monthly college loan payment."

Rose was now glancing at the menu. "The prices aren't that bad. Thirty bucks for a nice steak dinner."

"So Rose . . . just out of curiosity . . . how rich are you?" Kayla asked.

"Rich enough that I can do whatever I want with my life. Well . . . within reason."

"No college loans? You are lucky."

"Lucky? I would trade it all to get my parents back."

"Ladies, are you ready for another?" The bartender glanced at the three women.

"Yes . . . but let's celebrate," Kayla offered.

"Celebrate . . . I thought that's what we were already doing?" Tia held her drink up.

"How about three Jager Bombs?"

"Shots? You wanna do shots? I don't do shots well," volunteered Tia.

"I'm in," slurred Rose.

The three turned and looked at the bartender. "Three Jager Bombs coming up."

"Ever been married, Rose?" Kayla asked.

"Nope."

"Why not . . . I mean you're in your forties, right?"

"Early forties. Never found the right person, I guess. Happily ever after is a scary prospect."

"You are interested in men though, right?"

"You mean versus women?"

"Well I'm sure we've all experimented with another woman. Like back in college . . . right?" Kayla was shifting her eyes back and forth at Tia and Rose.

"No."

"Not really."

"Woops . . . too much information."

"Way too much."

"Here you go ladies. Three Jager Bombs."

The women each grabbed a drink as if it was their first of the night and not their fourth. Rose raised hers. "We've developed an excellent hypothesis. I think we are going to impress the hell out of Dr. Landis tomorrow."

"For three dumb blondes I think we did okay."

"Speak for yourself, Kayla."

"But just to be safe, maybe all three of us should wear something sexy tomorrow."

They laughed, clanged their glasses together, and downed the shots.

10

"Mama . . . why are you crying?"

"Reece . . . it's about your papa."

"Did Papa's cut stop bleeding?"

"Oh honey . . . your papa . . . your papa has gone away."

"When is he coming back? Will he be here for my birthday?"

"No honey . . . he won't be. He's gone to . . . he's gone to heaven."

"Mama, don't cry. How far is heaven? Will he be back for Thanksgiving?"

"No honey . . . your papa won't be back for Thanksgiving either."

"Papa . . . is that you?"

"Shhhhh . . . "

"MAMA. MAMA. MAMA."

"Honey, what is it?"

"It was Papa . . . I just saw Papa. He was standing right next to the bed. He leaned over and gave me a kiss. On the cheek. It was him."

"Honey, you know your papa is . . . your papa is in heaven."

"Mama, he was here."

"Honey, you were dreaming."

"No, it wasn't a dream. I know it wasn't"

"It was a dream."

"NO!"

"Honey, it was . . . "

"Mama . . . no it wasn't. I could see him. I could hear him. And I touched him . . . when he kissed me I touched him."

"It was a dream, Reece."

"If it was a dream, how come his smell is on my fingers where I touched him? Old Spice. Here . . . smell."

"Mama . . . Mama . . . "

"Reece, stop pounding on the door. I'll be right there."

"Mama . . . "

"Reece, what's wrong?"

"I heard voices. They were coming from your room. Mama, is someone in there with you?"

"No honey. There's no one in my room. You must have been dreaming again."

"Mama, it wasn't a dream. I heard you talking to someone. It was a man."

"Honey, there is no one in my room. See. You must have been dreaming. Come on, let's go get you tucked back in."

"Mama."

"Yes dear."

"I know Papa's in heaven. But the voice I heard . . . I thought it was Papa."

"Well see . . . you must have been dreaming."

11

"How did you guys do?" Kayla asked as they approached the three men walking toward them in the hall just outside of Landis's office, although by the look on their faces she thought she knew what their response would be.

"I hope you guys have better luck than we did," answered Joseph, the obvious leader of the team since his six-three, two hundred and fifty pound football player frame towered over his two teammates.

"What happened?" Tia asked as she, Kayla, and Rose faced the three men.

"I guess we should have been doing a little more work and less partying. He said our hypotheses were weak and not well thought out. We've got forty-eight hours to come up with a more suitable idea, one worthy of the stipend we are being paid."

"He said that?"

"I don't think he's in too good a mood today. Must have not gotten laid last night."

"We heard no one has gotten their projects past him."

"Well, we are keeping up the trend . . . five up, five down."

"Good luck."

"Thanks."

"You're going to need it."

As the three men walked down the hall one of them mumbled, "Those dumb blondes don't have a chance."

The women watched the three men walk down the hall, heard them laugh, and turned to face one another. "That's not encouraging." Tia was the first to speak up.

"We've got a great idea," Rose responded.

"Come on. Let's go kick some ass," added Kayla.

They turned, walked down the hall and knocked on the dook to Landis's office.

"Come in. Team six I take it? Come in."

"Rose Stone." Rose extended her hand.

"Rose . . . nice to meet you."

"Tia Diaz."

"Tia . . . nice to meet you."

"Kayla . . . "

"Dexter. Nice to finally meet you." Their handshake lasted slightly longer than the other two.

"Please, sit down." Reece pointed to the rectangular table surrounded by eight low-back black leather chairs, four on each side, and one high-back black leather chair at one end. "So, are you all settled into your rooms? Is everything okay?"

"Yes."

"Great."

"Have you had a chance to check out any restaurants?"

"Some, but we've been busy working on our project."

"Well, you really need to check out the restaurants and bars in Armory Square. There is quite a selection to choose from."

"We've heard there are a lot of great places – perhaps sometime we could pick your brain on where to go?" By the way Kayla was staring at Landis, Tia and Rose knew what she really wanted to ask Landis was, "Are you free for dinner tonight?"

"Actually, I have a list here someplace. I'll get you a copy. But first, let's get down to business. I asked you to come prepared to discuss three potential ideas or hypotheses to conduct your research on. I would like you to summarize those, starting with your third priority. I will give you ten minutes to present each of your ideas at which time I will give you my feedback."

As they had previously agreed, Tia presented their idea regarding trying to implicate government involvement in the assassination. Throughout the presentation Reece periodically scribbled notes on a yellow pad on the table in front of him. He continued writing for several seconds after Tia had finished, then looked up. "I would agree with you that there is a significant amount of circumstantial evidence to implicate both the CIA and FBI in the assassination, unfortunately I don't think you are going to find anything else in the literature that hasn't been found in the past fifty years. What evidence there was has either been destroyed to cover up those involved, or has been hidden and won't be exposed for another fifty years, or well past the lifetime of those involved. My own feeling is both the CIA and FBI had nothing to do with Oswald or the assassination, other than being totally incompetent in not letting the Secret Service know that a potential threat existed along the motorcade route, specifically, that Lee Harvey Oswald worked in the Texas School Book Depository Building. Incompetence . . . not conspiracy.

"What's next?"

"Our second hypothesis," Kayla stared at Reece, "has to do with JFK's personal life, specifically his many . . . "

"Affairs with other women including strippers, call girls, married women, communist spies, stewardesses, and movie stars," Reece interrupted Kayla. "We know the president swam naked in the White House pool almost every day at one in the afternoon. We also know that he sometimes had female companionship – even several at once. We know Mrs. Kennedy and the children spent most weekends out of town, supposedly to allow her husband the freedom to enjoy his extramarital activities without the fear of her walking in on him unexpectedly. Things were arranged by his brother. The Secret Service swore their allegiance and kept guard. The press turned their backs on it, and even the public at large refused to believe anything out of the ordinary was happening. How else could the most glamorous sexpot in Hollywood get away with singing a sexy, teasing, and taunting version of Happy Birthday Mr. President in front of a crowd of hundreds? There is not a doubt in anyone's mind what his birthday present was that evening."

"And we believe," Kayla took a risk and interrupted, "that some factions may have thought that the indiscretions were getting out of hand and their exposure would take down many in the government hierarchy. The FBI had a file on him. In it were the details of his sexual affairs, including photographs."

"Were these factions concerned enough to conspire to kill the president?"

"Our hypothesis is they may have decided to subtly decrease the protection afforded the president opening up a greater opportunity for someone to harm him. A trip to the deep south where Kennedy was not well liked. To Dallas where he was hated. Riding in an open top limousine without its bullet-proof bubble, no Secret Service agents on the bumper, through streets lined with tall buildings perfect for a sniper's nest, and traveling a route where the motorcade was required to make turns that slowed them to a crawl. And as you said, the advance Secret Service team doing a less than adequate job finding out who might be in harm's way along the route.

"We believe people may have not done the job they were supposed to do, which by implication made them a co-conspirator, one that would be almost impossible to prove."

Reece stared at Kayla. He hoped his silence would make her talk more. It didn't.

"Interesting hypothesis. Lower the veil of protection. Increase the risk that if someone tried to harm the president there would be a higher probability they might succeed. There had already been two attempts on the president's life. The first attempt was made after he was elected, but before he was sworn in. It was a Sunday morning in December, 1960. JFK was staying at his home in Palm Beach, Florida. A would-be suicide bomber, Richard Pavlick – yes, a suicide bomber in 1960 – was parked, and unnoticed by anyone including the Secret Service, less than a block away, his car loaded with explosives. He came within seconds of murdering the president-elect as he left for church. At the last minute he changed his mind when Jackie and Caroline appeared at the front door of the house. The second attempt was in Chicago just weeks before the trip to Dallas. This second scenario was eerily similar to Dallas – a sniper in a building shooting at the presidential motorcade. There, the would-be sniper got cold feet.

"These are the ones that we know about. After all, if Oswald had not pulled the trigger that day, or if he'd have pulled the trigger and the rifle had jammed, we would have never have known about the assassination attempt. Or if the FBI had done their job and told the Secret Service about Oswald, or if his coworker had been more curious about the 'curtain rods' Oswald carried into work that morning, or if someone had seen him setting up his snipers nest, or a dozen other things had happened, Dealey Plaza would have passed away into obscurity."

"But our hypothesis suggests there would have been another Dealey Plaza."

"Perhaps . . . but we are trying to solve this case, Ms. Dexter, not invent a new one. What's your last and hopefully best hypothesis?"

The three women looked at Landis. They had a sinking feeling their best idea was doomed before it was presented.

12

"I'm sorry . . . did I wake you?" Reece had been staring at his mother for the past five minutes wondering if a person, whose brain was being devoured by Alzheimer's, could still dream, which memory the dreams were from, and did it make any difference?

"No . . . you didn't wake me. I wasn't really sleeping. I just needed to rest my eyes for a few seconds. You look nice all dressed up in a suit and tie."

"Thank you."

"Most professionals don't dress up any more. They should. They would get more respect from people."

"I would have thought that having a DR in front of your name would be enough."

"Oh, my dear . . . don't get me wrong. I of all people know how hard it was for you to earn that title."

"Yes, you do."

"But . . . along with that title comes responsibility."

"I agree."

"And respect."

"Yes, respect."

"And if you want me to look up to you and show you respect, then I feel you should dress the part."

"I agree with you one hundred percent."

"Good . . . now what were we talking about?"

"We were talking about how great I looked in a suit."

"No, I mean before that? Before I rested my eyes?"

"I . . ."

"I'm sorry. You're confusing me. Sometimes I forget you know. What was your name again, Doctor . . . ?

13

"Woo-hoo! We did it."

"To the only team to get their project approved."

"These shots are damn good."

"I thought you didn't do shots, Tia?"

"Actually, what I said was, I don't do shots . . . well."

"Well, you're doing them just fine tonight."

"What should we try next?"

"How about a Red Headed Slut?"

"Woo-hoo."

Their final pitch to Landis, which they felt was their best idea, was presented by Rose. She had actually come up with the idea months ago when she learned she was accepted into the month-long seminar at S.U. She had degrees in photography and computers. When she was studying law she was fascinated by how much our everyday movements were captured on video. Cameras were everywhere. And although these videos were being used more and more to solve crimes, the quality of the recordings – which captured only one out of every three seconds of the actual sequence of events to save on data storage – resulted in a poor quality of recordings. Although software had existed for years to computer enhance a photograph, it did nothing more than lighten or darken the individual pixels that made up the image. Rose had actually developed a simple computer program that, like the human brain, tried to interpret what the object was in the photo, then use that information to help enhance the image.

As soon as she began to explain the theory behind how her code worked, Landis fell silent.

"I tried to duplicate with software how the brain interpreted images. As you know, the human brain doesn't always interpret correctly the image that falls onto the back of the retina of the eye. Instead the brain makes assumptions about what the eye is seeing."

Rose handed Reece a piece of paper with what at first glance seemed to be a bunch of misspelled words. "Would you please read this out loud?"

Reece looked at the paper, hesitated a moment, then began to read.

> Fuor yaer old Rceee Lndais sotod jsut tewtny feet form Psdiernet Kndneey as the sohts rnag out in Dleaey Pzlaa on Nebvmoer 22, 1963. Ftify yares leatr, taht secne, lkie a rcoecruirng darem, is siltl as cealr to Rceee as it was tehn. Ask ayonne who was fuor yares of age or oedlr on taht day, 'Wrehe wree you wehn JFK was soht?' and tehy wloud llikey slitl be albe to tlel you ectxlay werhe tehy wree and waht tehy wree dnoig.

Kayla and Tia watched the reaction on Landis's face. It was the same reaction they both had when Rose asked them to read the paragraph. Reece looked up at Rose.

"As you can see your brain took in the images from your eyes, made some assumptions based on the information previously stored in your memory, then came to a conclusion as to what the information on the paper was trying to tell you.

"As it turns out, in order for your brain to determine a specific word, what is important is that the first and last letters be correct. The rest of the letters don't need to be in the correct order because the human mind doesn't read letters. It looks for words. And when the words are grouped to form a sentence, it even makes assumptions as to what the next word might be from a previously read or even heard phrase. For example, if I said, 'See Spot . . . ', most people would end the sentence with the word, run. Or if I said, 'Pepsi hits the . . . ', or, 'I'd walk a mile for a . . . ', most adults would know how to complete the phrase. We may have read or heard the statement thirty or forty years ago, yet our brain uses logic to determine what was trying to be conveyed and fills in the missing information.

"My software tries to mimic that function as it looks at not words, but a photograph. What we propose to do is analyze the photographs recorded from the JFK assassination to determine if there is any new evidence hidden in them."

"Rose, you are a genius. By the end of your presentation you had old Landis wrapped around your little finger."

"Actually, Ms. Dexter, she had Dr. Landis wrapped around her little finger."

In unison they turned to see Reece leaning on the bar just next to them.

"Dr. Landis, I . . . "

"I'm kidding, ladies. Please . . . continue celebrating. Come on . . . what you do on your own time is your own business. Besides, you deserve it. You probably know you are the only project I approved. I know news like that travels fast. So congratulations. And you did have me wrapped around your finger. Is someone going to say something?"

"Would you like to do a shot with us?"

Reece dropped his head down, raised his eyebrows, and peered at Kayla as if he was looking at her above a pair of reading glasses. "Why not . . . but only if I buy."

"You won't get an argument from us."

"And if I can pick the shot." Reece motioned to the bartender. "Four Blood Transfusions please."

"What's in a Blood Transfusion?" asked Tia.

"I actually know." The three of them stared at Rose. "One part 151 rum, one part cherry brandy, and one part sour."

Kayla and Tia turned to Reece. "I'm impressed."

"You mean she's right?"

"I used to be a bartender too."

"I don't remember seeing that on your resume, Ms. Stone."

"One of many talents that I didn't think was going to help me get into this program."

"Au contraire . . . you never know when your past experiences might come in handy."

"Four Blood Transfusions."

Reece handed the bartender a fifty. "To team six . . . here's to a successful investigation." The four of them clanged their glasses and downed the drinks.

"That was good." Tia had a big grin on her face.

"Would you like another? Four more please. So, I see you took me up on my suggestion to try out a restaurant in Armory Square. What did you think of BC?"

"The food was great," volunteered Kayla. Tia and Rose nodded in agreement as they watched Kayla inch her way closer to Reece.

"I like the open format of the place. Plus you are right Kayla, the food is great here."

"What brings you here?" Kayla asked. She was now standing next to Reece.

"I'm waiting for my . . . "

"Hi honey . . . you beat me here." Meeka nudged between Kayla and Reece, put her arm around Reece, gave him a kiss, and moved in close to him giving the ladies the once-over.

"Ladies, this is my . . . friend, Meeka. Meeka, this is Kayla, Rose, and Tia. This is the team I was telling you about over dinner."

"Oh . . . the wonder-women. You must have really impressed my

Reece, because he couldn't stop talking about you over dinner. Nice to meet you." Meeka shook each of their hands then reached behind Reece and draped her hand on his shoulder.

"Four Blood Transfusions."

"You're doing shots?"

"We're celebrating . . . would you like one?"

"Here come Dean and Gerry." Meeka pointed to the couple and then to the bar. "I'll order a drink down there. Nice meeting you ladies and good luck with your project."

"Again ladies, congratulations." Reece held up his glass and the others joined him.

"I could get use to these."

"Me too."

"Ladies, be safe tonight. Don't celebrate too much. And, Rose, you'd better warn them about the drink."

The three of them watched Reece walk to the other end of the bar.

"Man he's got a nice ass."

"Why don't you say it a little louder, Kayla. I don't think he heard you."

"What did he mean, warn them about the drink?"

"The drink tastes great. So you wanna keep drinking them. But that 151 will knock you on your ass."

"How are you ladies getting back to the Sheraton?" Reece had snuck up on the three women without them noticing. "You're not driving, are you?"

"Taxi."

"Nonsense. I'll take you. I need to stop by my office anyway."

"No . . . that's okay. We'll take a . . . "

"Thank you, Dr. Landis. That would be great." Somehow Kayla managed to respond without slurring her words. "But, what about Meeka?"

"She's driving separately. I'll get the car and meet you out front in a few minutes."

"We gotta pay the bill."

"That's all taken care of."

"Thank you."

"Anything for my number one team. See you out front."

"What are you driving?"

"A yellow Camaro, 2013. Back seat is tight, but we'll be fine."

The three of them stared at Reece as he walked out the front door.

"I'm sitting in the front seat."

"I hope I don't puke in his car."

14

"Thank you for the ride, Dr. Landis."

"You're very welcome."

"Are you sure you won't come in for a nightcap?"

"Thanks, but I'd better be going. Take care ladies."

The three of them didn't take their eyes off the car until it disappeared down the street.

"He was staring at me all night."

"Don't you mean you were staring at him, Kayla?"

"Was not."

"Then how do you know he was staring at you?"

"I think we almost had him convinced to come in for a drink."

"I think we scared him off."

"Maybe he thought we wanted to do something kinky . . . like a foursome?"

"I definitely would not throw him out of bed for sexting."

"Don't you mean texting?"

"No . . . I mean sexting."

"He's probably got a promise from Meeka."

"Yes, Meeka. She'll probably be waiting for him on her knees."

"Lucky bitch."

"Come on ladies. Let's go in for one more blood infusion . . . I mean transmusion . . . transfusion."

The three of them spun around toward the hotel.

"Damn . . . you scared me."

Meeka was standing an arms length in front of them holding a cigarette to her mouth between her long thin fingers. She slowly pulled the cigarette away from her mouth, exhaled smoke in the direction of Kayla who was standing in the middle of the three, dropped the butt to the pavement, and looked down and stepped on it. She then raised her head.

"Ladies . . . I'm only going to say this once. If I ever catch any of you fucking with my man . . . " Without looking she reached into her purse, pulled out an onyx handled switchblade, held it up, and squeezed, exposing the five inch silver blade with a clinking sound loud enough to cause the three women staring at it to blink. "I'll use this to shave any bush you might have on your pussy, then I'll grab your clit between my fingers and squeeze, yank, and twist it until you beg for me to cut it off."

15

Reece knew he was getting laid. Meeka couldn't keep her hands off him all night. He hoped his flirting with the wonder-women would spark the jealous streak she had and make her act even sluttier than her usual slutty self. As they parted for their separate cars earlier, Meeka had whispered, "I'm gonna use you until you are too sore to be used anymore."

As he drove home he fantasized about her riding him. It was her favorite position. She liked to be in control as she grinded herself on you, teasing herself by varying the speed and depth of penetration, making it last as long as she could before she succumbed to a very noticeable, for both you and her, pulsating orgasm, its peak, if she were really horned up, lasting well over a minute. She would always put on a show for her partner, her motive being to keep him turned on enough to stay hard, but not so turned on as to make him cum. Of course she also had an ulterior motive. Her bouncing breasts, tugging on her, as well as his, nipples, sometimes very hard, sliding her fingers along the base of his wet shaft, then plunging them into both their mouths, and when things got overly lubricated for her liking, dismounting and licking and sucking his shaft, then remounting and kissing and sucking his lips, she did to please herself. To make her already strong orgasms, of which she would have many, more intense.

And if you should happen to cum before she was done, which was always the case, she was very understanding. She would slide off within seconds of you going soft, smothering your face as she positioned herself on your face, and push down until she found your flicking tongue. She would periodically reach back to stroke you, knowing she could enjoy several orgasms from your tongue before you were hard enough to remount. And experience told her, when you were ready, she would be in for a much longer ride than the first.

When Reece walked into the dimly lit kitchen and eyed the note on the counter he knew his "I'm gonna use you until you are too sore to be used anymore" fantasy was not the same one Meeka had in mind. That was too bad. He was so looking forward to lying on the bottom and being used by her. He knew he was still going to be on the bottom. And she was going to use him. He smiled realizing he'd made her more than jealous.

Reece stood under the spotlight in the center of the room. He followed the instructions exactly as she had written in her note. He drank the three shots – Blood Transfusions heavy in 151, light in sour – quickly. He stripped naked then walked down the circular stairway and stood beneath the light in the center of the room. He then reached down with his right hand and stroked himself hard. The note indicated he would be told when to stop.

Although he couldn't make her out with the brightness of the light and darkness of the room, he could periodically see the orange glow of a cigarette coming from the leather Barcalounger located in the far corner of the room.

Meeka snuffed out her cigarette, got up, and walked toward Reece. As she approached the outer edges of the spotlight glow, Reece was able to finally make out her outfit. He knew by the way she dressed what kind of an evening he was in for. As the light shown on the bottom of the six inch thick black platform and twelve inch spiked heal, Reece closed his eyes. He didn't need to see any more to know what she had on. The rest of the black leather boot, stretched tight against her leg by the full length zipper along the back, extended to her mid-thigh. He knew she had nothing else on, except for a clip that held her thick long naturally red hair on the top of her head. Her face would be covered with so much makeup, enough black eye shadow to look as if she had a mask on, even he wouldn't recognize her, and in fact didn't the first time she dressed like this for him. From that experience he knew exactly what the outfit meant and what he was in for this evening.

"You're gripping yourself harder."

Reece opened his eyes to see the normally five-eight Meeka towering over him, her large dark brown nipples at eye level, as she stood next to him in her stilt-like boots. She placed her right hand on his shoulder.

"Do you know how I know?"

His grip was not only tightening, he was stroking faster, and his breathing had deepened.

"Your head turns a darker shade of purple. Probably from all that blood you keep pumping into it. There's also pre-cum dripping out of your hole. You're close to shooting off, aren't you?"

"Yes." Reece didn't hesitate answering as his stroking and breathing increased even more.

"Good." She leaned forward with her lips almost touching his ear. "Now stop . . . I said, STOP!" Her left hand fell hard on his wrist and yanked his hand from his shaft.

"Ahhhh . . . fuck."

"You are lucky this fuck'n thing didn't shoot off." She slapped his still stiff erection hard with the palm of her hand.

"Ahhhh."

"Get into position."

Reece turned and walked over to the bar, leaned on it with his arms outstretched and spread wide, then spread his legs. He saw Meeka reach for the leather glove, the one she owned long before she met him, the one that was still soft on the top, but hardened and cracked on the palm, then disappear behind him.

"Do you know why I'm so fuck'n pissed?"

"No."

A second later he felt three sharp stings from her leather clad hand on his left ass cheek. He wanted to scream out but didn't, knowing it would deprive her of the satisfaction she was seeking.

"No?"

"No."

This time the three slaps landed on his right cheek, with greater force than the first three, based on not just the pain that shot through his body, but by the cracking sound that echoed around the room.

"No?"

"No."

She leaned in so close her lips brushed against his ear. "I am not going to stop until I break you. And you know I will eventually break you. I always do." She stood back behind him and in rapid succession slapped each cheek, alternating back and forth, and sometimes not to throw him off guard. After two minutes, during which Reece did not move or say a word, Meeka stopped, not because his ass was beat-red, but because her hand was stinging.

"Turn around and lean against the bar. Spread your arms out to the side and rest them on the edge of the bar." She reached down with her gloved hand and squeezed his already burning ass cheek. The hard cracked leather dug into his skin. "Push your hips out. You obviously like showing that thing off. Stick it out." Still gripping his ass, she placed her un-gloved hand on his shaft and slowly stroked it. "What a girth . . . I can barely get my fingers around it. And how big are you again?" When he didn't answer, she squeezed his ass harder.

"Eight . . . ahhhh . . . eight inches."

"That's right . . . eight inches. Now I remember measuring it. Eight inches was with the ruler resting on top of your shaft." She ran her long fingernails along his length, over his ridge, and down the head letting the nail rest at the entrance to his hole. "Now when we measure on the bottom." She reached under, letting his erection rest in her palm, then slid her hand until her middle finger dug into his soft ball sack, making him flinch. "And shove the ruler here, your cock measures nine inches." She ran her fingernails along the bottom of his shaft, again stopping at his hole. "That's why when I'm asked, I tell my girlfriends I'm getting fucked by nine thick inches. Gets 'em jealous. You know what that's like . . . making someone jealous . . . don't you?" She loosened her grip on his cheek and removed her hand knowing the sting would bite as bad as when she first grabbed him. She reached over and picked up the second leather glove from the bar, its palm also hardened and cracked, and slipped it on her left hand. She then stood in front of Reece, put her finger under his chin, and tilted his head back so he could look into her eyes as she stared down at him.

"I will ask you again . . . do you know why I'm so fuck'n pissed?"

"No."

She reached down with both hands, gripped his still stiff shaft like you would a baseball bat, squeezed and twisted her hands back and forth in opposite directions, letting the cracked hard leather scrape his skin raw.

"Ahhhh . . . ahhhh . . . ahhhh . . . "

"No?"

"No."

"Ahhhh . . . ahhhh . . . ahhhh . . . "

She loosened her grip and rested his still stiff erection, but now pink and scraped raw, in the palm of her hand. "Oh look . . . I said look at it. Just as I promised . . . nice and sore."

She reached for the black leather flogger, hesitated for a second, and then dropped it back on the bar. "Turn around and put your hands behind your back." Reece did so without hesitating. She reached for the chrome handcuffs on the bar and locked them on his wrists. She walked back to the leather Barcalounger, sat down, took a sip of her now watered-down drink that had been sitting on the side table, and lit up a cigarette.

"Come over here. Stand in front of me." Meeka reached up and started stroking his now half-limp shaft. It didn't take her long to get it erect. She took another drag of her cigarette and blew the smoke onto him. She held the cigarette up to her face. "I thought about branding this thing, actually the tip." She took another long drag, holding the hot orange glow close enough so he'd feel its heat on his tip, which he did because he backed away. "But I'd be willing to bet that you'd yell the safeword and our fun would be over for the night. And if you let me do it, you'd be out of commission for a few weeks and my fun would be over."

She stopped stroking, put her cigarette down, took a sip of her drink, then pulled the leather gloves tighter onto her hands.

"Look at me." Their eyes were now locked on one another. "Do you know why I am fuck'n pissed?"

"No."

Still staring at him, she grabbed his shaft with both hands, squeezed and twisted in opposite directions.

"AHHHH!"

"No?"

"No."

She twisted again.

"AHHHH!"

"NO?" This time he did not answer, so she squeezed him harder and started to twist again.

"YES . . . "

She loosened her grip. "Yes?"

"YES . . . you're fuck'n pissed because I was flirting with the blondes."

"Flirting? They think you wanna fuck 'em. Do you wanna fuck 'em?" She squeezed and twisted.

"NOOOO!"

"And how did you introduce me? I'm your friend?" She twisted again.

"AHHHH!"

"Those whores wouldn't know what to do with this." Another twist.

"AHHHH!"

“The next time you meet with your wonder-women, I want you to remember this.” She kept her grip, but slowly slid her gloved hand off his shaft.

“AHHHH!”

“The next time you think of me, I want you to remember this.” She leaned forward, gently flicked the tip of her tongue on his hole, swirled it around his head, then opened wide and shoved his full length down her throat until her nose was buried in his pubic hair.

16

"I'm sorry . . . I sometimes forget things. What were we talking about?"

"You were telling me how you met your husband, Carl."

"Oh yes. I was living with my aunt and uncle on their farm outside of Dallas. My father died in the war. In the last days. The Battle of the Bulge. They say he was a hero. I was two when he joined the army. I never knew him.

"Life was hard for my mom, being a war-widow and all. We eventually moved in with her brother, my uncle, and his wife. My mom died a few years later. I want to think it was from a broken heart, but it was probably the alcohol. Some of the moonshine made in the back woods of Texas was more comparable to kerosene – drink enough and it'd kill you. And she did drink enough, so it did. I ended up being raised by my aunt and uncle.

"I'm sorry . . . what did you ask me?"

"Your husband . . . Carl . . . how did you meet him?"

"Oh yes. I was a senior in high school. They needed help on the farm. Carl was the hired hand. I was seventeen. He was a year older. I remember when I came home from school that first day that I saw him. I was a quiet one in school. I had friends, boys and girls, but never a real boyfriend. I heard about love, at least love through a teenagers eyes, and sex, just the real basics, from my friends. My aunt and uncle weren't going to tell me about those things. They didn't have any kids of their own, so at the time I didn't think they even knew what sex was. Don't get me wrong, they loved me like I was their child. And I loved them. But, they never told me about the facts of life. The only thing I remember auntie saying when I came home that day was, there's gonna be trouble. She said she saw it in our eyes. She was so smart. And she was right.

"We were married a year later. It was two weeks before Carl was to report for duty in the Marines. We didn't have sex, I mean real sex, penetration, at least with his, you know, penis, until our wedding night. We were both glad we didn't give in to those temptations in the hay barn. Not to say we were prudes either. I mean we touched each other and made each other feel good. But we didn't actually do it. Anyway, we must have known what we were doing because Reece, our son, was born nine months later.

"After basic training Carl was stationed in Japan. It was no place for a wife and newborn, so I lived with my aunt and uncle on the farm. We didn't see much of one another for those three years he was in the Marines. When he got out though, things seemed to fall into place for us. We found our own place. Outside of Dallas. Carl got a good job using some of the skills he learned in the Marines. We made up for lost time. I mean we were doing it all the time. But even though we both wanted more kids, nothing happened. The Doctor said we were doing it too much. We should rest a day or two to let, you know, his sperm supply build back up. We tried, but couldn't do it. I mean, not do it.

"Then, after two years, everything changed."

"You mean Carl's death?"

"We didn't have a choice did we?" Dora reached for the hand of the man sitting across from her. "Please tell me we did the right thing."

"We did . . . " Before he could finish, Dora pulled her hands away.

"I'm sorry . . . I sometimes forget things. What were we talking about?"

"I was just saying that I should be leaving."

"Will I see you again tomorrow?"

"Of course you will, Dora. You know I stop in to see you every day."

"Oh that's right . . . to make up for lost time."

"That's right . . . to make up for lost time."

17

"Team ten . . . come in. Have a seat. Just because your team number is ten didn't mean you had to be the last to get project approval."

"We were jinxed."

"Jinxed?" Reece glanced back and forth at the three men sitting in front of his desk. "Ryan . . . how did your random number generator come up with a team like this? We've got Joseph, a lawyer who wants to be a football player. Paul, with two engineering degrees and an MBA who wants to be a bartender instead of a corporate executive."

"In the Caribbean . . . at least for a few years. Until I . . . "

"Mature?"

"Funny . . . that's what my father says."

"With age comes wisdom . . . and jealousy. We wish we would have done it before we started our careers. Nothing wrong with enjoying life while you're young and can still enjoy it."

"I'll drink to that."

"And Ryan, our statistician, who can't wait to get to Wall Street so he can make his first million before he's twenty-five. You have to admit you are quite a combination."

"Like I said . . . we're jinxed."

"I don't know if you are jinxed, Joseph."

"Hey, someone has to be last."

"Spoken like a true statistician. Okay, what have you guys come up with?"

"We'd like to analyze the acoustic evidence to try to determine from a statistical perspective how many shots were fired and where they came from."

"Before you shoot us down, hear us out."

"Who said I was going to shoot you down?"

"Dr. Landis, we've been before you two other times presenting five different proposals to you. We know that look."

"What look?"

"That one."

"Okay. I won't say a thing until you are done, but . . . "

"Thank you. We know a lot of other studies have looked at eyewitness testimony to try to determine how many shots were fired, and more importantly, where they came from."

"We also know eyewitness testimony is usually the least reliable."

"Especially during stressful situations."

"Like when you think gunshots are going off all around you."

"But when you look at it from a statistical perspective, you can start to at least draw some meaningful circumstantial evidence from this kind of evidence."

"All of the studies of the eyewitness testimony taken after the assassination, taken from the Warren Commission Report, and subsequent interviews of witnesses in Dealey Plaza that day came to a very similar conclusion. That is, about forty percent of the witnesses thought the shots came from the Texas School Book Depository Building. Forty percent thought the shots came from the grassy knoll area, and twenty percent from various other locations or they had no idea where the shots came from."

"What about the echoes in Dealey Plaza making it difficult . . . sorry, I said I wouldn't . . . proceed."

"Excellent point, Dr. Landis. As you know there have been several tests performed since 1963 measuring the echo patterns in Dealey Plaza.

We also know there was a significant amount of testing presented to the Warren Commission about echoes in Dealey Plaza and their impact on your ability to determine where shots were fired from."

"And these same echoes can also impact how many shots you believe were fired in Dealey Plaza."

"That's why most experts rely on the physical evidence found in Dealey Plaza that day. There were three empty cartridge cases found on the sixth floor of the Texas School Book Depository Building."

"But the eyewitness testimony . . . "

"We know it is not as reliable as the physical evidence, however, the eyewitness testimony indicates at least some percentage of witnesses, much less than five percent . . . "

"More like one percent . . . sorry. Hey, you guys are getting me excid-ed. Proceed."

"Okay, one percent believes four shots were fired, not three."

"And other evidence, like photographs, shows about an equal number of people running in the direction of the Texas School Book Depository Building and the grassy knoll, presumably to look for the shooter."

"Look guys . . . you are obviously excited about this, but what is it that you propose to do with this evidence that hasn't already been looked at thousands of times before? I'm sorry, but I'm not hearing any-thing new here."

Joseph and Paul both looked at Ryan with a please save us look on their faces.

"Ryan . . . I guess the other two are looking for you to answer my question."

"We would like to put together a three dimensional computer model of Dealey Plaza, and then model how the sound waves would travel throughout the Plaza from shots fired from various locations. We would then like to analyze the evidence, both physical evidence and eye wit-ness testimony, to see how statistically correlated the data is. That is, for example, how does the eyewitness testimony support the hard evidence, and if it doesn't, how might we explain it."

"How accurately can you model the sound waves and echoes?"

"It's all math and physics. And it's actually a relatively straight forward problem to model and should be extremely accurate. We are going to use some of the same modeling techniques that the Navy uses to interpret sonar signals aboard the Trident subs."

"And you know this how, Paul?"

"If I told you, I'd have to . . . "

"Never mind."

"I'm kidding. It's off the shelf software. Nothing proprietary. I'm going to tweak it a little. I've used the software before. Consulting."

"Consulting? I don't recall that on your resume?"

"It was for a rock band. They were playing a concert in a domed facility, similar to the Syracuse University Carrier Dome, but smaller. It was noted for its terrible acoustics. I told the band that I could tweak their amplifiers and speaker outputs to compensate for the building's acoustics. It worked."

"And it's not on your resume because?"

"I got paid with free concert tickets. Front row seats."

"So, what do you think Dr. Landis?"

"Well Joseph . . . and Paul, and Ryan . . . the logical side if me says this issue has been studied to death and there is nothing left there to find."

"But, Dr. . . . "

"Let me finish. But my gut tells me that if there is something hidden out there, the only way it is going to be discovered is with something new. Something not used before. Something not available until now. And . . . more often than not, I go with my gut.

"But what has really sold me has been your enthusiasm over this. I believe all three of you are invested in this."

"We are."

"And with only three weeks left, you are going to need to be. You're behind, but I expect great things from you. Congratulations."

18

"Here they come."

"CONGRATULATIONS! WOO-HOO!" The cheers and clapping from the twenty-seven seminar participants, along with the cheers from the dozen strangers in the bar who clapped because everyone else was, greeted Joseph, Paul, and Ryan as they walked into The Blue Tusk.

"Come on over here guys."

"I thought we were only meeting a couple other guys here?"

"I guess they lied."

"Here ya go . . . a shot for each of you."

"It looks like you've all got one."

"We do . . . thirty shots."

"What is it?"

"We couldn't think of an appropriate drink to celebrate your project approval . . . "

"Some of us wanted champagne."

"Yes . . . some wanted champagne. But others did not think that was appropriate. After all, you weren't the first to get approved . . . "

"Or the cutest."

"But, we are the best!"

"That's right, Joseph. And for being the best we thought the appropriate drink would be The Four Horsemen. As you may or may not know, The Four Horsemen, as described in the Book of Revelation, ride on white, red, black, and pale horses, and one of their missions, as summoned by God, is conquest. We won't mention the other things they are supposed to do. Since we only have three person teams, we hope Paul, as white, and Joseph, as black, and Ryan, as red . . . "

"What?"

"His hair . . . it has a reddish tint."

"That's really stretching things."

"And pale, well . . . for two of you anyway, since in order to catch up to the rest of us they will not see the light of day for the next three weeks . . . we hope they achieve the conquest they have set out for. To team ten."

Thirty drinks went into the air, each team of three clanged their glasses, and the shots were downed, some faster than others.

"What was in that?" Tia whispered to Rose.

"Liquor."

"That I could tell . . . you mean all liquor? No non-alcoholic anything?"

"Tequila, rum, jager, and peppermint liquor."

"I could go for another one of those." Kayla stared at her empty glass.

"Everyone put your glass on the bar . . . we're having another."

"Who's buying these?"

"Who cares."

"I don't think I want another one . . . yuk."

"Tia . . . get one anyway. I'll drink it."

"You know what I'll have instead . . . a Blood Transfusion . . . what?"

"You won't drink this, but you'll drink one-fifty-one."

"It's not the alcohol . . . it's the taste. If you're gonna drink alcohol, it might as well taste good. Otherwise, if it's just the buzz you want, do one of those alcohol enemas."

"What?"

"You mean Tia and I know about a drink that Rose the bartender doesn't know about?"

"Well, it's really not a drink."

"I hope not."

"Seriously . . . you've never heard of butt chugging?"

"Come on?"

"What . . . you insert a tube into your rectum and alcohol is poured directly into the colon."

"You can use an enema bag or an alcohol soaked tampon too."

"Tia . . . how do you know that?"

"It's a pain-free way to get blitzed. It happens fast since the alcohol enters the bloodstream directly, bypassing the liver . . . a high-intensity buzz. It's the latest craze on college campuses."

"Do you know you could get alcohol poisoning doing that?"

"People have."

"And die."

"People have."

"And do you administer this to yourself, or do you need help? And who helps you?"

"The bartender."

"Not this bartender. I am glad I was a college freshman back in the early nine . . . back before people started inventing all this weird stuff. I mean people drank, but not non-stop shots until you passed out. What fun is that?"

"Another toast."

"Tia . . . just take it."

"May all the magic bullets we encounter be silver."

"What the hell does that mean?"

"Magic bullet . . . get it?"

"That was lame."

"Don't look now Kayla, but Joseph is headed this way. I think he likes you."

"I don't know Tia . . . I think he likes you."

"He's not my type."

"Too big for you?"

"Probably."

"He's still headed this way. I wonder whose lucky night this is going to be? Kayla or Tia? Kayla or Tia? Or maybe, Kayla and Tia?"

"I need another drink. I'm buying."

"How about another Four Horsemen?"

"Anything."

"Tia . . . you're blushing."

"Must be the alcohol."

19

"This isn't working out like I thought it was going to, Tia."

"Rose, we're not even done with half the photographs. And we still need to analyze the Zapruder film and the others taken in Dealey Plaza that day."

"It doesn't matter if we had a thousand photos and a dozen movies to analyze, Tia. Garbage in — garbage out."

"What?"

"Sorry, computer jargon."

"Seriously?"

"Yes it is. No matter how good the computer code is, if the data you enter is flawed, or garbage in, the information you get out will be flawed, or garbage out."

"Ah . . . I get it. So what's wrong with the photographs we are analyzing?"

"Where the hell is Kayla. This is getting ridiculous. We've been working on this project for almost two weeks and as each day goes by Kayla shows up later and later."

"Where do you think she is?"

"How would I know. Hasn't she been with a different guy every night? She's like a kid in a candy store. You would think she has never been around a bunch of men before. So, there are only seven women in this program. Does she have to try to fuck every one of the twenty-three men, and probably some of the women, who are left? What is she up to anyway . . . at least five?"

"It hasn't been five."

"Why are you defending her?"

"I'm not defending her. It's just that for the past week she's been with the same man. If you'd lift your head up once in a while you'd know what was going on around you."

"Then who the hell would do the work that needs to get done around here. Have you forgotten we have a project that needs to get done? And we have a little more than a week to do it. I don't want my name going on something that whoever reads it in the future is going to wonder what bimbos wrote this report."

"We're both putting in extra effort to cover for Kayla."

"This is the exact issue Landis lectured us about the first day. The reason why there were three person teams. So we'd know if someone wasn't carrying their load and we could do something about it."

"So Rose . . . what do you suggest we do?"

"How about we get a hold of Kayla's phone and text Meeka. Thanks for letting me borrow Reece – he's great in bed, but I'm done with him. Then let Meeka take care of it."

"That's not even funny."

"It would put her out of commission for awhile and she could devote fulltime to the project."

"I think I know how important that part of her body is to her. I don't think she'd be interested in working on this."

"You're right."

"When she's here, she works her butt off."

"It doesn't make up for the time she isn't here. She better hope Landis doesn't find out."

"You're not going to say anything, are you?"

"Don't be ridiculous. Of course not. Look, I like Kayla. But if Landis catches wind of it, not that she's messing around with someone else in the program, but not pulling her weight, he could pull her stipend. It's happened before. Then with just the two of us left, our project could be in jeopardy. I just wish she would do her part.

"So who is she having this new long term, one week, or I should say one week's worth of nights, relationship with?"

"You'll never guess." Tia stared at Rose with a smirk on her face.

"Ryan, the math expert."

"No!"

"Not Landis."

"No, not Landis."

"Well, that's a relief. You had me scared there for a second. So who?"

"Joseph."

"Joseph? The six-three two hundred and fifty pound ex-football player? The black ex-football player?"

"That would be the one."

"Without her heels, what is Kayla, five-four, tops?"

"If that."

"And a hundred and ten pounds?"

"Tops."

"I can't picture that."

"At least she doesn't have to kneel down to suck him off."

"Tia!"

"Well?"

"Actually, that wasn't what I was picturing. You know what they say about black men. What hole would she have that is big enough? Can you imagine how stretched out she must be? A week, huh? She must be doing something right. Better her than me."

"Speak of the devil." Tia turned and walked to the door. "Nice of you to make it."

"Sorry . . . long night."

"I bet it was."

"Can we get back to work?"

"Sorry I'm late Rose . . . it won't happen again."

"You said that last time, Kayla. Rose and I are not going to carry you on this."

Rose looked at Tia, surprised, but glad she was speaking up.

"I know, it won't happen again."

"Why are you so sure?"

"Joseph's team is pissed at him too."

"So as long as you are doing it with him you are going to show up on time?"

"We'll see how long this relationship lasts."

"Oh, I don't think you have to worry about that."

"Why's that?"

"He's like that . . . " Kayla held up her hands.

"Too much information." Rose slapped her hands down.

"I'll never be able to look him in the face again. I'll be staring down there."

"He likes you too, Tia."

"He does?"

"And you too, Rose."

"He's not my type."

"Landis is not your type. Joseph is not your type. Are you sure you were totally honest with us about liking men?"

"What did he say about me?" Tia was blushing.

"Ladies, can you two work on this later. Obviously there's enough of him there for the both of you. We've got a problem we have to solve here."

"Why, what's wrong?"

"Rose thinks there's something wrong with our analysis."

"We're almost two weeks into this. There can't be something wrong."

"Well Kayla, there is."

"Why, just because we haven't found anything? We knew the probability of finding something was small."

"I did some research last night. I didn't get a lot af sleep either last night. I think there is a problem with the data we are looking at. We need to set up a meeting with Dr. Landis."

"Meet with Dr. Landis? I'm up for that."

"Did you forget about crazy Meeka?"

"We're meeting with him, not screwing him."

"So much for the long term relationship."

"Seriously Kayla . . . what did Joseph say about me?"

20

“I can’t be late this morning, Joseph. Stop it.”

“I can’t keep my hands off of you.”

“You would think after what I did to you last night you’d be drained and limp.”

“I don’t know about the drained part, but . . . ”

“I can see you’re not limp. Sorry . . . it’ll have to wait till later.” She reached down and stroked him. “Maybe we can break away at noon for a little afternoon delight?”

“I hope I can wait that long.”

“You’ll have to. I’ve got to get going. We have a meeting with Landis this morning.”

“Fuck.”

“What?”

“I was supposed to call Dr. Landis yesterday to reschedule our meeting for today. We need to finalize some things before we meet with him. We’re supposed to work on that this morning. Damn.”

“So call him now.”

“Fuck, my phone is dead. This is not my day.”

“I don’t think you were saying that an hour ago. Here, use my phone. I’m jumping in the shower.”

“Thanks.”

“Dr. Landis? This is Joseph.”

“Yes Joseph . . . what’s up?”

“We were wondering if we could reschedule our meeting for this morning to later this afternoon.”

“I’m booked for the afternoon. How about we do lunch?”

“That’s perfect.”

“Great . . . see you then.”

21

"Who was that?"

"Someone needed to reschedule a meeting."

"They're calling you at home now?"

"Excuse me, but I'm usually in the office by now. The only reason why I'm not is because of you." Reece walked over to Meeka, loosened the towel she had wrapped around her and let it fall to the floor, placed his naked body against hers, which was still damp from the shower, and kissed her.

"You're not complaining, are you?"

"Not at all." He kissed her again.

"By the way . . . you taste like me."

"You're not complaining , are you?"

"Not at all." She kissed him.

"My meeting for this morning got rescheduled." He pushed his hips into her. "I have an extra hour."

"Sorry." She reached down and stroked him. "I'm already an hour late for work. The other nurses are covering for me."

"Tonight then?"

"Not till late."

"Huh?" He pulled her hand away.

"What? I told you we were going out after work tonight . . . V's birthday."

"V's birthday . . . yes, I remember."

"What time will you be home tonight?" She reached down and started stroking again.

"I should be home by seven. Please . . . stop."

"I won't be home until midnight. So . . . you'll have plenty of time." She tightened her grip. "You know what I want you to do . . . don't you?"

"Yes."

"Leave the glass on the counter and be waiting for me in bed . . . ready. I don't want to have to waste time getting you stiff. I'm gonna be horned up. Five sluts . . . the cocks are gonna be hanging all over us all night. I'm gonna need to get off bad, that is if I don't before I get home." She pulled her hand away, kissed him, took a step back, looked down, licked her lips, then looked into his eyes. "I suggest a cold shower."

Meeka opened the bathroom door. "What are you doing in there?"

"Taking a shower."

"Are you sure that's all you are doing?"

"Fucker."

"I gotta go . . . I'll see you tonight."

"Okay . . . be safe."

"Always." She closed the door and as she walked by the bed, Reece's phone, resting on the nightstand, caught her eye. Ever since she saw Reece flirting with the wonder-bitches, she felt, for the first time in their three year relationship, threatened. And she had reason to be. After all, she had pursued and stolen him from his previous bitch. It had been easy. She sensed he was not happy and once she got him into her bed she knew exactly what she had to do to keep him there. Was it now her turn to be the bitch?

Who was his lunch date with? She picked up the phone, looked up the last call received, jotted down the number, and threw the note in her purse.

22

"What if four shots were fired? If there were four, they couldn't have all been fired by Oswald. The physical evidence of three shell casings on the sixth floor of the Texas School Book Depository Building doesn't support it. Also, the Zapruder film places the shots in a six second window, too fast for Oswald to have fired four shots."

"Guys, we've been debating this three shot, four shot question for days."

"Isn't that what your model is telling us Paul?"

"Hey, back off Joseph. It's not my model. It's our model. I didn't build it. We built it."

"It was your idea."

"Yea, and if it wasn't for this idea, we'd still be trying to convince Landis of a project to work on."

"Time out . . . take a deep breath."

"Okay . . . what is the model telling us versus what the eyewitnesses are telling us?"

"Forty percent of the eyewitnesses felt the shots came from the Texas School Book Depository Building, forty percent felt the shots came from the grassy knoll, and twenty percent felt they came from other areas."

"There is a high correlation, like 0.7, between where you were standing in Dealey Plaza and where you thought the shots came from. Those closer to the School Book Depository Building thought the shots came from there, and those closer to the grassy knoll thought they came from that location."

"But still, twenty-five percent of the people near the building thought that the shots came from the grassy knoll, and fifteen percent of the people on the grassy knoll thought that the shots came from the building. Some statistical significance, but not anything I would hang my hat on."

"But look what happens when you factor in our analysis of where the sound waves would have traveled with shots fired from the sixth floor versus shots fired from the grassy knoll. Slightly more people standing near the building should have heard shots fired from the grassy knoll area than the other way around."

"Which is consistent with the eyewitness testimony."

"Yes . . . but statistically it's too small of a variation to be significant."

"Joseph, what did you conclude from the other twenty percent of the eyewitnesses who thought the shots came from someplace else other than the building or grassy knoll?"

"If the model is correct . . . "

"The model's correct."

"The model indicates for about eighty percent of those eyewitnesses, they were probably hearing sound waves that bounced off of other solid surfaces. In other words, echoes. In fact there is a very high correlation, let's see, 0.6, between where they thought the sound came from and where we predict the actual sound wave, from the model, came from."

"You know, when you think about it, those are some pretty powerful statements that I don't think anyone has been able to make before to that level of confidence."

"There's only one problem. If we just model shots coming from the building, we get a definite sound wave pattern that should be received by those eyewitnesses on the grassy knoll as shots coming from the building. Yet forty percent of those eyewitnesses don't think that. That's a statistically significant number. So what are we missing?"

"You know what's wrong? Fuck. I can't believe we didn't see it."

"You're killing me Joseph . . . what?"

"Just a minute . . . there. Look at the question they asked the eyewitnesses. Where do you think the shots came from?"

"So."

"They were leading the witness. Where do you think the shots came from? Don't you think they should have asked first, do you think all the shots came from the same place, then where?"

"But if we assume more shots came from the building than the grassy knoll, why did so many people on the grassy knoll think the shots, and we need to assume all the shots, came from the grassy knoll?

"That's easy. It's the same reason why eyewitness testimony isn't reliable. Think about it. If you heard three or four shots being fired, when you didn't expect any shots to be fired, from two different, but still close locations, with after echoes indicating even different locations, all in six seconds, which shot would make the biggest impression on your brain?"

Paul and Ryan stared at Joseph for a few seconds before Paul spoke up. "The loudest one."

"The loudest one. And where would the loudest gunshot come from?"

"Most likely the location you were closest to."

"Which is what the data shows."

"It's why the eyewitnesses are so confused. Gunshots, coming from different directions, located at different distances away, with echoing issues. It's a wonder there is any correlation at all."

"You know . . . this sound wave model is so accurate, if we knew the actual orientation of each eyewitnesses ears, which we obviously don't, but if we did, I bet we could correlate to even greater accuracy which direction the witnesses should have heard shots coming from."

"Forget it."

"I know . . . I'm just thinking out loud."

"So what are we concluding here?"

"I think we are saying there appears to be enough circumstantial evidence to indicate more than three shots were fired, and from two different locations."

"If that's the case, we have two other problems that would need to be addressed."

"Paul, you're gonna make a great boss some day. You're always inventing more work."

"Well . . . I'm the abstract guy. You're the logical thinkers."

"So what new problems do we need to solve?"

"Two shooters, firing from two different locations, tells everyone there was a conspiracy. True conspirators would not want you to find out about the conspiracy. And from the first seconds of the shots being fired until now, fifty years, not a lot of hard evidence has surfaced to suggest a second shooter on the grassy knoll."

"What about the Moorman's Polaroid picture?"

"You can't make out anyone in that picture. It's a black blob."

"We better figure something out. We meet with Landis in two hours."

"Can't we delay the meeting until later in the afternoon? We probably only need a few more hours to put something together."

"The only time he's available is lunchtime."

"Great . . . Landis is gonna bury us."

"Wait . . . I have an idea."

"Is it something we can do in two hours?"

"I think so."

23

"Can you get us access to the National Archives?"

Reece was leaning back in his well-worn – although he liked to call it comfortable – black leather chair, staring at Rose only because she was first to speak up among the three woman sitting before him on the opposite side of his desk. No, hello? No, thanks for meeting with us on such short notice? No, we've run into a problem we'd really like to discuss with you? No . . . not with this team. With this team it was, we've got a problem, we've already figured out how to solve it, and we just need you to do your part to help us.

He liked that about them, although he would be the first to admit he doubted them from the beginning. But they had turned him around by the end of their first meeting. Their project was the kind of out-of-the-box idea he wanted these bright young minds to bring to him. It had been almost fifty years since the assassination and twenty for him running this seminar. Every conspiracy theorist's conspiracy theory had either been disproved or shown to be totally ridiculous. Since most of the available evidence had been looked at many times over the years, the probability of finding something new was extremely small. However if something were found it could be the one missing item that changes now-circumstantial evidence, that points to something other than a lone loser gunman killing JFK, to real evidence, or the most important finding in the fifty years since the assassination. Low probability events with high consequences have always been ignored because they are too difficult for the human mind to comprehend. A building sized meteor striking the earth and destroying civilization – a low probability, high consequence event until it happened to the dinosaurs. A human induced nuclear accident killing anyone – a low probability, high consequence event until it happened at Chernobyl in 1986. A 100 year hurricane destroying dikes that had protected a city for decades – a low probability, high consequence event until it happened in New Orleans in 2005 with Hurricane Katrina. The remnants of a hurricane coming up the east coast of the US, combining with a full moon high tide at the exact instant it strikes land – a low probability, high consequence event until it happened in New York City in 2012 with Hurricane Sandy.

The wonder–women's project was such an idea. Like finding a needle in a haystack. But if they did find the needle . . .

"Good morning to you too, ladies. No problem squeezing you into my busy schedule this morning. So can you explain why the normally proprietary database I was able to get you access to that contains every known photograph and video of the JFK assassination in Dealy Plaza on November 22, 1963, is not adequate for your analysis?"

Kayla and Tia turned to Rose who was sitting between them.

"Kayla, what's wrong with the data I've given you?"

"Rose be . . . I mean we believe the technique that was used in 1963 to develop, especially photographs, relied too much on the judgment of the person actually developing the film and therefore the negatives may have captured more information than what shows up on the photographic print."

"I'm listening."

"In the early sixties, although some automated film technology existed, most of the developing was performed by hand. This left a lot of latitude for the person doing the developing, specifically the process for producing the actual print. The first part of the process was to develop the actual film from the camera, which was a negative image – that is the brighter the light image was that hit the film, the darker the film got – of the actual image captured on the film. The second part of the process was to take the negative and print the actual pictures on photographic paper. This is where we believe the human played a big part in the process. They could manually adjust the image projected from the negative onto the photographic paper. Logic would tell you that the most important part of the photograph would be the information captured in the center of the picture being taken. Therefore the person doing the developing would fill the print paper with the negative image, and to make sure he filled the entire paper available, would overlap part of the negative image outside the paper. In most cases this would not be a problem because, again, you are interested in what is in the center of the picture, not on the edges. If something were lost from that part of the picture, it is likely no one would care."

"And all of the pictures in the database are already developed images . . . you think there could be something on the negative?"

There was a long pause before Tia spoke up. "Our research indicates only the actual developed photographs were given to the Warren Commission. We also cannot find any reference in any of the analyses we've looked at that indicates anyone considered looking at the negatives.

"We understand that even though all of the original photographs were returned to their owners following the Warren Commission investigation, many of the owners donated them to the government and they are being held in the National Archives."

"But the negatives . . . "

"We understand that in many cases the negatives were also donated."

"But Tia . . . the probability of the photograph and the negative being one that has something on it . . . "

"From what we have been able to determine about fifty percent of the photographs and something less than fifty, let's say thirty percent, have their corresponding negatives. We think we will be able to narrow our search down to something less than fifty photographs – those associated with the grassy knoll, the limousine, and the Texas School Book Depository Building.

"When we first presented our proposal to you, do you recall the question you asked regarding . . . "

"Your probability of success?"

"And we answered . . . "

"Less than one in a million."

"Well, if the population of photographs now available for analysis is only one third of what it was before . . . "

"Your probability of success is one in three million . . . "

"Versus one in one million."

"And the one in one million figure was only an educated guess to begin with," Kayla interjected. "It could be one in one hundred thousand, or one in ten million. Looking at it that way, we are still within the range we estimated when we first decided this project should be a go."

"Very convincing, ladies. And, yes, I do have a contact at the National Archives. Plus, she owes me a favor. But . . . they're not going to let you just rummage through their files. I need to have a plan describing what you want to do . . . " Kayla reached down into her briefcase. "And . . . you need to describe what potential damage or harm may come to the negatives, including how much their lifespan might be reduced."

Kayla continued to reach into her briefcase, pulled out a bound ten page report, and handed it to Reece. "The only part of the document that may change is the list of photographs we would like access to. That should be finalized in the next day or two. When we have finalized it, we will email you an electronic copy of this document."

Reece reached for the report, thumbed through it, and laid it back on the desk.

"You have one week left in this program. If you want any chance of getting into the National Archives early next week, which will still only give you a few days to finish your research, I'll need the list of photographs you want access to by the end of the day."

"Today?"

"You'll have it by the end of the day."

"Ladies . . . I'll see what I can do."

"Thank you, Dr. Landis." They stood up, shook Reece's hand, first Kayla, then Tia, then Rose, and walked out of the office. Five steps down the hall Kayla turned and gave the high-five first to Tia, then Rose. "What kind of a high-five was that, Rose? You got everything you were looking for."

"Wait here. I've got to ask Landis something." Rose turned and knocked on the door jamb to Landis's office.

"Dr. Landis."

"Yes, Rose."

"Can I ask you something?"

"I wanted to make sure your teammates were carrying their share of the workload. I see that they are . . . it's why I didn't call on you . . . isn't that what you were going to ask me?"

"No. I knew what you were doing. Thanks, but everyone on the team is working very hard."

"Okay . . . what then?"

"The black and white drawing hanging on the wall behind you . . . is that Dealey Plaza drawn from the perspective of the grassy knoll?"

Reece turned and looked up at the drawing. "Yes it is."

"And those two figures, in the background, behind the limo, the man and the child, is that . . . "

"Yes." Reece turned and looked at Rose.

"I've seen the photograph. It's one of the Marley photos."

Reece turned his chair a quarter turn, and pushed it back revealing the five by seven inch black and white picture framed in a thick black wooden frame on the credenza, previously hidden from view by the leather chair. It was the picture of Dealey Plaza replicated in the sketch hanging on the wall, except the only part of the silhouettes showing in the photograph were the shoes – obviously of a man and a child.

He turned again and they both stared at one another.

"It's one of the photographs we are hoping to enhance."

24

“Come in, come in. Let’s sit at the table. I got us salads. Two topped with spicy shrimp, two with spicy chicken, and one with pulled pork. I hope that’s okay with you. And I got an extra one for you, Joseph.”

“These look great. Where did you get them from?”

“Dinosaur. You guys been there yet?”

“We went there the first week. It was on your must go list.”

“I don’t think you’ll have a bad meal at any of those places on the list.”

“We haven’t . . . they’ve all been great. But I didn’t know the Dinosaur delivered. We could be having this for lunch all the time.”

“They usually don’t. But for five salads and trimmings, they’ll sometimes make an exception. So it was a good thing it was your team I was meeting with at lunchtime.”

“Thanks, Joseph.”

“Thanks for getting me two.”

“No problem. Please, dig in. We’ll have to talk and eat at the same time. I have another meeting at one. So, what’s on your mind? How is your modeling working out, Paul?”

“It’s actually not Paul’s model anymore . . . it’s all of ours.”

“Great, Joseph . . . I’m glad to see you’ve all bought into it. You will either all sink or swim together. Perfect.”

"We've actually completed modeling Dealey Plaza. It was a lot more complicated than we first thought. I handled the geometry. Things like the topography, building shapes, and other structures. Joseph determined all of the sound reflection constants for the various materials."

"There were over a hundred. Different bricks and stones, wood, glass, trees, grass, smooth and rough concrete."

"And Ryan handled placing all the eyewitnesses in the right locations."

"We only modeled those that we had testimony from indicating where they thought the shots came from."

"So, what did you come up with?"

"Before we get to that, Ryan wants to discuss some of the statistical analyses we performed."

"The first thing we did after we put everything into the model was to try to duplicate what the eyewitnesses said about where they thought the shots came from. When we modeled the shots being fired from the sixth floor of the Texas School Book Depository Building, the sound wave traveled a path such that the people standing near the building should have said they heard the shots coming from the building."

"Which makes sense. But what about the people standing near the building who thought the shots came from the grassy knoll?"

"I'll get to that, but first let's look at three other cohorts of witnesses. First, those witnesses who were on the grassy knoll and thought the shots came from the Texas School Book Depository Building. Because of where many of them were standing, there is a high probability that the sound waves they heard were from the Building.

"The second cohort is those witnesses who were near the building, but thought they heard the shots coming from elsewhere in the plaza, but not the grassy knoll. Because of where these people were standing there was a high probability they heard sound waves that echoed off other surfaces. That's why they thought the shots came from elsewhere.

"The third cohort is those witnesses who were standing on the grassy knoll and thought they heard the shots coming from elsewhere in the plaza, but not the sixth floor. Again, because of where these people were standing there was a high probability they heard sound waves that echoed off of other surfaces. That's why they thought shots came from elsewhere."

"Let me see if I understand what you just said. You've described four groups of witnesses. One near the building who thought the shots came from the building. One near the grassy knoll who thought the shots came from the building. One near the building and one near the grassy knoll who thought the shots came from elsewhere in the plaza, but not the building or grassy knoll."

"That's correct."

"When you say high probability, what kind of correlation coefficient are you coming up with? Greater than 0.5?"

"From 0.6 to 0.8."

"Really. So that . . . "

"And . . . sorry to interrupt."

"No, go ahead Joseph."

"We might be able to improve that even further. Paul had the idea to orient where the person was facing during the shots. Since the human interprets sounds directly ahead best, and only to one side or the other next, we thought we could model that to see what it does to the results."

"How will you get that orientation? You have some photos, but . . . "

"I had the idea that most witnesses were probably facing the president's limousine. So that might be a good first guess."

"Great assumption. I'd like to know how that impacts the correlation coefficient. The closer you can get to 1.0, or a perfect correlation, the more credible your analysis.

"But as I was saying, that leaves two other groups of witnesses, doesn't it? One near the building who thought they heard shots coming from the grassy knoll and the other on the grassy knoll who thought they heard the shots coming from the grassy knoll."

"That's correct." Ryan responded, but then waited silent with the others.

"None of you want to speak up and I think I know why."

"For the last two cohorts, we modeled . . . "

"No Paul, let me tell you what I think you found. For the cohort of witnesses near the building that said they heard the shots coming from the grassy knoll, you couldn't find a pattern of sound waves emanating from the sixth floor that would explain that eyewitness testimony. And for the cohort on the grassy knoll that thought the shots came from the grassy knoll, you also could not find a pattern of sound waves emanating from the sixth floor that would explain that eyewitness testimony."

"That's correct, Dr. Landis."

"What was the correlation coefficient?"

"Less than 0.2."

"Are you going to tell me what you modeled next, or do you want me to tell you?"

"You're on a roll, Dr. Landis . . . go for it."

"You modeled shots coming from the grassy knoll."

"Yes."

"And the correlation coefficient for those last two cohorts increased."

"Yes."

"To what?"

"Between 0.6 and 0.8."

The three watched Landis as his eyes shifted back and forth among them. They wanted him to experience the same feeling they had when they first saw the numbers. This was now more than just eyewitness testimony about shots coming from the grassy knoll. This was statistical analysis of the data which now indicated to a high level of confidence that the root cause of why people thought shots came from the grassy knoll area was not echoing, but actual sound waves from a gunshot coming from the grassy knoll.

"And you are confident it is not echoing we are dealing with here?"

"These individuals certainly heard some echoing. Everyone in Dealey Plaza that day did. However, these witnesses heard the sound of shots that dwarfed any echoing sounds. And the sounds came from somewhere other than the sixth floor."

"And why didn't the other witnesses on the grassy knoll hear the same shots?"

"The same reason why forty percent of the witnesses near the building thought the shots came from the grassy knoll even though we know to a high level of confidence that shots did come fron the sixth floor above them."

"And what's that, Joseph?"

"Actually, you said it before yourself. It's because we, humans, make terrible witnesses. You have the surprise of the shots ringing out. Many first thought it was the sound of firecrackers or a car backfiring. The last thing anyone thought, even several secret service agents, was that it was gunshots. You have the echo chamber effect of Dealey Plaza making a single shot sound like several and coming from different directions. Then you have people running in two different directions to where they thought the shots came from. And finally you lead the witness when you question him with 'Where do you think the shots came from?' instead of asking first 'Do you think all of the shots came from the same direction?'

"All of this conflicting information confuses the human mind, and our brain does not like to exist in a confused state. It doesn't like ambiguity. It will try to make some sense of it all. It will, if it has to, force a decision. It will come to a conclusion one way or another. That is, with or without even ourselves realizing it."

"How confident are you that this really does model the correct sound wave patterns?"

"Sound waves emanating from a source follow a very predictable pattern. We know how sound waves behave when they strike objects. We know how much of the sound wave is absorbed and how much is reflected. The model is based on sonar technology. Instead of sound waves traveling through water, in our model it travels through air. It's a reliable predictor of what happens in the real world."

"As I remember, any movie I've seen where a submarine, for example uses sonar, a single ping is sent out and the reflection of that sound is what is read to predict if an object is detected. Is that correct?"

"Yes."

"In Dealey Plaza that day, we are fairly certain based on the Zapruder film that the shots, wherever they were fired from, were all discharged in a six second window. Correct?"

"Yes."

"When you performed your analysis I assume you modeled the sound from a single shot?"

"Yes."

"But that's all we needed to do since if you assume the shots came from essentially the same spot, the sound wave pattern would be identical."

"That's true, but if the shots were fired close enough to one another, couldn't the echoed sound wave from one shot interfere with the sound wave produced by a second follow-on shot? After all, isn't it possible to produce two sound waves that essentially cancel each other out such that the human ear hears nothing?"

"Like a confounding effect?"

"Exactly. As I recall my physics, sound travels about four times faster in water than air. So with sonar, with faster sound waves and greater distances, you probably don't have to worry about any kind of feedback, or waves interfering with waves. But in air, with waves traveling slower over much shorted distances, with complicated echoing, couldn't you get interference and potentially sound waves being interpreted much differently by the human brain?"

"Potentially, yes."

"I suggest you go back and look at this issue."

25

"Hello." Reece had been standing in the doorway watching his mother staring out the window. He wished there was some way he could tell which mother he was going to meet and more importantly if she was the right one, would she stay that way for the entire visit?

"Where have you been? Oh my dear . . . it's you."

"Sorry to disappoint you. Were you expecting someone else?"

"No . . . no, of course not. Come over here and give me a hug. You know me . . . sometimes my brain doesn't know why it says the things it does."

Reece looked at his mother. He couldn't remember if he'd ever known her to tell a lie directly to his face, other than say a white lie about a surprise birthday party, but he had a suspicion she was doing so now.

"You are my son, right?"

She's lying to me. And it's her, not the disease.

26

"Five more Electric Lemonades."

"Alright . . . but then we do a Slippery Nipple."

"Oh, ladies . . . don't all look at once, but you should see what just walked in at the other end of the bar. I said don't all look at once."

"O M G . . . he waved to us."

"Of course he did V . . . Happy Birthday. We all pitched in and got him for you."

The five women erupted in laughter.

"Happy birthday V." They downed the shots.

"We need some Slippery Nipples."

"You're kidding, right?"

"No . . . Slippery Nipples are next."

"No, no, no . . . I mean . . . him."

"Who?"

"Him."

"You mean, did we get him for you?"

"Yeah."

"Why . . . do you really want him?"

"So, you didn't."

"You sound disappointed."

"No . . . not really."

"Hold on. Make that six Slippery Nipples."

"Six?"

"Yes . . . send one down to the big guy at the end of the bar. Tell him it's a Slippery Nipple from the birthday girl, V."

"No, don't."

"Too late . . . I already poured them."

"Let's see if we can get V laid tonight."

"I don't have any trouble getting laid all by myself, thank you."

"By something like that?"

"Well . . . he's looking over here again. He downed the shot. Oh no . . . he's coming over here."

"You ladies look like you're having way too much fun. I'm Joseph." He extended his hand.

"Hi, Joseph. This is Darla, Julia, Elise, V or Victoria . . . "

"The birthday girl."

"Yes, the birthday girl . . . and I'm Meeka."

"Hi, Meeka. Nice to meet you all. And I guess it would only be appropriate for me to buy you a drink. So in response to your Slippery Nipple, I would like to get you . . . bartender . . . six Red Headed Sluts, please."

"You're not trying to get us drunk so you can take advantage of us, are you?"

"That thought never crossed my mind."

"It didn't . . . why not?"

All five women were now staring at him.

"Well . . . um . . . I don't know?"

"Do you have something against white women?"

"Not at all. In fact I'm . . . "

"Because we don't have anything against black men."

"In fact . . . some of us really like black men."

"Are you married?"

"No, are any of you?"

The women were now looking at each other.

"Would that make any difference to you?"

"I guess that depends what you have in mind? I mean if we were just going to enjoy each other's company here at the bar, I guess it doesn't make any difference. If we were . . . "

"Well, tonight may be your lucky night. Tonight we have about as varied a choice as you can imagine. One of us is married, relatively happy, but could be tempted. One is in a relationship, but is always looking. One of us is recently divorced and enjoying her new found freedom. One has never been married, because she likes variety. And one is into only satisfying other women."

"It's not hard to tell who is who."

"Go for it."

"Obviously, Julia is married."

"The ring?" She held up her left hand.

"Yes, the ring."

"I told you I should take it off when I'm with you guys."

"And what if you lost it?"

"Or you forgot to put it on when you got home?"

"Ronald would kill you."

"Darla is recently divorced."

"How did you know that?"

"You've got a ring on every finger except the ring finger on your left hand."

"Damn."

"V is single, Elise is into women, and Meeka has a guy, but strays."

"How did you know?"

"I don't stray . . . I look, but don't touch."

"Never?"

"Never say never."

"Uh-huh."

"Seriously, how did you know?"

"I don't know. My gut told me. Call it men's intuition."

"So, we're here for a birthday celebration. If you're not here to take advantage of us, why are you here?"

"I'm taking a course up on the hill at S.U. We're almost done so we're doing some celebrating. I'm supposed to meet some guys here. Dolce Vita is a great place to eat. We come here a lot, being it's so close to the hill. I just happen to get here early."

"To check things out?"

"You guys don't give up, do you?"

"We're trying to get V laid."

"And if she doesn't want to, Darla has second dibs."

"Then Meeka."

"Then Julia."

"Then me . . . but only if we make it a threesome with one of them too."

"I told you it was your lucky night."

"So how many drinks would it take to make that happen?"

"Ah . . . we've got a kinky one here."

"You brought it up. I'm just trying to fulfill a birthday wish."

"Uh-huh."

"How about another shot. My treat again."

"Step one . . . he's getting us drunk."

"When does step two start?"

"Anytime you want it to, V."

"So what do you ladies do for a living?"

"We're all nurses."

"Yeah . . . so if you want to get kinky, you've met up with the right bunch of women. We nurses can do things to your body you wouldn't believe was possible."

"I know the perfect drink for a nurse. Bartender . . . six Blood Transfusions, please."

"Are you following me to the bathroom, Meeka?"

"Actually, I am."

Joseph turned and faced Meeka.

"In case you are interested. Well, I have this friend. She is into some pretty kinky stuff. BDSM. I don't know too much about it. But, she really gets off on it. And she's really into doing it with . . . black men. Especially, big black men. Like you. She likes dominating them. Here's her card."

"Zaria . . . first name, last name?"

"Only name. If you are interested, give her a call. Like I said, I don't know much about it, but I don't think you'll be disappointed."

27

"Do you believe we are stuck here on a Friday night working on this project?"

"Sorry to cut into your party time Kayla, but if we don't get this list to Dr. Landis . . . "

"I know Tia, I know. We won't be going to the National Archives."

"If you two guys wanna take off, I can finalize this by myself. There's not much more to do."

"Really?"

"No way, Rose . . . Kayla."

"I was just kidding. The night's still young. It's still light out."

"It's the longest day of the year Kayla. It's quarter to ten."

"Still early."

"Your man must be lonely without you. What's that . . . the tenth time he's texted you?"

"And I noticed, you haven't been responding lately."

"Rose, she's been too busy to respond. You're working her ragged."

"He can be such an asshole. I don't know why he thinks he has to make me jealous. I do any fuck'n thing he wants. You know what I did last night . . . "

"No."

"I got him off . . . "

"No. We mean no, and we don't want to know."

"Too much information again?"

"Yeah."

"So, if you're doing anything he wants, then how is he making you jealous?"

"He texted me from Dolce Vita earlier saying five horny nurses were all over him and maybe I should come join him."

"If they are hanging all over him, why would he want you there?"

"Ménage a trios material."

"Too much information again."

"Men are stupid. They don't know when they have it good."

"Who said it's him."

"Too much information."

"Hey guys, look at this."

"Whatcha got Tia?"

"I've been looking at frame 313 of the Zapruder film."

"Is that the gory one . . . the frame that caught the bullet striking the back of JFK's head?"

"Well, that's part of the debate. Some believe it was frame 312. But most people believe the bullet struck his skull between these two frames, at one-eighteenth of a second before frame 313, which makes sense because, yes it's the gory one, the head is already blowing apart in frame 313. But look at this."

"Is that frame 312?"

"Yes. I computer enhanced both of these frames. We can clearly see his head moves slightly forward between these two frames. In fact it moves a little over 2 inches."

"That's the evidence people use to prove that the bullet that struck JFK's head came from the rear, or the direction of the Texas School Book Depository Building."

"You're not disputing that, are you?"

"No, but look at this. Just behind JFK's head, in frame 313."

"What is that? It looks like something shining on top of the curb."

"Maybe it's something on the top of the curb reflecting light."

"That's what I thought at first too. But then I went and looked at frame 314, when I computer enhanced it . . . "

"It's gone."

"Exactly."

"Is it an imperfection on the film?"

"Could be. Don't forget this is a copy of a copy of a copy we are looking at."

"Did you run it through my software?"

"I did."

"So what did it tell you it was?"

"That's what's weird. There's a ninety percent probability that it's an imperfection on the film, and less than a ten percent probability that it's a reflection of some kind."

"Well we know it can't be a reflection. It's gone in the next frame."

28

Meeka paced herself tonight. She thought about getting shit-faced. That was right after calling the number she'd copied from Reece's phone earlier today and getting Kayla's voice mail. But if she did, she probably wouldn't remember anything she was going to do to Reece when she got home. And she wanted to savor what she had planned.

She saw the wine glass sitting on the counter as soon as she walked into the kitchen. By the amount of liquid in the glass she was pretty certain Reece hadn't had sex with Kayla at their lunch-time meeting. She dipped two fingers into the glass, then slipped her hand into her pants, and shoved her fingers into herself. She repeated the process several more times then drank what was left of the liquid.

"You better be fuck'n thinking about me." Meeka stood next to the bed, naked, watching Reece lying on his back, also naked, his right hand slowly stroking himself.

He hadn't heard her come in and his already pounding heart picked up a beat. He wondered how long she had been standing there. It couldn't have been too long. A minute or two ago he had been staring at the two MILFs, taking advantage of their young stud as much as he was taking advantage of them, on the widescreen on the wall. Then his eyes closed as he fantasized not about the movie scene, but what he hoped would happen later in the evening when Meeka would fulfill his long requested fantasy of a threesome. It was a perfect opportunity with several in her group of nurse friends being very acceptable, including probably a very horny, recently divorced, Darla.

"Why do I think you're not? Get your fuck'n hand off there." She slapped his hand away, climbed on top of him, and mounted his face as she held onto the large wooden headboard. "Oh yes . . . flick it good you bastard. At least you're good for something. Like the taste of my snatch? I had a half dozen studs to pick from tonight. Oh . . . yes, right there. I picked the . . . oh fuck. I picked the . . . ahhhh . . . the black one. Ohhhh . . . " She rubbed herself onto his flicking tongue. "Don't stop . . . make it last." He did, for several minutes.

"Get up and get over here." Meeka placed hand cuffs on him, stepped on the small stool, and yanked up his arms. "Up on your tiptoes." She looped the chain from the cuffs over the hook that was attached to the bracket mounted on the wall – the same bracket that normally held the spider plant – and closed the hook. Unlike most of the BDSM props they normally played with, ones that with enough effort were usually loose enough to escape from, this was Houdini-proof.

Meeka walked over to the nightstand, lit up a cigarette, then moved the chair, from the corner of the room, in front of Reece, and sat down. With the same hand she had the cigarette in she gripped his swollen head. "Do you remember what I did to you the last time I had you like this?"

Reece squirmed just thinking about it. He didn't look down, even when he heard the unfamiliar clicking sound. Seconds later he flinched from the pinprick-like pain he felt on his shaft.

"Oh, honey . . . I wouldn't move if I was you."

The second time he felt it, he tried not to move, but felt the urge to look down. "What the fuck are you doing?"

"Oh, honey . . . I told you not to move. Now look what you've done. You're bleeding. And you know with the amount of blood in this thing, you could bleed to death."

"What the fuck is that?"

"Oh, this little thing? It's my switchblade. I picked it up a few weeks ago. For protection. You never know when you might need it." She placed the point back onto his shaft.

"Fuck . . . you're cutting me."

"Isn't that what you're supposed to do with a knife?"

"Ahhhh . . . I'm fuck'n bleeding. YELLOW, YELLOW, YELLOW!"

"YELLOW! Fuck you with your safeword. This isn't a fuck'n game I'm playing with you tonight." She pulled the knife away, lowered it, and pricked one of his balls.

"Ahhhh!"

"I wouldn't move if I was you."

"Ahhhh!"

"I wonder what's worse . . . having your balls . . . "

"Ahhhh!"

"Or this cut off?"

She pulled the knife away, let go of his head, flicked the ashes from her cigarette onto his shaft, took a puff, and blew the smoke onto his pubic hair. She stood up and moved in close to him, resting her breasts on his chest.

"I'm going to ask you a question. And even though I already know the answer, I wanna see if you've got the balls, while you still have balls, to tell me the truth. Were you with that slut Kayla today?"

"Yes . . . but not the way you . . . AHHHH!"

29

"Rose, do you believe it's almost one o'clock?"

"Kayla didn't leave until after eleven."

"She didn't want to leave."

"We got the information to Landis by the end of the day. What?"

"A minute before midnight?"

"It was still Friday. And if Kayla hadn't of stayed until eleven we wouldn't have made it."

"She wanted to stay."

"I know she did."

"No, I mean she wanted to stay after that."

"There was no need to. The most important thing got done."

"I think she wanted to be here in case we found something."

"Well, the probability of that happening was pretty low. Let's see . . . the probability of answering the JFK assassination conspiracy question, I'd say, pretty close to zero. The probability of Kayla getting laid tonight, I'd say, pretty close to one. So who're the stupid ones."

"Rose, are you jealous of Kayla?"

"Not so much jealous as . . . well who's been the smarter one over these past three weeks? We've spent all our time, except for when we've gone out to dinner, focused on this project. And what did we get out of it? What have all thirty of us gotten out of it? We've all proved the null hypothesis, that there is no smoking gun. No conspiracy. Has it been fun? Kayla has it right. She works on the project to get some enjoyment out of it, and, she finds time to enjoy life too. Life-balance. She's a lot smarter than us."

"You've enjoyed working on this, Rose. We both did. Otherwise we wouldn't have spent so much time on it."

"I'm just saying there is probably a better balance out there."

"In hindsight there always is."

"Tia, the philosopher."

"Well, think about it. What if we would have found something on frame 313. How many people do you think have looked at that frame . . . a million? Has anyone else noticed what we noticed?"

"What did we notice, Tia? We've analyzed the crap out of all the frames showing that location on the curb. Nothing. It's probably just a defect on the copy of the copy of the copy we are looking at."

"I guess we will find that out when we get to review the film at the National Archives."

"They're not going to let us look at the original. I don't care who Landis is, he doesn't have that kind of clout."

"No, maybe he doesn't. But if we can get closer to the original copy and the speck disappears, we then know for sure it's a defect."

"And if it doesn't, then what?"

"We'll have to see if we can go back further, I guess."

"Fat chance."

"Let's cross that bridge when we come to it."

"We're done here. We've got an hour before the bars close. Let's go get buzzed. I'll even let you buy the first one, Tia."

"Who knows, maybe we'll get someone else to buy."

"The probability goes up the closer you get to two you know."

"Is that supposed to make me feel good, Rose?"

30

"How about domination?"

"Domination . . . I thought you wanted to do a threesome?"

"I thought you were the one who wanted to do the threesome?"

"I didn't hear any objections from you when I brought it up, did I Joseph Whitmore?"

"Do you think any man would object to his girlfriend . . . "

"Oh, now I'm your girlfriend? You're making a huge assumption there, mister."

"What . . . you're not my woman?"

"Woman! You're digging a deeper hole, Whitmore."

Joseph reached out, put his hands under Kayla's armpits, picked her up, and pulled her naked body against him. She spread her legs and wrapped them around his waist, grinding herself into his rock-hard washboard stomach. Her arms surrounded his neck. He slid his around her back. She placed her open mouth on his forcing her tongue into it. Their breathing deepened and she flexed her legs tighter, grinding herself into him.

"Shall we try again?"

"Sure." She tightened her legs some more.

"How about domination?" He reached down with both hands and

slapped each of her ass cheeks.

"Mmmmm . . . I feel like I'm being dominated whenever you're on top of me. Do you know you weigh more than twice as much as I do?"

"How often am I on top?" He slapped her again, only harder.

"Fuck . . . so it's not because you like to lay there and let me service you . . . you're looking out for my well being?"

"Exactly. And I think you kind 'a like being on top." Another slap, even harder.

"Kind 'a? That stings." She grinded herself into him.

"So what about the domination?" Another hard slap.

"Son of a . . . the way you order me around sometimes, I'm already being dominated anyway. I guess I could get into a fantasy about it." More grinding.

"No, Kayla . . . I don't think you understand. I want you to dominate me."

"Me? Do you? Now that . . . I think I could really get into that. Little me having big you . . . to do whatever I want to me? And I do whatever I want to you? I'm getting wet just thinking about it. Although, I don't know too much about the real thing. I mean BDSM. Could you teach me? Tell me what you want me to do?"

"Hold on. I'm no expert at it either." He slapped her again.

"Oh fuck . . . you could have fooled me."

"But . . . I may happen to know someone who might be able to help us out."

"I don't think we need any help. You're doing just fine."

31

"Tia . . . why Shifty's?"

"It's close, cheap, there's a band, and it's still crowded. Plus I hear it's a pick-up bar. You said you wanted to have more fun."

"Oh good. A pick-up bar. Just before two."

"I like to watch. Like take that guy at the bar. I bet when we walk up there, he'll move right out of the way and let us get a drink. Then he'll strike up a conversation with us."

"That's just being polite."

"Bet?"

"He's kind 'a cute, Tia. Okay . . . go for it."

"Excuse me."

"No problem."

"I only need a minute to get a few drinks. I'll be in and out before you know it."

"No problem. Did you ladies just get here?"

"We did."

"I'm Dixon."

"Tia . . . and this is Rose."

"Nice to meet you, Tia and Rose."

"How's the band?"

"Cookbook . . . they're great."

"Looks crowded out there."

"I think they only have a few more songs. People are trying to get their last dances in for the night."

"Rose, what would you like?"

"Snake Bite . . . double."

"What's in it?"

"Just try it."

"Two Snake Bites, please."

"You're brave. Having a drink without knowing what's in it."

"Rose was a bartender . . . I trust her. Plus, we not only just got here, but it's our first drink of the evening. We need to catch up to everyone else."

"Well a double Jack and Jack will do the trick."

"Wouldn't that be a quadruple Jack?"

"That's good Tia."

"Would you like to dance?"

"Sure . . . Rose could you hold our spot."

"When you said you might get someone else to pay, I didn't think you meant me."

"Wish me luck."

"Have fun."

"That'll be fourteen . . . out of a hundred."

Rose picked up the glass, hesitated a second, then downed the drink. She pushed the glass to the back of the bar and nodded to the bartender.

"Those things will knock you on your ass you know."

She turned to her right and came face to face with an unkempt used looking character – stubble faced, long disheveled salt and pepper hair, cutoff sweatshirt with what looked like drippings from chicken wing hot sauce, and matching beer breath, although he did have an overbearing scent of Old Spice, probably to try to cover up another scent – holding a bottle of Bud. In her sandaled feet he was still two inches shorter than her and might not have weighted as much. She concluded he was probably harmless, and if not, she could probably beat him up.

"I'm looking for a quick buzz."

"That'll do it, but tequila's a lot smoother."

"Good point. Would you join me?"

"Sure."

"Two Patron's, please."

"Whoa . . . top shelf kind 'a lady. You're out of my league, honey."

"Now how do you know what league I'm in?" Rose nudged in closer to him, trying to catch a whiff of his cologne and ignore his breath.

"You and your friend walk in here, take over the bar, throw a hundred up, and order rich-bitch shots . . . that's how."

"You want training wheels with that."

"No way."

"Not me." Although she did.

"That'll be sixteen."

"Take it out of here." Rose pointed to the bills on the bar. She picked up both glasses and handed one to the guy, which he didn't hesitate to take. "To rich-bitches."

"To rich-bitches."

"Another?"

"Honey, I been drink'n all night. Buy'n that shit for me is like piss'n in a toilet. And if you're look'n ta get laid tonight, that stuff does a job on my pecker." He held up his hand, index finger straight, then, let the finger drop down. "You know what I mean?"

She got close to his face. "I know what ya mean. How about a Bud then?"

"Now you're talk'n. That has just the opposite effect." He held up his hand and slowly stiffened his index finger.

"I bet it does." She pushed the glasses and empty bottle toward the back of the bar.

"Another round?"

"One Patron and a Bud, please."

As Rose leaned over the bar she turned her head to the right. Slouched at the end of the bar, with one elbow leaning on it, hunched over an empty glass, talking to the other bartender and staring at her healthy cleavage, was Dr. Landis. The bartender turned away, and in unison, as if he knew she was staring at him, Reece turned and waved at Rose.

"That'll be eleven."

Rose pushed a twenty toward the bartender, turned and started to wave, but Landis was gone.

"Thanks for the beer, honey. I don't even know your name."

"Those were some great songs, but I'm dying. It's hot in here. Hi . . . I'm Tia."

"Tia . . . Spider."

"Spider?"

"Was scared of 'em when I was a kid. Brothers used to yell spider at me all the time. Stuck ever since."

"Interesting. Is that my drink?" Tia reached in, grabbed the glass, and poured it down her throat. "Those are awful."

"I switched to tequila . . . want one?"

"Anything but that." She placed the glass on the bar.

"Where's Dixon?"

"Boy's room." Tia leaned into Rose. "Spider?"

"What?"

"Spider?"

"What the hell are you talking about?"

"So, Spider, I'm ready for another, are you?"

"What the hell." Spider put the full bottle to his lips, letting it empty into his mouth. "I guess I am."

Tia and Rose leaned into the bar. "Sorry, we hadn't gotten to names yet."

"I saw you do a shot with him."

"I wasn't writing him a letter. I was drinking with him. Don't need a name to do that."

"Two tequila's, a Bud, and a gin and tonic, no fruit."

"Patron's?."

"Yes."

"I got this one."

"So, how's Dixon."

"He's nice."

"Nice?"

"I've only known him for three dances."

"Two were slow."

"Do you mind if he takes me home? We're gonna do breakfast. I mean you can come too."

"I'm not gonna join you on your first date."

"It's not a date."

"Uh-huh."

"Two Patron's, a Bud, and a gin and Tonic. That's twenty-four. From here?"

"I got it. Keep the change. Here ya go Spider. To the longest day of the year."

"Excuse me ladies . . . gotta wiz and catch a smoke."

"Two more tequilas."

"You better slow down. You're drinking those on an empty stomach."

"I'm trying to get a buzz."

"For you or for Dixon?"

"Yes."

"Ohhhh."

"Besides, you got Spider."

"I don't know. He already warned me he might not be able to get it up tonight."

"What a gentleman."

"Actually, you'll never believe who's here."

"What are you two doing at Shitfy's?" Reece put his hands on Tia's and Rose's shoulders. They each turned around. "Don't you know this is one of Syracuse's premium pick-up bars, especially on a Friday night?"

"Dr. Landis?"

"We're here for the band."

"I saw you dancing up a storm out there Tia. If you'd like I could introduce you to the band. The lead singer, Ava, is a friend."

"Two Patron's. That's sixteen."

"Molly, make it three. And I got 'em."

"Here you go Reece." Molly flashed a wink.

"Thank you, Dr. Landis."

"I hope I'm not intruding? Were you doing shots with Spider?"

"I . . . um."

"Yes, she was." Tia reached down and poked Rose in the ribs. "And what are you doing here, Dr. Landis?"

"I'm celebrating."

"And where is Meeka? Isn't she here celebrating with you?"

"What should we toast to? Did you ladies get the file over to me?"

"Beat the deadline, actually."

"Great . . . to beating the deadline."

"Molly . . . three more."

"I don't know if I should."

"I thought you wanted a buzz?"

"Okay . . . one more."

"Three Patron's."

"Thanks Molly. Keep it."

"Thank you, Reece."

"Excuse me. I'm gonna try and find the guy I bought this drink for." Tia reached for the gin and tonic, and Patron, after pinching Rose on the leg. "Thanks again, Dr. Landis."

"Good luck."

"Yes . . . good luck Tia." Rose winked at Tia.

"Tia stepped behind Reece, where he couldn't see her, and mouthed, "You too, Rose," then winked.

Reece picked up his drink and motioned to Rose who did the same.

“To the National Archives.”

“Did you . . . ”

“Yes. Pending review of your plan, which I will send them first thing in the morning.” Reece clanged Rose’s glass and they both drank up. “It looks like the three of you should plan on flying down on Sunday afternoon and spending Monday morning at the Archives. I hope you can get your work done by early afternoon . . . ”

“We will.”

“Good, because that was the only window available for me to get you in there. Then plan to fly back that evening. That should still give you time to finalize your report by Friday.”

“Thank you, Dr. Landis.” Rose reached out and hugged him, but pulled away quickly. “Now this really does call for a celebration.”

“Rose, do you mind . . . ”

“Tia, we’re going to the National Archives.”

“Really . . . that’s great.” Tia and Rose hugged. “Thank you, Dr. Landis.”

She hugged Reece.

“Rose, do you mind if I go to breakfast?”

“No, of course not.”

“Thanks. And thanks again, Dr. Landis.” She hugged Rose and whispered, “I hope you are going to thank him properly.”

“I’ll see you later too. Have fun.”

“So . . . you never did say what you were out celebrating tonight?”

“My manhood.”

“I’m sorry?”

“Long story . . . I think we are going to need another drink.”

32

"Tia . . . Tia . . . open the door." Rose knocked on the door, hopefully loud enough to wake Tia and not anyone else who might be staying in the adjacent rooms. "Tia." She stopped knocking. It was almost four. What if Tia wasn't back yet? What if she was still at breakfast with Dixon? What if she went home with Dixon? "Tia." She went to knock again, then stopped. What if Dixon was in the room?

"Boo!"

"TIA!"

"Shhhh."

"You almost gave me a heart attack."

"Don't push me . . . what the hell are you doing here anyway? What if I brought a guy home with me?"

"Don't push me . . . you don't have a guy."

"What if I did?"

"Then he'd be excited thinking we were going to have a threesome."

"Right . . . so what do you want anyway?"

"Let's go in your room."

"You got anything to drink?"

"Vodka."

"Perfect."

"Ice?"

"No."

"Lemonade?"

"No."

"Say when."

"Grey Goose?"

"What?"

"We go out and you bitch about the price of drinks, but when you drink alone you drink Grey Goose."

"Who says I drink alone?"

"Tia."

"Well . . . if I ever don't drink alone, I want him to think I'm expensive."

"Always thinking."

"Probably too much. Bottle's half empty and I'm the only one who's drank it."

"How did you make out with Dixon?"

"We didn't . . . he was a perfect gentleman. I kissed him on the cheek."

"He wasn't interested, huh? I'm sorry."

"We're going out to dinner tomorrow night. He's picking me up at seven."

"You go girl."

"Now what was so important that you needed to break my door down at, holy crap . . . it's almost four in the morning."

"You're not gonna believe it."

"What? Wait a minute. Last time I saw you, you were with Dr. Landis."

"Uh-huh."

"Shut up. You did something with Landis?"

"No."

"I didn't think so."

"Why not?"

"First, it wouldn't be ethical. Second, he's not your type. And good thing, because third, did you forget about crazy Meeka?"

"Well, he may not be my type . . . but he could 'a been tonight."

"Shut up."

"Actually, he could 'a been anyone's tonight."

"What happened to Meeka . . . did they get into a fight?"

"I guess you could call it that."

"What?"

"Well . . . remember Meeka's threat to us?"

"Remember . . . I had nightmares about it. I still say we should have told Landis about it."

"I don't think that would 'a been such a good idea."

"Why not . . . what kind of a sicko makes a threat like that? Although I think she was all talk and no action. Bitch."

"Oh . . . I wouldn't be so sure about that."

"Why . . . did she show up there tonight? Did she see you with him? O M G . . . are you all right?"

"I'm fine. Nothing happened. She didn't show up."

"Then why don't you think she was just BS'n us?"

"Because she almost cut off Landis's dick earlier tonight."

"What! You mean right in front of you?"

"No . . . it happened earlier."

"And you know this how?"

"He told me."

"He told you. He told you his girlfriend almost cut off his dick? And this just came up in the evening's conversation. Like between ordering drinks. Or during a lull in the conversation. Hey . . . guess what? My girlfriend almost cut off my dick tonight."

"Yup . . . with a switchblade. Sound familiar?"

"I told you she was a nutcase. We should 'a warned him."

"Warned him of what? She threatened to use the knife on us, not him."

"So, why did she try to use it on him tonight?"

"He wouldn't share too many details . . . "

"Oh, he confided that she almost sliced his dick off, but couldn't tell you why?"

"I get the feeling that once he saw the blood . . . "

"Blood! You mean she really cut him down there?"

"He said once he saw the blood and realized she wasn't kidding, he managed to break free and . . . "

"Break free? She had him tied up?"

"I'm assuming that's what he meant. I mean think about it. How else would she be able to . . . to you know . . . do it?"

"Well . . . how did he let her tie him up to begin with?" They both stared at each other.

"My thought exactly."

"He's not only gorgeous, but kinky too."

"Sounds it."

"So tell me . . . does that now make him more your type?"

"Tia!"

"Well . . . you said you could 'a had um."

"He was in a vulnerable state. He kicked her out of his house. Then he took all her clothes and dumped them in her driveway."

"Sounds like something a woman would do."

"He was pissed because her car wasn't there."

"He tells you all this, but doesn't tell you why she wanted to cut it off?"

"He only mumbled something about she accused him of cheating on her."

"That would be reason enough for me to cut it off. Except, I wouldn't leave it laying around like that woman did with . . . who was it?"

"Bobbit."

"Yeah . . . Bobbit. I wouldn't leave it laying around so the bastard could get it sewn back on. I'd . . . I'd slice the damn thing up. Or maybe throw it down the garbage disposal."

"Tia . . . it sounds like you've given this some thought."

"I'm just say'n. Any man who pulls that shit deserves what he gets."

"Make sure you let Dixon know that."

"We're only going out to dinner."

"Well, Reece was . . . "

"Reece?"

"What . . . he told me to call him Reece."

"I guess when a guy is talking to you about his dick, the least he could do is let you call him by his first name."

"Anyway . . . he seemed pretty broken up about the whole thing. I don't think he was cheating on her."

"You have a few drinks with the guy and you can tell if he's being honest with you?"

"I just don't think he's that kind of a person."

"Rose Stone."

"What?"

"Are you smitten for the Dr. Landis?"

"He's not my type, remember."

"Uh-huh."

"I just feel sorry for him. I think he's depressed too. He kind 'a indicated this might be his last year with the seminar."

"Shut up."

"Yup."

"Another vodka . . . I mean, Grey Goose?"

"Yup."

"Why?"

"Because I got a damn good buzz go'n and I don't want it to be over yet. Although I'm gonna regret it in the morning."

"No . . . why does he want to stop doing the seminar? I mean he's a legend. He's famous."

"After fifty years he says all the JFK conspiracy theorists have been proven wrong. If something were out there to be found, we would 'a found it be now. And who would know better than him? He believes most of the conspiracies out there, aren't. Lincoln, 9/11, moon landings . . . "

"What?"

"Moon landings. You mean you never heard of that? Oh to be young. Lots of people think the moon landings were all staged on a Hollywood set. That's why the footprints look like sand and not moon dust. American flag fluttering in the what . . . moon wind? And supposedly the 400,000 people working on the space program all conspired to keep it a secret for more than forty years."

"I think it would probably be easier just to go to the moon."

"Exactly. So all these conspiracy theories are just that . . . theories that stretch the truth with no real factual evidence behind them."

"Do you think what we are doing is a waste of time?"

"I didn't . . . that is until earlier this evening."

"Why don't we just ask Dr. Landis what he thinks?"

"Yeah, right. I don't think I'll ever be able to look him in the eye again. At least sober anyway."

"So, do you want some more Grey Goose?"

"I'm not done with this."

"Well, I suggest you drink up. Have you forgotten we're meeting with Dr. Landis . . . I mean Reece . . . in less than ten hours."

33

"Mama?"

"Yes Reece."

"What did Papa do?"

"He was a photographer."

"Is that why he had a lot of cameras?"

"Uh-huh."

"How do you learn to be a photo grafter?"

"You mean a photographer?"

"Yes, that."

"Well . . . your papa learned when he was in the Army."

"Papa wasn't in the Army."

"Sure he was."

"No he wasn't. He was in the Marines."

"I'm sorry . . . you're right. The Marines. I didn't think you knew what the Marines were."

"Sure I do. Papa told me. He said the Marines were the tough guys and the Army guys were sissies."

"Oh he did. Do you know what a sissy is?"

"Is it a girl?"

"Your father . . . always one to simplify things."

"What?"

"Nothing . . . yes, it's like a girl."

"Did Papa take his cameras with him to heaven?"

"No, they burned . . . I mean, why are you asking so many questions today?"

"I don't know. So did he?"

"Yes . . . yes he did. Why?"

"Because I was looking in the black trunk . . . "

"How many times have I told you to stay out of that trunk. Those are your father's things."

"But mama, the lock wasn't on it, so I . . . "

"Don't you ever go in that trunk, do you hear me!"

"Yes mama."

"Oh come here . . . stop crying. Stop now."

When Reece awoke the first thing he noticed was his tear-soaked pillow.

34

"Landis has us off on a wild goose chase."

"Not really, Joseph. It didn't take us long to model which way the eyewitnesses were facing versus the direction of the sound waves from the sixth floor and grassy knoll. And it improved the correlation coefficient. He wants us to get as close to 1.0 as we can. So he helped us there."

"Wait. That was Paul's idea. Landis just forced us to do the modeling."

"And he was right."

"No . . . we knew it was going to improve the results."

"I don't know why you guys think he is trying to sabotage us."

"Come on Paul. He's doing it to every team. He's shot down every team's findings . . . "

"You're wrong, Joseph. He's asking good common sense questions. Questions any opposing council would ask."

"You really think he's helping us?"

"What about everyone else? They've all gotten more work dumped on them. Most of it to disprove all the work they've done over the past three weeks."

"Now you sound like the conspiracy theorists."

"What's that supposed to mean?"

"Joseph, it's one thing to come up with a theory . . . it's another to come up with credible evidence to support it. I think we are onto something here. No one else has ever done an analysis like this. It's based on physics, not what somebody dreamed up about what happened in Dealey Plaza."

"Okay, great. But what about this analysis Landis wants us to do. Intersecting sound waves that cancel each other out. Sounds like a bunch of busy work to me."

"Actually, I've given this some thought and he may actually be right, Joseph. Think about it. If the phenomena existed in Dealey Plaza that day, that is sound waves canceling each other out, then that's probably more proof that the sound waves came from two different sources."

"Why is that?"

"I need to think it through a little more, but if the phenomena did exist that day it could explain why twenty percent of the eyewitnesses thought the sound came from someplace other than the sixth floor or the grassy knoll. And more importantly, the ideal conditions for the phenomena to exist involve sound waves coming from opposite directions or perpendicular to one another." Joseph and Ryan looked at one another. "Ryan . . . go ahead."

"The sound waves can't be coming from opposite directions. That would mean a shooter in front, which no one has ever claimed. Plus any shooter would be out in the open. There is really no place for them to hide directly in front of the presidential limousine. But perpendicular sound sourses fits our sixth floor, grassy knoll theory."

"Very good, Ryan. And guess what other question this analysis might answer?"

"Why do I sense more work here."

"Joseph . . . it won't be at all."

"Miracles do happen."

"And better yet, Landis's request that we look at the sound wave interaction, instead of killing our theory, is going to further support it."

"How so?"

"Well, in order for this phenomena to occur, it has to be from shots fired very close to one another. Echoed sound waves have dissipated too much energy when they reflect off a surface, especially a coarse one, like a building facade. They have far too much less energy to interfere with an oncoming direct source sound wave. The bottom line is, the only way for the sound wave to have canceled out another is if they both reach their target at the same time. The only way for that to happen in Dealey Plaza is if the shots are fired close to one another."

"Our three shot, four shot question."

"Bingo. Remember the Zapruder film places the shots in a six second window, too fast for Oswald to have fired four shots. What if the fourth shot was fired from a different location. A location perpendicular to the sixth floor."

"Like the grassy knoll?"

"And what if that shot was fired within the six second window of Oswald's shots. There could be a high probability . . . "

"Hold on . . . I know where you're coming from . . . a sixty-six percent probability."

"Thank you Ryan. A sixty-six percent probability that the shot was fired within a second of one of the other three shots, making it difficult, with the echoing phenomena in Dealey plaza, and now this sound wave interference phenomena, to determine if there were three or four shots fired and making it difficult for those in Dealey Plaza to determine from which direction the shots were fired from."

"I thought we proved to a high probability that the eyewitness testimony matched where the sound waves came from?"

"We did Joseph. But thanks to Landis's request we can now answer why so many other eyewitnesses thought the shots came from elsewhere and that in all likelihood there were four shots, not three."

"So Landis's wild goose chase may have backfired on him. I'd love it if it did."

"Don't celebrate so fast, Joseph. We still have some work to do."

"I knew it."

"Actually . . . I think this is something I need to work on by myself.

I think it would be better if we limited the number of people working on the model at the same time."

"Sounds good to me, Paul."

"I hope you're not right, Joseph."

"About what?"

"I hope this doesn't end up being a big waste of time."

"Why do you say that?"

"Because no matter what we come up with I don't think Landis will ever believe there was a second shooter."

"Paul's right. He's got fifty years of bias."

"He was a four-year-old eyewitness. How good do you think his eyewitness testimony is? And in any event, I don't think he ever gave any testimony. There's nothing in the Dallas Police, FBI, Secret Service, or Warren Commission files. No testimony by anyone named Landis. Not even his father's testimony."

"Anyone ever ask him about that?"

"Maybe we should, Ryan."

"Go ahead, Joseph."

"Maybe I will. It's a fair question, right?"

"And if he never gave any testimony, maybe we should get it from him now."

"Oh sure . . . fifty years after the fact. Let's see . . . a four-year-old's eyewitness testimony fifty years later."

"Sounds like credible admissible evidence to me."

"If I were the opposing council, I'd allow it . . . not!"

"I just had a crazy thought."

"I don't like that look on your face, Paul. Is this going to mean more work?"

"It might."

"No . . . Landis has given us enough to do."

"I think you both might like this one."

"What?"

"What if Landis was never in Dealey Plaza on November 22, 1963."

35

"Mama . . . who was that?"

"Reece . . . you are full of surprises lately, aren't you. Weren't you just here yesterday? You almost never visit me two days in a row. And on a weekend? I would have thought you would have been at your cabin. Is there something wrong with you?"

"No . . . nothing's wrong with me."

"Is there . . . is there something wrong with me that you're not telling me about?"

"No Mama . . . everything's fine."

"Thank goodness for that."

"So . . . who was it?"

"Who was who?"

"The man I saw leaving your room. I just got out of the stairwell and saw a man leaving your room."

"Oh him. I have no idea . . . he had the wrong room. Now come over here and give me a hug."

"You look very nice today, Mama."

"Well . . . thank you, I think."

"Why, I think?"

"Because I think I look nice everyday. Everyday you come to see me."

"You know what I mean, Mama. You look like you're ready to go out on a date."

"Actually, I'm going to have lunch today out in the garden area with some friends of mine."

"Margaret and June?"

"Yes, they will be there. Would you like to join us?"

"Sure . . . but I have to leave a little before one. A meeting."

"Oh, I'm sorry . . . but we aren't getting together until one. But maybe we can do it some other time."

"I'd like that."

"How about Monday?"

"This is the last week of my seminar . . . "

"I know . . . always hectic."

"Exactly . . . so maybe the following week, if we don't go up to the cabin."

"You know where to find me."

"So, you remember that I was here yesterday?"

"Of course I do."

"It's just that I thought . . . I mean you seemed . . . "

"Was she here?"

"Sometimes I can't tell."

"Maybe we should have a safeword."

"A what?"

"A safeword . . . not that kind of safeword."

"What do you mean?"

"Reece, I may have Alzheimer's, but I still know how to read. And I haven't lost my mind totally, at least not yet. I still remember what I read. Well . . . most of it anyway. Are you telling me you haven't read about . . . oh, great . . . I can't remember the title. Three books . . . a trilogy. Oh, Fifty . . . "

"I know what you're talking about, Mama."

"You've read them?"

"Yes, I have."

"Has your friend, Meeka?"

"I don't know . . . "

"Then you know what a safeword is. It would be a word that hopefully I would know . . . of course I would have to remember it . . . and she wouldn't. Then you would really know if you were talking to me or not."

"I'm not sure if it works that way."

"Well, let's conduct our own little experiment. Come on . . . it'll be fun. So, what can we have as our safeword?"

"Mama . . . "

"No, that's too common. It's got to be a word that we normally wouldn't use in conversation. How about a color . . . my favorite . . . "

"Purple."

"Very good. You remembered. Then purple it is."

"How do you know she doesn't know the word?"

"We don't, that's why it's an experiment."

"And, how do I know you're not her right now?"

"Oh . . . I could be her, who knows the safeword, hoping the real me doesn't know it. If you ask me what the safeword is, and I don't know it, you'll think I'm her. And if I do know it you'll think I'm the real me, when I'm her."

"See what I mean?"

"Honey, do you honestly think if I was her I would be able to explain what I just explained to you?"

"No . . . but I'm not sure my mama could explain it either."

36

"I never thought I'd see the day that Rose Stone would be late for a one o'clock meeting."

"And she's not only late . . . she looks like death warmed over."

"Thank you, Tia. I feel like I'm dead. And thank you, Kayla. Yes, I'm late."

"I understand you had quite a night last night."

"I'm sure Tia has filled you in on all the details."

"She did . . . except of course about the sex. She said you would explain that part."

"Funny."

"I don't know, Rose. I understand you know a lot about Dr. Landis's, or should I say Reece's, sex organ."

"Tia . . . is nothing sacred between us?"

"We're a team, aren't we?"

"How am I gonna face him today? I'm gonna be so embarrassed."

"You . . . what about him?"

"Can't you guys meet with him without me? Tell him I'm not feeling well. Which would be the truth because I feel like crap."

"No way girl . . . we're a team. Remember. Plus, if he makes it to the meeting today with his injuries, what could you possibly be suffering from that would cause you not to show up?"

"Why are you in such a good mood? Usually you're hung-over?"

"Maybe if you got what she got last night, you'd be in a better mood too."

"Never mind . . . I can just imagine."

"Come on . . . let's go. We gotta meet with Dr. . . . I mean Reece."

"Yea . . . I want to ask him how his injury is."

"I'm not going."

"Come on . . . we're just kidding."

"Wait . . . okay, I've got my key. Let's go."

"We're gonna be late."

"It's less than a five minute walk. We'll be fine."

"So, Kayla . . . you and Joseph . . . what's the story?"

"What do you mean?"

"Well . . . this doesn't look like a one-night-stand to me."

"No . . . its been many one-night-stands."

"Tia, I'm trying to be serious here."

"Actually, I was gonna say the same thing."

"Kayla."

"What do you want me to say? I don't know."

"You two seem pretty serious."

"Right now we're just enjoying each other's company."

"Is that what you call it?"

"Yes, Tia . . . that's what I call it."

"What about next week?'

"What . . . what about next week?"

"We're done. The seminar is over. What then?"

"We haven't talked about it."

"No way."

"I told you, one day . . . "

"Night?"

"Yes . . . one night at a time."

"What do you want to do?"

"Seriously?"

"Yes . . . if you could wave your magic wand . . . "

"I wouldn't want this to end."

"You got it bad, don't you?"

"Let's not talk about it."

"We're here. Door's closed. You knock."

"You knock."

"Oh for cripe sakes." As Rose stared at Kayla she lifted her hand to knock on the door, not noticing it open, and knocked on Reece's hand he had raised to block her fist from hitting his chest. "I'm sorry Dr. Landis."

"No need to beat me, Ms. Stone. I haven't changed my mind about letting you go to Washington."

"We had a one o'clock appointment with you." Kayla finally spoke up.

"Yes . . . go right in. Have a seat. I'll be back in a minute." Reece disappeared down the hall.

"Should we sit at the table or in front of the desk?"

"Desk. I'm hoping this is going to be a very short meeting."

"Rose, you almost hit him."

"I told you I shouldn't have come."

"I'm surprised he didn't ask you for help."

"What are you talking about?"

"He obviously had to go to the bathroom. In his injured state he probably needs your help."

"Kayla, shut up."

"Kayla's right."

"Tia."

"Did you see the way he was staring at you?"

"You mean because I almost hit him, or because he's just as embarrassed as I am about last night? Now will the both of you shut up before he hears us."

"I hear footsteps."

"Kayla!"

"Okay . . . I hope I have everything here. The people who handle our travel arrangements normally don't come in on a Saturday, but I sweet-talked them into a favor.

"So, here are your receipts for your tickets. Pick them up at the airport kiosk. You fly out tomorrow afternoon. You can use the Metro to get to the hotel. Let's see . . . Crystal City Marriott, perfect. Then you can take the Metro the next day to the National Archives and back to the airport. All the directions are in here. There's one for each of you. And, here's a cash advance for meals and incidentals. Your contact when you get there is Liz Conway. She's expecting you at nine. Don't be late. You have a four hour window. Sorry, but that's all I could get you.

"Any questions?"

"Our procedure for viewing the pictures and negatives . . . "

"As long as you follow the procedures you outlined in the document you gave me yesterday, you won't have any problems. There will probably be somebody in the room with you at all times. It's normal operating procedure, so don't worry about it.

"Any more questions?"

"I don't think so." Rose looked at Kayla and Tia who were shaking their heads.

"Great." The four of them stood up and Reece walked around his desk and shook each of their hands. "Have a safe trip and happy hunting."

"Thank you, Dr. Landis."

"You're very welcome." Reece opened the door to his office and the women exited, Rose being last. "Ms. Stone." All the women turned around. "Could I speak with you for a minute?"

"I'll catch up."

"We'll be in Kayla's room."

"Sounds good."

Kayla and Tia watched from the hall as Rose disappeared into the office and the door closed shut.

37

"Joseph . . . what are you doing here?"

Joseph leaned over, gave Kayla a kiss, then whispered in her ear, "How about a little afternoon delight?"

"Tia's here."

"Hi Joseph."

"Hi Tia. No problem . . . Ryan's with me."

"Hi Kayla. Hi Tia."

"Hi Ryan."

"So, what are you doing here?"

"Part of team ten would like to meet with team six."

"Only part of team six is here."

"Where's Rose?"

"She's . . . she should be here soon."

"Where's Paul?"

"He's working on something for our project."

"Come on in. What did you want to meet about?"

"We'd like to know if you would be willing to help us with something?"

"Depends on what it is."

"Well, you guys have been looking at a lot of photographic evidence from Dealey Plaza and we've been looking at a lot of eyewitness testimony from Dealey Plaza. We were wondering if maybe we could join forces to help us prove a theory we've come up with?"

"You guys don't have enough work to do?"

"This is just a little side project . . . "

"So, you don't have enough work to do."

"No, Tia . . . we've got plenty to do. This issue happened to come up and we were curious about it. I think you will be too."

"So, what is it?"

"We don't believe Dr. Landis was in Dealey Plaza on November 22, 1963."

"Shut-up!"

"Hear us out . . . Ryan."

"You know how Landis is always harping on the importance of hard evidence versus circumstantial and eyewitness testimony."

"It's not just Landis. Every lawyer is taught to prioritize evidence that way. It's common sense."

"Right, Tia. So what evidence exists to support that Landis was there?"

"He says he was there."

"No better than eyewitness testimony. From a four-year-old by the way."

"Lots of articles have been written saying he was there."

"Again, most of those were based on him telling the interviewer he was there. No hard evidence."

"I remember reading an article where his mother was interviewed . . . "

"Eyewitness testimony, Kayla. Plus hear say. She said he was there based upon what he told her."

"What about testimony from his father? He was there with him."

"We couldn't find any testimony that was taken from anyone named Landis by the Dallas Police, FBI, Secret Service, or the Warren Commission. And that obviously begs the question, for two witnesses who were supposedly standing twenty feet from JFK when he was assassinated, why didn't anyone bother to interview at least the father?"

"Well, this is stupid. Why would somebody say they were in Dealey Plaza if they weren't."

"It's the same reason why millions claim they were at Woodstock even though we know the number was closer to a half million."

"And what's that?"

"Bragging rights. You can say, I was there. In the case of Landis, he now becomes an expert or authority on the topic. As is the case with Woodstock, if you say you were there, and you're halfway credible, like the right age, it's almost impossible to prove you weren't."

"This is crazy. Did you check to see where he was born? Where he lived at the time?"

"Still circumstantial, Tia. Just because you live in or near Dallas doesn't mean you were in Dealey Plaza twenty feet from the president when he was assassinated. And unlike Woodstock, this should be a lot easier to prove one way or the other."

"Is that somebody knocking?"

"I'll get it. It's probably Rose. Well . . . it's nice of you to join us." Kayla looked down at her watch. "This should be an interesting story."

"So should this. What's going on here?"

"Hi Rose."

"Joseph. Ryan."

"Rose, you're going to like this. Team ten would like our help to prove that Dr. Landis was not in Dealey Plaza on November 22, 1963."

"Really?"

"Yes. They claim there is no hard evidence to prove he was there."

"Really?"

"No pictures, no direct testimony given by him or his father who was supposed to be there too."

"I have a picture."

"Of Landis . . . in Dealey Plaza . . . on November 22, 1963?"

"Yes, yes, and yes. It's the same picture that's on the credenza in his office. You probably looked right at it when you met with him. And did you ever notice the pen and ink sketch on the wall above his credenza? That's a sketch of the picture, slightly modified."

"Do you have a copy of this picture?"

"I happen to have one right here." Rose reached into the folder she was carrying, pulled out an eight-by-ten black and white photograph, and laid it on the round table where Joseph, Ryan, and Tia were sitting.

"This?" Joseph slid the photograph toward the end of the table where Rose was standing.

"Yes . . . this."

Ryan slid the picture toward him. "Well . . . it certainly could be Dealey Plaza. And it's probably November 22, 1963 since that looks like the president's limousine with JFK, Jackie, and Conley. But . . . where's Landis?"

Rose leaned over and pointed to, if you looked close enough, two pairs of shoes, one noticeably smaller than the other, and the first few inches of legs sticking out of each pair, again one pair noticeably thinner than the other.

Ryan hunched over the photograph and pointed his fingers at the shoes. "You mean that? That's supposed to be Landis, and I take it that's supposed to be Landis's father?"

Everyone looked at Rose

"By your silence, I think you realize how ridiculous you would be if you had to submit this as evidence and then try to prove who it was. This is like holding up an old album cover that has an arial shot of the crowd at Woodstock and pointing to a speck saying, that's me."

"What does this have to do with Woodstock?"

"You missed that very enlightening conversation, Rose. Probably not as enlightening as the conversation you probably had with . . . "

"Okay, I'm in."

"You're in what, Rose?"

"I'll help work on this with you, Joseph, and Paul."

"Great. Tia, Kayla . . . you in on this?"

"Why not."

Tia stood up and whispered into Rose's ear, "What the hell happened with Landis?"

38

"The garden is so beautiful in the summer time."

"It's not too warm for you?"

"No . . . I love being outdoors. I'm going to eat lunch out here more often this summer. Like I used to do last year and the year before. I need to enjoy the outdoors more often. I don't like being cooped up indoors. It's the one thing I don't like about this place."

"Your freedom?"

"Yes . . . my freedom."

"But . . . "

"I know. I know. I can't be trusted."

"It's not that you can't be trusted."

"The other part of my brain can't be trusted."

"That's a good way to put it, but it really doesn't matter. We really can't have you walking out of here and getting lost again."

"I know. I just wish we could go away for a weekend. Like we used to."

"Don't even go there, Dora. You know we can't."

"We could."

"Dora."

"You've been thinking about telling him."

"No . . . we, actually mostly you, discussed telling him."

"Well, if we are going to tell him, wouldn't it be better to do it sooner versus later. I don't know how much longer . . . "

"You're doing fine."

"But . . . "

"No buts. I think you are doing great. I see you everyday. I'd know better than anyone how you are doing. If you were getting . . . you are doing great."

"If I were getting worse, you wouldn't tell me anyway."

"I would."

"No, you wouldn't. You'd say you told me and then say it was probably the other me you told. Even though you of all people know, better than anyone, when it is me or her."

"And that's why I know you are doing great."

"Still . . . I would like to enjoy a little of the outside world again before . . . before I can't remember enjoying it."

"In a few weeks you'll be enjoying the great outdoors with Reece."

"I meant spending it with you. Creating memories with you. If we told him . . . "

"Stop."

"But, if we told him then we could be together."

"We are together."

"You know what I mean."

"Dora . . . we've discussed this a million times."

"I could slip you know."

"You're not gonna slip."

"I could tell him everything."

"You're not . . . "

"She could tell him. What happens if she tells him everything."

"She's not going to tell him either. And besides, if she does tell him, he'll know it's her and not you."

"How are you so sure he'll know it's her?"

"How do I know? Because I've thought about that happening. I think about it everyday."

"And you're not concerned?"

"No."

"Why not?"

"Because it doesn't matter if you tell him or she tells him. He's not going to believe it anyway."

39

"Your guy is one demanding dude."

"Most of the time Joseph is a big teddy bear. It doesn't take much for me to have him wrapped around my little finger."

"Rose . . . I can't believe you agreed to work with those guys on this. What happened with you and Landis?"

"Oh yeah . . . what did he say? Did you talk about his . . . injury? Did he apologize? Did he try to do something to you?"

"Don't get excited, Kayla. Nothing happened. Yes, he apologized. No, he didn't talk about his injury."

"That's it?"

"No."

"Well, come on . . . tell us."

"He gave me the picture. It's a duplicate of the one in his office. He's really hoping we'll find something at the National Archives to prove that it is him in the photo."

"Why? Doesn't he think it's him?"

"Oh . . . he's certain it's him. And his father. But like Ryan said, it's not very convincing evidence. And this is not the first time someone has questioned whether he was really there or not."

"He told you that?"

"Yes. Even though he was only four, he does remember being there. But he also realizes that's not enough to convince the skeptics. So he's hoping we'll come up with something."

"What about his father? Was Ryan correct? He never provided testimony?"

"His father died before he could testify. In fact, he died on the evening of the assassination in a car accident."

"Woo-hoo . . . aren't there some conspiracy theorists who claim that the eyewitnesses to the assassination in Dealey Plaza have themselves been assassinated? Could this have been the first one?"

"That whole theory has been shot down. In fact, it was investigated by one of the seminar teams years ago."

"His father's death was a freak accident."

"What about his mother?"

"She's in a nursing home. Alzheimer's."

"Wow . . . talk about a conspiracy theory. It looks like someone is trying to cover up the fact that he was in Dealey Plaza."

"I think you're stretching things a little there, Tia."

"See how easy it is to invent a conspiracy."

"Like I said . . . woo-hoo."

"So why did you agree to work with Joseph, Paul, and Ryan?"

"If we're lucky on Monday, maybe we'll come up with something that puts this issue to rest. And it doesn't hurt to work with them so we know what they're up to."

"Why are you so intent on helping Landis?"

"I'm not."

"It looks like it to me that you are. Have you taken a liking to our Dr. Landis?"

"I'm just trying to complete our analysis."

"Uh-huh."

"Besides, he's . . . "

"We know, we know. He's not your type."

"So, any plans for dinner?"

"You're not with Joseph tonight?"

"He's doing dinner with the guys. We're meeting up later. So, how about dinner?"

"You mean you don't know about Tia's date?"

"What date? With who?"

"Are you telling me you spent the whole time earlier today talking about me and you didn't tell Kayla about your date last night and dinner date tonight?"

"Date? Dinner date? With who?"

"It wasn't a date."

"And tonight?"

"With who?"

"I'll do dinner with you, Kayla. Hope your ears don't ring too much, Tia."

40

"I was hoping it was you guys."

"Paul . . . who else would be banging on your door in the middle of a Saturday afternoon?"

"I've had a few lady friends . . . "

"What is it about you and older women?"

"I told you. I'm in my late twenties . . . "

"On Friday you told us you were really thirty."

"I was drunk."

"You showed us your drivers license."

"Okay . . . I'm thirty. Anyway, I've had my share of women, but my recent encounters with older women have been very, very enjoyable."

"How old are we talking about?"

"Early forties."

"On Friday you said fifties. Late fifties."

"Even sixties."

"I was drunk."

"Uh-huh."

"What? Did I show you their driver's licenses too?"

"I'm sure they have all been perfect MILFs, but why are you so excited to see us?"

"I am convinced now more than ever that there were two shooters in Dealey Plaza."

"Whoa . . . we leave you for a few hours and you make the discovery of the century?"

"Our results have been pointing to this since we first put together this model. And every time we tweak it by throwing in another variable that we think is going to negatively affect the results, instead we get just the opposite. Our conclusions get stronger and stronger."

"What the hell did you find?"

"I looked at what Landis wanted us to analyze. Echoing and interacting sound waves. I put together a crude time-dependent model. I looked at the sound wave patterns at tenth of a second intervals. I'll probably have to decrease the interval to say a hundredth of a second to eliminate any . . . "

"Dude . . . bottom line."

"What I'm trying to say, Joseph, is what I did wasn't perfect, but it was close enough to approximate what was happening in Dealey Plaza that day, and the correlation came out stronger yet for the two shooter scenario."

"So Landis's wild goose chase actually improved our results?"

"It doesn't matter how the results changed. Landis doesn't believe there are two shooters. Therefore he's gonna come up with as many reasons as he needs to shoot down whatever we come up with. I'm beginning to think this is a big fuck'n waste of time. I'd rather spend the week we have left trying to bury Landis. And we've got team six's support."

"They're gonna help us?"

"We just left them. They're on-board."

"I wouldn't be that confident about it, Joseph. They agreed to help. I think they feel like they still have something with their project. Landis is sending them to the National Archives in Washington. He must feel they are on to something."

"Bull. They're chasing a ghost. Landis knows they're not going to find anything. He's just doing it to appease them. They'll come back empty handed and he'll force them to conclude they have nothing. Another conspiracy theory laid to rest, just like the almost two hundred before us. That's why I want to nail the guy. Beat him at his own game."

"But I think our project is different."

"Not as far as Landis is concerned it isn't"

"Screw Landis. We've got a solid analysis here. It explains why the eyewitness testimony varied like it did. And the explanation, a statistically valid explanation I might add, is that there were two shooters in Dealey Plaza that day, both firing within the same six second window, from two different locations."

"Paul, you know how Landis is gonna respond."

"Ryan, screw Landis. You of all people should understand how strong these conclusions are."

"But its basis is still eyewitness testimony."

"No . . . we are trying to explain why the eyewitness testimony appeared to be so confusing. We've explained it. Two shooters."

"Landis will say two shooters means there was a conspiracy. True conspirators would not want you to find out there was a conspiracy."

"And we haven't."

"What are you talking about . . . we just did?"

"It's taken fifty years."

"Not true. People thought there were two shooters as soon as the shots were fired that day. Connally said they are gonna kill us all. Johnson said the same thing. Eyewitnesses hearing shots from different directions. People in Dealey Plaza running in different directions toward the shooters. Even a movie of the murder can be interpreted as showing shots from different directions. It's what fueled the conspiracy theorists within hours of the assassination."

"And fifty years later it's still all circumstantial hearsay. It took someone with new investigative techniques, technology that didn't even exist until recently, to put together a statistically valid explanation of the events. I agree that the conspirators didn't want anyone to find out there was a conspiracy and so far, for fifty years, they have been successful."

"This is what I don't get. Landis has been working on this probably longer than anyone on this planet. He's been running these seminars for twenty years and has coordinated, what, six hundred people, two hundred different teams, and two hundred different projects. Out of all these he hasn't found any hard confirmed evidence to support anything other than what was found by the Warren Commission. So why after all this time and analysis did we come up with something?"

"That's easy," Ryan was quick to respond. "It's the fundamental principle that's the basis of all statistics. The more you do something, the higher the probability you will achieve what you are trying to, or find what you are looking for. Buy twice as many tickets in a raffle and you double your chances of winning. Keep playing golf and you improve your chances of getting a hole-in-one. Look hard enough and you'll find a defect in any product, process, or service. Look long enough and you'll find a weakness in the Warren Commission Report."

"So, what are you saying."

"There may be a method to Landis's madness."

"And we may be the ones to finally hit on something that he can't shoot down."

41

"Hi Dean."

"Reece."

"What can I get ya?"

"What are you drinking? Never mind. Don't know why I asked. What do they have on tap? Oh, perfect. I'll take a Blue Moon."

"Traci . . . when you get a chance, a Blue Moon draft, and I'll take another. Thanks."

"Isn't The Retreat a little out of the way for you?"

"Not really. I had to be on-campus today. It's only ten minutes away. Plus, you live in Liverpool. It was convenient for you."

"You used to live here once, too. Until you made the move to the other side of Syracuse."

"We used to have some pretty wild times here. Isn't this where you met Gerry?"

"Yes it is. It's a great pick-up bar."

"I'm sure she'd like to hear that."

"She knows. She thinks it's a great pick-up bar too."

"Thanks, Traci."

"Put it on your tab?"

"Yes."

"Thank you . . . to wild times."

"To wild times."

"When did you get here?"

"Just missed the start of the Yankees game."

"The game was over an hour ago. Why didn't you tell me you were getting here so early? I would've come over sooner."

"You set the time."

"You still could've told me when you were getting here. Have you had anything to eat?"

"No, why?"

"You okay?"

"Why the third degree?"

"We've been friends since high school. I know when something's wrong with you. Plus, you look like crap."

"Gee . . . thanks. You'd look like crap too if you just broke up with Gerry."

"I was just going to ask about Mecka. Not like you to be out on a Saturday afternoon without her. What happened?"

"She went off the deep end."

"I thought you liked it when she went off the deep end?"

"Well . . . this time she went a little too far."

"When did this happen?"

"Last night."

"You guys have broken up before. And from what you told me the making up part is kinky."

"Not this time . . . it's over."

"We'll see. What else is on your mind?"

"What makes you think something else is on my mind? Isn't that enough?"

"Something else was bugging you last time we were out for dinner. Is it your mom?"

"You do know me."

"What else?"

"Fuck."

"What else?"

"I think I'm burned-out."

"Burned-out? You're a college professor. How could you be burned-out?"

"Funny."

"Hey . . . talk about burned-out. Try being a psychologist."

"No thanks. Seriously. Teaching is getting to be a bore. And this seminar. When I was asked to do it twenty years ago, I was so psyched. I thought we were going to solve the mystery that surrounds the assassination. But now, after twenty years, I'm convinced there is no mystery. I'm tired of the whole fuck'n thing. The whole effort has been a farce. A waste of time and money. I'm getting paid handsomely to do it, but it's just to carry on a myth. One not based on any kind of reality. And that's probably one of the reasons why I'm feeling burned-out. I'm tired of the whole thing. Think about it . . . fifty years."

"So, why don't you take a sabbatical? Take a year off. You're lucky you have the type of job that you can even do that. Take advantage of it. Go write a book."

"Write a book? On what? I just told you, there's no mystery to be solved."

"On what? On what? Man . . . you're a legend. You were there when JFK was assassinated. Remember how many drinks people bought you when they found out you were there? You should write a book about it."

"There have been thousands of books written about it already. There isn't anything more I could add."

"No . . . how about how it's affected your life? Think about it. How different would your life be if your father hadn't taken you that day to Dealey Plaza? Or better yet, what if he hadn't gone there that day?"

"What if he hadn't gone there? You know . . . I've asked myself that before. But now that my mother is disappearing, the question takes on a much different meaning."

"My suggestion . . . take some time off. You deserve a sabbatical. Spend it with your mom. Spend it writing a book. And, I'll tell you what. I won't charge you for this session. But if you write a best seller, I want my cut of the royalties."

42

He raised his hand to the doorbell button, and then hesitated. The four Jaeger Bombs he downed in his room just before he left that were supposed to increase his confidence, still hadn't kicked in. He was having second thoughts. He took a deep breath, exhaled slowly through his mouth, then pushed the button. He was about to push it again when he heard the door creak and watched it slowly open, only a few inches.

"May I help you?" The woman spoke with a slight Russian accent.

"Yes. I had an eight o'clock appointment with Zaria."

"Joseph?"

"Yes."

"Come in."

The door opened wider and Joseph walked into the dark entranceway, which appeared even darker to him since his eyes had not adjusted from the still bright evening light. As soon as he was inside the door closed. He turned to his right and came face-to-face with a jet-black haired, slender woman dressed in a one piece skintight black leather jumpsuit.

"Welcome." Zaria draped her hand in front of him. He reached up, clasped her fingers, pulled her hand to his mouth and kissed it. "This way please."

As he followed her down the dark hall, lit only by two small candles in glass holders resting on wooden shelves on either side of the aisle, his eyes moved down her body. She was several inches taller than his six-three frame helped by a mane of hair piled on her head and what appeared to be twelve inch spiked platform shoes on her feet. How could she even walk in them? He followed her through a doorway on the right into a small windowless room. The walls were covered with black velvet drapes that went from floor to ceiling. There was a black leather chair with a round back tucked in each corner of the room facing toward the center. Next to each chair was a small dark wooden round pedestal table. Each table had a large white candle in the center of it, each with three lit wicks surrounded by liquid wax, providing the only light in the room and keeping the interior space a few degrees warmer than the hallway.

Joseph's eyes had adjusted to the darkness and when Zaria turned and faced him he could now make out features of the woman that had appeared featureless before. Eyes were outlined with so much eye shadow, extending back along both sides of her face disappearing under her hair, that it appeared she had on a mask. Dark red lipstick covered her puffy lips. The leather suit looked painted on, clearly exposing the fullness of her breasts and large hardened nipples.

"Why don't you take a seat," Zaria pointed to the chair in the far left corner of the room, "and I will get you a drink. When we spoke on the phone I believe you indicated Captain and Coke?"

"Yes."

"I will be right back."

Joseph waited for her to exit the room before he sat down. Although he was dressed in a white short-sleeved silk shirt and light cotton slacks he was beginning to perspire from either the candle warmed room, the warm leather chair, the bombs finally kicking in, or some combination of the three. He took a handkerchief from his back pocket and wiped his forehead. As he put it back into his pocket he took in a deep breath of air. He was certain he could smell the faint odor of pot.

Joseph stood up when Zaria entered the room and reached out and took the drink she handed him. The coldness of the large glass felt good in his hand. He followed Zaria's lead when she raised her glass, then stopped when she did.

"There is only one thing I like more than a gentleman." Her eyes roamed down his body then back up to his. "It's a black gentleman. And there is only one thing I like more than a black gentleman . . . it's an obedient black gentleman." She raised her glass and clanged his. "You may take your seat." He did so, but not until she sat down.

"From our conversation you indicated that you were interested in learning about bondage and domination, is that correct?"

"Yes."

"Do you even know what those terms mean?"

"Well . . . "

"Be honest with me. The more I know about you, the better training program I can devise for you."

"I'm not that familiar with any of it."

"Would you consider yourself a virgin . . . I mean with respect to bondage and domination?"

"Yes."

"Is there anything in particular that you are interested in experiencing?"

"What are my options?"

"There are many. Bondage and domination are two very broad areas. There's also discipline, submission, sadism, and masochism. Are you interested in being a sex-slave, a top, a bottom, or maybe all three? What types of things do you want to experience? Humiliation, masturbation, fellatio, torture, servitude, whipping, spanking, flogging, cock and ball torture, nipple torture, wax play, golden showers, strap-ons, anal intercourse, genital clamps, nipple clamps, butt plugs, dildos, vibrators, fisting, beads. The list is almost endless. And there are many variations of each, all the way from mild or playful, to some very extreme role-playing."

"I think we are interested in things closer to the extreme end."

"We?"

"I have a friend who I would like you to . . . "

"Male or female?"

"Female."

"Would you consider her to be a virgin too?"

"Yes."

"I am certainly willing to teach you both whatever it is you want to learn about. I have worked with many couples in the past. I do suggest though that I first work with you alone. So we can experiment a little. Try different things. Things that you might even be embarrassed doing in front of her. Things you might not think you would enjoy, until you experience them and find out you enjoy them. I can almost guarantee that you will find some things you thought wouldn't be enjoyable, very enjoyable. To the point of begging for it. Men always do. You just need a good teacher. That should only take a few sessions at most."

"I was hoping that I would be able to bring her next time."

"Why don't you let me make that determination? Trust me . . . in the end you will both be very satisfied with what I show you. Are you ready to begin?"

"Yes."

"Good. The first thing I always do with a new client is a thorough examination. I need to determine how far I can push you . . . physically I mean. Before we start that, we need to agree on a safeword."

"Safeword?"

"Yes. Especially since you indicated you were probably interested in the extreme end of things, we need a word that you can say to tell me you want me to stop."

"Why can't I just say, stop?"

"As part of the fantasy, there will be times when you will beg for me to stop, but I know you really won't mean it. So stop, or no, or I can't take anymore, or I've had enough, are not good safewords. But if things do get too intense for you, we need to have a word, that when spoken, means you absolutely can't take anymore. You are at your limit. You need to stop. Good words are colors, or the name of a state or city. Whatever it is, it must be something you can remember easily. Can you think of a word?"

"Jets."

"Jets?"

"Yes, jets."

"Jets, it is. Oh . . . there is one other rule that I have for the use of your safeword. Once you use it . . . our session is over. And I do not mean just for the evening. You will never be allowed back into my room. So, you need to think very carefully before you call out, jets. Is that clear?"

"Yes."

"Are you ready to get started?"

"Yes."

"There is a small room across the hall. You will find a robe. Strip down to your underwear and put on the robe. Knock when you are ready and I will tell you when you can come out." Zaria stood up, walked out the doorway and across the hall. She opened the door to the room and turned on the light which was barely bright enough to illuminate the doorway opening. Joseph rose from his chair, took a step, and then stopped. "Is there something wrong?"

"I'm a . . . I'm not wearing any underwear."

She walked over to him and reached down between his legs with her right hand. She rubbed the back of her hand against his inner thigh, then moved her palm to the right until she found what she was looking for. "You know what they say about men who let it hang loose and to the right, don't you?" She squeezed the tip with her fingers.

"No."

"No? You're going to find out."

It hadn't taken him long to strip off his clothes and put on the black silk robe, but it seemed as if he'd been standing there forever since he had knocked on the door. He heard noises, he thought, coming from the room across the hall. She must have heard his knock. He looked around the room again. The only things in it were a small bed, twin-size, covered with a black sheet and two large pillows, also black, and a small three drawer nightstand. He didn't doubt what the room was used for and wondered if he would be back in it later.

"You may come out now, Joseph."

As he walked across the hall and entered the room, he thought he was in a totally different place. The black velvet drapes were pulled back from what were the walls directly in front and to the left revealing a room twice as large as the one before. The leather chairs had been moved against the wall to the right, each with its own round pedestal table, as if four spectators were about to enjoy a relaxing evening watching what was about to take place. He wondered if during some future evening Kayla would be sitting there.

Joseph stopped in the doorway and glanced around the enlarged room, dimly lit by dozens of randomly placed candles. He recognized a few things hanging on the walls. Black leather whips, chains, ropes, handcuffs. Other things, he had no idea what they were. In the far corner was a chair, mounted on a pedestal.

A light on the ceiling slowly illuminated in front of him and he noticed Zaria sitting on a swivel stool, the kind that might be in a doctor's office, one on wheels. Next to her was a small stainless steel table with things he couldn't quite make out on the top of it. As the light got brighter he could see that Zaria had changed out of her leather jumpsuit. She did still have on her twelve inch spiked platforms, but from what he could tell, nothing else. He thought he caught a glimpse of her breasts. By the size of their dark centers he thought she might have been wearing pasties.

"Step under the light." Zaria reached behind to the dimmer switch on the wall and adjusted the light down slightly. She rolled the chair in front of Joseph and adjusted its height down until she was almost eye level with his crotch. Without looking she reached over to the table and raised a small light that was attached to it, flipped on the switch and adjusted the beam so it was shining directly on Joseph's crotch area. Joseph had been staring down at Zaria and at the same time glancing at the table to see if he recognized any of the instruments laying on it. He didn't. He glanced back at Zaria, but the table light now made it difficult for him to make out anything but her face. She was staring up at him. "Are you ready for me to examine you?"

"Yes."

"Yes, Mistress."

"Yes, Mistress."

She reached with both hands for the cord that was tied around his waist holding the black silk robe to his body and pulled it loose. She reach up, spread open the robe, and stared.

"Take off the robe."

"Yes, Mistress." He let the robe drop to the floor.

"You're a fast learner . . . and obedient."

She leaned forward to pick up the robe, letting her hair brush against his shaft, and tossed it aside. She sat back up, again brushing against him, and pushed her chair back several feet. "Turn around . . . slowly."

"Yes, Mistress." He turned around, stopping when he was again facing her.

"Put your hands behind your back, clasp them, and spread you legs apart."

"Yes, Mistress."

She rolled the chair in close to him. With her left hand she picked up a pair of clear rubber gloves from the table and slid them onto her hands. She reached behind his hanging shaft, gripped it, and began stroking.

"Do you shave your pubic area everyday?"

"Yes, Mistress."

"How many orgasms do you average a day?"

"Two to three, Mistress."

"When was the last time you had an orgasm?"

"This morning, Mistress."

"Was it with your friend?"

"Yes, Mistress."

"Were you in bed?"

"No, Mistress."

"Where were you?"

"In the shower, Mistress."

"What did she do to give you an orgasm?"

"She knelt down in front of me and . . . "

"Is she able to take you down her throat?"

"No, Mistress."

"No?"

"No, Mistress."

"Has she tried?"

"Yes, Mistress."

"Would you like me to teach her how to take this down her throat?"

"Yes, Mistress."

"See how much I can learn from my examination, Joseph?"

"Yes, Mistress."

"Did she have an orgasm?"

"Yes, Mistress."

"How?"

"She was standing in front of me with her side facing me. I had lathered up with soap and was rubbing her back and breasts. I slowly worked my way down and before I knew it my fingers were inside her, both front and back at the same time. It didn't take long."

"There's another thing I've learned about her . . . she likes double penetration."

"I never really thought about . . . "

"There . . . " She pulled her hand away. "That obviously got you very excited. I needed you hard for the next part of my examination." She reached over with her left hand and picked up the Wartenberg Pinwheel off the table. "Have you ever had someone use one of these on you?"

"No, Mistress."

"Do you know what this is?"

"No, Mistress."

"It's called a Wartenberg Pinwheel. It is used to test for sensitivity. It is a very common instrument in a physician's office. Many of the things we use are. We roll the pinwheel across the skin. The more pressure applied, the greater the sensation. The parts of the body I plan to use it on I already know are sensitive. But I want to know how sensitive." She put her right hand under his stiff shaft and placed the needled wheel just below his bellybutton, dragging it down his belly to the base of his shaft, then along its length to its tip, stopping just before the flair of the head. "Breathe. That's it. Now . . . take a deep breath and hold it." She then dragged the wheel over the ridge of his head and down toward the tip, pushing the wheel much harder into the skin.

"Ahhhh . . . "

"There . . . that wasn't so bad, was it?"

"No, Mistress."

"Did you enjoy that?"

"Yes, Mistress."

"That's good, because I'm going to be focusing a lot of my time on this." She squeezed his shaft hard and yanked her hand away.

"Ahhhh . . . "

"And, these." She reached down with her hand and wrapped her fingers around his sack and pulled on his balls.

"Ahhhh . . . "

"And of course, this." She reached between his legs and up to the crack of his ass, then inserted the tip of her middle finger into him.

"Ahhhh . . . "

"Do you like that?" She pushed her finger in as far as she could.

"Yes, Mistress."

"How about this?" She slowly pulled her finger out, rested it on his opening, then pushed it back in, again as far as she could, then flicked the tip of her finger.

"Ahhhh . . . yes, Mistress."

"Do you have anal sex with her?" She flicked her finger again.

"Yes, Mistress."

"She sounds like a real slutty one. Just my type. I can't wait to meet her. But first . . . " She pulled her finger out, flicking the tip, pushed back her chair, slipped off the gloves, and tossed them on the table. She then stood up and stepped in front of Joseph. They were so close they could feel each other's body heat and for the first time Joseph was able to get a glimpse of her breasts. They were as big as he had imagined, perky, and they were nipples, not pasties, large and dark. "First . . . " She leaned in so her lips almost brushed his. "First, I need to finish my examination of you. Are you ready?"

"Yes, Mistress."

43

“Joseph really has a bug up his ass about Landis, doesn’t he?”

“I think he’s frustrated with the whole project. It took them forever to get approved, they think they are on to something, and they feel Landis is throwing roadblocks in front of everything they try to do.”

“But, Kayla . . . going after his integrity? That sounds like a lot more than being frustrated.”

“I think there are some other things going on too.”

“Like?”

“Well . . . for one, I don’t think he has his heart set on being a lawyer.”

“Kind ‘a late . . . ”

“Can I get you ladies another?”

“I’m ready.”

“Me too.”

“He’s gorgeous.”

“You mean . . . he could actually be your type?”

“I didn’t say that. I said he was gorgeous. Besides, I could be his mother.”

“What difference does that make? Younger men seem to be into older women now-a-days. You said it yourself. The experience factor.”

“Here you go ladies.”

"Thank you."

"Thank you . . . you can take it out of here."

"So . . . would you do him if the opportunity came up?"

"Kayla . . . I think he heard you."

"Good . . . I wanted him to. So . . . would you?"

"Yes."

"Rose Stone . . . we finally found out who your type was."

"I didn't say he was my type . . . I said I'd do him. Well . . . I'd let him do me too."

"So . . . why don't you go for it."

"How come we never came here for dinner before? There seems to be a lot of great restaurants on North Salina Street."

"Don't change the subject."

"I'm serious. This place was really nice. The food was great. Asti Caffe. Have you eaten here before?"

"Yes. Joseph and I had dinner here once before. Stop changing the subject."

"What other restaurants are around here?"

"There's Francesca's, just up the street. Farther up Salina is Frankie's Bistro. One block beyond that is Attilio's Restaurant."

"And you've been to all of these places?"

"Rose, we've been here for three weeks. And Joseph doesn't want to go to the same place twice. So we've tried a bunch of places. Covered all the ones on Landis's list and then some. We probably could have gotten paid to rate them. Fortunately, they've all been great. I can't think of one bad meal. We've had great times in every one of them."

"You're really into him, aren't you?"

"Who'd a thunk. Although, he was a football player and I was a cheerleader."

"And they attract somehow?"

"That was my experience."

"Why am I not surprised."

"This is different though."

"I know I asked you this before, but have you thought about . . . "

"No! I mean, yes. I mean . . . "

"You have got it bad."

"We've got a week to figure things out. Neither of us has a job yet. We know we will be a sought-after commodity when the program is over. We'd like to take the summer off and start work somewhere in the fall. That was each of our plans before we were a we. It's tough enough to find a job in the legal profession when you are an I . . . a we is almost impossible."

"So you have talked about it?"

"A little."

"It sounds like he's got it just as bad as you do."

"I hope so. No . . . I pretty much know so."

"Talk about a whirlwind romance."

"Tell me about it."

"So . . . it's not just the sex."

"Oh . . . it definitely started out that that way. More like a dare."

"A dare?"

"Yeah. Can a five-four one hundred and ten pound woman pin . . . "

"Pin?"

"Yes, pin . . . as in hold down and completely control, a six-three two hundred fifty pound man."

"And?"

"He was no match for me."

"How come I can picture that?"

"I told you . . . he really is a teddy bear. A great big teddy bear."

"Just out of curiosity, how big is he and how do you . . . "

"I think you ladies might be ready for another?"

"I think you are right. We'll take two more."

"Very big, and you learn to take it."

"I'm sorry?"

"No . . . I was talking to my friend. By the way . . . what was your name again?"

"Grant." He reached across the bar to shake Kayla's hand.

"As in Cary?"

"As in Grantham . . . my grandfather's name."

"Hi Grant. I'm Kayla, and this is Rose."

"Kayla and Rose, nice to meet you. Let me get those refilled for you."

"I told you he could hear us."

"Good, then maybe he will hear me when I say I'm glad he's your type."

"Let's get back to Joseph. The conversation was just getting interesting."

"What happened to way too much information?"

"Now I'm curious."

"Well . . . let's just say, I was very surprised I could take it in all the places I've taken it."

"Okay . . . too much information."

"Here you go ladies."

"Thanks, Grant."

"I think you should go for it, Rose. Have some fun."

"I'm not into one-night-stands."

"Who says it will end up being a one-night-stand? Look at me and Joseph."

"I'm not into a month of one-night-stands either."

"Thanks a lot."

"You know what I mean."

"No, I don't."

"Kayla . . . you said it yourself. You don't know what's going to happen after next week. Aren't you scared?"

"Yes . . . yes, I'm scared. You never know what's going to happen with any relationship you start. Any one of them could end up being a one-night-stand, or a month of one-night-stands. I am scared. But I believe that if he and I are meant to be then somehow it will happen. We'll make it happen. But, I would have never known that unless I tried."

"So, you're saying I should just go out there and try?"

"Yes. I mean no. I mean, not necessarily with the first person you meet for the night."

"I used to do that you know."

"What?"

"Screw around. A lot. A real lot."

"You?"

"What? Don't look so surprised. I was a bartender. I could have, or I should say did have, several men a night if I wanted to. Flashback twenty years ago, with this body in a tight tank top, no bra, when I didn't need a bra, and I could have my pick."

"You still can. You look great for a . . . "

"For a what?"

"You look great. You could have any man you want if you'd just try."

"I don't mean for the night, Kayla."

"You've been burned, haven't you?"

"Too many times."

"So, you're never gonna try again?"

"Haven't for two years."

"Two years!"

"It's not that bad, Kayla. It's not like I turned back into a virgin or something."

"You must have really been hurt."

"Hurt? I thought this was the one. Finally, after two previous relationships I thought this one was it. This was real. Two years of bliss. Happiness. Love. Sex at least twice a day. I did anything he wanted, and he did the same for me. And it was fun. And nasty. Sometimes, very nasty. And very fun."

"What happened?"

"We went away for a long weekend. A cabin in the mountains. I thought he was going to propose. I fucked his brains out. Drained him dry. And for what? The drive home on Sunday evening was quiet. I knew something was wrong. He waited until we got home to tell me that he didn't think things were working out between us."

"What did you do?"

"My first thought was to beg him, plead with him. What did I do wrong? I'll make it right. What didn't I do? Tell me. I'll do it. But I didn't. I hadn't done anything wrong. I'd done it all. I'd given it my all. I realized it wasn't me. It was him. Or someone else. I moved out that evening."

"Did you ever try to contact him again?"

"As a matter a fact I did. I thought for sure he would call me. Tell me it was all a mistake. That he still loved me and wanted me more than ever. Two weeks went by and nothing happened. I got drunk and went over to his place. He was just getting out of his car. With another woman. Younger. Much younger. They walked into his place. I drove away. See . . . it wasn't me."

"Screw him!"

"I did . . . a lot."

"No . . . I mean forget him."

"I have forgotten him."

"No you haven't."

"Why do you say that?"

"The way you are talking about him. The way you act toward other men. Because you haven't tried with another man for two years. The way you say, he's not my type."

"It's over."

"We just need to convince you of that. We need to get you back in the saddle."

"Isn't that what you are supposed to tell the man to do?"

"Fine Rose . . . we need to get you laid."

"Nice Kayla . . . Grant looked over here when you said that."

"I hope so, because he's the one who's gonna do it."

"Okay . . . let's make it happen." She raised her drink and clanged it against Kayla's.

"Are you serious?"

"Never been more serious in my life."

"This is gonna be fun."

"You're not gonna be watching, Kayla."

"Okay . . . let me think about this for a minute. How do we get him into bed with you?"

"No offense Kayla, but I used to be pretty good in that department. I think I can figure something out."

"The night's still early, and we want a high probability of success, so we need a plan."

"While you're thinking about how to snare this guy for me, can we talk about something serious first?"

"Sure, what is it?"

"Are you going to pay attention to me?"

"I am."

"Then stop staring at Grant."

"Fine . . . what is it?"

"I think you should tell Joseph to be careful about going after Landis."

"Why? You were the one who agreed to help him."

"Landis could have a lot of influence on Joseph getting a job in the legal profession. That's why most of the people are taking this seminar, I mean besides for the challenge of it. It's a big plus to have this on your resume and to have Landis as a reference. If he pisses him off . . . "

"I don't think he's too concerned about it."

"Well . . . he should be."

"What if he doesn't want to be a lawyer?"

"What's he gonna do with his life? Especially since he has invested so much time into becoming a lawyer?"

"He wants to play football."

"He already played football. I don't think he can go back to college and play again. There are eligibility rules in college sports."

"Not college . . . pro."

"Really?"

"Yup."

"Are you saying a pro team is interested in him?"

"Unfortunately, no."

"Who would he like to play for if he had the chance?"

"The Jets . . . the New York Jets."

44

"You are one horny bastard tonight . . . what's gotten into you?"

"You're not complaining, are you?"

"No. It's just that . . . I'm not sure I'm satisfying you."

"What! Why would you say that?"

"No matter how hard I make you cum, within minutes you're stiff again. And all three of your orgasms have been in my mouth, so I know you're not faking it. So what gives?"

"First of all . . . why would I want to fake it? Second, I think I've cum three times in one night before with you."

"Not in two hours."

"I would think you'd take that as a compliment. In fact, it sounds to me that you are more than satisfying me."

"I just want to make sure it's me."

"What do you mean? Who else would it be? I'm here with you."

"We've been together for almost three weeks and you've never acted . . . well, like this before."

"Like what? I've lusted you like this before."

"And you want it again." She reached down and wrapped her hand around his already half-hard shaft. "And the night's not even half over."

"Again . . . I would take that as a compliment if I were you. And speaking of orgasms, how many have you had?"

"I can remember number six, but then in the heat of things, I lost count. At that point you hadn't even had your second, so figure it out."

"And again, you're not complaining . . . are you?"

"No."

"Good." Joseph rolled onto his back and pulled Kayla onto his chest, sliding her sweaty body against his until their tongues found each others in the candle lit room. He slid his hand down her back, placing it on her ass cheeks, then quickly lifted his hand and slapped her.

"Mmmm . . . " She arched into him. "And, I'm not complaining about that either." She licked his lips with her tongue. "You've been doing some research."

"You like it?" He slapped her again.

"Fuck . . . that stings."

"You like it?" He slapped her again.

"Do I like it?" She reached down with her hand, stuck three fingers into herself, pulled them out, rubbed her wetness over his lips, and then shoved her fingers into her mouth. "Do I like it?"

"Mmmm." He slapped her again. "Ride my tongue."

She reached for the headboard with both hands, pulled herself up onto his chest, spread her legs and lowered herself onto his pink tongue. It didn't take long for his flicking tip to find her spot.

He reached up with his hand, slid his index finger down her back, then along her crack, and stopped at her warm opening, still lubricated from his entry into her. He pushed his finger in flicking the tip in unison with his tongue just as he had been taught earlier that evening.

45

"Hello Morgan."

"Bill, do you know where Jason is?"

"Hopefully, he's on his way down Blue Mountain, or on his way up the next one. This was his big climbing weekend in the Adirondacks. Six peaks in two days."

"Damn . . . I forgot that's where he was going. That explains why he isn't answering any calls or texts."

"I don't think there is very good service where he's going. I think he said he wasn't even going to keep his phone on. Why, what's up?"

"I think I found something and I wanted to get the team together before our status meeting with Landis on Monday."

"The meeting's not until Monday afternoon. We can meet to talk about it in the morning. Besides, I don't think he'll be back until late this evening. Very late."

"I think we need to meet this afternoon, even if it's just you and me."

"What did you possibly find in the last twenty-four hours that we didn't come across in the past three weeks? I mean, the six degrees of separation exercise sure sounded exciting when we proposed it. But, we really didn't find anything that wasn't already known to the rest of the planet."

"That's why I need you guys to go over this. I think I found something and you're not going to believe who is in the middle of it."

"There's a Yankees game on at one. A bunch of us are going to The Varsity to watch it and have one last binge on wings, pizza, and beer. Unless you've found something more important than that, like the proverbial link between Oswald and Tippit, or better yet among Oswald, Ruby, and Tippit, my vote would be it can wait until Monday."

"I can do better than that. How about Oswald and his, before now, unknown accomplice, the one who was with him in Dealey Plaza that day."

46

"You do know your restaurants, Rose."

"I was hoping you would like the Lafayette. I was here years ago. Not much has changed though. Was I right about the steaks?"

"Like cutting through butter."

"I don't know why they gave us these?" Kayla held up the expensive looking, thick bladed, steak knife.

"For show."

"I've never eaten across from the White House."

"I've never eaten in a restaurant where there are no prices on the menu."

"Don't worry about it, Tia. We're on an expense account."

"Kayla . . . we've been on an expense account for the past three weeks."

"I know. I think I'm going to have to go into detox or something starting next week. I'll probably max out all my credit cards thinking someone else is going to still reimburse me for all my expenses."

"Seriously, Rose. How do you know about these things and places? You know your drinks. You handle yourself well around men. You've eaten in a restaurant with no prices on the menu."

"Don't forget, Tia. She's lived twice as long as we have."

"Thanks, Kayla."

"Think about it. You've experienced twice as much of life as we have. Anything I've done you should be able to top and then some."

"That I doubt, Kayla. Some things, maybe. Anything . . . no way."

"What? Sex? You told me that you used to screw several men a night."

"What? How come I'm just learning this now?"

"Key word is screw."

"Who did you screw? What do you mean several?"

"Are you saying you don't suck . . . and swallow? Just as I thought. You do it just as much as I do it."

"Who are you doing?

"Show me a woman who doesn't suck, and I'll steal her man."

"I did some sucking last night."

"Did you do some sucking last night, Rose?"

"Rose? With who?"

"Did you even try to pick Grant up after I left?"

"As a matter a fact, I did."

"Who's Grant?"

"Did you sleep with him?"

"That's one difference between you and me. When I was your age, I wouldn't have had a second thought about sleeping with a man I'd just met, including fucking, sucking, and swallowing. But with age also comes wisdom. We had coffee. He asked if I wanted to go back to his place. I got the feeling he felt sorry for me. Either that or he had a MILF fantasy. I wasn't sure. Anyway, I'm not that hard up."

"You need to get over him."

"Get over who?"

"The guy she was going to marry."

"Marry?"

"And by the way, I didn't have sex the first time I slept with Joseph. He wanted to, but I said no. Drove him nuts. Drove me nuts. Neither of us got any sleep that night. He told me later he jerked-off in the shower after I left."

"Does that make you some kind of a saint?"

"No . . . I'm just saying . . . I . . . I'm more show. Not that I haven't had my share of men . . . I have. But, I put on a good show too."

"You like people to think you're a slut?"

"No . . . I like men to think I'm a slut. Given the choice between a princess and a slut, which do you think a man would choose?"

"For the night, or forever?"

"Give 'em what they want for the night and they'll come back the next, and the next, and the next. It won't be a one night stand, as long as you keep giving it to them."

"I don't know. I kept giving it to him. It still wasn't enough. He still dumped me for a younger and probably tighter model."

"Giving it to whom? Who dumped you?"

"You've gotta keep coming up with new things all the time. Keep 'em interested. Keep 'em guessing."

"Believe me . . . we did new things all the time. Sometimes, very kinky new things. And here I am, so I guess none of it worked."

"Like, what kind of kinky things?"

"Some guys are just born assholes, Rose. You can't blame yourself. It was his loss."

"Then why do I feel like . . . like I'm the lost one?"

"I'll say it again. You need to get over him. And the only way that is going to happen is . . . "

"I know, I know. I should have listened to you and gone home with him."

"You mean Grant, right?"

"Yes, you should have. I bet he would have done some new things you never had done to you before. And you would've loved it. And, you'd be glowing right now."

"What kinds of things are you guys talking about?"

"Look at Tia. She's been acting like a school kid after her first date."

"How was your date with Dixon?"

"Yes, Tia . . . how was your dinner-date?"

"I don't know, Kayla. By the way she's been glowing, I think it was more than a dinner-date?"

"Now she's blushing."

"You got laid, didn't you?"

"Wait . . . did you say a minute ago that you did some sucking last night?"

"I was wondering if either of you was listening to me."

"Tia Diaz! You . . . you went down on a guy on your first date?"

"Technically, it was our second date. We went out to breakfast the night before. I count that as a first date. And Dixon agreed."

"Dixon agreed? Did you have a discussion with him about it? Did you tell him you don't give oral sex on a first date and then ask him his opinion as to whether he thought this was your first or second date? I'm not a betting person, but I think I know how a vast majority of men would have answered that question."

"It was a mutual decision."

"And where did this sex act take place? Don't tell me you did him in his car."

"Did I tell you he drives a Porsche?"

"You didn't."

"No . . . his bedroom."

"You slept with him?"

"Yes . . . but I went down on him before we got into bed. I need to get to the gym more. My knees and thighs are sore. And . . . we didn't get much sleep."

"You go girl."

"You're a slut, Tia."

"Really!"

"No, I mean a slut."

"Thank you, Kayla. No one has ever called me that before. And, especially coming from you . . . "

"What's that supposed to mean?"

"So, how was it?"

"How was it? She only knew this guy for what, twenty-four hours, and she had oral sex with him."

"Kayla . . . you wanted me to have sex. I assume it meant oral sex too. With a guy I had only met two hours before."

"That's different."

"Why is it different?"

"Because . . . because . . . "

"I'm a princess? Is that what you wanna say, Kayla? Well, I'm not. I may not have had as many men as you have. And I might not be as experienced in bed. But, I do enjoy it. I enjoy it a lot. It just has to be with the right guy. Last night it felt like it was the right guy. And Rose . . . it was fuck'n great."

"Well, that's just perfect."

"What now, Kayla."

"I try to get you laid and Tia ends up in the sack."

"So . . . what are these kinky things you two keep talking about?"

"Woo . . . looks like Dixon might need some help in bed."

"Not really. In fact . . . he was an animal. My knees aren't the only part of my body that's sore. And I almost missed the flight."

"There must be something in the Syracuse water because Joseph was the same way last night. I mean . . . more than his normal lustful self. He wants to try some kinky stuff . . . "

"You guys keep saying that . . . like what? Give me some specifics."

"Role-playing. Bondage. Whipping."

"You mean BDSM?"

"You've done it, Rose?"

"More role-playing. Nothing too serious. I know it's the big rage now. I think people are more curious than anything."

"And maybe, bored."

"It'll pass just like . . . other things passed from when I was in my twenties."

"What other things, Rose?"

"Too much information?"

"Anyway, he's either reading or watching some movies because he's been doing some new things . . . "

"Maybe he's a lot more experienced than you think?"

"No . . . if he knew about these things he would have done them to me the first time we had sex."

"There you go with the generalities again. I need specifics!"

"You mean men might have the same idea about give 'em what they want in bed and they'll keep you forever?"

"More like you'll come back for more."

"That's how I feel about Dixon and last night."

"Well . . . I don't care where he's getting it from. I just hope he learns more."

"More what?"

"And how are your meals this evening, ladies?"

"Fantastic."

"I will second that."

"But, I think we need another round."

"The same for everyone?"

"No . . . we need to celebrate."

"I thought you said we needed to take it easy tonight. Remember? The National Archives?"

"I know. But it's still early. We've only had two so far. And we have something to celebrate."

"What's the occasion, ladies?"

"Well . . . "

"How about a bottle of Dom Perignon Cuvee Vintage 2003."

"Excellent choice, madam. I will be right back"

"Showoff."

"Why does he keep calling me madam?"

"He probably thinks you're our mother."

"Thanks, Tia."

"Just kidding."

"No, you're not. See what happens when you get laid . . . you get cocky."

"I had cocky last night."

"Me too."

"You know Rose . . . play your cards right and I bet you could have his cocky tonight."

47

"Please, Mistress."

"Don't beg. I can't stand it when my slaves beg." Zaria tightened her grip on Joseph's shaft and twisted her hands in opposite directions, then back again.

"AHHHH!"

"Yelling and screaming are fine. Begging is not."

"AIIIIIII!"

"Your women have always given you pleasure, haven't they?"

"AHHHH!"

"Haven't they?"

"AHHHH! Yes, Mistress."

"And that doesn't satisfy you anymore, does it?"

"AHHHH!"

"Does it?"

"Yes."

"AHHHH!"

"What?"

"AHHHH! I mean no."

"That's why you are here with me, isn't it?"

"Yes, Mistress."

"You can't truly experience more pleasure by comparing it to other pleasures." She loosened her grip and started to stroke his shaft. "Because no matter what kind of pleasures I dream up, you only have so many nerve endings in even the most sensitive parts of your body, which eventually limits the total amount of pleasure you will experience. And when that happens, you think the only way you can find more pleasure is through someone else. Isn't that correct?"

"Yes, Mistress."

"But, when you have something to contrast that pleasure against . . . like pain."

"AHHHH!"

"It makes you appreciate the pleasure that much more, doesn't it Joseph?"

"Yes, Mistress."

"Do you like being in the position you are in, hanging from the ceiling, totally in my control?"

"Yes, Mistress."

"Of course, even if you weren't held up by those leather cuffs, if you were just standing here in front of me, totally free, you would still be under my total control, wouldn't you?"

"Yes, Mistress."

"You're enjoying what I'm doing to you, aren't you, Joseph?"

"Yes, Mistress."

"Are you enjoying looking at me?"

"Yes, Mistress."

"What do you like best about what you see?"

"Everything, Mistress."

"There must be something that turns you on more than anything else. The black leather platform boots? The arm-length fingerless leather gloves? My long fingernails, especially as they rub against this part of your . . . you're dripping again."

"Ahhhh . . . your nipples. Your nipples turn me on, Mistress."

"What do you like about them?"

"Ahhhh . . . they're big. Ahhhh . . . and dark. Ahhhh . . . and pointed."

"Are her nipples big?"

"Yes, Mistress."

"This big?"

"No, Mistress."

"Are they dark?"

"Yes, Mistress."

"This dark?"

"No, Mistress."

"This pointed?"

"Only when she's excited, Mistress."

"Her and I have a lot in common. Mine only get like this when I'm excited. Have you ever seen me not like this, Joseph?"

"No, Mistress."

"That must mean that you excite me. Do you like it when I rub these against you?"

"Yes, Mistress."

"Joseph . . . you are dripping again. I can understand you dripping when I'm doing this to you. But when I was whipping that hot ass of yours with my leather strap, I noticed you were stiff as a board and dripping. I assume by your screaming that you were experiencing pain. Pain, hard, and dripping. Can you explain that?"

"No, Mistress."

"Could it be that the pain you experienced from the whipping gave you pleasure?"

"I . . . "

"Or could it be that I wasn't whipping you hard enough?"

"No, Mistress. It was hard enough."

"Joseph, I know you can take much more than that. Don't you agree?"

"Ahhhh . . . yes, Mistress."

"Because, remember . . . we need to balance the pain with the pleasure.

Otherwise, you won't appreciate the pleasure. And don't think you can fake it with me."

"AHHHH!"

"Because, this is my barometer. If you're stiff and dripping, you are obviously enjoying it too much."

Joseph watched Zaria as she moved the stool and stainless steel table from the evening before in front of him. She sat down, turned on, and adjusted the light onto his crotch area. It was then that he noticed the surgical clamps, thirty, forty, he wasn't sure, laying neatly in two rows on the table. With her left hand she lifted and held his shaft against his belly. With her right hand she reached up behind his ball sack, closed her thumb and middle finger around it, and slowly pulled down.

"Ahhhh."

"You have a big set of balls."

"Ahhhh."

"Do you know what I'm going to do now, Joseph?"

"No, Mistress."

"I'm going to administer a unique combination of pain and pleasure to these things."

"Ahhhh."

"You're so big I had to gather up more surgical clamps. I hope I have enough." She stood up, picked up one of the clamps, inserted the fingers from her right hand into it like you would a pair of scissors, and held it in front of Joseph's face. "Have you ever experienced one of these?"

"No, Mistress."

"The unique thing about this is, they are painful going on." She reached for his left nipple with her free hand and squeezed it with her thumb and index finger exposing the tip. She placed the rubber tipped end of the clamp onto it and squeezed, each click of the clamps locking clasp indicating a tightening of the rubber tip onto the nipple.

"Ahhhh."

"As painful as this is going on, your nerve endings will eventually numb, and like a narcotic you will feel an erotic tingling as the weight of the clamp pulls on your nipple." She pulled her fingers from the clamp and let it hang freely. She repeated the process on his right nipple.

"Ahhhh."

"Feel good?" She reached up and tugged on each clamp.

"AHHHH! Yes, Mistress."

"As good as this feels now, just wait until the numbness sets in. It's exquisite. Of course, with every pain comes pleasure, and with every pleasure comes pain. If you thought these hurt going on, I can't wait to hear you scream when I take them off and those nerve endings come alive again. And what's even more erotic is, there is no getting around that part. The clamps must eventually come off. The thought of that future pain is going to drive you crazy. Believe me, I know." She tugged again on the clamps.

"AHHHH!"

"I am now going to put the rest of these clamps on your ball sack. Then I'm going to whip your ass again with my leather strap, only this time harder. We'll see if you are still stiff and wet after that. And, if you've been a good slave for me tonight, and after I let you practice on me, maybe I will let you take a few of these clamps home so you can use them on her tonight. Practice what you've learned, on her, like you did last night with what I showed you."

"That won't be necessary, Mistress."

"And why not? Didn't she enjoy it?"

"No, Mistress."

"What?"

"I mean, yes Mistress. She enjoyed it."

"Did she have a powerful orgasm?"

"Yes, Mistress."

"Tell her the next one will be even more powerful if she experiences pain first. And tell her she will never be an effective top unless she experiences being a bottom first. I don't care how much of a slut she is.

She must first experience pain before she can administer it. When I finally let her into this room, she will be my bottom and I will show her what it means to service me. But first, it would be better if you teased her . . . made her curious for me. I want her to beg for me to do her. Is that clear?" She tugged on both clamps.

"AHHHH! Yes, Mistress. But I can't do her tonight. AHHHH! She is out of town and won't be back until tomorrow evening."

"Are you saying you can slave for me for as long as I want this evening?"

"Yes, Mistress."

She reached down with both hands and gently started to stroke him. "Do you want to stay with me tonight?"

"Yes, Mistress."

"You may regret saying that." Zaria sat down, picked up the first clamp, placed it on the skin of his sack, squeezed, and waited for his scream.

48

"In summary, Dr. Landis, our model is able to capture what appear to be the inconsistencies in the eyewitness testimony from Dealey Plaza that afternoon. But, in fact, there are no inconsistencies. To a very high degree of confidence what the eyewitnesses say they heard could only be explained by two shooters, firing within the same six second window, perpendicular to one another, and at least one of their shots being in close sequence to one another, or both fired at almost the same instant."

Reece flipped back and forth among the tables and graphs that Ryan had handed him when he started his presentation to him almost thirty minutes ago. He looked up at Ryan and Paul. "Gentlemen, I must admit. I am impressed with your analysis. Your model is very convincing. I can't think of anything you left out of your analysis. I can't argue with your statistics. However . . . "

The two loud knocks echoed off the opening door, startling everyone. "Sorry I'm late." Joseph closed the door and sat in the empty chair between Paul and Ryan.

"As I was saying. Two shooters, firing at the same instant, from different directions, tells you that there was a conspiracy. True conspirators would not want you to find that out. And your theory is contrary to the principles of Occam's razor."

"Dr. Landis, I believe what we've come up with is totally consistent with Occam's razor." Ryan's voice was noticeably louder. Joseph and Paul, along with Reece, were staring at him. "Occam's razor tells us that, other things being equal, a simpler explanation is better than a more complex one. But, you should not utilize the simpler theory if it does not do as good a job of explaining the solution to the problem. That is, simplicity should not be sacrificed for better accuracy. I believe that is what we have done here.

"What if it wasn't a conspiracy? What if it was two independent shooters? Each one unknowing of the other. Each one firing from a snipers nest at the point at which their target was in the best line of sight, which happens to be in the same six second window.

"It explains witnesses equally divided as to what direction the shots came from. It explains a majority of witnesses hearing three shots. It explains witnesses running in two different directions, after the shots were fired, in pursuit of the assassin. It also explains all the other circumstantial evidence of someone being on and fleeing from the grassy knoll. And . . . it's supported by a scientifically developed model, that can be validated, and is statistically accurate."

"Give me a day to look over what you've got. Send me a copy of your write-up . . . "

"It's still in draft form."

"That's fine. Give me what you've got. Let's plan to meet again tomorrow at . . . let's see . . . what do I have open? How about four. In the meantime, I want you to come up with a plan on how you would actually validate your model. Have something by our meeting tomorrow.

"Thanks everyone . . . "

"Dr. Landis . . . there is one other thing we'd like to ask you about."

"Yes, Joseph."

"We still need to do some more work on that issue, Joseph."

"We've gone over all the eyewitness testimony from Dealey Plaza and we couldn't find anything from you or your father."

"That's because none exists."

"We can understand there being none for you. After all, you were only four years old at the time. But why was there never any taken from your father?"

"He was killed before he could make a statement. A car accident."

"Is there any direct evidence to support that you were in Dealey Plaza that day?"

"Actually Joseph, there isn't. Other than that." Reece turned around and pointed to the black and white photograph on the credenza, then turned back to Joseph.

"The evidence is very . . . "

"Weak? I agree. And even my recollection of being there has been clouded by almost fifty years of time and research, trying to convince myself what really happened there that day. If you're insinuating that I may have not been there, you wouldn't be the first, and I'm sure you won't be the last. To be honest . . . I'm not sure myself anymore."

"We weren't insinuating anything, Dr. Landis. Joseph is just trying to put all the evidence through the same rigorous process as we've been doing with our model."

"Well . . . if you find something gentlemen, please let me know. In the meantime I look forward to your draft report and our meeting tomorrow."

Ryan waited until they were down the hall before he spoke up. "Where the hell were you?"

"Sorry. I . . . I overslept."

"Your woman's out of town and you overslept?"

"You shouldn't have brought up the issue of Landis not being there."

"He dumped more work on us. Besides . . . I had him sweating."

"You missed the first part of the meeting, Joseph. I think we've got him convinced that our model works. He agrees with the results. Paul?"

"Ryan's right."

"Then why the additional work?"

“He’s dotting the I’s and crossing the T’s.”

“Besides, he’s right. We need to validate the model before we can publish anything on this.”

“Screw ‘em. I still enjoyed seeing him sweat.”

“I don’t know. I still say something’s not right.”

“How can you say that, Paul? The model came up with better results.”

“I think Landis knew exactly what we’d find when we enhanced the model. He knew the results were going to get better. He knows something else. He’s not telling us something.”

49

"Do you think Landis did her?"

"Who?"

"Ms. Conway."

"Why do you say that?"

"Did you see how she lit up when I said his name? I think they've had sex. Hot sex. Hot erotic sex. I can see it in her eyes."

"The professor and the librarian?

"Why not?"

"I can't see it."

"Oh, I can. She's probably wild in bed."

"Kayla . . . why do you say that?"

"Don't let those clothes fool you. She's got a tight body hidden under there. Yup . . . Landis did her. There's no doubt in my mind. Why do you think we got access to this place?"

"Alright ladies . . . enough of this sex talk. How are you coming on getting all the photos looked at? We have less than an hour left to finish up."

"Slave driver, Rose."

"We're waiting for Ms. Conway to bring us the last batch of photos and the Zapruder film. She is looking over us like a hawk. Won't let us have more than a half dozen photos at a time."

"Landis said it would be like this."

"I hope we have better luck with what's left to look at. So far we haven't found a thing."

"Quiet . . . here she comes."

"Ladies, here are the final six photographs you requested. Here is the Zapruder film. Two copies. These are first generation copies of the originals. I still don't understand why you wanted two copies, but here they are."

"Thank you, Ms. Conway. It was actually Dr. Landis's idea that we look at two copies of the film. You know how thorough he can be."

"Yes . . . I do. He can be very demanding at times . . . very demanding. Well . . . I'll let you ladies get back to work. I do need to remind you though that you have fifty-five minutes to finish up."

"We should be finished by then, but Dr. Landis said if we needed a few more minutes to finish up that we should ask you. He said to say that he would owe you one if you could accommodate us."

"Dr. Landis already owes me one for letting you in here in the first place. Not many people get to look at what you are holding in your hands right now. Please don't over extend your welcome. I will check back in a while to see how you are doing."

"I bet she can be a real bitch when she wants to be."

"Landis said we had a four-hour window. He never said we could ask for more time."

"He can be demanding . . . she can be demanding."

"What if she calls Landis?"

"I wonder who is more demanding when those two are together?"

"I bet she's calling him right now."

"Maybe he likes women who are demanding."

"If she does, we are in big trouble."

"Maybe she likes men who are demanding."

"Ladies . . . can we get back on task here. You help Tia with the film. Use that room. I'll stay here and check out the last of the photos. We've got to be out of here at one so move it."

"She'll let us stay longer. In fact, she's hoping we'll have to stay longer. Then Landis will really have to owe her. I bet she's sitting at her desk fantasizing about it right now."

"Kayla!"

"Talk about bitches."

"There it is, Kayla. Right on frame 313. Plain sight. And I haven't even computer enhanced it yet. This film is a lot crisper and clearer than the copy we've been looking at."

"It is a lot clearer, but if you hadn't pointed that thing out to me, I wouldn't have even noticed it. What is it anyway?"

"It's the same . . . flash, spark, reflection, that was on the film we have."

"So we can rule out an imperfection on our copy."

"And an imperfection on these copies. Whatever this is, it's on the original Zapruder film. It could still be an imperfection on the original film. But there is no way we are going to find that out. They would never let us look at the original."

"Let's see what it looks like when you computer enhance it."

"Give me a second. There. Wow."

"What?"

"On our copy of the film the program said there was a ninety percent probability that this, whatever it is, was an imperfection on the film. Now it's saying there's only a fifty percent probability that it's an imperfection."

"What's it say about the other fifty percent?"

"A spark or a flash of some kind."

"Tia, what's this on frame 314?"

"Where?"

"Right in the same spot on the curb where the spark or flash or whatever appears in frame 313."

"That doesn't show up on our copy of the film. That looks more like an imperfection on the film. That's strange."

"What?"

"The program says it's dust."

"Dust?"

"Dust."

"Is there anything on frame 315?"

"Let's see. I can't see anything. But look at the computer enhanced model."

"More dust?"

"Not as crisp, or as noticeable, as in frame 314. But there's no doubt about it. There is something there."

"What about the next frame?"

"Damn."

"Come on guys, we've got to wrap things up. Conway is coming right back."

"Rose, come and look at this."

"We've got five minutes to get out of here."

"Tell the bitch we just need a few more minutes."

"You'd better listen to Rose, because the bitch is not going to let you have a few more minutes."

"Ms. Conway, I . . . "

"You ladies have exactly four minutes to get packed up and out of these rooms. If you are not out in the hallway by then, I will confiscate all of this equipment and you will be escorted out of the building by security. Do I make myself clear?"

"Yes, Ms. Conway."

"Don't get pricky with me young lady. You think you're so smart. Coming down here. Rummaging through these photos. Looking at classified copies of the Zapruder film. I don't know what you expected to find that Dr. Landis has not already found? He's been through every one of these photographs. The exact ones you've looked at and more. He's spent hours, no days, going through them. Been down here at least a dozen times over the last twenty years. And I've been his escort for every one of those visits. And I do mean escort."

50

"Honey . . . are you sure that's the only thing bothering you?"

"The only thing . . . isn't that enough?"

"You forget who you are talking to, my dear. No one knows you like I do. No one's known you longer than I have. No other person on this earth. Come to think of it, that's a pretty scary thought. So . . . what else is bothering you?"

"Mama."

"Reece . . . how many times over the years have people told you that they didn't believe you when you told them you were in Dealey Plaza that day? And then add that you were twenty feet from JFK when he was . . . you know what I've often thought about? Fifty years ago the most important human being on earth was assassinated . . . no killed. Assassinated sounds too antiseptic. Anyway . . . the nation was in mourning. Within hours most of the people on the planet had heard about it. The world was in mourning. Yet I never heard of anyone going to a counselor, or counselors being available at schools to help kids through the grieving process, or anyone asking anyone how they were doing."

"Mama . . . you had your own grieving to get through."

"I know, but look at what we do today. Much lesser events occur and we react like everyone is going to have a nervous breakdown.

Counselors ready to talk to kids at school. Priests, ministers, and rabbis extending office hours, and people lined up looking for an easy, quick fix to feel better. Well it doesn't work like that. I think it's why the baby-boomer generation is a lot tougher than those that followed. You played on dangerous playgrounds, broke bones, ate worms, and drank water out of a garden hose. And you weren't coddled and comforted every time something bad happened."

"Maybe we should have been."

"I tried my best."

"I know you did."

"It was a terrible day for me too."

"How did we get through it?"

"I guess we were counselors to each another."

"I was in Dealey Plaza, wasn't I?"

"Yes you were, honey."

"But Mama . . . how do you know for sure?"

"Because I am certain your father was there. And I know you were there with him."

"But, there is no hard evidence of that. You didn't see us there. You're going by what someone else told you."

"Actually, by what two people told me . . . you and your father."

"I was four years old."

"Which is probably better than a forty-four year old? I don't think you had learned how to lie yet. And even if you had, why would you have?"

"I know I was there, but after fifty years it's hard to separate what I remember really happening from what I've read about and studied over the years. I'm not sure my brain is keeping very good track any more of what I experienced versus what I've read about."

"Now you're beginning to sound like me."

"It is hereditary you know."

"Oh, don't be silly. Your brain is working just fine."

"Then how come I'm having such a problem living in the present?"

"Present . . . there is no such thing as the present. There is only a past and a future."

"What's the safeword?"

"What?"

"There's only a past and a future? Where did that come from?"

"Think about it. The past is everything that has happened up until now. The future is everything that will happen after the now. But there really is no now . . . no present."

"No present?"

"Nope. Just a past and a future."

"And you learned about this from?"

"I was just sitting here and it came to me."

"It came to you?"

"What do you think I'm doing when I'm sitting here staring out the window all day? I'm contemplating life. And I came to the conclusion that there was no present."

"If there is no present, then what are we living in?"

"I really haven't figured that out yet. But answer me this. How long is the present?"

"How long is the present?"

"Yes . . . how long does the present last?"

"I don't know."

"A day, hour, minute, second, micro-second?"

"An hour."

"Can't be an hour. Anything that has already happened, let's say, ten minutes into the hour is already the past and anything that hasn't happened yet in the next fifty minutes is the future. Our memory contains all our past experiences. It also contains the things we want to experience in the future. But the present is the interface between the past and the future. As soon as we experience the future, it becomes the past. The present, in essence, doesn't exist."

"What's the safeword?"

"I'm trying to be serious here."

"What's the safeword?"

"Don't be silly. I'm your mama."

"Prove it. My mama doesn't think those kinds of philosophical theories. Are you sure you're her?"

"As you grow old you have the time to think about things you never thought about before. That's one of the advantages of sitting around here all day. I get to philosophize. Unlock the mysteries of life. Maybe that's what the purpose of Alzheimer's is. Maybe all us old people looking like we are just sitting around vegg'n out are really experiencing the true meaning of life. And maybe I'm not supposed to be sharing this with you? I'm supposed to just sit here and be quiet about it."

"I've never known you to be quiet about anything. If the plan is to keep it a secret, it's not working with you."

"Maybe . . . maybe because I'm still . . . you know . . . she hasn't taken all of me yet."

"Mama." Reece put his hand on his mother's. "I think she's the one who should be worried about being taken over. You are one tough broad."

"Reece Landis! Is that any way to talk to your mama?"

"Well?"

"I am a tough broad, aren't I!"

"What's the safeword?"

"Reece . . . I think . . . I have been feeling better lately."

"That's good."

"No . . . I mean . . . I . . . I think I'm beating her."

"Why do you say that?"

"Oh . . . because I . . . never mind. So . . . now that we've concluded that you were definitely in Dealey Plaza that day, what else is bothering you?"

"Mama."

"Spit it out, dear." Dora put her other hand on top of his which was still on top of hers.

"Well . . . "

"I knew it. Your mother always knows."

"I broke up with Meeka."

"Oh, is that all." She pulled both hands away.

"You asked."

"I thought it was something important."

"You never did like her, did you?"

"I'm not saying anything."

"Why not?

"How many times have you broken up with her?"

"I don't . . . "

"Exactly. I've held my tongue every time. And it was a good thing I did. You ended up making-up with her. Imagine if I would have said something."

"So you don't like her."

"Don't put words in my mouth, Reece Landis. I didn't say I didn't like her. Anyway, what matters is if you like her or not. My thoughts and feelings are secondary."

"The way you are beating around the bush, you must really not like her."

"She's all right . . . I guess."

"You guess?"

"Well . . . if you want me to be honest."

"You mean sometimes you're not?"

"When I think it's in your best interest I might bend the truth, but only a little . . . and very infrequently."

"That's good to know. So . . . why don't you like her?"

"It's not that I don't like her. It's just that . . . well . . . first . . . "

"First? There's more than one reason?"

"First . . . she broke up your previous relationship with . . . "

"She did not. We weren't compatible. We were drifting apart way before Meeka came along."

"If you say so, dear."

"I think I was a little closer to the situation than you were."

"Maybe you're right."

"Maybe?"

"She speeded up the process. And who knows . . . maybe you would have made it if she hadn't come along."

"We wouldn't have . . . what else?"

"Second . . . "

"Second? I can't believe you have to number them."

"Second, I never thought she was good enough for you."

"Did you ever think any woman I dated was?"

"Of course I did."

"Who?"

"Let's see . . . there have been so many."

"Funny."

"Third . . . "

"How many do you have?"

"This is the last one."

"Whew."

"Third . . . I thought she was a . . . a . . . "

"Spit it out."

"Slut."

"Mama!"

"You wanted the truth."

"Slut?"

"What? You don't think I know what a slut is?"

51

"Team three . . . sorry I'm late. Time got away from me." Reece unlocked the door to his office, pushed it open, backed into the hall, and motioned to the three to enter the room. He followed and turned on the lights. "Time got away from me. That's a funny saying, isn't it? How can time get away from you? Time is a constant. It doesn't speed up or slow down. Have you ever thought about how long the present lasts? I mean . . . we can measure the past in recorded units of time, and we can talk about how far into the future an event might occur, but how long, or how much time, does the present last?"

Bill, Morgan, and Jason just stared at Reece.

"Never mind . . . let's sit at the table."

"We sent you the latest draft of our report on Friday."

"Yes, Jason. I read it over the weekend. I think you've addressed all of the questions and issues I raised at our last meeting. And I did see that you've added a new section on your six degrees of separation exercise. As we discussed last time, it was probably good that you formalized the analysis, but as you concluded, and as we previously surmised, nothing new came out of the effort."

"Actually . . . that's what we wanted to talk to you about. Since we sent you that report, we've, actually Morgan, has performed some additional analysis . . ."

"Look Jason, and Morgan, and Bill. I appreciate you going the extra mile and performing this analysis this late in the program, but as I stated the last time we met the issue of who knew who with the individuals closely involved, and for that matter even remotely involved, in the JFK assassination has been studied to death over the past fifty years. Sure there are some interesting relationships that have surfaced. Take George de Mohrenschildt, a well-educated ex-Russian who was living in Dallas at the time of the assassination. He was a close friend of Jackie Kennedy's aunt Edith Bouvier Beale and knew Jackie when she was a child. He may have had connections with the CIA, although no direct evidence has been found. He was the one who introduced the Oswalds to Ruth Paine who eventually rented an apartment to the Oswalds. It was Ruth Paine who got Oswald the job at the Texas School Book Depository a little over a month before the assassination.

"Now the six degrees of separation theory would tell us that any person on the planet is just six introductions away from knowing any other person. Therefore you wouldn't expect anything out of the ordinary that de Mohrenschildt, just because he had all these connections, was somehow linked to an assassination attempt on JFK. Yet the conspiracy theorists will say there was. They make ridiculous statements like Oswald was placed in the Texas School Book Depository building by the CIA, through de Mohrenschildt, through Ruth Paine, to assassinate JFK, even though Oswald started working there on October 16, weeks before the actual motorcade route was even determined.

"Six degrees defines links among people, not true relationships. The links do not explain the true meaning of the relationship that exists. Someone knows someone. But we don't know how strong the relationship is. And the greater the links, remember the theory says up to six, the higher the probability you will find the link or connection."

"What if the link is one-to-one with Oswald?"

"That certainly is the strongest possible connection, Morgan. But you still need to define the relationship that goes with the connection. Was it a chance connection, or was there a more defined connection from which you can conclude something else? Starting within hours of the assassination those links were hypothesized and analyzed, and have been so for the past fifty years, especially with Oswald. Oswald and the CIA. Oswald and the FBI. Oswald and the Secret Service. Oswald and the mafia. Oswald and the KGB. Oswald and Cuba. The list is endless."

"None of those are relationships with actual individuals."

"Oswald and Ruby. Oswald and Tippit. Oswald and every eyewitness in Dealey Plaza that day. They've all been looked at. Maybe it wasn't called six degrees of separation, but the links have all been analyzed. Believe me. I know. I've looked at every one of them myself. There is nothing there. I suggest you three stop wasting your time, and mine, and finalize your report. Everything needs to be closed out by Friday."

"We believe there was someone else in Dealey Plaza that day who had a close one-on-one relationship with Oswald. We believe this person may have played a role in the assassination."

"You believe, or you have proof?"

"We have proof of the one-on-one relationship, but . . . "

"Oswald had one-on-one relationships with many people, but none of them were in Dealey Plaza on November 22, 1963."

"We have circumstantial evidence that proves someone was . . . "

"Every conspiracy theorist has circumstantial evidence that proves their theory is real. Circumstantial evidence is what has kept this issue alive for fifty years. I refuse to deal with circumstantial evidence anymore. Unless you have irrefutable, hard evidence, our meeting is over."

"Actually, that's where we were hoping you could help us out."

"Don't pull me into this, Morgan."

"But, Dr. Landis . . . you're part of the link that we've uncovered."

"Link? What the hell are you talking about? How can I be part of a link to Oswald? I was four years old at the time."

"Actually, our analysis indicates you were two degrees away from

Oswald." Morgan handed Reece a copy of their four page stapled report.

"You're saying I knew someone who knew Oswald directly?"

"Yes."

"And that someone was in Dealey Plaza?"

"Yes."

Reece flipped over the cover page and started reading the report, although he had already determined in his own mind the only person who could have possibly been one degree away from both him and Oswald.

52

"Stop it!"

"Stop what?"

"Stop hiding behind your Alzheimer's."

"Reece . . . I have no idea what you are talking about. And please . . . there is no need to yell at me. I may not remember things, but I'm not deaf."

"Damn it Mama . . . I want the truth! And I'm not yelling!"

"Reece . . . calm down."

"I am calm."

"Just listen to yourself. Three hours ago you were in here telling me you didn't think you were even in Dealey Plaza on the day of the assassination. There was no hard evidence, as you put it, to prove that you were there. Now, three hours later mind you, you're accusing me of keeping secrets from you about your father's involvement in the assassination. Three hours later, you believe you were in Dealey Plaza the day of the assassination, and that your father was there, and that he had something to do with the assassination. Honey . . . think about what you are saying."

"I am thinking . . . I know exactly what I am saying."

"No . . . no . . . you are thinking, but what you are saying isn't consistent with what you are thinking. Your brain is going a mile a minute. You're trying to process more information than you can handle."

"You of all people should not be providing advice as to how another person's brain is functioning."

"If I didn't know any better I would swear that's not my son standing there. My son would never talk to his mama like that."

"And sometimes I swear you are not my mama. My mama would never lie to me."

"Sometimes I am not your mama."

"There you go hiding again. I thought you said you thought you were getting better?"

"I'm just saying that . . . sometimes . . . sometimes protecting your child is more important than the truth. And when a mother isn't honest with her child, she isn't being a bad mother . . . she doesn't intentionally want to be a bad mother. But to ease the pain of lying she pretends to be someone else."

"Mama . . . are you saying it's true?"

"What I'm saying is . . . yes . . . there have been times when I have not been honest with you."

"Mama . . . did Papa know him?"

"But, I did it to protect you."

"Mama . . . what are you saying?"

"To be honest Reece, I don't know what I am saying anymore. I'm getting old. And when you get old, you get tired. And when you get tired, your brain doesn't work as well as it use to. And when your brain doesn't work as well you start to blur fact with fiction, reality with fantasy, truth with lies. But the worse part is you forget. What were the real facts? What really happened? What was the truth? All of that becomes intertwined with the story telling, the fantasy, the lies. And it gets harder and harder to remember what really happened."

"Mama . . . did Papa know him?"

"I'm sorry Reece . . . I can't . . . "

"How could you forget something as important as that?"

"Reece . . . I can't . . . "

"I don't believe you kept this from me. Lied to me. All these years. Especially when you knew my whole life has been consumed trying to find the truth. And now . . . you are too old to remember?"

"Reece . . . I didn't say I couldn't remember. What I want to say is . . . I can't lie to you any more."

"Then don't Mama. Please . . . tell me the truth. You need to tell me before . . . "

"She takes over completely?"

"You said you were getting better." For the first time since Reece stormed into the room earlier, he sat down in the chair next to his mother and reached for her hand.

"I really think I am getting better, but . . . "

"But what?"

"What if I'm not getting better? What if I only think I'm getting better because the only things I can remember anymore are what I experience? What if I don't remember what happens when she has me? What if it's just her taking more and more of me?"

"Mama . . . that's why I think it's important that . . . "

"I know . . . I know. Before it's lost forever. Only I think some of it is already lost."

"Mama."

"Please don't be angry with me."

"Mama . . . I could never be angry with you."

"Who was that yelling and screaming a minute ago?"

"You must have been hallucinating."

"Oh, now I'm hallucinating? Great!"

"Just like you have a her, maybe I have a him inside of me. It was him yelling at you, not me."

"I don't doubt it was. It's convenient isn't it? Having him around."

"Very."

"I was always planning to tell you . . . the truth . . . some day. Then she entered my life. And now . . . now I'm not totally sure what the truth is anymore?"

"Then it's important that you tell me. I need to know. Mama . . . you may be the only person left who can . . . "

"What they told you is true. Your papa did know Lee Harvey Oswald."

53

"Hey . . . team six finally made it home."

"Did you get to meet the President?"

"Did you smuggle the Declaration of Independence out like I asked you to?"

"Joseph, you better stop hustling the bartender. Your woman's here."

"Don't call me his woman." Kayla reached up with her hand, clasped the back of Joseph's head, and pulled down until she could seal her lips onto his.

"Is she tonguing him?"

"I think he's tonguing her."

"Keep back . . . these two have been away from each other for almost, what, thirty hours? They're probably going to do it right here."

Without moving his lips from hers, Joseph reached down, wrapped his arms around Kayla, and raised her off the floor. She wrapped her stocking covered legs around his waist, her black strapped spiked high heels almost stabbing into Ryan's back as he sat watching the show in the bar stool behind Joseph.

"I told you they're gonna do it here."

Cheers erupted from around the room.

Kayla pulled her lips away. "I assume you had something to do with planning happy hour at the Library Lounge?"

"Why would you think that?"

"A bar in the Crowne Plaza? A hotel? I assume you have a room waiting for us?"

"Woops."

Kayla pushed away, as Joseph relaxed his grip, and stood back on the floor. "I guess somebody missed somebody more than somebody else did."

"Maybe I have something else planned for us this evening. I think you should have a drink. Maybe several."

"This sounds like it's going to be kinky. Let's not waste any time . . . make it a double."

"Hey, Rose."

"Hey, Paul."

"What can I get ya. We've got a tab running."

"How about a Grey Goose and Sprite with a lime. Tia got me hooked on Goose the other night. But . . . make it a double."

"How was your trip? Did you uncover any secrets?"

"The trip was long. I didn't sleep well last night. It was hot and muggy in Washington. We got rocked around by a thunderstorm on the flight back. The person behind me threw up. And any secrets hidden in the photos at the Archives are still hidden. So overall, I guess you could say the trip sucked."

"Sounds like you could go for a nice relaxing soak in a hot tub and then a back, or maybe body rub. I've even got a special drink I've been aging in my room for the past two weeks. It will be ready to drink at midnight. It's called a Moscow on the Hudson. Ever hear of it?"

"Can't say I have. What's in it?"

"It's a lot more complicated than that. Two weeks ago I placed a half dozen quartered lemons in a two quart glass jar, covered the lemons with one cup of brown sugar, and put the jar in the refrigerator. A week later I added a liter of vodka, in fact it was Grey Goose, then placed the jar on the floor in the corner of my room, behind the chair. It needed to be kept in a cool dry place. I've kept my room at sixty-five for the past week. It will be ready to drink at midnight tonight. All we need to do is strain it through a piece of cheesecloth, which I already obtained, pour over ice, and . . . what can I say! Are you in?"

"No."

"No . . . to what? The hot tub, body rub, or drink?"

"No to it all, although you do have me intriqued about the drink."

"Come on, Rose . . . why not? We have so much in common."

"We're both bartenders."

"Sounds like a match made in heaven to me."

"I told you . . . "

"I know, I know, I'm not your type."

"Paul . . . you know I like you. Can't we just leave it at that? By the way, why are we having a happy hour on a Monday night? Especially during our last week here. I would have thought everyone would be trying to finalize their project reports."

"That's right . . . you guys have been on a plane all afternoon and probably haven't heard."

"Heard what?"

"Team three, Bill, Jason, and Morgan uncovered a new conspiracy. It appears there was someone else in Dealey Plaza on November 22 who knew Oswald. And you'll never guess who it was?"

"Okay, I give up. Who?"

"Carl Landis. Dr. Landis's father."

"What? Wait a minute. Yesterday, weren't you working on a theory claiming that Landis and his father were not in Dealey Plaza. Now you're saying . . . "

"I'm not saying anything. Team three is saying he was not only there, but he was also a friend of Oswald's. He was stationed with Oswald in the Marines in Japan. Atsugi Naval Air Base. It was 1958, or maybe 1957. They may have worked side-by-side for several months. Monitoring U-2 spy plane flights over the Soviet Union. Then five years later they both end up in Dealey Plaza on November 22, 1963. What are the chances of that happening?"

"Probably pretty small."

"Ryan has been trying to calculate it. Not having much luck though. And it gets better."

"What?"

"Did you know Landis's father was killed on the evening of November 22, 1963? It probably has something to do with why he is so obsessed with the assassination."

"Ya think?"

"Like I said, they may have uncovered the best conspiracy theory in years. That's why we are here celebrating."

"Have they talked to Dr. Landis about it?"

"Oh yeah."

"And?"

"Well . . . after he turned white, he asked them to provide him with all of the information they had on the topic. A few minutes after the meeting he stormed out of his office and hasn't been seen since."

"Hi Paul."

"Hi Tia."

"Rose, Kayla wanted me to tell you that she left with Joseph. And I wanted to tell you that I'm leaving with Dixon. So we won't need rides."

"Did you hear about what team three found today?"

"No, but I can't talk now. I'm really not leaving. Dixon got a room upstairs. I'll see you tomorrow. Hope I make the ten o'clock meeting."

"Tia, wait! We need to talk."

"Gotta go, Rose. Priorities. Life-balance. We'll talk in the morning, I hope."

"Looks like the rest of your team is finding other things to do for the evening. Are you sure . . . "

"I'm sure."

"Another drink?"

"Yes, please."

"A double?"

"Yes, please. And don't think it'll loosen me up either."

"The thought never crossed my mind."

"Uh-huh."

"Rose . . . we're two mature adults enjoying each other's company."

"Is Morgan here? Or Bill? Or Jason?"

"Of course . . . we're celebrating their big discovery. Here's your drink."

"Thanks. There they are. I'll be back."

As Rose made her way through the crowd, her phone rang. A restricted number. She hesitated, then decided to answer it. "Hello?"

"Rose?"

"Yes."

"It's Reece."

54

"Stop yelling at me."

"I'm not yelling!"

"You're the second person that's said that to me today."

"Damn it . . . we had an agreement. We wouldn't tell him . . . we wouldn't tell him about anything unless we talked about it first. And we both agreed on it. We both agreed that was in his best interest. What else did you tell him?"

"That's all."

"And he was satisfied with that? He didn't want to know about anything else?"

"Now what do you think?"

"So . . . what did you tell him?"

"That I was tired and that was all I wanted to talk about today."

"I wish you hadn't have done that. You've opened up Pandora's Box. He's going to want it all now."

"Maybe it's time we told him."

"No! How many times have we had this discussion? We decided long ago that it was best not to."

"It's been fifty years."

"And everything has been fine for fifty years. Why did you have to go and do it?"

"Because I'm forgetting. And I want him to hear it from me. I want to tell him before . . . before . . . "

"Dora . . . you're fine. You said so yourself. You think you are getting better, not worse. And I think you're right. I see it too. Who else but me would be a better judge of that?"

"An MRI. Of my brain. Before and now. That's the only way to truly know."

"You've been reading too much."

"Reading's good for you."

"I wish you hadn't have . . . "

"But I did! It's too late! I did! Nothing we can do about it!"

"Maybe there is."

"No . . . we said we would only do that as a last resort."

"We may need to."

"Please . . . the real thing has been hard enough to deal with. I don't think I can . . . "

"You want to protect your son, don't you?"

"You need to ask me that? I've been protecting him for fifty years . . . FIFTY YEARS!"

"Do you have another suggestion?"

"How about the truth!"

"It's too late for the truth."

"It's never too late for the truth."

"Dora . . . "

"There has to be another way."

"We've gone over this . . . a million times. You know there is no other way."

"I can't bear losing him any more than I already have."

55

"Does that feel good?"

"Mmmmm . . . yes . . . flick your fingers . . . oh, yes . . . just like that."

"Just like that, what?"

"Just like that, Mistress."

"How do these feel?" Zaria reached up with her other hand and pulled down on the lead weights hanging from the short chain attached to the nipple clip that was clamped on the tip of her right breast. Then she reached over and pulled on the weights hanging on her left breast.

"Ahhhh . . . you were right. The burning sensation on my nipples has gone away. How did you know?"

"How did you know, what?"

"How did you know that the . . . AHHHH! How did you know, Mistress."

"I told you . . . I've been doing this for a long time. The initial pain, that sharp bite, then burning, fades to a quite pleasing feeling. Something I suspect you've never experienced before. But the best is yet to come." She pulled again, this time on both of them.

"AHHHH! Are you sure you're not adding more weights. It feels like they're getting heavier. AHHHH! It feels like they're getting heavier,

Mistress."

"Those young perky things of yours are holding up just fine, honey." She pulled again on the right one. "When these are worked on by your man do you get a sensation down here?" She flicked her fingers harder.

"Yes . . . a tingling . . . and I get wet, Mistress."

"That I can see." She pulled her black rubber gloved hand out, raised it, and placed it in the woman's mouth. "Clean it off. You've tasted yourself before, I mean not because you licked your juices off a man's shaft, but like this, off your own fingers, haven't you?"

"Yes, Mistress."

"Have you ever done it in front of your man while he was watching you?"

"No, Mistress."

"You will tonight. And he will do the same for you. Would you like to see your man lick his own juices?"

"Yes, Mistress."

Zaria reached down and pulled on the six surgical clamps, three clipped to each side of the inner lips of her sex, and pulled.

"Ahhhh . . . please, Mistress."

"Are these feeling better?"

"Yes, Mistress."

"And how about this?" She inserted her fingers until she found the now swollen clit and gently rolled it between her thumb and index finger.

"Mmmmm . . . Mistress, please don't stop."

"Does your man take care of this?"

"Yes, Mistress."

Zaria reached down with her other hand and placed it on her slaves warm pink ass-cheek.

"Ahhhh!"

"Did you enjoy the whipping I gave you earlier?"

"Yes, Mistress."

"You don't mind it that your man brought you here to me this evening to be my slave, do you?" Zaria squeezed her fingers together.

"Mmmmm . . . no, Mistress."

"I want you to promise me something."

"Mmmmm . . . anything, Mistress."

"No matter what happens the rest of this evening, I want you to come back here some night soon, alone. I promise you won't be disappointed. Will you do that for me?"

"Yes, Mistress."

"Very good. Now . . . would you like to see what I have done to your man?"

"Yes, Mistress."

Zaria backed up and stood next to the black velvet partition that was separating her two slaves. They had each been hanging from the ceiling for the past hour, naked, while she attached various clips and weights to their nipples and genitalia. She proceeded to whip them with a well used, and therefore slightly hardened, twenty-four-inch, thick, black leather slapper. With the bite of the clamps still fresh, each lash of the slapper resulted in a loud scream, a jerking body, and an even harder bite as the weights swayed back and forth tugging even harder on the clamps. She alternated between each of her slaves, increasing the intensity of each lashing as she moved from one to the other, until either could take no more.

Zaria pushed the partition away. For the first time that evening Joseph and Kayla were able to stare at one another. A smile came to both their faces.

"I see that you both enjoy what you see."

"Yes, Mistress." They both responded at the same time.

"Good. Let's see how much you enjoy what comes next. I am going to let both of you down and I want you to remove the weights and clips from each other, alternating between you, starting with your nipples."

56

"Yes, I've been drinking."

"I didn't . . . "

"You didn't need to. I saw you walk in. A while ago. You've been staring at me."

"I had to go to the . . . "

"And then you were staring at me."

"Only two shots worth."

"Patron."

"I know."

"How . . . oh . . . bartender. One of your many secrets that didn't show up on your resume."

"I wouldn't say many."

"Would you like another, Dr. Landis?"

"Yes, but a Jack and Diet. And what can I get you?"

"Grey Goose and Sprite, please."

"Fruit?"

"Yes, lime please." Rose sat on the barstool next to Reece.

"So, are you saying there are no interesting facts about your past that you left off your resume?"

"I'm four . . . I'm more experienced . . . let's just say I've lived a lot more of life than could fit on the no more than two pages you allowed us to submit with the application summary of our education and job history."

"You could have used smaller font. I had an applicant once who fit over six normal pages of information in that two page space."

"Did you accept him into the program?"

"Her . . . and, no."

"Here are your drinks."

"Thank you, Daniel."

"Thank you, but could I get a lime please?"

"Sorry."

"That's okay . . . thanks."

"He gave me the lime instead . . . which I didn't want." Reece grabbed a small napkin from the holder on the other side of the bar, placed the lime in it, wadded it up and laid it on the bar.

"Most people would have just thrown it on the bar."

"Not very considerate of the bartender."

"It's a tough job."

"I don't doubt it. Taking care of people like me is."

"Takes special skills to be a good one. For example, he remembered he had to put a lime in one of the drinks, and just mixed up which one. A good bartender wouldn't do that. A good bartender would have listened carefully, remembered what was ordered, and made and delivered the correct drinks. And if he was uncertain about it, he would re-verify with the customer, not guess."

"And you have those skills?"

"I like to think so. And with the tips I used to end up with at the end of the night, I believe I did."

"So, you're saying the tips had everything to do with your listening and execution skills and not your . . . not what you were wearing, and . . . well . . . in some cases, what you weren't wearing?"

"Well . . . I will admit to a slight correlation . . . "

"Correlation?"

"When I took statistics, we had to do a semester project. I did mine on that very subject."

"And?"

"My conclusion, to as I recall a 0.82 correlation coefficient, was that there was a positive correlation between the amount of cleavage showing versus the amount of tips at the end of the night."

"That must have been a very interesting presentation."

"It was great. I was, as usual, the oldest in the class. I was dead serious with my presentation. Charts, graphs, schematics."

"Pictures?"

"No pictures."

"Good grade?"

"An A."

"Did the professor hit on you?"

"Yup."

"I bet he did."

"She."

"Even more interesting."

"So did half the guys in the class. Funny how many showed up later that evening at the bar I worked at. Clear across town. I made a lot of tips that night. Too bad they were all ten years younger than me."

"I would think you'd take it as a compliment."

"They didn't want to marry me. They wanted to . . . "

"You don't like younger men?"

"I prefer . . . "

Reece broke the uncomfortable silence by holding up his drink. "Here's to . . . I hope your day was better than mine." They clanged glasses and drank.

"I heard you had quite a day."

"Gotta love this instant messaging society we live in. Can you imagine what it would have been like if all this technology existed on November 22, 1963? There would have been a hundred Zapruder-like movies. Security cameras on every corner would've captured the entire event. No street signs, trees, blocking the view. People in Dealey Plaza would have been pointing their smart phones in every direction they thought the shots came from. Oswald, or anyone else involved, would have been caught in the act. All the evidence needed to close the case would have been sent around the world before Kennedy was pronounced dead. Fifty years of analyses and investigations by thousands, maybe even millions of individuals could have been better spent finding . . . finding the cure for cancer, or solving world hunger, or poverty, or who knows what else. Think of what we could have done with all that brain power.

"Instead we come up with new interpretations of the same old evidence and spin a new theory that sometimes defies logic."

"We're just trying to find the truth. It's something we crave as human beings."

"Truth? Do you know in less than four hours today I had two groups of very bright intelligent people . . . do you know how much time I spend to make sure only the best of the best and the brightest of the brightest get into this program? Two groups of the best of the best and brightest of the brightest came to me, within four hours time mind you, and one group told me I was not in Dealey Plaza on November 22, 1963, and the other said I was not only there, but the person I was there with, my father, may have had something to do with the assassination."

"I think they said he may have known Oswald, not that he had anything to do with . . . "

"Oh, I suppose you were involved with this analysis?"

"Actually, I was only involved with the first one . . . the one that said you weren't there."

"And you played along with me . . . the picture . . . did you find anything?"

"I wasn't playing along with you."

"But you knew about team ten and what they were looking at? And you were working with them?"

"Yes . . . I knew what they were doing and I was working with them . . . ”

“Then you played me.”

“No . . . I only agreed to work with them so I could prove them wrong.”

“And?”

“Nothing . . . the only photograph there is the same as the one you have. No negative.”

“Excuse me . . . I didn’t mean to interrupt, but can I get you guys another round?”

“Yes, but make mine a double, please.”

“Mine too . . . and no lime.”

“I thought I was going to blow their hypothesis out of the water.”

“I’m kind ‘a glad you didn’t. I’m beginning to think it’s better not to find evidence that I was there.”

“But you were.”

“Prove it!”

“Here you go, doubles, one with fruit, one without.”

“You’re gonna get drunk guzzling Goose like that.”

“Were you playing me for a fool?”

“What?”

“The picture. You knew what was in the Archives. That it was the same picture you had. You knew the negative wasn’t there.”

“I wasn’t sure if the negative was there or not. I didn’t know about how pictures were printed from negatives and your stupid theory . . . ”

“It’s not stupid!”

“Fine . . . about your theory that there may be something on the negative. I never paid attention to the negative. And I didn’t remember if it was there or not. So no . . . I didn’t play you for a fool.”

“And I didn’t play you for a fool either.”

“Let’s drink to that. Cheers.”

“Cheers.”

“How did you know?”

“Know what?”

"That the picture was the same."

"Your girlfriend."

"Meeka?"

"Liz."

"She's not my girlfriend."

"I thought Meeka wasn't your girlfriend any more either?"

"She isn't. And neither is Liz Conway."

"But you have done her."

"Ms. Conway and I are very good friends. She's been very gracious over the years to let me do my research in the Archives with little more than having to buy dinner at some of the best restaurants in D.C.

"Oh please."

"What?"

"Her eyes lit up every time your name was mentioned. If I didn't know any better I'd say her panties got wet too."

"Excuse me . . . I told you not to guzzle. You're getting goosed."

"Be honest with me . . . you did, didn't you?"

"You don't understand. She gave me access to things . . . "

"I bet she did. They say you should never underestimate those librarian types. Just tell me . . . yes or no?"

"I may have . . . "

"I knew it. Actually Kayla was the first to suggest it. Did you do it in the Archives? She said you've spent a lot of time in there."

"I was doing research."

"So you did! You did her in the National Archives."

"Stop! If you get off about me telling you what I did and didn't do with a librarian, I'd be glad to tell you about it sometime. But, that's not why I asked you to come down to Joey's on one of the worst days of my life. I think I know where the negative is."

"What? Where?"

"Saratoga, New York."

"Where is Saratoga, yew nork? Fuck . . . I think you were right about the Goose. It's goosing me."

"Eastern part of the state, near Albany. Less than three hours drive."

"How do you know? And why didn't you try to track it down before?"

"I have a friend in the FBI."

"Of course you do."

"She's the granddaughter of the woman who stood on the grassy knoll and took the picture."

"The FBI person?"

"No, the woman in Saratoga."

"You mean she really knows someone who was on the grassy knoll? That's a joke. Like whenever someone is looking for a place for something to happen, the grassy knoll is often mentioned. Woodstock is too. Do you know if you add up all the people who said they were at Woodstock that there would be like millions and millions. And there was like, half a million."

"Maybe we should talk about this tomorrow."

"No . . . no . . . I'm fine. I tend to talk a lot when I drink . . . a lot. But I'm not drunk. Maybe I should have some peppermint schnapps . . . on the rocks . . . with a splash of water. That sobers me up."

"Grey Goose with Sprite to straight peppermint schnapps sobers you up?"

"I said with a splash of water."

"Daniel, can we get a Jack and Diet and a peppermint schnapps on the rocks with a splash of water."

"Only a splash."

"Got it. Double on the Jack?"

"Yes, please."

"And why didn't you try to track this negative down before?"

"I guess you're not as drunk as I thought."

"Wait till the schnapps kicks in. So . . . "

"I never had a reason to . . . until your stupid theory."

"I told you, it's not stupid."

"Well . . . we'll find out tomorrow."

"We? Tomorrow?"

"If you are willing to go with me. To Saratoga. My last meeting ends at two. We could be there by five. She said she has a box of old photographs from her grandmother. There are some dated from 1963. We are welcome to look at them, but we can't take anything. The negatives are there too. We'd be back here by nine, ten at the latest. I'll drive. What da ya say?"

"What do I say? Yes. Of course. Yes . . . I'll go. That is if you want me to."

"I wouldn't have asked you if I didn't want you to."

"Your drinks."

"Thank you, Daniel."

"Aren't you nervous?"

"About what?"

"What we'll find."

"I'd like to know, one way or the other."

"You already know."

"But I can't prove it."

"This may not give you the answer either. It still may not be enough evidence."

"I'll take that chance."

They both lifted their glasses and sipped from them, eyes locked on each other.

"You're afraid of me, aren't you?"

"Why would you think that?"

"Two reasons."

"I'm listening."

"First, I think you like older men. And second, I think I excite you."

"Don't flatter yourself."

"Actually there's a third reason . . . you excite me."

57

"What the hell was that all about?"

"I have no idea."

"Could that have been any . . . "

"Hotter?"

"You were an animal."

"So were you."

"Are you feeling . . . "

"Tingling all over?"

"I guess that's a good way to describe it. And all over, yes. But some places are tingling more than others."

"I bet I could name exactly where those places are."

"Do you know it's three o'clock in the morning? We've been at it for over two hours."

"How did you stay hard for so long?"

"How did you stay so wet?"

"You started ripping my clothes off me as soon as we walked in the door."

"You're lucky I waited until then. And look what you did to my clothes."

"No . . . I mean rip. You tore the buttons off my top. I just bought that too."

"Sorry."

"I'm not . . . it was hot."

"You like it a little rough, don't you?"

"I guess I do. Who knew? What about you?"

"Definitely."

"Did you wanna think about it?"

"I have been . . . for a week."

"I have a feeling it's been longer than a week."

"Are you glad I did something about it?"

"Very."

"Did you wanna think about it?"

"Nope."

"Are you sure? I mean . . . I had . . . "

"Sex with her?"

"Yes."

"I don't look at it that way."

"You don't?"

"No."

"Really?"

"Really." Kayla, who was lying on her back next to Joseph who was lying on his back, rolled to her side and pushed her body into his. She draped her arm onto his chest and slowly and lightly ran her fingernails over his still damp skin. "The way I see it is, you were the student and Zaria was your teacher. How else would you, and then me of course, have learned about those things? I've been reading about it, and I thought I was at least curious about it. Curious enough to want to try it. But, try what? Until I actually experienced it tonight with her, then you on me, and me on you, I had no idea it would be that exciting."

"And erotic."

"And nasty."

"And hot."

"And tingly."

"Still . . . I was with her."

"She was showing you how to do things. She was your teacher and you were her student."

"Yes . . . but . . . "

"There wasn't anything more than that between you, was there?"

"No! Absolutely not."

"I mean . . . I'm not stupid. I know that when you went to see her that she . . . she did things to you. And that you probably excited her and she excited you. Just like tonight when you were on the other side of the curtain. I wasn't sure what she was doing to you, I could only fantasize. Then, when she came over to my side and started working on me, I knew exactly what she had done to you. She was doing the same thing to me."

"What about you?"

"What?"

"There's nothing between you and her, is there?"

"No . . . no . . . "

"How come I sense some hesitation in your voice?"

"She was hot, that's all. And slutty."

"Very."

"So admit it. She turned us both on."

"I agree . . . both."

"Then we came back here and went at it like whores in heat."

"So, she's just spicing things up . . . for you and me."

"Exactly! Tell me. Were you with her this past Saturday evening?"

"Why do you say that?"

"You said you had something to do. I went out to dinner with Rose. When we got back to the room that night you were . . . you were like you were tonight. An animal. Insatiable."

"You don't want me to give away all my secrets, do you?"

"No . . . but I do want to make sure it's me you're lusting, not someone else."

"I think I just proved that for the past two hours, didn't I?"

"Yes, you did." Kayla crawled on top of him and pushed her tongue deep into his mouth.

"Do you want it everywhere again?"

"Yes." She tongued him deeper and harder.

"Kayla Dexter, you're getting sluttier than when I first met you."

"As slutty as her?"

"Yes."

"Don't lie. I know I'm not . . . but I intend to be." She slowly slid herself down dragging her flicking tongue on his still clammy body.

58

"I've read all of the information you guys, and gal, put together, and I'm impressed. Morgan, Bill, Jason . . . great find."

"Thank you. We weren't sure how you would react since it is your father who was potentially involved . . . "

"And you only have three days left to complete your analysis and wrap things up. I want answers over these next three days, not hypotheses. Is that clear?"

"Yes."

"Good. Now first, have you heard about the hypothesis that team ten has come up with?"

"We've heard parts of . . . "

"I want you to meet with them. We need to resolve that issue or your hypothesis ends up being a nice discovery with little meaning."

"We will do that."

"Second, I want you to contact everyone who is still alive from Oswald's platoon when he was stationed at the Atsugi Naval Air Base. I realize some of them were interviewed by the Warren Commission, but not everyone. Here is a contact at Marine Corps Headquarters in Quantico, Virginia. I already spoke with him and he's expecting your call. He's looking through the records now for the names of everyone in that platoon. There should be enough background information for you to find many of them, those that are still alive anyway. Ask them if they recall if Oswald worked on the same shift with or hung around with my father. Fifty years is a long time, but maybe there is something there."

"Depending upon how much background information there is and how lucky we are with our search, this could take . . . "

"If you need some more bodies to help you, team two is essentially done with their final report, and they can help you. I've already spoken to them."

"Daren, Raji, and Andrew?"

"Yes."

"Great."

"Third, as you know there has been an extensive timeline put together of Oswald's life, from his birth until his death on November 24, 1963. I want you to do a search of the literature. As much as you can over the next two to three days. Look at his timeline for the final year leading up to the assassination. Knowing what you know now, that a possible link might exist between Oswald and my father, is there anything in the timeline to suggest that link exists? I know it's a long shot, but who knows. There might be something there that we didn't see before."

"We can try some keyword searches to start with."

"Excellent."

"Dr. Landis, we also thought about contacting any close friends or relatives of Mr. Landis to see if they recall him ever mentioning Oswald."

"I already thought of that too. Unfortunately my father was killed within hours of the assassination. An automobile accident. If he was somehow involved, I doubt he would've said anything to anyone. If he wasn't involved, I'm not sure he had heard that Oswald was the suspect. In any event he only had contact with three people that day. Me, my mother, and a friend of his who was staying with us. I'm not even sure what his real name was. I am trying to question my mother about it. Unfortunately she is suffering from Alzheimer's, so we'll have to tread lightly there. I'll do the best I can, but I'm not too hopeful.

"Anything else that you can think of?"

"That was the only other suggestion we had."

"We don't have much time, so let's get to work. And again, great find!"

59

"Are you saying Rose, this hypothesis has been a big waste of time?"

"No Kayla. What I'm saying is the photographic information we looked at in the Archives didn't reveal anything."

"Sounds like a big waste of time to me."

"Not really. Most of the photographs had negatives that had a lot more information on them than what was on the developed picture. Unfortunately, nothing showed up of any interest on the unexposed negative."

"Sounds like a big waste of time to me."

"You're a bitch today. Didn't you get enough sleep? Usually when you don't get enough sleep it's because you were getting laid. You might be tired, but at least you're in a good mood."

"Screw you, Tia. Just because you're in a good mood doesn't mean everyone else has to be. I guess you must of got laid? Oh wait . . . you did . . . Dixon got a hotel room. Now you're an expert on the after effects of getting laid. Well, I got laid too. For hours if you must know. That's why I'm exhausted. And bitchy."

"Who said I wanted to know?"

"Ladies . . . great. You both got laid last night. You should both be in good moods. So can you get into them. We meet with Landis in two hours."

"I'm in a good mood."

"I'm in a good mood too. No, I'm in a great mood. But I'm tired and bitchy too. I'm just asking, has this whole exercise been a waste of time?"

"I'm in a great mood too."

"Tia!"

"I just want to be clear about that."

"Kayla . . . it hasn't been a waste of time. We found new evidence, photographic evidence, that no one even knew existed."

"With nothing on it."

"Which still proves something. Didn't you ever hear of the null hypothesis?"

"A statistics term, or something?"

"We assumed that there would be new photographic evidence that would contain some new revelation about the assassination. As it turns out the new information did exist, but it didn't reveal anything new. But what it did do was confirm what we already knew. It proved the null hypothesis."

"You lost me. Statistics wasn't one of my strongest subjects."

"Ryan would know what I'm talking about."

"Let me try, Rose."

"Go for it Tia."

"Let's say you had invented a drug that you thought was going to cure breast cancer. That's your hypothesis. You conduct your study and you determine the drug doesn't cure breast cancer. You proved the null hypothesis, that the drug does not cure breast cancer."

"I get that. The drug was a failure. The study was a waste of time."

"Yes, the drug was a failure, but the study was not a waste of time. Finding out something doesn't work is sometimes just as important as finding out what does work. In this example, if you had breast cancer and were taking the drug, wouldn't you want to know if the drug worked or not?"

"Okay, I get it. We found new evidence, but we didn't find anything to support a new theory about the assassination. So the most credible hypothesis, Oswald acted alone, still stands."

"You got it, Kayla."

"I knew talking about breasts would help."

"Sorry I've been so bitchy this morning. But honestly, I didn't get any sleep last night. I'm exhausted."

"Any?"

"Almost none."

"Good for you, girl."

"I didn't get a lot of sleep either."

"Good for you too, Tia."

"But Red Bull's got me flying. You should try it, Kayla."

"I already had two."

"You're both going to crash later. Just make sure it's after our meeting with Landis."

"That's not till one. I can get a good hour nap in and still look good for the meeting."

"Maybe I'll try that too."

"I'll put something together for the meeting, so you both can nap. Before you nod off, what about the Zapruder film? Anything new Tia on the imperfection on the film?"

"I wish we could get a hold of the original. If we could confirm it's not on the original, then we know it's just an imperfection made during copying. That's the likely scenario, because I can't come up with it being anything other than an imperfection. If it is on the original, we are in the same place we are now. But it would help to know we weren't chasing a ghost."

"Well that isn't going to happen."

"Your Dr. Landis isn't as important as everyone thinks he is. Hasn't got enough clout to view the original film?"

"He's not my Dr. Landis. And if we came up with a good enough reason to need to view the original, he probably could somehow make it happen."

“I’m sure he could work something out with his lady friend at the Archives. A little dinner and . . . ”

“I don’t think the original is even there.”

“Whatever.”

“What do we tell Landis?”

“We’ll brief him on what we found and tell him we’re still working on it.”

“That’s not going to go over well.”

“Then you better do some sweet talk’n, Rose.”

60

"I'm just asking, Doc, if bringing up a traumatic event from one's past could somehow affect memory in a patient with Alzheimer's?"

"Reece, that's such an open ended question."

"I realize that, but is it possible?"

"I'm sure that it is. After all, the literature is full of references where healthy people have blocked out traumatic events that they have experienced or witnessed. Rape victims, witnesses to murders, soldiers in combat zones, even children in dysfunctional families. If a healthy person's brain can do it, I'm sure someone suffering from Alzheimer's could have the same thing happen to them. Why do you ask? Has something happened with your mother?"

"I'm not sure."

"I just saw her yesterday during my morning rounds. She seemed fine to me. In fact, especially these past few weeks, I've never seen her better. If anything, I would swear she was getting better, not deteriorating. Of course we would need to do some testing to confirm that, and I'm not sure what baseline test results are in her file."

"Dr. Sanger, I'm not asking you to do any testing. Yesterday morning my mother seemed fine. In the afternoon we had a discussion about some events that took place years ago. The discussion seemed to disturb her. Fifteen minutes ago I visited her and she is a completely different woman from yesterday. For the first time in a long time she doesn't even remember who I am."

"That isn't uncommon for someone with Alzheimer's."

"But could our discussion yesterday have done something to . . . "

"It's possible. But so could a dozen other things. There is so much we don't know about this disease. I wouldn't blame yourself. Whatever she is going through is probably not permanent. It will likely all pass in an hour, or a day, or a week. Who knows"

"It's just that . . . the change from yesterday to today was so dramatic. She didn't even know me."

"If you are that worried about it, there's an easy fix. Don't ever bring up again whatever topic it was you were talking about."

61

"So, what do you guys want to do?"

"They've got a lot a balls coming in here and telling us to drop our theory due to lack of evidence when their own theory is hypothetical at best."

"Joseph, they came up with a huge find. The link between Oswald and Landis's father. That's gonna reinvigorate the conspiracy movement. And all on the fiftieth anniversary of the assassination. This is big!"

"And look how much bigger their find would be if we dropped our find."

"I'm not sure what we even found?"

"We found that two pairs of shoes showing up in a photograph isn't enough evidence to prove that Dr. Landis was in Dealey Plaza on the day of the assassination."

"He says he was there."

"Testimony from a four-year-old, remembering fifty years later."

"He's said it all his life."

"I thought I was Superman for a lot of years of my life. Doesn't make it true."

"Paul, you've been awful quiet over there. What do you think?"

"I'm not sure . . . which answer does Landis want to see come out of this?"

"That's easy. He doesn't want everyone to think he's been lying for the past fifty years about being there. His reputation would be shot. His career would be over. He wants the answer to come out that he was there."

"But if this other theory is true, and his father knew Oswald, and they were in Dealey Plaza, that opens up a whole new scenario. Was he there working with Oswald? Was he a conspirator in the assassination? Don't you think that would be even more damning to his career, to find out your father was part of the JFK assassination? And not an observer, but a co-conspirator."

"So, he wants their theory to be wrong?"

"But they have hard evidence to prove his father knew Oswald. There is a lack of evidence to prove whether they were doing something together in Dealey Plaza or not. Again, which answer does Landis want to see come out of this?"

"He's fucked either way."

"But what if there was a third scenario?"

"Good, Paul. How could there be a third? He was either there or he wasn't there. One or two, not three."

"Or maybe he was there and for fifty years he's been using that as a diversion for the real truth. The truth about his father and Oswald."

"And he thought this up as a four-year-old?"

"No. At first, the only thing he knew was he was there. He builds his whole career around that life changing event. Then at some point, maybe during one of these seminars, someone or maybe even Landis, discovers the link between Oswald and his father. But to protect his father, and his career, he has to hide that discovery. It becomes easy for him to do because he makes everyone focus on him. This person standing before you was in Dealey Plaza and witnessed JFK being assassinated. You're blinded to everything else that could have happened around him. Keep the story alive, still be a legend, and protect his father. It's easy for him to pull it off."

"Then why run an annual seminar to try to find out what happened on November 22, 1963? He was playing Russian Roulette. At some point someone was bound to find something."

"That's true, Ryan. I don't have an answer for that."

"I think I do."

"Let's hear it."

"What if Landis was there . . . "

"But Joseph . . . what about your theory?"

"Okay . . . I was wrong. What if Landis was there and he didn't know about the link between Oswald and his father. As you said Paul, he builds his whole career around being there and it blinds everyone to the truth hidden behind it, including himself. It's right under his nose, but he doesn't see it. So what if, and here it comes, someone else was responsible for making sure that secret stayed a secret, to the point that even Landis didn't know he was being used?"

62

"Did you mention anything to team ten about the negative in Saratoga? To Paul, Ryan, or Joseph?"

"No."

"To Kayla?"

"No . . . you told me not to mention it to anyone. I didn't. Why?"

"I just got an email from them. They now believe they don't have enough evidence, circumstantial or otherwise, to support their theory that I wasn't in Dealey Plaza."

"That's good. You never really believed them anyway, did you?"

"I told you last night Rose, I don't know what I believe anymore. In a way, I was hoping they were right. If my father and I weren't there, then it might not matter if he knew Oswald. Being there is now much more complicated."

"Hopefully we'll have an answer to that by the end of the day."

"I hope so. Where's the rest of your team?"

"I think they . . . they're under the weather and I don't think they are going to be able to make it."

"Oh, by the way, we aren't going to be able to leave at two. I need to stop by and see my mother before we leave."

"Is everything okay? I could go by myself, or we could go another day."

"I'm sure everything is fine. I just need to check up on her. And, I don't want to be late getting to Saratoga."

"Well . . . I don't have much to report. I already told you about the photographs and we are still analyzing the Zapruder film."

"Cutting this meeting short isn't going to help. I have a meeting after this."

"Well, there was one thing we wanted to ask you. Is there any way we could view the original Zapruder film? With your connections . . . "

"It's not in the Archives. My connections there won't be able to help us with this one. Although, if I asked her for a favor, knowing I would then owe two in return, she would try her damnedest to get a hold of it."

"I bet she would."

"She would probably even make it look like some special request from the National Archives."

"I bet you can be quite demanding when you want to be."

"I've been told that in the past."

"So . . . is there a chance?"

"No. We'd need a very compelling reason to even try. And it would likely have to be through the courts. So forget about it. You'll have to work with what you've got."

"We'll do our best."

"If that's all, I'll see you about three."

"Three it is."

63

"Reece! You startled me. What are you doing here?"

"What am I doing here? I'm visiting my mama, that's what I'm doing here."

"But you were just . . . "

"I was just what?"

"Nothing."

"I was just what, Mama? What were you going to say? Were you going to say I was just here this morning?"

"Were you?"

"Mama, do you remember that I was here this morning?"

"I . . . I can't . . . no wait . . . I think . . . I can't remember. Were you here? What are you doing?"

"I thought I saw someone walking into your room."

"There's no one here. You don't believe me?"

"I believe you."

"Then why are you looking in my closet?"

"I could have sworn I saw someone walk into your room. Then I saw you step out into the hall. I think you saw me."

"For heaven's sake Reece. You probably saw Lilly next door. She's always getting visitors. Sometimes you can hear them through the wall. Especially if you use a glass. Put it up to your ear. Like this. Want to try?"

"No, I think I'll . . . "

"Really, Reece! You're going to look under the bed? Fine, go ahead. Call your mama a liar right to her face. There's not much worse you can do than call your mama a liar to her face."

"I believe you Mama. Don't cry. You're right. I must have been mistaken."

"Come hug your mama."

"You smell good. Do you have perfume on?"

"Yes, I have perfume on. And don't I always smell good?"

"Yes, you do."

"What do you think I should smell like, an old person?"

"An old person?"

"You know what they say about old people. Old people don't remember things. Forget to shower, to wash up, to brush their teeth, to comb their hair, to wash their clothes, to wear deodorant, or perfume. Pretty soon they smell . . . like an old person."

"Mama . . . you've been reading to much again. Besides, like I said, you always smell good."

"You wouldn't tell me if I smelled bad anyway."

"Yes I would."

"You'd hurt my feelings like that?"

"No."

"Good. Come, sit. Visit with your mama."

"I really can't . . . I'm off to another appointment. I just came by to see how you were doing."

"I'm doing fine. I think I told you yesterday, or maybe the day before, that I was doing fine."

"Do you remember that I was here this morning?"

"I seem to recall something. How long ago was it?"

"Ten o'clock. About five hours ago."

"Five hours ago. I seem to remember you being here five minutes ago, not five hours ago. But you know how time speeds up for us old people, so maybe it was five hours ago."

"Mama, time is a constant. It doesn't speed up or slow down."

"Reece, do I need to share with you another one of those secrets?"

"You mean like past, present, and future?"

"Yes."

"Will it take long?"

"No."

"I'm listening."

"Pay attention, because I'm only going to say this once. From the instant you are born, every future second, minute, hour, day, week, month, or year that you experience, it doesn't matter what increment of time you use, is interpreted by your brain to have taken less time to experience than it did in the past. Are you following me?"

"I heard what you said, but it didn't make sense. Time is a constant."

"Let me provide you with a simple example."

"Please do."

"When you are five years old each year of your life represented twenty percent of your life. When you experience the next year of your life, going from five to six years old, that next year does not represent another twenty percent of living. To your brain, it only represents about seventeen percent of your life. Do the same calculation going from twenty-nine to thirty and that year is only worth about three percent of your total life lived. From forty-nine to fifty, it's about two percent, and from sixty-nine to seventy, it's about one percent. So as you get older your brain thinks each successive increment of time is speeding by faster and faster, based upon the only thing it has to compare it to, its own memory of past experiences.

"Does that make sense?"

"I hate to admit it, but it does. Where did you read about that?"

"I didn't read it anywhere. Just like I didn't read about past, present, and future."

"Then where . . . "

"I told you. Sitting here, thinking, everyday. I don't know how to explain it, but you experience an inner peace. Things . . . things just come to you."

"Do you remember if I was here this morning?"

"I think so . . . but I'm not totally certain."

"Do you remember me being here yesterday?"

"I . . . I think so . . . but I'm not totally certain."

"Do you know who I am?"

"That I do. Of course I know who you are. You are Dr. Reece Landis, my dentist."

Reece stared at his mother.

"Got ya, didn't I! Come give your mama another hug."

64

"Where did Rose say she was going?"

"She didn't. Just said she had something to take care of. Wasn't sure when she'd be back."

"That's not like her, Tia."

"You don't think she has a date?"

"With who?"

"That guy you tried to set her up with the other night. When you were out to dinner. Young guy. Saturday night."

"Yes . . . Asti Caffe. Cary. No, Grant."

"Cary Grant?"

"No, Grant. As in Grantham."

"Grant. That's right. You told us at dinner in D.C. You think she might be out with him?"

"She did say she thought she made a mistake by not going home with him that night. Although she also said he wasn't her type."

"Who is her type, Kayla? I mean, every guy we've ever pointed out hasn't been her type. Maybe she likes women?"

"No. I mean she might like women too. We didn't talk about that. But, she definitely likes men. She thought she was going to get married."

"No? Wait . . . didn't we talk about that at dinner in D.C. too? I must have been feeling good. Married?"

"Yup. Dumped her on the weekend she thought he was going to propose."

"No wonder no man is her type."

"Tia, it was two years ago. She hasn't gotten laid in two years. She hasn't even dated another guy in two years."

"So . . . she's not over him yet."

"He dumped her. He's going out with other women. Two years have gone by. She needs to move on."

"Well . . . I know how she feels. I've been dumped. You never wanna see another man. And if you do see one the only thing you want to do is cut off their . . . "

"Two years!"

"Okay . . . she needs to get over it. So, maybe she is out with . . . "

"Grant. And I don't think so. Too young."

"You'd think she'd wanna show off she was going out with someone younger than her."

"No . . . I mean way too young. Like almost half her age."

"Even more to brag about. Men do it all the time."

"Only . . . I think she likes older men."

"So she does have a type. How do you know?"

"The guy who dumped her. Mr. Right. I think he was older."

"How much?"

"She didn't say exactly. But just the way she talked about him. He sounded, you know, well to do. Like he'd already made it."

"Doesn't mean he was older."

"Plus, he dumped her for someone younger. She made that clear. I don't know . . . he just sounded older."

"I hope I look half as good as she does when I'm her age."

"You and me both. Paul thinks she is one hot MILF. So does Joseph."

"I have a feeling every guy in the program thinks the same thing. But I don't think she likes being called a MILF."

“I don’t think she minds the ILF part, it’s the M she doesn’t like.”

“Son of a . . . ”

“What?”

“No way?”

“You’ve been staring at that screen for over an hour. Did you finally find something?”

“I’m not sure. Look at this. No wait. Let me go back. To this frame.”

“Is that 313?”

“Yes.”

“I don’t like looking at that one.”

“There’s the, whatever it is. Reflection, or imperfection on the film.”

“I think we ruled out reflection because it’s gone on the next frame.”

“We did, but here’s the next frame. Frame 314.”

“No reflection, or imperfection.”

“Right. But what were we all looking for on this frame?”

“The reflection, or whatever it is.”

“Or what else?”

“No reflection?”

“Exactly. We were looking for one or the other. But look what happens when I computer enhance the frame and zoom in on that part of the curb where we think we’d see a reflection.”

“I don’t see a reflection.”

“That’s right, you don’t. You don’t see the reflection. But look closer.”

“It looks like a . . . a gouge in the curb. I don’t remember seeing that before.”

“It’s because you were experiencing inattentional blindness. Actually, we all were. It’s when we don’t see what we are looking at because we are focused on a different issue. In this case, we either wanted to see a reflection or not see a reflection. Because of this inattentional blindness we didn’t see what was really there, a gouge in the curb.”

“Is that like the video I remember viewing in Psych class with the two groups of players passing basketballs. We were told to count the passes between members of one of the groups. Because we were so focused on that many of us in the class did not see the guy in the gorilla suit walk between the players."

"Exactly. It explains why as humans we sometimes don't see what's right in front of our faces."

"So, what's the gouge? Could it explain the reflection?"

"I don't know, but look at this. It's from earlier frames of the film right before Kennedy's head blocks that part of the curb. I've computer enhanced them."

"I don't see a gouge on the curb."

"I can't be certain if we are looking at the exact spot on the curb because Zapruder is following the limo with his camera as it passes by. But it appears the gouge somehow appears after the limo, or I should say Kennedy's head, passes by. And here's one more strange thing. This is frame 314 again. No reflection, but when I zoom out from the curb to right about here, then sharpen the image, look." Tia pointed with her finger in a circular motion over the screen.

"What is that? Wait . . . dust. That's what we saw in the Archives. Just before bitch Conway threw us out."

"That's exactly what Rose's software says it is. Dust, or fog, or smoke. It's centered on the gouge. And with each successive frame, 315, 316, and 317, it fades away."

"I think I know what it is, Tia."

"What?"

"Hold on . . . let me call Joseph. Hi, it's me. Are Paul and Ryan with you? Can you guys come over to Tia's room? I think we may have some evidence that you are going to find interesting."

65

"There must be a thousand, no two thousand photographs in this box. No order to them either. And no markings on the envelopes to indicate the date they were taken or developed."

"She said it was a box full of photographs."

"Yes, but Dr. . . . I mean Reece, this is going to take a lot more than a few hours . . . "

"Might take . . . think positive. We could get lucky and find the negative in the first envelope."

"Well . . . it's not in the first envelope. Besides, she's not even certain the negative is here."

"She said she remembers her grandmother talking about being in Dealey Plaza and that some of her photographs were used in the Warren Commission investigation."

"Well . . . it's not in the second envelope either."

"You would think they would stamp the date on these photographs when they developed them?"

"It wasn't until the early sixties that large photographic developing centers were established. And that was only because of the introduction of color film which was more complicated and costly to develop. Most film, which was still black and white, was developed by one-man operations, especially in the smaller towns. That's why there was so much variability in the printing of pictures from negatives."

"And that's what you are hoping with my picture?"

"First we need to find the negative. Then yes, I'm hoping the person who developed the photograph decided to focus on the important part of the negative . . . "

"Thanks a lot."

"Well . . . what he felt was important at the time. I'm hoping your sneakers and your father's shoes were not what he focused on."

"You don't feel comfortable when you're with me, do you?"

"No, I'm . . . I don't know what you mean?"

"You seem to be uneasy and nervous around me. And even more so when we are alone. Like now. Or earlier when we were in the car. You become more guarded."

"I don't know what you are . . . "

"For example, when we are around other people you look me in the eye. When we are alone you tend not to."

"I don't think that's true."

"You're looking at me now because I brought it to your attention."

"I'm looking at you now to prove a point that I am able to look at you when we are alone. I wasn't looking at you prior to that because I was going through these photographs. I can't look at you and these at the same time."

"Nice excuse."

"Yesterday you accused me of being afraid of you. Now I'm nervous and uneasy around you. If those things were true, if I was so uneasy around you, why would I have come with you today knowing we'd be alone together for hours?"

"Your curiosity about the negative."

"Curiosity killed the cat you know."

"And curiosity is what drives humans to do things they probably shouldn't do too."

"That and the seven deadly sins."

"Some are deadlier than others."

"Depending upon the circumstances, I suppose. And by the way, excite is not one of the seven."

"So you do remember last night? I thought maybe you were too . . . "

"Drunk?"

"Goosed."

"Were you trying to get me drunk?"

"No, just goosed. I find that drunk women are not as . . . "

"Exciting?"

"That too . . . but I was going to say that my experience with drunkenness is it leads to one of two things, passing-out or puking, either of which is undesirable to me. Plus you have to deal with the next day's depression."

"So get 'em drunk, but not too drunk?"

"Sometimes, yes."

"Well . . . I do remember last night. And I was going to say something to you about it today. So maybe that is why I appear uneasy or nervous. I can assure you that you do not . . . not . . . no way . . . "

"No way? If I don't excite you, then why can't you even say it?"

"I mean, no. Not that. Not excite . . . this."

"What is it? Is that it? The negative?"

"I need to get my equipment set up."

66

"Tell Tia what you mentioned to me last night."

"That I thought she'd be hot in bed?"

"Come on, Joseph . . . I'm serious."

"So am I."

"Paul, Ryan, do you want to give this a try?"

"Absolutely."

"Yes."

"Well?"

"You mean both of us at the same time? And here?" Paul and Ryan looked at one another, then started to walk across the room toward Tia.

"I don't think that's what she had in mind."

"You jerks!" Kayla stepped in front of them and put her hands on their chests stopping them. "I'm trying to be serious here. Will one of you explain to Tia, to us, about your second gunman theory?"

"Joseph . . . have you been sharing our results with Kayla?"

"I can't tell a lie . . . she forced it out of me. She might be small, but she can be quite persuasive when she wants to be. Right, Kayla?"

"Ahhhh! I give up. Screw you guys."

"I thought that's what we started to do?"

"We'll find a way to do it without you."

“I bet it would be more fun to do it with us.”

“What is it that you wanted to do?”

“Provide you with the hard evidence you need to confirm your theory about a second gunman on the grassy knoll!”

67

"You know I love you."

"And I do you."

"I wish we didn't have to . . . "

"But we do."

"It feels so wrong."

"At one time you found it exciting."

"That was years ago."

"You mean it's not exciting now?"

"It's exciting. It's always exciting. But in a different way."

"Is it still the excitement of getting caught?"

"It used to be the excitement of getting caught. Now it's the fear of getting caught."

"That's what makes it exciting."

"No, it doesn't."

"Oh, Dora. That's one of the reasons why I love you so much."

"I'd like to see how you would explain your way out of this if we ever got caught."

"I have a story all worked out."

"Mind letting me in on it? What if we are interviewed in two different rooms? Shouldn't we tell the same story?"

"I'm not worried about that."

"Why not?"

"Well, whatever story I tell will be the truth."

"That hurts."

"The truth sometimes does."

"So . . . it doesn't matter what story I tell because I'm the nut-case, right? They're not going to believe me anyway."

"Bingo."

"Still, it would be nice to know what you'd say."

"Don't worry . . . I got it all worked out."

"Really?"

"Got it covered."

"So . . . how would you have explained being under my bed earlier today?"

68

"You were right. Thanks for pushing the issue. I was starving. It was a great restaurant. Lillian's?"

"Yes, Lillian's. Great steaks."

"Is she the owner?"

"Lillian was supposedly a madam who associated with many gangsters and gamblers of the time. It was when Saratoga not only condoned, but actually encouraged, gambling, prostitution, you name it."

"She sounds like a woman ahead of her time."

"Yes she was. I was hoping you would like the place."

"I did. Again, thanks for forcing me to go. Plus it's not that late. We'll still be back by . . . "

"Midnight, maybe a little later. Besides, we needed to celebrate your finding, Rose."

"My finding? You knew where the negative was."

"Negative was useless without your knowledge of film developing in the early sixties."

"Somebody else would have thought of it at some point."

"Rose Stone. No one's thought of it in the past fifty years. The chance of somebody thinking of it in the next fifty is even smaller. Bits and bytes make up a photograph today. Few remember how it used to be done with chemicals and the human hand. We are losing that institutional memory. It's happening every day. In every industry. Every corporation. We are starting to come across problems that came up years ago not realizing someone already solved them. The current generation doesn't have the knowledge or memory."

"Maybe."

"No maybe. Congratulations."

"Before we celebrate victory, let's complete the analysis. We still have some work to do."

"What are you talking about? He lopped off a major portion of the negative when he printed the picture. I know that's me. Those are my legs, my sneakers, my pants. I can prove it."

"Your mother saved your clothes from when you were a kid?"

"Better than that. You'll see."

"Before you get all excited . . . "

"Too late."

"I can see that. But . . . can we wait to complete the analysis of the negatives we copied before we come to a firm conclusion on this?"

"Fair enough. When will you be finished?"

"I should have something by noon tomorrow."

"Call me as soon as you are done."

"I don't know why you are so excited about this? It's only going to prove something you've already known."

"No . . . you don't know how important this is to me. I've been starting to doubt the past fifty years of my life. Things that I thought were true may not be. Do you know how scary that is? Not knowing if the past, as you think you know it, is what really happened?"

"I can't, but it must be how people with Alzheimer's feel. Lost. Scared."

"Did I say something wrong?"

"No . . . why?"

"You haven't been this quiet since I got in your car earlier this afternoon."

"I'm usually very quiet when I drive. It relaxes me. I use the time to think. Contemplate life. Heavy stuff."

"Then you won't mind if I relax too. Except when I relax I close my eyes."

"I don't mind at all."

"It might look like I'm sleeping, but I'm not."

"My mother has Alzheimer's."

"Uh . . . I must have . . . "

"I'm sorry . . . did I wake you?"

"No . . . no. You already told me about your mother. How is she doing?"

"Even though she started exhibiting symptoms several years ago, she's actually doing quite well. In fact she thinks she's getting better."

"Who is to say she isn't? After all, we know so little about the disease. Some people's immune systems might learn how to fight it just like any other disease."

"Maybe? Anyway . . . she thinks so."

"I think my mother . . . did I wake you?"

"No, not at all. I just had my eyes closed. You were saying about your mother?"

"I think my mother might know something about my father and Oswald that she's never shared with me."

"Why do you think that?"

"Her reaction. The other day. When I visited her. She lives in an assisted living facility. Loretto. It's a few miles from the office. Anyway, I confronted her with the findings from team three. About my father and Oswald. She didn't seem at all surprised by it. Like . . . no reaction at all."

"Are you sure she knew what you were . . . "

"She knew. She might have wanted me to think she didn't, but she did. I think she does it on purpose."

"What?"

"Her Alzheimer's. I think she sometimes uses it to her own advantage.

I know that's probably a mean thing to say, but my gut tells me she does. And usually my gut is pretty damn good at figuring things out."

"Maybe it's just her way of coping with it. The disease I mean."

"But if she does know something, something she's kept from me, to protect me she says, I might never learn what it is. It will be locked inside her forever, never to be let out."

"What do you mean, protect you?"

"I have no idea."

"One other thing. Sorry . . . sleeping again?"

"Just resting."

"I think she has a friend."

"I'm sure she does. People make lots of friends in assisted living residences. My grandmother was in a home and she . . . "

"No . . . I mean a man-friend."

"And she hasn't told you?"

"No. I've never seen her with anyone, at least not directly. I keep thinking I see things. Maybe it's just me. Then again, I see the same face. At least I think it's the same face. It's probably nothing."

"Probably."

"About last night. Our discussion at the end of the night. I'd like to apologize. I don't really think you are afraid of me. At least I hope you aren't afraid of me. And I don't know how you feel about older men. In any event I'm really not that much older than you, so you probably wouldn't think of me as an older man, anyway. I mean if that's who you like. And the excite part . . . well . . . that was the Jack talking. So . . . again . . . I apologize and I hope you will accept it.

"Rose?"

"Yes."

"Do you . . . "

"No . . . I'm sure your mother would have said something to you about having a friend."

69

"Tia . . . I'm coming." Rose opened the door to her room and Tia flew past her.

"Where the hell have you been?"

"Good morning to you too."

"I've been trying to get a hold of you since yesterday evening."

"Sorry . . . my phone went dead. Didn't notice it until this morning. Just got it on the charger. What's up?"

"What's up? Only the biggest discovery in the past three plus weeks of this program. Hell, maybe the past fifty years of . . . of . . . since the assassination."

"I thought Dr. Landis's father knowing Oswald was the biggest discovery?"

"That was Monday's news. Yesterday we found something that . . . I don't know what? You've gotta come with me up to Ryan's room. We're meeting to put the finishing touches on our presentation to Landis."

"Ryan? What does team ten have to do with this?"

"Come on, Rose. We need to get you caught up."

"I can't. I'm in the middle of something."

"You gotta believe me. Nothing that you are working on could be more important than this. Come on."

"I promised Dr. Landis that I would get the results of our analysis to him by noon."

"Rose, Landis being in Dealey Plaza isn't an issue any more. Everyone agrees he was there. You can forget about that."

"I promised to get it to him . . . "

"Landis's stuff can wait."

"But . . . "

"Rose! We found evidence, hard evidence, of a second shooter in Dealey Plaza. Now . . . are you coming?"

70

"Hi Mama."

"Reece, for heaven's sake. It's not even ten yet. You are dropping in on me at all hours of the day. Are you checking up on me, or something? Trying to catch me doing something I'm not supposed to be doing?"

"If you're feeling guilty about something?"

"That's one of the benefits of Alzheimer's . . . anything I might feel guilty about I just forget. So what can I do for you on this beautiful Wednesday morning? Doesn't it look glorious out there? We're having lunch in the garden. Can you join us?"

"I'd love to Mama, but I can't. I've only got a few minutes until my next meeting."

"Always rushing. You need to slow down. Enjoy life. Remember what I said about time speeding up as you get older?"

"So that was you."

"Or I could be her? The other me. You never know, do you? So what can I do for you in a few minutes?"

"Where are all our old photographs?"

"They are on the bookshelf in your den. Don't you remember? We moved them there when we sold the house."

"Not the ones . . . the ones when Papa was alive."

"They are . . . they are in a box. No, two boxes. How many times did I say to myself over the years that I should put those old photographs into albums. Never got to it. Anyway, they were in the storage closet. Not sure where you put them."

"I know where they are. With the junk drawer boxes. They're in the closet in the spare bedroom. I didn't even think to look there this morning. Thanks Mama . . . gotta go."

"What kind of a kiss was that? And no hug? What do you want with those old pictures anyway?"

"Evidence."

"Honey . . . you . . . you do remember that all the pictures you and your papa took that day were destroyed in the accident?"

"I remember Mama. The pictures I need were taken before that day."

71

Reece looked up from his desk when he heard the knocking on his door and motioned to Rose, who was staring through the window, to come in.

"Rose, come in."

"Thanks for seeing me on such short notice."

"Let's sit at the table. I know I told you to call me as soon as you finished analyzing the negative, but you sounded so frantic on your voice mail. What did you find?"

"We've been working with team ten and I think . . . "

"No, I mean with the negative."

"This other issue is more important."

"Right now nothing is more important to me than verifying with hard evidence that I was in Dealey Plaza on November 22, 1963. Good or bad, I want to know what you found."

"I really think you should . . . "

"Rose!"

"I'm sorry, there wasn't much there." Rose reached into the blue folder she had placed on the table and slid the eight by ten photograph in front of Reece. His eyes locked onto it.

"What are you talking about? This is . . . this is the evidence I've been looking for."

"But Dr. . . . Reece. It doesn't show much more of you and your father than the photo behind your desk."

"That photo only shows two people from the ankles down."

"And this one shows those same two people, only the boy from the waist down and the man from his knees down."

"And that's all I needed to verify that this is me and that's my father."

"You're going to have to explain to me how this is the hard evidence . . . "

As she spoke Reece placed a three by five black and white photograph on the table just above the other picture.

"I take it that's you?"

"And my father." Reece placed a second, third, and fourth photograph on the table on each side of the larger picture. "Notice anything about the photographs?"

"You mean besides they are all better than the middle one because they show the entire silhouette of a person and not just the bottom half of their legs?"

"Besides that."

"All taken around the same time?"

"Yes. The first three were taken within a month of the assassination and the fourth, the one just of me, was taken three weeks after the assassination."

Rose leaned over closer to the table and looked at each picture. After a minute she sat up and looked at Reece. "Were those P. F. Flyers?"

"No. We couldn't afford P. F. Flyers."

"So you put different colored shoe laces on each sneaker?"

"Black on the right."

"White on the left."

"I couldn't afford P. F. Flyers, but I could still be . . . I'm not sure what we called it back then, cool?"

"And the ripped fabric just below the right knee on your jeans?"

"Fell in the barn about a month before the assassination. Ripped my brand new pair of jeans on the chipped concrete floor. Mama whooped me good. Said she wouldn't sew them. I'd have to wear them like that until I grew out of them to teach me a lesson to be more careful."

"Still circumstantial."

"But?"

"But . . . I think any court of law would be convinced."

"I knew it! I knew I was there." Reece stood up, and so did Rose.

"But, I don't understand? You always knew you were there?"

"But now I have proof. Thanks to you I have proof." Reece reached over and grabbed both of Rose's hands. "Thanks to you." He pulled her closer and kissed her, probably lingering longer than he should have. "Thank you."

Rose pulled away from him. "Reece . . . I mean Dr. Landis . . . I mean Reece, this wasn't the reason why I wanted to meet with you. We found something . . . "

"Who gives a damn what else you found. Don't you understand . . . I was there."

"But team ten . . . "

"Fuck team ten. They have no idea what they're talking about. All their analyses just confirms to another factor of ten beyond the decimal point what others have been saying for fifty years. The acoustics in Dealey Plaza make it impossible for eyewitnesses to pinpoint where the shots were fired from. But the hard evidence, like a sniper's nest, a gun, empty shell casings, and a nut who wanted to be famous all point to the sixth floor of the Texas School Book Depository Building."

"We found new evidence."

"Who the fuck do you people think you are? You don't know shit about finding new evidence. What kind? Circumstantial?"

"No."

"Of what?"

"A . . . a second shooter."

"You can't even say it without . . . where . . . where is this new evidence?"

"On the Zapruder film."

"The Zapruder film? The Zapruder film. Are you crazy? A movie that's been analyzed by a million experts over the past fifty years? You found something no one else did?"

Rose reached down and picked up the large photograph off the table and held it up in front of Reece's face. "Yes, we are capable of finding new evidence."

72

“Morgan, Bill, Jason, come in. Sit at the table. I was surprised you wanted to meet this morning. Let’s see . . . twenty-six hours since we last met? And less than forty-eight hours since you dropped your bombshell on me about my father and Oswald? So, what do you have for me now?”

“We wanted to let you know that we’ve essentially completed the three things you wanted us to look into and thought it would be good to report out ASAP in case there was something else you had for us to do.”

“I’m surprised you got it done so fast.”

“Andrew, Daren, and Raji helped.”

“You should have had them come here with you.”

“We asked them to, but they needed the time to finish up their final report.”

“So, what did you find?”

“I handled the first item, Bill coordinated the second, and Morgan handled the third.”

“Then let’s take them in order and start with you Jason.”

“I met with team ten as you requested. After looking over their data I didn’t feel there was anything there. I was able to convince them that they didn’t have enough firm evidence to prove their theory that you weren't in Dealey Plaza."

"Just to let you know they did leave me a voicemail indicating that."

"They said they were going to. However, they also wanted me to make it clear to you that if there were ever a trial, there was not enough circumstantial evidence to support, without a reasonable doubt, that you were there."

"I understand. I am willing to concede that at this point, but only to save face for them. What has come out of this is their analysis has strengthened my resolve to find evidence, firm evidence, to prove I was there. Without their willingness to question things, I would have never gone down that path. You can tell them that, and I will too. But you can also tell them I will gather the evidence to prove I was there."

"Bill will now cover the second issue."

"This is where team two helped us out. I spoke with Major Dennison at Quantico. He was able to provide me with the names and enough records on the other men in the platoon to enable us to track down over eighty percent of them. Of those identified, over half were deceased. From the remaining, we were able to speak directly with seven of them. Of those seven, two had been previously interviewed by the Warren Commission staff. We asked all seven about any connection, first with Oswald and anyone, then with Oswald and Mr. Landis. None of them were able to recall anything specific, but two of them did indicate that everyone in the platoon rotated through the night shift on radar watch and that meant you were at some point paired with everyone in the platoon, including Oswald."

"So we can conclude that my father definitely knew him."

"Yes, but it appears no more, or no less, than any other member of the platoon."

"Anything else?"

"Yes, it sounded like the men were coached, or at least had spoken with one another about it, because three of them volunteered that they believed Oswald was a complete nut and in their opinion no one would have conspired with him, especially to assassinate a president."

"Because of their personal relationship, I'm sure these men have read more than the average person has about the assassination and Oswald. So who knows when they formed that opinion about him."

"I agree, but thought I would mention it. I will provide you with a write-up of all the conversations including transcripts of each call."

"Excellent. Thanks Bill. And please thank team two. Make sure their names are on the report. Morgan, I guess you're next."

"I went back and reviewed several sources that have been put together over the years that reconstructed Oswald's life. I focused on his final year. There are several gaps, but nothing out of the ordinary. I also did not find anything that could connect him with your father. I especially focused on the last month when you would have expected some interaction with a co-conspirator, if there was one. Again, nothing."

"Thanks, Morgan."

"I will have my report finalized by mid-day tomorrow."

"Great. Is there anything else?" Both Bill and Jason looked at Morgan which invited Reece to do the same. "Morgan?"

"I wasn't sure what information you had regarding your father's death . . . "

"Ironically, I have very little information. Only a newspaper article about the accident. I never saw any need to look into it any deeper. Why?"

"We know conspiracy theorists have speculated over the years that many individuals connected with the assassination were silenced . . . "

"You mean either murdered or died suspicious deaths?"

"Yes. And we also know that the theory falls apart because most of the deaths take place after the individual has told their secret about what they knew about the assassination."

"Why kill them after the fact?"

"Correct. But some of the deaths fall into the category of being suspicious, none the less, such as . . . "

"Oswald?"

"Yes, Oswald. He may have been the first to be silenced."

"Or killed by a patriotic Jack Ruby."

"Yes, or killed by a patriotic Jack Ruby. But in any event he was killed before any confession as to his involvement in the assassination. So his death does not fit the profile of the other so called mysterious deaths."

"How does this involve my father?"

"If you hypothesize . . . "

"It's very dangerous, Morgan, to hypothesize things based on circumstantial evidence."

"I agree, Dr. Landis. But let's for a moment hypothesize that your father's death was something more than a random automobile accident."

"And what proof do you have of that?"

"I obtained a copy of the newspaper account of the accident as well as the police report and photographs of the accident scene. The police concluded that your father lost control of his car, slipped off the right hand side of the road, down an embankment, hit a tree head-on, and the car burst into flames."

"The road where the accident occurred was loose gravel, there were no such things as guardrails along these types of roads back then, and you are talking about a 1958 Pontiac Catalina, not one of the best handling cars of its time. Believe me, I was a passenger in the back seat of that car and drove down that very road many times."

"I am not disputing the circumstances of the accident itself. What I am disputing is what I found in one of the photographs taken at the scene." Morgan laid an eight by ten black and white photo on the table in front of Reece. He glanced at it then turned back to Morgan. "This photograph was taken the morning following the accident after the body was removed. It is a shot taken through the driver's side window of the interior. According to the investigation report, the only thing removed from the car, or moved in the car was the body."

"Your point?"

"On the passenger side of the seat, now just the springs revealed after the fire, there are the charred remains of a camera."

Reece again glanced at the photo. "That was one of my father's cameras. He was an amateur photographer."

"'The issue I have is, if the car had slipped down the embankment and crashed head-on into a tree, why didn't the camera fly off the seat and land in the passenger foot well, where it would have burned?"

73

"Thanks for stopping by, Rose. I apologize for yelling at you . . . and everything else I did. You were right. I've been so obsessed and blinded by this notion of not being there that I'm ignoring everything else around me. Plus with all the other personal things in my life . . . "

"Your mother?"

"That and Meek . . . yes, my mother."

"We've proved you were there."

"Right. We've proved what I've known for fifty years. A lot of wasted effort with nothing new to show for it. A waste."

"Not a waste if it was something you needed to do to convince yourself you were there."

"Or to prove to myself that I wasn't going crazy."

"That I'm not so sure you can prove one way or the other."

"Rosetta Stone . . . show some respect."

"What did you . . . how did you know?"

"I told you, we do a thorough background check on all of the participants in this program. I know much more about you than you let on in your resume. And of course social media can provide us with a wealth of information about your character. Don't look so distraught. Many applicants have done worse things than you. Hey . . . we let you into the program, didn't we?"

"I'm beginning to wonder why? I'm not anywhere near as bright as the rest of the people here, and . . . and . . . well . . . my background isn't as pristine."

"I beg to differ . . . well. Okay, your background may not be as pristine, although looking at some of the things people have posted on the internet, that might be debatable. But your name certainly seems to define the way you think and analyze problems. Your ability to take a small sample of something and use it to interpret the larger whole. Your critical thinking skills. They are everything we look for in people for this program. And diversity."

"But . . . the other things? What exactly do you know about my background?"

"I didn't ask you to come to my office to talk about that. I need your skills . . . your Rosetta skills . . . to help me with something." Reece walked over to the table and pointed to the photographs scattered on it.

"What are these? Photographs of an automobile accident?"

"My father's accident. Fifty years ago. Was deemed an accident by the local Sheriff. Of course, my father died on the same day as JFK. There were a lot more important things to worry about."

"What do you want done with them?"

"I want you to see if you can identify the camera." Reece put his finger on one of the photos, then another, and another. "I realize these are terrible digital images of the originals, and the camera was burned in a fire, but do the best you can."

"Can I ask why?"

"Sure. The car hit a tree, head-on. If nothing was disturbed in the car, how could the camera still be in the front seat? But more importantly, I don't think that camera was my father's."

74

"Let me see if I've got this right?" Seated at the end of the table in his office, Reece flipped through each paper copy of the power point slides until he came to the pages summarizing the results, folded over the pages, and placed them side by side in front of him. He looked to the right of the table where Joseph, Paul, and Ryan were seated.

"You are saying that your acoustics analysis indicates to a very high probability that four shots were fired, and the shots likely came from two different directions. You also believe that if three of the shots came from the Texas School Book Depository Building, the fourth came from the grassy knoll area, and it was the fourth of the four shots, but coming close behind the third shot. This would make it even more difficult for an eyewitness to determine how many shots were fired.

"Did I summarize that correctly?"

"Yes." All three responded in unison.

"Reece then looked to his left at Kayla, Tia, and Rose who were seated at that side of the table. "And you are saying that from your analysis of the Zapruder film, you believe something may have hit the curb sometime during frame 313 of the Zapruder film, which was about when the third and fatal shot hit the president's head. If what they are saying about the fourth shot being fired from the grassy knoll is correct, you believe the shot missed the president's head and struck the curb. Hence the flash that appears in frame 313 and the gouge and cloud of dust that appears in frame 314, and less so in later frames.

"Did I summarize that correctly?"

"Yes." Kayla and Tia responded, with Rose just nodding her head.

"And with either analysis, by itself, you are not able to conclude to any level of certainly that a fourth shot was fired . . . "

"Except the acoustics analysis seems to suggest with a high correlation that eyewitnesses heard a shot coming from the grassy knoll area," interrupted Ryan. "If three shots were fired from the sixth floor of the Texas School Book Depository Building, and if a fourth shot was fired, it is a high probability it came from the grassy knoll."

"I will give you that. But the acoustics analysis is still circumstantial. It's based on eyewitness testimony . . . confusing eyewitness testimony. But . . . but . . . if the Zapruder film captured a fourth bullet hitting the curb, you now have hard evidence, and that evidence would lead you to believe another shot was fired and the shot came from the grassy knoll area, if you assume the shooter was aiming at the president's head.

"So . . . without the acoustics analysis, you do not know what caused the flash, gouge, and cloud on the Zapruder film. And without the Zapruder film you have no hard evidence to back up the acoustics analysis indicating a fourth shot was fired from the grassy knoll."

"And until we combined the results of our analysis together, we weren't sure what we were seeing," Joseph added.

"The two separate analyses were interesting, but wouldn't stand up on their own. However when viewed together, you get synergy. One and one ends up equaling three." Everyone was now staring at Kayla.

"The problem, Kayla, is each one still relies too much on the other to be credible. In order to get the synergy you are looking for, we need to obtain some other corroborating evidence that links the two. It's the only way one plus one is going to equal . . . might equal ten. So what do you suggest we do to firm up this crazy hypothesis? Whatever it is has got to be completed in the next forty-eight hours."

"We have three things we think should be pursued." Tia passed a piece of paper to Reece and let him look at it for a few seconds before she spoke up again. "First, we should review the other one hundred and ninety reports from the previous seminars to see if there are any other theories that, on their own might seem innocuous, but when combined with our theory might support it."

"More synergy, Kayla?"

"Exactly, Dr. Landis."

"I will also pass along to you the eight other draft reports from this year's seminar. There may be something there."

"Our second recommendation is to incorporate the second shooter, using the new information we now have from the Zapruder film, into the three dimensional model developed by team ten."

"And redo your acoustics analysis, Paul?"

"Yes."

"Third, we recommend we go to Dealey Plaza to verify the curb . . . "

"You think it's still there after fifty years?"

"Granite curbs have an infinite lifetime, especially in the south. The only reason to ever replace them is when the road's path is changed, or widened. There has been a conscious effort by the city of Dallas to keep Dealey Plaza as it was on November 22, 1963. We believe the curb, and the gouge, is still there. We also recommend we reconstruct the line of fire from the grassy knoll to the curb and into the hill on the other side."

"No research can be done in the Plaza without a permit from the city. That takes weeks. How do you plan to accomplish this in forty-eight hours?"

"Stealth."

"Stealth? You mean illegally, don't you?"

"We prefer the word, stealth."

"I'm listening."

"We think we can perform this entire operation in less than five . . . "

"Three!"

"Three minutes. We will need three people. One to place and aim a small handheld laser near the fence on the grassy knoll, one to place a small mirror on the curb over the gouge, and one on the hill to mark the location where the laser strikes the ground."

"You're going to try to determine the bullet's trajectory onto the hill? You don't seriously think there's a bullet someplace on, or in, that hill, do you?" Reece looked around the table at each of them. It was Tia who again spoke up.

"We'll get a photograph of the laser trajectory."

"You're planning on doing this at night?"

"Then, using a small metal detector, we'll scan the area on the hill."

Reece stared at the paper Tia had handed him for over a minute before he lifted his head and spoke up. "Who was the one to make the connection between the two analyses?"

"I did," Kayla was quick to respond.

"Ten teams working in silos has always fostered a competitive spirit and produced some great studies. But I suspect in the future I will have to consider the synergies that could be gained when competing team members come into closer contact with one another during this one month process." Reece kept his eyes on Kayla until the end of his statement when he quickly glanced to his right at Joseph, then back at Kayla. "Therefore, I concur with your first recommendation. I suggest this effort be headed up by you, Kayla. Does anyone have a problem with that?"

Kayla glanced around the room before she responded. "I can do that."

"Good. I also concur with your second recommendation regarding incorporating this new finding into the acoustical model you've developed. I think that should be Paul. Is everyone okay with that?"

"I would be glad to, but I want to give credit to Joseph and Ryan too for their help in putting this thing together."

"I know it was a team effort, but with so little time left I think it is better if we only have one set of hands tweaking the model at this point."

"I agree," Joseph and Ryan responded in unison.

"Good. Now as far as recommendation three is concerned, I cannot condone or sponsor any activity, stealth or otherwise, that has the potential to tarnish the reputation of this program or . . . "

"But Dr. Landis, without that evidence, what we have come up with carries no more weight than what any one of a thousand amateur conspiracy theorists has postulated."

"I will not dispute that, Joseph. But there are ethical standards that must be maintained. I cannot knowingly allow you to break . . . "

"But . . . "

Reece held up his hand. "This is my program and I cannot condone such an activity."

"This is bull . . . this could be the most important discovery . . . "

"I'm sorry, Joseph."

"Dr. Landis."

"Yes, Rose."

"Isn't it true that what we do on our own time is our own business?"

"Absolutely."

"And if we were to travel to Dallas on our . . . "

"Rose . . . what you do on your own time is your own business."

75

"I still don't see why Tia had to go with them?"

"Don't you mean you don't know why you didn't get to go?"

"No, Rose. I know why I couldn't go. Although I still think Landis tricked me into it."

"What are you talking about, Kayla? I would think you'd be flattered. It shows he has confidence in you. This is an important effort."

"He knows Joseph and I are fucking."

"Who doesn't know?"

"He's keeping me here and sending Joseph to Dallas to keep us apart."

"Kayla . . . we've got two nights left to go in the program. Do you really think Landis planned this to keep you two out of the same bed for one of them?"

"Well . . . why did Tia have to go?"

"Are you jealous? Do you really think something is going to happen between . . . "

"Joseph is always talking about her. How hot she is."

"I thought you said he thought I was hot too?"

"I'd feel the same way if you were on your way with him to Dallas."

"You wouldn't have to worry about me, and I'm sure you don't have to worry about Tia."

“It’s not Tia I’m worried about.”

“Don’t be crazy. Joseph lusts you. I wish I had a man who lusted me like that. Nothing’s going to happen.”

“Better not, or Landis . . . ”

“Stop blaming him. He didn’t choose who was going to Dallas. Hell, he doesn’t even condone the trip, remember?”

“Still pisses me off.”

“Look at it this way. You and Joseph have been asked to work on something for Landis, last minute. I bet you could use this to your advantage in getting a recommendation from him for a job . . . I mean both of you together . . . if that’s what you want?”

“Two days left and Joseph and I still . . . ”

“What! What are you waiting for?”

“I think we’re going to take the rest of the summer off. Do some traveling around the country.”

“Sounds like talking about it to me.”

“Visit each other’s parents,” mumbled Kayla.

“What did you say?”

“You heard me right.”

“So, this is getting serious.”

“As long as Tia doesn’t fuck it up.”

“Kayla!”

“Rose!”

“Do you know what time they are supposed to get into Dallas?”

“Eight-fifteen their time, nine-fifteen ours.”

“Let’s assume an hour to get to their hotel.”

“They aren’t checking any baggage. Didn’t want to risk losing it.”

“What about the laser, and metal detector?”

“They’re going to use a laser pointer. Looks like a pen. Paul said it should work just fine. The metal detector is a miniature one. Almost looks like an electric shaver.”

“So, an hour to the hotel . . . ”

"Then they were going to get a quick bite to eat."

"So, they won't get into Dealey Plaza before ten-thirty their time, eleven-thirty our time."

"Maybe even later. They figured the later they were the less noticeable they would be."

"When do you think you'll be done with your review?"

"So far I've been averaging ten minutes a report. I'm reading the executive summary and if I find something interesting I dig deeper into the report. At this rate the whole thing should take about fifteen hours. If I work late tonight I should be able to finish by early afternoon tomorrow."

"I've got some other stuff to work on for Landis . . . "

"Landis? What other stuff?"

"Some clean-up work on some photos."

"Uh-huh."

"When I'm done with that I'll stop back by here to see how things are going. Then I plan to go over to Ryan's room around midnight. They were going to transmit all their data back to him and he was going to plug it into his model. I'll see if he needs help doing that."

"Have we set up a time to meet with Landis tomorrow?"

"I have to leave him a message to let him know what time we'll be ready. Do you know what time they're getting back from Dallas?"

"Two-fifty tomorrow afternoon."

"I'll set up the meeting with him for five. That will give us all day tomorrow to work on this and brief them before we meet with Landis."

"If we've got until five, I just might go out tonight for a little while."

"Kayla . . . this is not the night to go out partying."

"Only for a few, and only for a little while."

"This is not the time to fuck things up!"

"Don't worry."

"Just be ready to brief those guys when they get in."

"Landis isn't going to want to wait until five to know if we've found something."

“He was okay with late afternoon. He did say we should use our judgment in contacting him beforehand if we found something of interest.”

“Like what?”

“I would think if they found a bullet in the ground on the other side of the grassy knoll, he’d want us to contact him.”

76

"He sent a team of people down to Dallas."

"Uh-huh."

"They're gonna perform some kind of a test to duplicate what happened. A shooter on the grassy knoll."

"Let 'em."

"How come you're not concerned about this? For years you've been worried about him uncovering the truth, and now I don't even get a reaction out of you. Will you stop watching TV."

"What?"

"A couple of days ago you were upset with me because I told him about, you know . . . Oswald."

"You don't have to whisper, Dora. No one can hear you. And even if they did hear you, they wouldn't have any idea what you were talking about."

"Why were you so upset with me before, and now you don't care?"

"It's not that I don't care. I was upset because you told him something we both agreed we would never tell him."

"You mean without talking about it. We never said we would never tell him. We said we wouldn't tell him without talking about it first."

"And, we didn't talk about it!"

"What about this . . . this going to Dallas? What if he finds . . . "

"He's not going to find anything."

"How can you be so sure?"

"Because, I am."

"But . . . "

"Dora, it's taken him fifty years . . . no wait, it's taken the world fifty years to get to where they are now with their investigations. And even though they keep picking away at things, they still don't know jack-shit."

"Watch your language."

"Well . . . they don't."

"Then why can't we tell him . . . "

"Because . . . because, damn it."

"Watch your . . . "

"Sorry . . . because on his own . . . anyone on his own . . . will never get to the truth."

"He's getting closer."

"Fifty years."

"He's . . . "

"Not on his own. And that means without your help."

"At some point we need to . . . "

"Dora!"

"You promised."

"Not now . . . in the future."

"But it has to be before she takes over completely."

"Yes . . . before that, I promise."

"Why are you so sure about Dallas? That they won't find anything?"

"I told you . . . because I am."

"Did you do something?"

"You don't remember?"

"No . . . I . . . I don't."

"Good . . . I think it's better that way."

77

"They were almost totally consumed in the fire. Only the nonflammable portions of the camera were left. And although it's very difficult to determine from the photographs, it looks as though they burned on the seat."

"You keep saying, they?"

"I believe there were two cameras."

"Were you able to determine what kind?"

"No, the remains were too burned up."

"Were the lens and lens housings still in tact?"

"Yes, they were."

"How big were they . . . could you determine their size?"

"They were about an inch across. If you'd like I could get a better measurement."

"Do you think they were thirty-five millimeter cameras, like a Nikon or a Pentax?"

"That I can definitely rule out. The lenses were far too small."

"Did one of them look like a movie camera?"

"Definitely not."

"And why do you conclude the cameras burned on the seat and weren't moved there at some later point?"

"It's the way the weight of the cameras appeared to depress what was left of the metal undercarriage of the seat. That could have only have happened if the cameras physically burned on the seat, along with the seat."

"Any theories, Rose, as to how the cameras were on the front seat if the car was involved in a head-on collision with a tree?"

"The only thing I could come up with was the cameras were moved to the seat after the collision took place, but before the fire started."

78

"Kayla. Kayla. Are you in there?" Rose knocked again, this time harder, on the door to Kayla's room. After a minute she turned, started walking down the hall, grabbed her phone from her purse, and speed-dialed Kayla.

"Hi. You've reached Kayla. Leave me a message. Thanks."

BEEP.

"Kayla, it's me. I just tried knocking on your door. On my way to Ryan's room. Hope you're sleeping, but if you're not, give me a call. Bye."

79

"Hold on . . . someone's at the door. It's Rose."

"Is that them?"

"Yes. No . . . I was talking to Rose. Hold on. Let me put you on speaker. Can you hear me?"

"Yes we can."

"Hi guys."

"Hi Rose."

"Can I assume you aren't calling from a jail cell?"

"You can."

"Just got your email, Joseph. I'm opening the attachments now."

"Ryan, I'm sending you a second email. It's the GPS coordinates for the location of the laser, mirror on the curb, and where the laser beam hit the hill."

"Got it, Joseph."

"Was there a gouge on the curb?'

"Hi Rose."

"Hi Tia."

"There was. Unfortunately, it was much bigger than what we saw on the Zapruder frame. It was as if someone purposefully gouged out the area with a hammer."

"Any other marks on the curb?"

"No."

"What about . . . any luck with the metal detector?"

"Nothing, but Paul wants to keep searching."

"Okay, but remember. Stealth."

"Got it. We'll call if we find anything."

"Okay. Have a safe trip if I don't talk to you again tonight."

"Bye, guys."

"What do we do now, Ryan?"

"I'm going to input this data into the model. It's going to take about a half hour."

"The Citrus is still open. Want something?"

"You buying?"

"Wouldn't be asking if I wasn't."

"Jager Bomb. Double. Make it two."

"Taking advantage of me?" Ryan glanced at Rose. "Be right back."

"Here you go. Two Bombs. Doubles. Hope you don't plan on sleeping."

"They don't keep me awake."

"Really?"

"Really."

"What do you have there?"

"Jack and diet, double, pint glass."

"New drink? I've never seen you drink that before."

"You've been keeping track?"

"I notice details."

"Did you finish?"

"Here it is."

"Wow. Can you rotate, you know, the image?"

"Sure. What perspective do you want to see it from?"

"From the shooter's perspective. On the grassy knoll."

"That is unbelievable. You're a genius."

"Well . . . okay, say it again."

"I'd slow down on those. They're doubles."

"Can't help it. I'm thirsty."

"Are all the eyewitnesses modeled in here?"

"Yes."

"Where's Landis? And his father?"

"They aren't in the model."

"Why not?"

"We only modeled eyewitnesses that provided testimony about where they heard the shots coming from."

"Can you put them into the model?"

"If you know where they were standing."

"I'll be right back."

"On your way back, mind refilling these drinks?"

80

"So . . . you finally decided to call me. I thought you enjoyed yourself so much, what was it . . . Monday, that you would have been back here the very next night. Instead . . . here it is two nights later. I guess I didn't turn you on as much as I thought." Zaria turned the left dial from three to ten and quickly back to three on the micro controller momentarily increasing the size of the pulsating electric shocks traveling down the wires to the two clips, each one clamped to the damp inner lips, hanging down between Kayla's spread legs.

"AHHHH!"

Zaria turned the right dial sending a jolt to the clips attached to Kayla's swollen nipples.

"AHHHH!"

"I take it you enjoy the pulsing shocks better at this setting than you do the other?"

"Yes, Mistress."

"The two women stared at each other, neither one blinking. They were dressed like twins. Wide black leather garter belts, dark seamed stockings, and black stiletto platforms, except Zaria's were several inches taller than the six inch ones worn by Kayla making her tower over her.

"Personally, I prefer the other setting. I like to watch those young perky breasts of yours twitch as you hang there in front of me. And, I like to watch this twitch too." She reached down between Kayla's legs. "And you obviously like it too. Twitches almost like an orgasm, doesn't it?"

"Yes, Mistress."

Zaria pulled her fingers out and placed them in Kayla's lips. She eagerly licked the juices off of them. "Did you enjoy making love with me?"

"Yes, Mistress." She continued licking.

"Am I a good lover?"

"Yes, Mistress."

Zaria took her fingers out of Kayla's mouth, reached down between her legs again, and moved them in a slow circular motion. "Did you enjoy what I did to you with my tongue down here?"

"Yes, Mistress."

"You, too, have a skilled tongue yourself. It wasn't your first time, was it?"

"No, Mistress."

"Did you enjoy what I did to you with my strap-on down here?"

"Yes, Mistress."

"Was it big enough for you?"

"Yes, Mistress."

"I told you I could do you as good as your man does. And with the varied shapes and sizes, I can make you feel like you're getting it by a different stud every night. Plus . . . we could do it for hours and I'd never go soft on you. How does that sound, Kayla."

"It's getting me hot, Mistress."

"You fuck'n slut . . . what doesn't get you hot?" She turned both knobs to the off position.

"Thank you . . . "

Before Kayla could finish the sentence Zaria yanked on all four wires pulling the clamps from the skin pinched between them.

"AHHHH! JETS! I've had enough."

Zaria knelt down, leaned forward, and buried her tongue into Kayla's opening. She swirled her tongue, first clockwise, then counter clockwise, for several seconds, repeating the process until Kayla started first moaning, then pushing herself onto Zaria's tongue. "Are you sure you had enough?" Zaria whispered, her face still buried between Kayla's legs.

"No . . . no, I haven't had enough, Mistress."

"You never get enough, do you Kayla?"

"No, Mistress."

Zaria reached her hands around Kayla's butt-cheeks, spread her crack open, pulled forward, and speeded up her swirling tongue.

"Please, Mistress. Don't stop . . . please . . . I'm going to . . . "

Zaria pulled herself away and stood up.

"NOOOO!"

Zaria locked her lips onto Kayla's open mouth and felt her tongue lap up the wetness. Zaria backed away. "Do you trust your Mistress?"

"Yes, Mistress."

Zaria reached up and grabbed both of Kayla's swollen nipples, squeezed, and pulled on them. "Do I give you intense pleasure?"

"Oh . . . yes, Mistress."

"And," she squeezed harder and pulled, "intense pain?"

"AHHHH! Yes, Mistress."

"And . . . do you desire both from me?"

"Yes, Mistress."

"And . . . do you want to continue to be my bottom tonight?"

"Yes, Mistress."

Zaria knelt down in front of Kayla again and without prompting Kayla spread her legs and pushed her hips forward.

"That's the kind of bottom I'm used to having hang in front of me in my playroom." She carcfully attached the four clips, wires dangling, directly onto and as near as she could to her opening, making sure the clips did not touch each other. She then stood up, turned both knobs to one, and tucked the controller into Kayla's garter belt.

Kayla froze, staring at Zaria. She could feel herself pulsating as if she was having an orgasm, but it was without the intense pleasure she normally experienced. “Please, Mistress.”

“Please what, Kayla?” She reached and turned the knobs from one to two.

“Oh . . . fuck.”

“Oh, fuck what, Kayla.” She turned the knobs to three.

“Oh, fuck, Mistress.”

“Do you want me to fuck you again, Kayla?” She turned the knobs to four.

“Oh . . . yes, Mistress.”

“Is your clit throbbing, Kayla?” She turned the knobs to five.

“Oh . . . fuck . . . yes, Mistress.”

“Does it throb like that when you orgasm?”

“Yes, Mistress.”

“Did it throb like that when I fucked you?”

“Yes, Mistress.”

“Does it throb like that when your man fucks you?”

“Yes, Mistress.”

“Your bitch-stud stays hard for you, doesn’t he?”

“Yes, Mistress.”

“And he recovers quickly, doesn’t he.”

“Yes, Mistress.”

“Do you know how I know, Kayla?” Zaria turned the knobs to six. “I had him bottoming for me one night. He was like a stud-bull. I’ve never had a man cum so much or so often. And when he thought he couldn’t get it up anymore, I proved him wrong with this.” She turned the knobs to seven.

“AHHHH . . . Oh . . . fuck . . . please, Mistress.”

“You should have seen his shaft throb with these things connected to it. It was a gorgeous sight.” She reached up and pulled on Kayla’s nipples. “Feel good, Kayla?”

"Yes, Mistress."

"How do you feel about me fucking your man?" She turned the knobs to eight.

"AHHHH . . . fuck . . . please, Mistress." Kayla's hips now started to visibly twitch involuntarily with each pulse that shot into her.

"I don't know about you, Kayla. But if another bitch fucked my man . . . " This time the Russian accent was gone from her voice.

Kayla froze when she heard the clicking sound, and then stared as Zaria raised up her hand and slipped the onyx handled switchblade into her garter belt. She then bent forward, removed the black haired wig, brushed her long red hair with her fingers, and stood up, her hair whipping back behind her head.

"Meeka?"

Meeka reached for the switchblade and held it up to Kayla's face. "I know you didn't fuck with my man, or at least I don't think . . . "

"I didn't, Meeka. I swear . . . "

"And, I'm sorry I fucked your man . . . actually, I'm not sorry at all. He was one fine fuck." She turned the knobs to nine.

"AHHHH!" Kayla's hips started to twitch again.

"But, I do blame you, and your blonde slut friends, for fucking up my relationship. And for that," she waved the knife, "I'm not going to do any permanent damage to your clit."

"Please, Meeka."

"But, I am going to put you out of commission for a while." She turned the knobs to ten.

"AHHHH!"

"Give it a few minutes, honey. Your clit is going to get very numb. Almost as if it was getting a shot of Novocain. You'll be like that for a week or two. No matter how hard your man tries, you're not going to have an orgasm."

"Please . . . no . . . stop."

"If you want me to turn it off, I will. But then I'd have to use this."

She waved the knife. "Your choice . . . just as I thought."

She lowered the knife, walked over to the table, lit up a cigarette, walked back and stood in front of Kayla, and exhaled smoke in her face. "Rest assured, as soon as you bitches are gone I will be back in my man's bed. I know his weaknesses and how to exploit them to my advantage. But since I don't have him now, and I'm horny as hell, before you leave you're going to satisfy me. Is that clear?"

"Yes."

Meeka reached up and pulled Kayla's right nipple. "Yes, what?"

"AHHHH! Yes, Mistress."

"And one more thing." She leaned in close to Kayla's face. "If you tell anyone about this," she reached down into her garter belt, pulled out a picture, and held it up, "this picture, dozens more like it, and several movies of you and your stud will be posted to the Internet."

81

"Is she okay, Dr. Sanger?" Reece had been racing down the hall towards his mother's room when he finally looked up and almost ran into the doctor in front of him.

"Slow down, Reece." The doctor put his hand up. "She's doing fine."

"I didn't get your message until I got into the office this morning. I got here as quickly as I could."

"We're not sure exactly what happened. It appears she may have blacked out or fainted. One of the attendants found her on the floor this morning. I've ordered blood and urine analyses, but I don't expect to find anything out of the ordinary. She seems to be eating well and getting exercise, so I don't think it's a physical issue."

"Then what?"

"There's so much we don't know . . . "

"Mental? The Alzheimer's?"

"She appears to have had another setback, similar to what she experienced two days ago." Sanger glanced at the chart he was carrying. "Yes, Tuesday. She is having a difficult time remembering things."

"That's exactly what happened on Tuesday. One minute she was fine, and the next she was a different person. When I was with her yesterday, she was fine."

"As I've said, there is so much we don't know about the disease. Why, for instance, in some patients it's a steady progressive deterioration, and in others it's so erratic. The last time we met you were concerned that maybe it was something that you said that may have upset her. Did anything like that . . . "

"No. I was only with her for a few minutes yesterday. I asked her if she knew where some old photographs might be. Funny. I couldn't remember where I put them, but she did. That was it. I was gone."

"I've ordered increased observation of her. I don't want to move her to another room."

"That would devastate her. She still has some freedom. That's very important to her. She would know she was . . . was slipping away."

"I'm not saying we need to do that . . . yet."

"Can I see her?"

"Of course. She's up and dressed. Doesn't remember anything, so I suggest you don't bring it up. Another benefit of the disease, I suppose. We'll be in touch." Sanger extended his hand to Reece.

"Thank you, Dr. Sanger."

"My pleasure."

Reece stared at his mother who was sitting in her chair looking out the window. A feeling of guilt overtook him. Although he hated watching his mother disappear before him, he hated worse the thought that she was doing so without first telling him the truth about the lies.

82

"It appears you and your father were standing very near where the fourth bullet hit the ground."

"Hypothesized fourth bullet, Rose."

"Reece . . . what additional evidence do you need to consider this hypothesis a credible one?"

"Additional evidence presumes you are adding to already existing evidence. I'm sorry . . . but I don't recall either the former or the latter."

"Excuse me, Dr. Landis. What additional circumstantial evidence do you need to consider this hypothesis a credible one?"

"Certainly much more than what you've presented, Ms. Stone."

Rose had been sitting in the chair in the front of Reece's desk for the past fifteen minutes summarizing the preliminary findings from the Dallas trip. She also reviewed what she and Paul had worked on until after two in the morning – incorporating Reece and his father into the model. That analysis, made difficult because their exact location on the hill across from the grassy knoll could only be estimated, had a wide margin of error, but it did conclude that the hypothesized fourth bullet likely hit the ground close to where they were standing. Civil conversation had steadily deteriorated as their voices grew louder with each sentence spoken. She was now staring at Reece wondering who would be the first to blink.

“Is this whole effort a farce?”

“Excuse me?”

“You heard me. Is this whole effort . . . this seminar on the JFK assassination . . . is it a farce? An exercise in futility? Someone, or some foundation, spending its money on it because it doesn’t have anything better to do with it? A big waste of time and effort? In other words, a bunch of bullshit? Because that’s what it feels like to me. You don’t want the truth. You don’t give a rats-ass about the truth. You want . . . you . . . I don’t even know what you want anymore.

“Here’s our draft report.” She stood up and threw the papers she was holding onto his desk. They slid across the desk onto his lap. “You’ll have the final by our five o’clock meeting. I know you think this is a bunch of crap, but you might want to look at the attachment to the email I sent you this morning. It’s a three hundred and sixty degree view of the fourth, excuse me, hypothesized fourth shot that took place in Dallas. On second thought, don’t waste your time. Just delete the fuck’n thing.”

Rose picked up her purse from the desk, turned, and walked toward the door. As she opened it and pulled the handle toward her, it suddenly slipped out of her hand as the door slammed shut with a loud bang. She turned around to see Reece hanging over her, his arm extended and hand resting on the closed door. Her heart, already pounding in her chest from the sound of the slamming door, went ballistic when Reece used his body to push her up against the door, placed his hands on her cheeks and kissed her, forcing his tongue into her now open mouth. Her arms went limp to her sides and her purse fell from her hand onto the floor.

83

"You promised . . . you promised you would let me tell him before . . . before I . . . before I went totally crazy."

"Dora, quiet down."

"Don't tell me to quiet down. You promised."

"There is nothing wrong with you. We still have time."

"WE! There is no WE here. You may have the time, I don't. Don't you understand. Next time . . . next time I might not come back. It scares me to death to think I will leave this earth before I've told him."

"You're out of juice again."

"Juice? I'm having a nervous break . . . fine, go get your juice."

"I'll be right back."

"Are you feeling better?"

"I've never felt better. Look at how beautiful it looks out there. Let's go for a walk. And how about lunch in the garden? Doesn't that sound nice?"

"Cranberry juice?"

"Yes . . . I'm thirsty." She sipped several mouthfuls from the glass.

"Are you sure you're okay?"

"Absolutely. Now . . . what were we talking about earlier?"

He had to be careful with what he said. Although it was Dora sitting there, he knew it was the other Dora who was now in control. He knew because Dora hated cranberry juice.

84

"I apologize. I don't know . . . I've been under . . . "

Reece backed away from Rose who stood motionless and glued to the door. The only thing connecting them now was their eyes. As he started to turn away Rose reached for his biceps, pulled him toward her, and in one quick motion spun him around so each was now standing where the other had been a second before. She pushed Reece against the door, hesitated for an instant as she stared into his eyes, then crushed her body against his as she reached up with her right hand, slipped it around the back of his head, and pulled him down so their mouths and tongues, still wet with each others juices, were again one. She pushed her heaving breasts tight to him and could feel him arch his pelvis into her.

Suddenly he pushed her away and took a deep breath. "Stop. I can't be doing . . . I'm your . . . you're my . . . this isn't right." She leaned in toward him again and he put his hands on her shoulders to stop her. "Rose. Please. This is my fault and I apologize. I didn't mean for this to happen."

Rose backed away and brushed the strands of hair from her face. "I'm sorry . . . I feel so stupid. I should go."

"No, wait . . . please, sit down."

Rose picked up her purse and they both went back to the same seats they were in before, sat down, and stared at one another.

"You are a student in my seminar. I have ethical standards I need to maintain. This has all been my fault and I am sorry. I can assure you that I have never done anything like this before, and I do not intend to start now with you. No matter how much I . . . please accept my apology."

Rose hadn't taken her eyes off Reece and hesitated before she responded. "I do . . . accept your apology. But only under one condition . . . that you accept mine. I am sorry for . . . "

"No . . . it's my fault. I started . . . "

"And I encouraged . . . "

Reece put his hand up. "I accept your apology. We were both at fault."

"Yes . . . but . . . "

"What?"

"Well . . . it was you who started it."

"Can we talk about who started it and who encouraged it some other time?"

"Sure." Rose stood up and started to walk toward the door.

"Rose . . . sit down . . . please. I . . . I need your help."

"I've done everything that you've asked?"

"No. I mean, yes. Yes, you have. Thank you. You, your team, all the teams, they've all been great. There is no doubt in my mind that this semenar group has made more discoveries, important discoveries, than all previous groups combined."

"But?"

"Yes . . . there always seems to be a but."

"With you there does."

"I'm just trying to be thorough. Anything that we find. Anything that we publish. It has to be credible. It has to stand up to scrutiny. It has to be based on evidence, and the evidence has to be interpreted correctly."

"You're worried about the Marathon Phenomenon, aren't you?"

"Yes, that's part of it. We're collecting more and more information, using today's technology, about an event that didn't occur seconds ago, but fifty years ago, and I believe we may be using it to jump to conclusions that are not correct. Just like people tried to interpret the events in Boston from all the factual data, hard evidence mind you, that was right in front of them, and most got it wrong. Accusing people, even groups of people, of being the bombers when they weren't. The social media spun out of control. They finally did get it right, but not before many others got it wrong. Those individuals who were wrong were never held accountable. I don't want to be like them. I want to get it right. I don't want a rush to judgment."

"Like the Warren Commission?"

"Yes. I mean, no. I mean . . . I believe they got most of it right. But . . . "

"Another but."

"But . . . there is just too much noise, conspiracy noise, for there not to be something that we missed. And . . . I think . . . maybe after fifty years . . . we've stumbled upon it. We've used today's technology to uncover evidence that we didn't know was there fifty years ago. But . . . "

"It's circumstantial."

"Just like all the other evidence that supports the conspiracy theories that are out there. Some hard evidence, and even most of that is left up to interpretation, AKA Boston, but most of it is circumstantial."

"So, how can I help?"

"You, your team, all the teams have come up with new evidence that I thought we could close out during the seminar, but I now realize that is not possible. There's too much there. It's too complicated. It's too overwhelming. Too many people have their hands on it. And Kayla is right, it's synergistic. That complicates things even more."

"Are you saying it is spinning out of control."

"Yes. And just like Boston, we need the expertise . . . "

"The FBI?"

"Well . . . FBI-like expertise to look at this and try to come to some kind of resolution of it."

"I'm not an expert."

"Don't sell yourself short, Rose. You are closer to this, to all of the most important issues uncovered, than anyone else including me. I need your help."

"There are others who could help too."

"Just about everyone else will be gone by the weekend. They've all made plans. Vacations, interviews, new jobs, new locations."

"What about me? Don't you think I've made plans too?"

"You are the only one who didn't ask me to line up an interview, or recommend you to a prospective employer. I just assumed . . . "

"Maybe I already have a job."

"I just thought that . . . "

"Or plans."

"If you can't . . . "

"Plans that I can't change."

"Rose, if you can't do it, I will get . . . "

"I didn't say I couldn't do it. I can. And I want to."

"Well . . . good. Thank you. I don't expect this will take more than a week to resolve."

"When do you want me to start?"

"I have some things that you could start looking into as soon as you get a chance. Here are my thoughts and ideas." They both stood up and he handed her a folder. "But, I would also be interested in your thoughts. Any questions before you go?"

"Yes. Just one. Is this effort still part of the official seminar?"

85

"Where the hell have you been, Kayla?"

"Good to see you too, Rose. Come in. Sorry for the mess, but as you can see I've been working."

"I tried getting a hold of you yesterday . . . "

"When?"

"About eleven. I stopped by."

"I went out for a while."

"I tried calling too. Tried again this morning. Got your voice mail."

Kayla walked over to the desk in the corner of the room, rummaged through her purse until she found her phone. "Woops . . . dead battery. Sorry."

"You mean you haven't talked to Joseph since yesterday?"

"I'm pissed at him, remember?"

"He's not doing anything down there that he shouldn't be doing. I happen to know that they were up until after two . . . "

"I bet they were. Well, so was I."

"In Dealcy Plaza. Looking for the fourth bullet."

"I was out looking for a bullet too. Actually, a magic bullet."

"By the way you look, I hope you found it."

"What?"

"You look like you were, well . . . let's say, out partying. Heavily. And took a bullet. Maybe several."

"What the hell is that supposed to mean?"

"I'm just commenting on the way you look."

"What's wrong with the way I . . . "

"You look like shit, Kayla. What the hell did you do last night? You know you were supposed to be working on . . . "

"I was. I mean, I did. Have been. Give me a break. I worked on it for most of the day, yesterday. I was more than half done, and I knew I had most of today to finish it, so I decided to go out for a while. I was lonely without my man here."

"How many bars did you go to?"

"I only went to one place."

"Well . . . you must have had a great time because you look like you were either used-and-abused, or you got sloshed and you've got a hangover."

"Maybe a little of both."

"Kayla, what about Joseph?"

"Rose, trust me. I didn't do anything Joseph wouldn't have approved of."

"You shouldn't have been doing anything." Rose pointed to the papers on the table. "This was your priority."

"Don't worry . . . "

"Why should I be worried? It's your ass that's on the line, not mine."

"I'm gonna finish."

"Now is not the time to let Landis down."

"I've finished reviewing one hundred sixty-five reports. Only twenty-five to go."

"Do you need any help?"

"No. Thanks anyway. I'll get it done. Don't worry."

"Find anything?"

"Not really. Well . . . I'm not sure. There was a report written about ten years ago by a team that looked at all of the alleged assassins that were in Dealey Plaza that day. The guy in the broken down truck on the overpass, the secret service agent following in the car behind who supposedly accidentally fired the fatal shot, the two bums in the rail yard behind the grassy knoll, just to name a few."

"I remember the report. When I was reading it I thought to myself if only half of those people were actually there, a dozen shots would have been fired at the president."

"Obviously, most of them, if not all of them, are theories with little or no data or evidence, especially hard evidence, to back them up. But, there is one in particular that stands out. There was an individual from Chicago, James Files, who claimed for years that he fired on the president in Dealey Plaza that day. He had been hired by the mob."

"But there wasn't much to back up his claims, was there?"

"No. He came out with his story years after the assassination, and other than his claims, there was no hard evidence to support them, just his say so. But here is what I find curious. He claims he was the person who fired from the grassy knoll. Under the tree, behind the fence."

"The location where Joseph, Ryan, and Paul say the fourth shot was fired from."

"Yes. But years later in some of the interviews Files gave he claimed that he shot at the president, but missed. Taken on its own, that doesn't mean much. But tie it in with the acoustic analysis from team ten, and our analysis of the Zapruder film showing a possible bullet hitting the curb . . . "

"And you now have more corroborating evidence."

"Circumstantial, but consistent with the theory we are putting together."

"Synergy?"

"One plus one equaling three."

86

"Mama?"

"Yes, Reece."

"Papa had a lot of cameras, didn't he?"

"I guess he had more than most, considering if a family owned more than one camera that would probably be unusual. We didn't have a lot of money back then, and every time he bought another camera I guess I gave him a lot of grief. But your papa worked with cameras and photography. He claimed he got a lot of his equipment used. Rich folk would buy an expensive camera, use it for a few months, and then lose interest in it. He'd get it on the cheap. Or so he said."

"Whatever happened to all his equipment?"

"Some of it, as I recall his best stuff, was destroyed in the . . . the accident."

"But he had more than that, didn't he?"

"I guess it just got misplaced over the years."

"Wasn't there a black trunk with his equipment in it?"

"The black trunk . . . yes . . . what happened to that thing?"

"I was hoping you could tell me."

"I . . . I have no idea. I guess it, too, just got misplaced over the years. Maybe it got lost when we moved up here? In fact, I don't recall ever seeing it in the house after we moved. Do you?"

"No, Mama, can't say as I did."

"Well . . . there you go. It must have gotten lost in the move."

"Guess so."

"Why are you so interested in that old thing anyway?"

"I guess it would be nice to have something to remember papa by."

"For some reason I don't think your papa would want you to have that trunk."

"The trunk . . . or what was in it?"

"Not sure. Probably both."

"Well . . . gotta go, Mama. I'll stop in sometime tomorrow."

"Reece, you don't have to stop in every day you know. But since you insist on coming by tomorrow, how about lunch?"

"Can't. Last day of the seminar and we have a lunch planned."

"Always something else."

"Don't forget, I won't be here to bother you all weekend. I'm going to open up the cabin. Are you getting excited about going up there in a few weeks?"

"The cabin. You know I hate that place."

"Mama . . . what are you talking about? You love it there."

"Your mama loves it there. I can't stand it. Out in the middle of the woods. Cold. Damp. Buggy. Yuck."

Reece stared at, her, staring back at him. In the past, whenever she would appear in his mother's brain she would always ease into place, subtly, and unless you were paying attention, you might not notice. This, this was an outright announcement that she was now there.

"Mama . . . are you okay?"

"Honey . . . your mama is just fine."

"But . . . "

"Reece . . . if I was you," she leaned forward and whispered, "I would take advantage of your mama not being here."

"But, who . . . "

"Your mama will never tell you where the trunk is. She promised not to."

"Promised . . . promised who?"

"That doesn't matter. What matters is she won't tell you."

"Mama . . . "

"Honey . . . you know I'm not your mama, don't you? Of course you do. And since I'm not your mama, I can tell you where the trunk is. That is, if I haven't forgotten."

87

"I feel like we're putting together a puzzle and we've gotten to the end, but there are a bunch of empty spaces and no more pieces left."

"I had an older brother who used to do that."

"Seriously, Tia. You put puzzles together?"

"My mom loves puzzles. You should try it, Kayla. It's very calming, and addictive."

"Maybe that's how we need to look at this."

"Tell me you did puzzles, too, Ryan?"

"No, but statisticians deal with these kinds of problems all the time. What puzzle piece do we need, and what's the probability of finding it? The probability that the next piece is the one that completes the puzzle goes up as you get to the last piece, but usually that last piece is the most difficult to find, especially when you have an older brother. In our case we only need one or two more pieces of hard evidence, like the bullet, to prove our hypothesis, unfortunately that last piece may prove impossible to find. After all, no one has found these key pieces in fifty years. And if someone has made sure the key piece never gets found . . . well, it may not."

"Even I can understand that, but how do you explain the things our teams have found in the past four weeks?" Paul asked.

"Dumb luck."

"Speak for yourself, Joseph. I think it was hard work."

"It was probably a little of both, Tia. That's why in statistics you sometimes come across the outlier. The five heads in a row when you flip a coin. Your name being drawn in a raffle. Spending a billion dollars developing a drug you thought was going to make two billion, only to find out it didn't cure what you thought it was going to, but instead addressed a problem no one knew was a problem and made billions more than you ever thought possible."

"You're talking about Viagra, aren't you, Ryan?"

"Tia, it's the number one selling prescription drug in America."

"Don't tell me Paul that you . . . "

"I bet your Dixon does too. And Joseph, what about . . . "

"Can we get back on track here guys? We're meeting with Landis in less than one hour."

"Why don't you handle it, Rose? He seems to trust you more than any of us."

"It's only because she's older."

"I like to think it's because I'm wiser."

"Well, then will you do it?"

"Fine. But we still have to figure out what we are going to say."

"I like the puzzle analogy."

"I do too."

"Me too."

"Alright. I think I can put something together, with Ryan's help."

"No problem. Tell me what you need."

"Well . . . if our theory is correct, what happened to the bullet?"

88

"Interesting theory. But, if it is true . . . what happened to the bullet?"

Rose, who was sitting at the opposite end of the table from Reece, glanced first to the left side of the table at Tia, and Kayla, and then to the right side of the table at Joseph, Paul, and Ryan. Tia was the first to start laughing, but in seconds the others joined in, except for Rose, who was staring at Reece.

"Sorry, Dr. Landis. You'll have to excuse these guys. After four weeks of WORKING HARDER THAN THEY'VE PROBABLY WORKED IN YEARS . . . I think they've finally cracked."

"No problem, Rose. I've seen this before with other teams. Classic case of burnout. OR TOO MUCH PARTYING EVERY NIGHT?" Reece's raised voice silenced the room.

"Sorry, Dr. Landis. We had asked ourselves that same question. What happened to the bullet? We knew you'd ask. It's why we are laughing."

"And your answer, Kayla?"

"We don't have an answer. But we thought we'd bury a couple hundred nickels on the hill, then publish a paper about our theory. We wondered how long it would take for the treasure hunters to dig up the hill."

"Funny, Kayla. Perverse, but funny. Did you come up with any other puzzle pieces we could look for?"

They all shook their heads no.

"Alright then. I can honestly say I have never worked until the final Thursday evening of the seminar trying to closeout not just an open issue, but one so intriguing as what you two teams have come up with. But, intriguing isn't enough, is it? Your theory might someday make a good plot for a book, but as you said, we still need a final piece to complete the puzzle to make it credible. Maybe someday. In any event, great job.

"Next, I need to remind you of the confidentiality agreement you signed when you enrolled in the program."

"You mean, we can't write a book?"

"That's right, Tia. Not for five years, anyway. But any follow-on work on this theory that gets published will certainly give credit to the six of you. Any other questions before we break up? I don't want you to be late for the dinner tonight. It certainly wouldn't look good if I walked in late.

"Questions? Great. See you all at seven."

"Thank you, Dr. Landis." They all got up and started for the door.

"Joseph, do you have a minute?"

89

“Landis knows how to do it right, doesn’t he?”

“Sure does. I don’t remember seeing the Arad Evans Inn on our must-go-to restaurant list.”

“It wasn’t. I guess he was saving it for our last bash.”

“The whole place is closed down just for us.”

“I know. It’s great. You can order anything you want off the menu. And have you looked at the menu? Unbelievable.”

“And open bar.”

“By the way, congratulations, Paul.” Ryan held his glass up and Paul followed.

“You too, Ryan. How’s it feel to be going to Wall Street?”

“It’s not a done deal, yet.”

“You already have the offer. It’s only yours to turn down.”

“Did you know Landis was going to do this for everybody?”

“I knew in the past he lined up interviews for everyone.”

“These aren’t interviews, Paul.”

“I know. Everyone I’ve talked to has a job offer.”

“And what about you?”

“What about me?”

“If I’d have known the sky was the limit.”

"You just need to be honest about what you want to do with your life."

"Paul . . . Barbados? He got you a job in Barbados?"

"It's what I want to do."

"Hi, guys."

"Hi, Tia."

"Seriously, Paul? Barbados? And you, Wall Street."

"Tia . . . everybody got what they asked for. What about you?"

"First choice was Atlanta. That's where I'm from."

"Nice. Gonna take it?"

"Not sure. Got my second choice too. Syracuse."

"Really."

"Yup. Think'n about it."

"Hi, Rose."

"Did you hear about Kayla and Joseph?"

"No . . . what? They both wanted New York City, right?"

"Kayla got the city."

"And, Joseph?"

"Landis got him something there too, but as his second choice."

"Second? Is Joseph pissed?"

"Not at all."

"How about Kayla?"

"Not at all either."

"What did Landis come up with for his first choice?"

"Cortland, New York."

"Where the hell is Cortland, New York?"

"About thirty miles south of Syracuse."

"What the hell is in Cortland, New York?"

"Jets summer training camp."

"As in New York Jets?"

"As in New York Jets."

"No way."

"Yes way. Landis knows someone high up in the Jets organization."

"Holy crap. Good for Joseph. And, what about you, Rose?"

"I didn't have anything picked out yet. I'm still up in the air."

90

"That was very nice what you did for Joseph."

"I just got his foot in the door, Rose. He's got a long way to go to actually make the team."

"Still . . . "

"I happen to know someone."

"You seem to know a lot of people."

"Comes with age . . . and experience."

"You never answered my question."

"What question."

"The follow-on work I'm doing for you . . . "

"With me."

"The follow-on work I'm doing with you. Is it part of the official seminar?"

"No."

"And the official seminar ends tomorrow?"

"Yes, at twelve. Why?"

"Nothing. Just asking." An uncomfortable lull caused Rose to speak up again. "You look great tonight."

"Thank you. So do you. You all do. And everyone seems to be in such a great mood."

"Probably has something to do with the alcohol and dinner, which by the way, was fabulous."

"Good. I'm glad you enjoyed it. This is one of my favorite restaurants. I don't live too far from here."

There was another uncomfortable lull again forcing Rose to speak up. "So, when would you like to get started tomorrow? I'm available right after the morning exit meeting."

"I have a few things I need to do after that meeting, so why don't we get started after lunch, say two."

"Sounds good."

"The first thing I'd like to do is brief you on some other issues I've uncovered."

"Other issues?"

"I've come across some things of my own."

"I hope they weren't things we could have used in our analysis?"

"I don't think . . . "

"You don't think?"

"Could we have two more, please."

"Jack and diet, and . . . ?"

"Grey Goose and Sprite." Rose turned to Reece. "I don't understand why you wouldn't want to share all the information you had with us? I thought we were all working together on this?"

"We were. I mean we are."

"Then why hold back?"

"Rose, you don't need to get upset."

"I'm not upset. I'm pissed. We worked our asses off for you, and . . . "

"Rose . . . quiet down."

"Your drinks."

"Thank you. Would you like a lime, Rose?"

"Here you go."

"Fine. We worked our asses off for you, and you hold back information we could have used to . . . "

"Hold on. I didn't say I was holding back anything that would have helped your analysis."

"Why hold anything back?"

"Because I'm not sure how credible the information is."

"You still should have vetted it with us. The whole team. Both teams. Let us make that determination as to how credible it might be."

"That's what I need you to help me with."

"I said team, not just me. Team. Synergy. You don't get it, do you?"

"Rose . . . "

"No! If I'm going to help you on this, you need to be open with me. I need to have access to the same information that you have. Otherwise I can't contribute to my full potential."

"I'm not sure how much I want to share . . . "

"You have to stop being so damn controlling."

"I can also be demanding."

"And demanding."

"Very demanding."

"Well," Rose leaned in closer to Reece, "this should be a very interesting next few days because I too can be controlling, very demanding, and . . . difficult to deal with."

"Difficult to deal with . . . or difficult to please?"

"Yes."

91

"Get on your fuck'n back. I'm gonna sit on your face."

"Kayla . . . we've been at it for an hour and . . . "

"Get on your back."

"You've had too much to drink."

"Are you gonna get on your back, or do I need to get someone else to lick me out?"

"I'm just saying . . . you've had a lot to drink. It's probably why you can't . . . "

"Don't tell me I can't!"

"I'm sure after a few hours of rest you'll be able to . . . "

"Get on your back, Joseph. I'm not resting until I have an orgasm."

92

As soon as Reece opened the door he froze at the smell of her scent. His initial reaction was to search her out – she would either be in the bedroom or playroom – and tell her to get the fuck out. However, his second reaction – the throbbing sensation in his groin – told him to wait and give it a little more thought.

It had been a week since he'd had any kind of sex. Considering over his past three year relationship with Meeka it had never been more than twenty-four hours between orgasms, he thought horny was not quite the right adjective to describe how he felt right now. He'd also had his share of make-up sex with Meeka. He throbbed harder thinking how that would likely more than satisfy his current urge. He wondered what she was wearing and if she was already on her knees waiting for him. He took one step, then froze again. The uncomfortable throbbing subsided as he thought about why he hadn't had a release in a week. He couldn't remember how many scabs he had left.

"What the fuck are you doing here?"

Meeka was kneeling in the circle of light in the middle of the darkened playroom naked except for a garter belt, stockings, and stilettos.

"Dr. Landis, if you can't figure that out without me telling you, it's going to be a much longer and hotter night than even I had planned."

93

"Grey Goose, Sprite, and fruit."

"You remembered."

"By the second one I usually get it right."

"Even a week later?"

"For good looking women, or . . . "

"Good tipping women?"

"Or good tipping women, yes."

"Which one am I?"

"That's easy . . . both."

"A true bartender. Able to lie with a straight face."

"No lie."

"So . . . when do you get off?"

"Midnight."

"Were you . . . "

"Surprised that you called me?"

"Yes." Her heart was beating so fast she could hardly answer him.

"No."

"No?"

"No."

"Awfully cocky of you, isn't it?"

"Not really. I think . . . last time . . . I piqued your curiosity."

"Curiosity killed the cat, you know."

"True. But in this case, I believe you are curious about what might happen if you . . . "

"End up in your bed?"

Grant placed the drink in front of Rose, and placed his hand on hers when she reached for it. "Actually . . . if I were you . . . I'd be just as curious about what might happen before we even get to bed."

94

"Were you really serious at this morning's exit meeting when you hinted that we might be the last seminar?"

"Hi, Rose. Hi, Reece. Welcome. Glad you found the place. Come in. Your house is beautiful, Reece. Thank you, Rose. I'm glad you like it. I thought it would be more relaxing to work here. Can I get you something to drink? Water, soda, iced tea?"

"Iced tea would be great. Lemon, no sugar." Rose walked through the doorway, past Reece, into the entranceway, then turned and faced Reece waiting for him to close the door and turn around. "Well . . . were you serious?"

"I was . . . I am."

"Then please tell me . . . why the hell am I here? If you truly believe that no more evidence is left to be uncovered, what do you need my help for?"

"Come on in. Sit. Let me get your iced tea and we can talk."

"Fuck the iced tea. And if you don't mind, I'd like to talk right here."

"Did you have a bad night last night or something?"

"No . . . why . . . no. That's none of your business."

"You're right. It's not. But something must have happened from the time I saw you yesterday evening, when you seemed excited to help me, to now, when you're about ready to walk out the door. That gives us last night, and this morning, for something to have happened that changed your mind."

"It wasn't last night. I mean it was this morning. I want to know if you truly believe there is nothing left to be found."

"Yes and no."

"Cut the lawyer bullshit."

"I believe we are on the verge of closing out this issue once and for all. But . . . "

"Then why . . . "

"BUT . . . I also believe that you may have uncovered something. Evidence, circumstantial evidence, but very strong circumstantial evidence, that there may have been another shooter in Dealey Plaza that day. But . . . yes, another but . . . before we can say with confidence that this theory is correct, we need to find the missing puzzle piece, as you so aptly put it."

"So . . . what is it that you are looking for?"

"I was hoping you would find something in Dealey Plaza, that is, a bullet. That didn't pan out. I was hoping you would find something in the twenty years of analyses, some synergistic evidence. Nothing there. What's left is my last puzzle piece. I need to either prove its existence, or prove it never existed to begin with. To do that, I need your help."

"What is it that you've been keeping from us?"

"You see . . . that's why I need your help. You have the critical thinking skills to look at evidence and know when something is not right."

"Don't try and flatter me . . . just tell me what you're hiding."

"The cameras. The ones found destroyed in my father's car. They were supposed to be the cameras he took with him to Dealey Plaza that day. The ones that would have contained the pictures with the grassy knoll in the background. The ones that might prove or disprove a second shooter located there."

"But . . . they were totally destroyed. The pictures you had me analyze."

"Those cameras were destroyed. But . . . those weren't the cameras my father had with him in Dealey Plaza. My father was an amateur photographer. He owned several thirty-five millimeter cameras. You verified yourself that the cameras that burned in that car were not large lensed, heavy bodied cameras."

"But, the quality of the pictures . . . "

"Come with me. I'm not going to attack you. I want to show you something." Reece walked past the kitchen area to a large teak dining table totally covered with old photo albums and stuff you'd find in a junk drawer, or in this case several junk drawers. He reached for the camera that was on the far corner of the table and handed it to Rose. "Be careful, it's . . . "

"Heavy."

"This is a Model 414PD Bell & Howell Zoomatic Director Series 8-millimeter movie camera. It's the same make and model used by Abraham Zapruder in Dealey Plaza. I think it's also the same model my father owned. The one he took with him to Dealey Plaza that day. The one he used to film the motorcade as it passed in front of him on Elm Street. One of the two cameras supposedly destroyed in the accident.

"Tell me, Rose. Was the quality of the photograph you looked at good enough for you to conclude, without any doubt, that this was not the type of camera that burned on the front seat of that car?"

"What is it that you want me to help you with?"

95

"Can we go over this again, Reece?"

"Rose, I've been over it . . . why don't you review it for me?"

"Okay . . . I'll give it a shot. Let's talk about the black trunk first. You are certain it's where you father stored his photographer gear. You are also certain the trunk was still around after your father died, but you do not recall seeing it after you moved from Texas to New York. How am I doing so far?"

"Good, except . . . the recollections you are talking about are from a fifty-four-year-old remembering what he thought he saw as a four-year-old."

"And, what your mother has told you."

"And that's questionable because I'm not sure if it was my mother, the disease taking over my mother, or a combination of the two."

"But your mother, or whomever, told you the trunk was real, still exists, and the answer to where it might be located is hidden in all this junk."

"She thinks it's hidden in all this junk. Look at all this stuff. Aptly named junk drawer. Except we had a few of them."

"And if the trunk still exists, you think it still contains the movie camera."

"That's the second . . . "

"Hold on . . . you asked me to summarize this for you. The second issue is the cameras. You don't think the cameras that were destroyed in the accident were the same ones that your father had in Dealey Plaza."

"And neither do you, based on your analysis."

"No . . . I don't think the cameras that were destroyed in the fire were thirty-five millimeter cameras, or a movie camera. I don't know what your father took with him to Dealey Plaza."

"Okay . . . I stand corrected."

"Only you, your father, and perhaps your mother knows that for certain."

"But, doesn't it make more sense that he would take his most expensive cameras to photograph the president? Plus, I remember taking pictures with the thirty-five millimeter."

"It does make sense, but without direct evidence or testimony from someone other than a four-year-old at the time, it's still circumstantial."

"What else?"

"You believe the photographs and movie you and your father took in Dealey Plaza may exist somewhere, and if they do they could help corroborate the second shooter theory."

"And, something tells me the black trunk is where we'll find that evidence."

"You're hoping an image of the black trunk will show up in one of these photographs? How many albums are here?"

"My mother liked to take pictures of me as I was growing up."

"There must be thousands of photos here."

"I'm hoping someone who has never seen the pictures before will spot something I didn't notice."

"Someone . . . or me?"

"You."

"If these were all in digital format, I could use a software recognition program to find a black trunk in no time."

"Sorry, the pictures go back well before digital imaging."

"I'll keep looking through the photos, but I'm not sure what you're looking for in all this junk."

"My mother said the key to finding the trunk is hidden somewhere in all this junk. Right now I'm just going through each piece, one-by-one, to try to figure out if there is any hidden meaning behind each one."

"You've probably got to look at it like a puzzle."

"That's exactly what I'm doing. Trouble is, this might just be a wild goose chase. I'm not even sure it was my mother talking to me."

"Is she that . . . "

"She has her good days, and bad days. Trouble is, it's getting harder to determine which is which."

"I'm sorry."

"Me too."

"Reece, who is this?" Reece walked over to Rose who was pointing to a man in one of the pictures.

"I have no idea. That was taken at a high school wrestling match. I wrestled when I went to Liverpool High. Might be my senior year. Probably just a spectator. Why?"

"Because, he shows up in a lot of photographs of you."

"Maybe he was a father of one of the other wrestlers on the team."

"No . . . look. This is of you at . . . what? Your high school graduation?"

"No . . . college."

"And this? And this? And this?"

"Are you sure this is the same guy?"

"There's probably ten to fifteen years of aging taking place during the time sequence of these photographs. I can't be certain without running them through my software recognition program, but I'd say it was."

"But the beards, hair color differences."

"Yeah . . . almost like he's purposefully trying to hide something."

"Well . . . I have no idea who it is. But maybe my mother does."

96

“Mama . . . are you sure . . . ”

“Reece, I don’t have to look at the pictures again. I have no idea who that is.”

“How could he be in so many pictures of me?”

“It doesn’t even look like the same person to me.”

“It is, Mama.”

“Can I help you?” Dora glanced over Reece’s shoulder at the woman standing in the doorway to her room.

“Reece, I . . . ”

“Rose, come in.”

“Reece, I need to see you.”

“Reece, you know this young lady?”

“Rose, come in. Mama, this is Rose Stone. She is working with me on closing out some remaining issues from the seminar. Rose, this is my mother, Dora.”

“Nice to meet you.”

“Very nice to meet you, Rose. What a lovely name, my dear. Is Rose your real name, or short for something like Rosalie? Or perhaps Rozanne?”

“Reece, I really need to speak with you.”

“I was just asking my mother about these pictures. She has no idea who this man is. She doesn't even think it's the same person."

"Reece, please." Rose turned and walked out the door and into the hall.

"Be right back, Mama."

"Reece." Dora motioned for Reece to come closer to her, then she whispered, "She's not another one of those demanding bitches like Meeka, is she?"

"Mama, what are you talking about?"

"I heard Meeka. At the cabin. Talking on her phone. To one of her friends. Telling her . . . well . . . things she was going to do to you. A proper lady would not repeat what she said. That's why I think she's a slut."

"Mama . . . I'll be right back." Reece stood, turned, and walked toward the door.

"Honey . . . you don't have to be embarrassed. I read the Fifty books you know."

"You were a little rude to my mother, don't you think?"

"Reece . . . "

"What!"

"I saw him."

"Who?"

"Him. The guy in the pictures."

"What?"

"He looked a lot older, but I'm sure it was him."

"Where?"

"Walking out of this building."

"How sure are you it was him?"

"It was only a second. We made eye contact. There was something about him. And, unfortunately." She held up her phone.

"It's a picture of the back of his head."

"I know. Sorry. That's all I could get without spooking him."

"Rose . . . you didn't see him. You wanted to see him. Your mind is playing tricks on you."

97

"You look . . . nice."

"What's wrong with what I have on?"

"Nothing. I said you look nice."

"Nice? I would have thought . . . "

"Sexy. You look sexy, okay?"

"Don't make me force it out of you."

"Hot. You look hot, too. What? Stunning, alluring, mysterious, provocative, attractive, spicy, suggestive, arousing, intriguing, tall . . . "

"Tall?"

"Six inch stiletto platforms. In public?"

"It's the style."

"Seamed stockings?"

"It's the style, too."

"And I'd be willing to bet the only thing you've got on under that short, very tight, very low-cut black dress of yours is . . . "

"Go ahead. Spit it out."

"Is a matching black push-up bra, garter belt, and G-string."

"Matching?"

"Yes. You are a woman who pays attention to details."

"And you are a man who seems to know a lot about what a woman needs to wear to . . . "

"Get a man's attention?"

"Must come with . . . "

"Experience."

"And, I bet you have a lot of that."

"I've had my share. I mean . . . of experience."

"Well . . . in this case, if we'd of bet, you would have lost."

"Doesn't match?"

"Oh . . . it matches. And, since you can see my bra-straps, and I saw you catch a glimpse of my garter belt strap when I sat down, I know you now know what part of the matching set I decided not to wear tonight."

"Dr. Landis, your table is ready when you are."

"I think we'll have another drink here at the bar, if you don't mind, Daija."

"Not at all, Dr. Landis. Just let me know when you are ready."

"It's a gorgeous Friday evening in the summer. This place is mobbed. We only decided to go out to dinner an hour ago. How did you get a table?"

"I've told you before, I know people. In this case, the owner."

"You know the owner of this place? The Prime?"

"He was a student of mine. Opened the restaurant a few years ago. I frequent the place a little. You want a prime cut aged steak that is soft as butter and tastes like the best steak you've ever had in your life, then this is the place."

"Why wasn't this place on your list of restaurants?"

"I like to keep it to myself. For special occasions."

"Special occasions?"

"Yes."

"And why is this evening so special?"

"We're done . . . with the seminar, of course."

"Well . . . actually, Dr. Landis. To be correct about it, we have until midnight before the seminar is officially over. You know me, a woman who pays attention to details."

"Midnight? What are you talking about, Rose?"

"You know. Students? Seminar participants? Ethical conduct?"

"I still don't . . . "

"You said you would never do it with one of your students. Ethical conduct. When I asked you, you said the seminar ended at midnight. In three hours I will no longer be your student."

"Rose . . . when you asked I said the seminar was over at twelve o'clock. I meant noon today. Not midnight."

"You mean . . . I've been. Excuse me, I've got to go to the ladies room."

"Would you like another drink?"

"Yes . . . a shot . . . of Patron . . . double."

"Melody, could I get another Jack and diet, and a double Patron, please."

"That was fast. Are you okay?"

"I'm fine." Rose sat back onto the barstool purposefully exposing her garter belt strap on both legs, and left them exposed. She picked up the glass of Patron and put it to her lips.

"I wasn't sure if you wanted training wheels . . . I guess not. Would you like . . . "

"Yes . . . yes I would."

"Melody." Reece pointed to the empty glass. "Thanks." He turned to Rose. "Are you sure you're okay?"

"I'm fine. But . . . I'm sorry that you aren't feeling well."

"What are you talking about? I feel fine."

"No . . . actually, you look like you're coming down with something." Rose reached up and brushed aside a strand of hair that had fallen onto his forehead.

"Dr. Landis, I'm sorry you're not feeling well. I've cancelled your reservation. You're all set. See you next time."

"Thank you, Daija."

"I hope you feel better."

"I'm sure once I get him home Daija, he'll feel much better."

98

"He's getting closer. To finding out. We need to tell him before . . . "

"Before what?"

"What if he says something? To someone. Before . . . before we get a chance to stop him. To tell him . . . "

"To tell him what?"

"We need to tell him. We need to tell him, before . . . "

"Dora . . . we need to think this through."

"Think this through? Don't you already have it thought out? You knew this day would eventually come. You have a plan, right? What is it? Damn it . . . tell me."

"I don't have a plan. I never thought he would find out . . . that he would figure out anything. That anyone would figure out anything."

"But, he has."

"No, Dora. He doesn't know. And, he can never know. It wouldn't be safe. For you, for me, or for him."

"But, you promised."

"He doesn't know. No one knows. I've made sure of that. We can't tell him. Do you understand?"

"Yes . . . yes, I understand. But, I'm warning you. She, doesn't understand."

99

No sooner had the door to the house slammed shut and Rose had Reece pinned against it, her body, pushing onto his, her lips locked onto his, her tongue searching then finding his.

"You were purposefully vague about the twelve o'clock, weren't you?"

"Why would I do that?"

Rose lifted her knee between his legs, stopping at the right spot. "To torment me." She jerked her knee into him.

"To torment you? How do you think I felt when you were over here this afternoon and you didn't attack me."

She jerked her knee again. "Attack . . . me . . . attack you?" She jerked again. "I was horny enough to. Wanted to. Almost did at one point."

"Then why didn't you? I thought you were a demanding bitch?"

She jerked again, this time harder. "And ruin your precious reputation. Compromise your ethics." She lowered her leg, reached down and replaced it with her hand, and squeezed. "I thought you were a dominating bitch." Their lips and tongues locked again.

Reece put his arms around her, lifted her off the floor and spun around, pinning her against the door. "You want a demanding . . . I'll give you . . . " He grabbed her shoulders, spun her around, gripped her wrists, and lifted her arms above her head pushing them against the door. He unzipped her dress, reached down and pulled the dress up over her body, head, and arms, then pressed against her as he moved her hair to one side and buried his lips into her neck. "You're gonna see what demanding is like. I haven't had sex in a week."

She first pushed her butt into him, and then her whole body, almost knocking him off balance, turned around, grabbed his head and crushed her breasts against his chest, and her lips to his. She backed away, and stared into his eyes as she started to unbutton his shirt. "If you're this demanding after a week." She opened his shirt exposing his chest, but left it hanging from his shoulders. "Then you're gonna know how demanding I'm gonna be with you tonight, since I haven't had sex in over two fuck'n years." She loosened his belt, undid his pants, lowered his zipper, and let his pants fall to the floor.

"Two years?" He backed away a half step and gave her an elevator stare.

She returned the stare. "No underwear?" She inched toward him.

"No G-string?" He inched toward her.

"One week. That pisses me off." She inched forward, reached down, and put her hand around his semi-erect shaft.

"Two years? That . . . that excites me." He reached down, put his hand between her legs, and curled his middle finger into her. "I can see why you didn't wear a G-string." He started moving his fingers. "It would have been soaked by the end of the evening."

"And, I can see why you didn't wear underwear." She moved her hand along his shaft. "Too confining . . . and it too would be soaked by the end of the evening."

"Try, beginning."

"I took mine off . . . oh, please don't stop . . . fifteen minutes after I got dressed. It was . . . oh, fuck."

"Soaked?"

"Yes. Soaked. Oh . . . fuck. You're beginning to un-piss me off."

"Really?"

"Oh, fuck. Really."

He reached behind her and pulled her to him, their lips and tongues again feeding on each other. He reached up with one hand and unclasped her bra. She let it fall between them, then resumed her slow stroking. He reached around to her breast with his free hand and kneaded it. Then he pinched her now erect nipple. She did the same to him, only squeezed harder.

"I'll do whatever you want." She sucked on his tongue, almost pulling it out of his mouth.

"Rose . . . I can be very demanding."

"Whatever you want."

"You may regret saying that."

She looked into his eyes and squeezed his nipple harder. "It's been two years. I'm begging you. Make me regret it." He squeezed her nipple harder. "I only ask one thing in return." She squeezed harder.

"That I do whatever you want?"

"Say it." She squeezed and increased the length of her stroking. He responded with his finger.

"I'll do whatever you want."

"You may regret saying that. I, too, can be very demanding."

He pulled his finger out of her and raised it to her other nipple squeezing both of them with equal pressure. She dropped her hands to her side. He released her nipples and did the same.

"Kneel down." She obeyed without hesitation.

He reached down with one hand and gripped the base of his shaft. He put his other hand on the back of her head. Just as he started to feel the hot breath from her open mouth on his tip, his phone, still in his pants around his ankles, rang. He froze.

"You're not seriously going to answer that?"

"I just need to see . . . "

"I'm about to suck your . . . and you wanna stop for . . . you don't even know who the fuck it is calling you." She swatted his shaft with the palm of her hand and waited for his response. "You bastard."

He reached down, groped for his phone, looked at the screen, then put it to his ear. "Hello. Yes . . . I'll be right there."

100

"Mama . . . are you okay?"

"Well look at you two all dressed up. Hello, Rose."

"Hi, Dora."

"Don't you look pretty. I love your dress. And those shoes. Hard to believe they are in style. Why, a few years ago anyone walking around in those . . . well . . . let's just say they were trying to attract attention. And they must be difficult to walk in. And Dance in, too."

"Mama?'

"Yes, Reece. Oh, you look handsome too. Although, your pants look a little wrinkled. Better take them to the dry cleaner."

"Mama . . . they said you were asking for me."

"They did? Who did? I don't remember."

"Mama, are you okay? You never call for me."

"Reece, I never call for you because you're always here visiting me. You're such a good boy. Why should I call you?"

"Mama, they said you were insisting on seeing me. Tonight."

"Oh, wait a second. That's right. I did want to see you. Silly me. I sometimes forget you know, Rose. I have Alzheimer's."

"Mama."

"Yes, dear."

"You wanted to see me . . . now, tonight."

"Yes . . . yes, I did. I was wondering if you found the key?"

"The key?"

"Yes, to the black trunk."

"I've been looking through the junk boxes, but I haven't found anything yet."

"Well . . . I know it's there."

"Mama . . . can you be a little more specific as to what it is I'm supposed to be looking for?"

"You mean the key?"

"Yes . . . what is the key?"

"What do you mean, what is the key?"

"What is the key that I am looking for?"

"It's to the black trunk."

"Mama, I know it's to the black trunk. But, what is it?"

"Reece, have you been drinking? I might be the one with Alzheimer's, but you are making no sense to me."

"Reece . . . I think what your mother is saying is, it's a key."

"I know it's the key."

"No, Reece. Not the key . . . a key."

"Actually, Rose, my dear. It should be two keys. One to the black trunk, and one to the storage unit it's being kept in."

101

“I don’t see why this couldn’t have waited until the morning.”

“She thought we should check it out tonight.”

“It’s almost five o’clock. The sun is coming up.”

“She’s your mother.”

“And I know when what she is saying makes some resemblance to . . . ”

“Not something crazy?”

“I know it sounds terrible, but yes. I know when it’s my mother talking, and when it’s . . . the other person. That was not my mother we were talking to tonight. And whoever it was is back there laughing at us driving around Syracuse and Onondaga County looking for a non-existent storage unit that contains a non-existent black trunk.”

“Then how do you explain these?” Rose held up her hand. “Two keys. One that looks like it belongs to an old Master padlock, and one that looks like it belongs to a newer lock. And this number? Seventy-four. Just like she said would be there.”

“These keys were in a junk drawer. Probably been there for years. Ten years. Twenty. Who knows. The vision of it popped into her brain. Probably all my talking to her about a black trunk. Who knows. With Alzheimer’s, no one knows. I only know that wasn’t her talking, and all this can wait until tomorrow.”

"She insisted on tonight."

"And, why did she insist on tonight?"

"She wouldn't say."

"She wouldn't say, or she couldn't say?"

"I don't know, Reece. I just think there was a reason, a good reason, why she wanted us to do this tonight."

"I'm glad after meeting my mother only hours ago, and spending what, less than one hour with her, you know when it's her or . . . the other her."

"Reece, if this is real . . . "

"It's not."

"But, if it is. Wouldn't you want your hands on it tonight?"

"It's not real."

"Here's the next storage place, on the left."

"Why are all these places out in the boonies?"

"It has a keypad. Five, five . . . "

"I know the number, Rose. Besides the fact that we've been to a dozen of these places tonight, it's my mother's old phone number. This one's got a star and a number sign button."

"Try them both."

"Number doesn't work. And star doesn't . . . "

Before he could finish, the light on the pole in front of them went on and two seconds later the gate started sliding open.

102

"Who was that?"

"Nobody."

"Nobody? No offense, Reece. If that was nobody on the phone, I'd hate to see how you are when it's somebody."

"It was the Foundation that funds the JFK seminar. They read my email about possibly not wanting to participate in next year's program."

"And, they're pissed."

"Very."

"So, how are you going to un-piss them off?"

"Un-piss off. You used that term last night. It was right when I was . . . "

"Can we not talk about last night?"

"Do you think we'll ever do it?"

"Do it. That sounds so mechanical."

"Have sex?"

"That sounds so casual."

"How about make mad passionate love until I can't get it up anymore, and you're too sore, everywhere, to want me to?"

Rose got up from the table, walked over to Reece, and put her arms around him. "Much better, but . . . can we not talk about it."

"You know it might be fate."

"What?'

"Us, not doing it."

"You mean like someone or something not wanting us to do it?"

"Exactly. From the stars aligning to . . . whatever."

"I thought when we were driving around last night visiting all those storage facilities that you said we'd go up to your cabin for the rest of the weekend. Even though we were going to open it up, that sounded semi-romantic to me."

"Semi-romantic?"

"Dust, bugs, bears, no running water . . . "

"There's running water."

"Okay, romantic. Quite frankly, after last night, I'd take the dust, bugs, and bears, too. We are still going, I mean after I finish looking at some more of these photos, aren't we?"

"Blame the stars."

"What?" She let go of him and backed away a step.

"Gotta go to New York tomorrow. That's what the call was about."

"Well . . . at least now I understand the yelling. Wait . . . on a Sunday?"

"Flying out first thing. Meeting with the Foundation Sunday afternoon."

"But . . . why Sunday?"

"Next week's July fourth. Lots of people off. They need to get it taken care of now. Guess they need to determine where they're gonna spend their money if not on this."

"When will you be back?"

"Probably won't finish up until Monday, so hopefully I'll be back Monday afternoon or evening."

"I'm getting pissed at the stars."

"Maybe this will un-piss you off."

"Maybe I don't wanna be un-pissed off." She walked back over to the table, sat down, and started looking at the pictures in the album in front of her.

"I have a plan."

"If it doesn't involve doing it, I don't want to hear about it."

"It's almost eleven. I'll make us breakfast." Reece walked into the kitchen and opened the refrigerator.

"Eleven. No wonder I'm starving. Do you know you never fed me last night?"

"Excuse me. You were the one who cancelled our dinner reservations."

"I thought what I had in mind was well worth canceling dinner over."

"Then don't bitch about being hungry."

"Wait . . . you didn't give me what I cancelled out for either. You reneged on both. So the lesson-learned is when you offer me food, I better take it."

"Even over sex?"

"Seems so, doesn't it? So, what's for breakfast?"

"Do you like omelets?"

"Cheese, mushrooms, and sausage or bacon?"

"I believe . . . I can do that."

"You believe?"

"No, I can."

"Sounds good."

"After breakfast, you can continue to run those photographs through your software scanner."

"Even if I work on this until late, I'm not going to finish it today."

"No problem. You'll have all day to work on it tomorrow while I'm in New York."

"Slave away while you'rc out bcing schmoozed over dinner in some fancy restaurant."

"Somebody's gotta do it."

"Wanna switch places?"

"That would really piss 'em off."

"What are you gonna do while I'm slaving away this afternoon?"

"I'm gonna try to get the security video from the storage facility."

"You really think they'll give it to you?"

"When I spoke with them earlier this morning, they told me the storage space was in my mother's name. I have legal proxy to act in her behalf. I'm going to tell them we think a theft took place last night."

"The flashlight?"

"Yes, the flashlight we found on in storage space seventy-four. Someone had to be there just hours before. That will limit the amount of video I need to look at, so hopefully they'll give it to me."

"Reece . . . how did your mother know? She knew someone else was going to go there last night."

"I know. I've been asking myself that ever since we opened the door to that storage space and saw nothing but a dimly lit flashlight. So the next thing I want to do this afternoon is visit my mom and ask her the same question."

"Reece . . . please be . . . "

"I will. I'm not going to do anything that would . . . you know . . . hurt her, mentally I mean."

"She's fragile. Be careful."

"I will. Then the next thing on my list is to cook you a romantic dinner. Do you like shrimp?"

"Of course."

"Good. How about a Japanese stir-fry dinner. Shrimp, snow peas, black beans, scallions, water chestnuts, bean sprouts, chicken broth, soy sauce, and a side of lo-mien noodles?"

"You can't ask a starving person a question like that. Yes . . . of course . . . it all sounds delicious."

"Then . . . "

"There's more? I think by then I'll be too exhausted for anything more."

"Then, we'll do it."

"Do it?"

"Have sex."

"Sex?"

"Make mad passionate love until I can't get it up anymore, and you're too sore, everywhere, to want me to."

103

"Mama, you seem like you are in a good mood today?"

"Why shouldn't I be? It's a glorious day out here. I'm having lunch with my son in this beautiful garden, although that salad is not much of a lunch for a grown man."

"I told you, I'm not that hungry. I had a late breakfast. Besides, I think I'm all grownup. I don't need to put on any extra pounds."

"Well . . . as I was saying, it's a beautiful day, I'm spending it with my favorite son . . . "

"Mama."

"Favorite son, and besides, I'm always in a good mood. Actually, I think I'm always in a great mood. Aren't I?"

"Yes you are, Mama."

"Let me put it to you this way. I really don't remember when I was in a bad mood. Oh wait . . . yes I do. It was when your papa . . . oh, but that was a while ago."

"Do you remember me visiting you yesterday?"

"Of course I do. You were here with that lovely friend of yours. Don't tell me . . . Rose."

"And, do you remember what we talked about?"

"Are you quizzing me? Am I . . . am I getting worse?"

"No, Mama."

"Then why all the questions?"

"I was just seeing if you remembered . . . "

"Pictures. You showed me some pictures. Of you. When you were younger. Well . . . am I right?"

"Yes . . . you're right. I showed you some pictures."

"There was more though, wasn't there? Don't tell me. Let me think. I'm sorry. I can't remember. Tell me."

"It's not important, Mama."

"It must be important, or you wouldn't be asking me about it. What is it?"

"I was wondering what you think about Rose."

"I told you. She's very nice. Much nicer than that . . . "

"Mama!"

"She's lovely. Isn't she one of your students? You could get into trouble over that you know."

"Mama . . . she was one of my students. She's not anymore. And no I'm not . . . "

"Reece . . . if you're not sweet on her you'd better be careful, because she is sweet on you. I saw how she looked at you. And Reece Landis, I saw how you looked at her too. You can't fool your mama."

"Well . . . "

"Reece?"

"Maybe a little."

"Just as I thought. Your mama is always right."

"I should be going. Thank you for lunch. It was wonderful. We'll have to do this some more."

As Reece leaned over to give his mother a kiss she nudged him to the side and whispered into his ear, "Did you find it?"

"Find what?" Reece whispered back.

"You know?"

Reece stood up, reached into his pocket, pulled out the keys, and held them up in front of him. "These?"

"So, you got it?"

"You mean, these?"

"No . . . the trunk."

"No."

"No! What do you mean, no!" Dora was no longer whispering.

"There was nothing in the storage locker when we got there."

"What do you mean there was nothing there!"

"Mama . . . quiet down."

"Don't tell me to quiet down! Didn't you go there last night, like I told you?"

"Mama. Shhhh."

"Don't shush me! Did you?"

"Yes we did. But by the time we got there, it was gone. Mama . . . how did you know . . . "

"Go . . . I said, go! I'm too upset to talk to you right now. GO!"

104

"I didn't even know this room was down here. When you said let's go downstairs, I though you meant the basement. Then of course I thought, I guess I wasn't as good as I thought I was."

"Oh . . . you were good."

"Good?"

"Fantastic."

"Better. So were you."

"What would you like to drink?"

"I'd ask what do you have, but that would be a stupid question, wouldn't it? Oh, I know. Something refreshing. How about a Blood Transfusion!"

"I guess you wanna live on the wild side."

"I thought we just lived on the wild side."

"It was pretty wild."

"And isn't this wild? I can't believe I'm sitting here naked at a bar, being served by a naked bartender."

"I'm naked. You're not naked."

"Garter belt, stockings, and stilettos is naked in my book."

"I guess I can't argue with that. Plus in this dim light those large dark . . . you look like you have pasties on."

"I guess I can't argue with that, either. Reece, this bar is beautiful."

"I built it myself."

"One of the many talents that I bet don't show up on your resume."

"No . . . I guess not."

"So, why is it okay for Reece not to list all his talents, but when Rose doesn't, it's a major crime?"

"I never said it was a major crime, Rose. I just said you should be honest about your work experience and talents on your resume."

"Dr. Landis, are the bedroom talents you just displayed in the last three hours also missing from your resume?"

"As are yours from yours, Ms. Stone."

"Touché."

"Here you go, Blood Transfusions."

"You too?"

"I figure I might as well join you on the wild side."

"What should we drink to?"

"How about to, doing it."

"And, doing it."

"And, doing it."

"And, doing it."

"And, doing it."

"Oh, and to doing it that way."

"Which way was that?"

"I think you know exactly which way I'm talking about, Dr. Landis."

"Actually . . . I thought there were several of those ways."

"Maybe you're right. No . . . not maybe. You are right. I am . . . well, let's just say you accomplished what you set out to do if your goal was to make me sore all over. And I do mean, all over."

"You didn't seem to mind when we were doing it."

"And if I had, would it have mattered?"

"I would have . . . "

"You would have what? Stopped?"

"Probably not."

"Probably not?"

"What about you?"

"What about me?"

"You didn't stop either."

"I just assumed those were screams of ecstasy."

"Uh-huh."

"And, that you didn't want me to stop."

"That's good . . . because, I didn't."

"So much for just going to bed and making love."

"That was making love."

"Three hours of hard-core sex is not making love."

"Then what is it?"

"I just told you . . . hard-core sex. Have you . . . have you ever done that before? I mean the things we did?"

"Have you?"

"I asked first."

"Yes . . . I have."

"Me too. But, not like that."

Reece walked around the bar and stood next to Rose who was seated cross-legged on the bar stool. "With one man?"

"So . . . you do know about . . . "

"Your movie career? Yes."

"Background check?"

"Background check."

"And I suppose you . . . you didn't happen to . . . "

"Watch it? Of course."

"Fuck."

"Yes, you did. Along with a few, actually many, other things. And to be honest, you seemed to enjoy it."

"It was a long time ago. I was broke. Couldn't, or I should say wouldn't, call my parents for a hand-out. It was easy money."

"Rose, you don't have to justify your past to me. I've done some pretty crazy things myself."

"I bet you were never in a porn movie."

"Actually . . . "

"You made a porn movie?"

"Well . . . not exactly."

"You set up a camera while you were having sex?"

"Yes."

"That doesn't count. Lots of people do that. That's not a porn movie."

"Are you saying I couldn't make a porn movie?"

"There's no doubt in my mind that you could make a porn movie. In fact, you'd be damn good at it. Is that what you were doing upstairs?"

"What?"

"Fantasizing?"

"About?"

"Doing it . . . with a porn star."

Reece inched in closer to Rose. "A second ago you were defending why you made a porn movie. Now you're claiming to be a porn star?"

"Answer my question. Were you fantasizing?"

"Did you know your nipples get hard when I look at them?"

"Were you?"

"Or is it because I'm standing next to you, naked."

"My nipples are getting hard for the same reason as you are getting hard."

"I'm getting hard because you just brushed your leg against me."

"Excuse me. You're the one who brushed that thing against my leg. See . . . you just did it again."

"Sometimes, it has a mind of its own."

"Looks to me as if it's asking for another do it?"

"Do you want to do it?"

Rose brushed her leg against his shaft. "I think that answer is obvious. But . . . I want to do it down here."

"Down here?"

"Have you ever done it down here? I take it by your silence that's a yes. And by the rise in this." Rose reached down and stroked his shaft. "And I thought you were turned on by fucking a porn star." She squeezed him harder. "What the hell happened down here?" She took her hand off him and looked into his eyes. "You might as well tell me." She reached down again and squeezed him. "If not, I have my ways of getting it out of you."

105

"Rose, my dear. What a surprise. Come in. Sit down. Is Reece with you?"

"No, he's . . . "

"Wait, isn't he in New York? Had to meet with the Foundation, right?"

"Yes, that's right."

"I thought he told me during lunch yesterday that he was going there." Dora pointed to her head. "Sometimes the brain works just fine. So . . . what brings you here, my dear?"

"Dora . . . I wanted to talk to you about the man in the pictures. The ones from your albums." Rose placed several pictures on the table.

"My dear, I already told Reece. I have no idea who that man is. Perhaps . . . "

"Dora, I think you know exactly who this is."

"My dear, my mind isn't as sharp as it used to be, but I am quite sure I do not know this man."

"He shows up in dozens of pictures in your albums."

"You must be mistaken, my dear. Why look at these pictures. That doesn't even look like the same person to me."

"I will admit, Dora, that to the human eye this does not look like the same person."

"Then you agree with me."

"But . . . to a computer . . . "

"A computer? My dear, what would a computer know about . . . "

"There is something called facial recognition software . . . "

"Facial recognition software. That sounds like hocus-pocus to me."

"Facial recognition software uses various facial attributes that are difficult to hide with disguises."

"Disguises? Are you saying this is the same man in these photos, but he's wearing different disguises? My dear, you have a very vivid imagination. Besides, these don't look like disguises. They're just . . . "

"Short hair, long hair, light colored, dark colored, curly, straight, glasses, no glasses, beard, no beard."

"Exactly, my dear. It looks like several different men to me."

"Except there are a number of facial features, such as the width of your forehead, cheek bone and jaw bone orientation, the distance between your pupils, that are difficult to change with a disguise. They are almost like fingerprints. The computer predicts with a very high correlation that . . . "

"My dear, I don't need a computer to tell me that these are not the same man."

"The computer says it is."

"The computer is one hundred percent certain?"

"No, but . . . "

"There you go then. If it's not one hundred percent."

"Nothing is one hundred percent."

"Is that my Reece in this picture?"

"Yes."

"Are you one hundred percent certain?"

"Yes, but . . . "

"And, in this picture. Is this not a picture of Reece?"

"It is not."

"Are you one hundred percent certain?"

"Yes, but . . . "

"There you go my dear. I do not trust computers. Never have. My eyes . . . that's what I trust. And my eyes tell me the men in these pictures are all different."

"How did you know someone was going to the storage facility the other night?"

"Are we changing subjects now? My dear, I didn't know . . . "

Rose pulled another picture from her purse and placed it in front of Dora. "This is a picture of the man who got there before us. The picture is grainy, and he never looks directly into the security camera outside the storage location, but his overall body features, shoulder width, leg and arm length, are the same as the man in these pictures."

"And from that you are one hundred percent . . . "

"No. In this case it is more circumstantial. Or should I say curiously coincidental."

"Finally . . . something we agree on."

"And that would be?"

"That curiously coincidental does not mean one hundred percent."

"It's the same man, isn't it Dora?"

"How would anyone possibly tell that from this picture?"

"Dora, you don't need a picture. You know it's the same man."

"My dear . . . "

"You knew he was going there."

"If I don't know who he is, how would I have known . . . "

"Dora, what was in the trunk?"

"Are we changing subjects again? You make it very difficult for a person to keep track of a conversation with you."

"Dora?"

"I already told you and Reece. Things . . . things that his father would want him to have."

"Then why have that man steal . . . "

"He didn't steal it!"

"Who is he?"

"I don't . . . "

"You said, he. Who didn't steal it, Dora?"

"Did I say, he? I don't remember saying, he. Why would I have said that? What were we talking about again?"

"Dora, don't hide behind your Alzheimer's."

"My dear, I have no idea . . . "

"Who is he, Dora?"

"Who is who, my dear? I really have no idea what you are talking about."

Rose reached into her purse and placed another picture in front of Dora. "Look at it."

"Not another picture. I thought we agreed . . . where did you get that? I said, where did you get that?"

"It was hidden behind one of the pictures in the album. No one would ever notice it unless they removed the picture on top."

Dora picked up the photo and looked at it closely. A tear dripped from her eye. "I . . . I don't . . . "

"Dora . . . that's you . . . and him. Standing side-by-side. Holding hands. Isn't it?"

106

Rose had just knelt on the floor under the dimmed spotlight shining down from the ceiling when she heard the door upstairs open and close, then the shuffling of footsteps. She took a deep breath. The text message from the restricted number earlier today was short and to the point. He would be home at ten. Be kneeling on the floor under the light dressed in something revealing with a blindfold on.

He didn't need to say anything more. They had shared some of their errotic fantasies with one another during the previous evening while sitting naked at the bar in the playroom. However their discussions kept getting interrupted by another round of doing it. Rose was curious to find out how dominating Reece could be, especially since he seemed to get excited talking about it. So she agreed to bottom for him when they opened the cabin early next week. Having him come home from New York earlier than anticipated provided an opportunity for her to experience him tonight.

She looked down. Her nipples were already hard, but she reached up and squeezed and pulled on them to make them stick out even more. Based on last night's experience she knew what that would do to him. She also decided last night's outfit fit the definition of revealing. As soon as she heard the footsteps on the circular stairway she lowered the blindfold over her eyes and waited.

Within minutes she was bound in leather cuffs, standing with her arms stretched above her head, and she assumed attached to a hook in the ceiling she had not seen the night before.

"Ahhhh! I guess you're not gonna start off slow, are you? Ahhhh! I've been whipped with a leather flogger before, but not one like that. Ahhhh! I guess if you're not going to talk, I won't either."

She stood as still as she could and decided after the fifteenth thwack to stop counting. She also wished she had downed more than the five quick shots of Patron.

"AHHHH! I hope you're fuck'n enjoying yourself. AHHHH! If you're stopping, thank you. My ass must be beat red. Ooooh. Your hands feel good. Is my ass nice and hot?

"AHHHH! What the fuck do you have on your hands? It feels like old cracked leather gloves. AHHHH! Fuck that hurts. You like squeezing my ass-cheeks apart? Why don't you lick down there like you did last night. AHHHH!

"No . . . please. Take the gloves off before you squeeze my nipples. AHHHH! Fuck. You like playing with those? Are they big enough for you? AHHHH! You like those big dark nipples, don't you. I had you worshiping those last night. AHHHH!

"Fuck . . . are those clips? AHHHH! AHHHH! No. Not weights.

"Things have been quiet for too long. Why won't you talk to me? My nipples are getting numb. What are you doing? What is that? Ooooh . . . I liked it much better last night when you stuck your tongue up there first. What fun is using K-Y jelly?

"What are you doing? What is that? Are you giving me an enema? No . . . it's . . . it's a butt chugger, isn't it? Baby . . . I would have done the shots. Anyway . . . I thought I showed you last night that I'd do anything for you. I took you everywhere. You don't need to get me drunk to slut for you.

"This silence thing you've got going is kind 'a . . . kind 'a . . . eee . . .

rrrotic. Fuck . . . I'm . . . I'm . . . I'm get'n . . . that thing is give'n me one buck'n fuzz. Baby . . . don't get me too . . . fuck . . . dizzy . . . I'm . . . dizzy.

"What are you . . . oh, yes. Tinger fit. I mean . . . finger . . . finger it. Drip . . . I'm drip . . . you get me . . . I'm wet."

"Are you ready?"

"Ooooh . . . pull on it. AHHHH!"

"Like that?"

"Who . . . Reece? AHHHH!"

"No . . . bitch. It's not Reece. You like me pulling on this?"

"AHHHH! No . . . please. Who . . . "

"You know who this is . . . don't you, bitch?"

"No . . . I . . . AHHHH!"

"I told you I would squeeze, yank, and twist this fuck'n thing if you fucked with my man."

"AHHHH! Please, Meeka . . . no."

"Keep begging, bitch. You know what's coming next, don't you?"

107

"That' was nice."

"Very nice."

"Sometimes . . . I just need you like that."

"Sometimes?"

"You know what I mean."

"Yes . . . I do."

"I know you do."

"Are you still mad at me?"

"Yes."

"Even after . . . "

"Sex doesn't make a problem go away."

"I didn't think it was a problem."

"We need to tell him . . . about what really happened. In Dallas."

"Dora . . . "

"You shouldn't have taken the trunk. You should have let him find it."

"We need to think this through."

"I have. It's time that he knows."

"I have just as much say in this as you do."

"You've had all the say for fifty years. Now it's my turn."

"I still have . . . "

"The trunk? What are you going to do? Destroy it? What about these pictures? They prove . . . "

"They don't prove a thing. They are pictures of some man."

"They are pictures of you."

"And if you don't say anything."

"And, what if I do? No one will believe me. Is that what you are thinking? No one is going to believe a woman who is out of her mind?"

"Dora . . . "

"Don't touch me. Go ahead. Destroy the trunk. He still has these pictures. And he will find you. Or . . . are you . . . "

"Dora . . . please."

"You'd walk out of my life, wouldn't you?"

"My whole life has been about protecting you and him. I'm not about . . . "

"Get out."

"Dora . . . "

"Get out. And this time, don't come back."

108

"You're awake."

"Is that what this is called? You could 'a fooled me. I feel like death warmed over."

"You look like death warmed over."

"Oh . . . my head."

"Don't get up. Here . . . take these."

"What are they?"

"Just take 'em."

"Reece . . . I don't take anything unless I know what it is."

"Pain pills . . . with codeine. Left over from a prescription I had. Just take them."

"Okay . . . stop yelling."

"Do you remember anything about last night?"

"The last thing I remember is you . . . you were a bastard. If that was your idea of . . . "

"Rose . . . "

"A hot erotic evening . . . "

"Rose . . . "

"You fucked up big time. I don't remember . . . "

"Rose . . . "

"Why did you do that chugging crap? I don't remember a thing after that. Did I pass out? You don't have to get me like that to make me do things for you. I might resist at first. But that's part of the game. I thought you liked it when I resisted? You know I'll give you what you want in the end. Oh fuck . . . my head. You know, that stuff's dangerous. You could get alcohol poisoning from doing that."

"I think that was the idea."

"And I had some pretty fucked-up dreams after that, too. More like nightmares. Your ex-bitch was . . . what do you mean that was the idea?"

"Now is not the time to talk about it. Someday I'll show you . . . "

"Show me? Did you videotape last night? I take your silence as a yes. Did you enjoy yourself?"

"It's not what you think."

"Right. Will I be shocked?"

"You'll be shocked all right. But this isn't the time. You need to get some rest."

"Good excuse. If my head wasn't pounding so much, I'd disagree with you. But since it is."

"Get some sleep."

"Oh . . . one other thing. Who is Sage Ventura?"

"Sage . . . how do you know that name?"

"I visited your mother yesterday."

"You what?"

"I went and visited your mother yesterday. I showed her some more pictures of the mystery man."

"Rose, she told us she didn't know him."

"You need to look at the pictures on the table. There's one with her standing next to the man. They're holding hands. She finally confided that his name was Sage . . . Sage Ventura."

109

"Rose. Rose. Wake up."

"What time is it?"

"It's three o'clock."

"In the morning?"

"No, afternoon. I just got a call from the nursing home. My mother is asking for me again. I need to get over there right away."

"I'll go with you."

"No. I think it's best if you stay here."

"Why?"

"Apparently, she's been upset ever since she saw you yesterday."

110

"Mama . . . don't cry." Reece reached across the table for his mother's hands. "Don't even think you have to apologize to me for anything you've ever done in your life."

"Yes . . . yes, I do."

"Mama . . . you've raised me single-handedly since I was four years old. For fifty years you have guided me. Inspired me."

"But, Reece . . . I've lied to you. I've been lying to you my entire life."

"I'm sure you had your reasons."

"I have. I mean, I did. But . . . in hindsight I'm not sure it was the right thing to do."

"Hindsight is always twenty-twenty. I'm sure at the time it was the right thing to do."

"We were scared. Everyone was scared. At the time we thought what we were doing was the right thing. We did it for your own good. Please Reece . . . please forgive me. It was for your own good."

"Mama . . . nothing you've done will ever make me change the way I feel about you."

"I can never make it up to you."

"I'm not asking you to."

"I know. But in the little time I have left, I'd like to try."

"Mama . . . remember what you said. There's the past and there's the future. You can't do anything about the past. The future is all we have that can be changed."

"You're right, my dear. And I'd like to change the future by starting with this." Dora got up from her chair, walked over to the other side of the room, and pulled the towel revealing the black trunk that had been against the wall.

"Mama . . . "

"This belonged to your papa. At some point he wanted you to have it. I guess fifty years has been long enough."

"Mama . . . I remember. Papa's trunk."

"Reece . . . Reece, listen to me. I am giving this to you and trust that you will use your best judgment to determine what should be done with it. As you will soon understand, people's lives are at stake. My life, your life, and others."

The silence was broken by the loud knock on the door as it swung open. "Reece, he's here. I saw him. Look. I got a picture. This time a front view."

"For heaven's sake, Rose. You scared the living daylight out of me."

"Rose, I told you to wait in . . . "

"Reece, it's him!" She held her phone up closer to his face.

"Is that a picture of Sage?"

"Mama . . . who is Sage?"

"Oh, you remember Sage, don't you Reece? He was papa's friend. He was there when papa was . . . "

"Is that the trunk?" Rose walked over to it.

"What is Sage doing here?"

"Don't you want to open it?"

"My dear, you just can't open . . . "

"Rose, before we open it I need to . . . "

"Reece! Do you hear what you are saying? This could be . . . this could be what you've been searching for your entire life. The evidence

. . . hard evidence. The answer to the one question . . . the one question everyone asks about Dealey Plaza could be in this trunk." Rose bent down and pulled on the padlock.

"Mama . . . why is he here?"

"Reece . . . this is an old Master padlock. Wait . . . the key!" She stood up and turned toward Reece. Then she reached into her purse, pulled out the two keys, and handed them to Reece. He didn't reach for them. "What's wrong?"

"We need to think about . . . "

"Three nights ago, if we'd of found this trunk in the storage locker, you wouldn't have hesitated a second to open it. I don't understand?"

"We don't know what's in it."

"It might be the answer you've been looking for."

"And it might have nothing to do with Dealey Plaza or November twenty-second."

"Are you . . . are you afraid to open it?"

"Of course he's afraid to open it, my dear. It's not very often you get a chance to go back in time and re-write history."

"What if . . . "

"There is no what if. You spent your whole life for this moment." Rose again offered him the keys.

"Mama . . . why is Sage here?"

"Why don't you ask him yourself." Dora pointed to the other end of the room. Reece turned to see a man walking through the doorway toward him.

"Hello, Reece." Sage walked over to Reece who already had his hand extended. "Sorry, I don't shake hands. Spreads germs. But I will take a hug." He reached out with both arms. Reece instinctively did the same. "I don't suppose you remember me. Sage . . . Sage Ventura. And you must be Rose." He walked over and gave Rose a hug. "Nice to meet you."

Sage walked over to Dora, hugged her, kissed her on the cheek, then stood next to her. "I see you've shown him the trunk. It's still locked. Do you need a key?" Sage started to reach into his pocket.

"They have a key, dear. Rose."

"What's the hold-up? I thought you'd have that old trunk opened and emptied by now."

"That's what I said."

"Maybe you should open it, Rose?"

"Hold on. Am I . . . am I the only one even curious as to what the hell is going on here?"

"Isn't that obvious? You've spent fifty years trying to find the answer to what happened in Dealey Plaza. The answer might be in that trunk. Go ahead . . . open it."

"Mama . . . you said people's lives were at stake."

"Don't pay no mind to your mama, boy. What could possibly be in that trunk that could cause anyone any harm after fifty years?"

"The truth."

"The truth, Rose? The truth isn't supposed to harm you. Lies and cover-ups harm you. Truth liberates."

"Not when the truth isn't in everyone's best interest."

"And when might that be, Rose?"

"When an event happens that is so shocking, that it has the potential to topple the very fabric of a nation."

"That's a good point. Or, how about when that event happens right when you and your enemy are looking for the slightest reason to be the first to push a button and hopefully annihilate the other before they can respond. Combine these two events and what do you think the leadership of a nation might be willing to do to preserve itself?"

"Hold on. The two of you sound like you're reading from the original writings of the first conspiracy theorists."

"Well, Reece. Isn't that when most conspiracies are born? During the first minutes, hours, or days following an event? When there is the most fear and confusion. When we are searching for an answer, and any answer, no matter how bazaar, is better than no answer."

"And you're saying this trunk has something to do with finding that answer? The real answer to what happened in Dealey Plaza?"

"That, I will leave up to you to determine. After all, you are the expert. What I can tell you is the camera you held in Dealey Plaza that day is in there. So is the movie camera your father held."

"But . . . where . . . why . . . why now?"

"Your father wanted you to eventually have it. Dora and . . . your mama felt after fifty years, now was the right time."

"I needed to give it to you before I . . . before I forgot what it was I was supposed to give you."

"Can we open . . . "

"Nothing is stopping you, Reece. Here's the key." Rose dropped the keys into Reece's open hand.

"What's in there has only ever been seen by me and your mother. It's yours now and you are certainly free to do with it as you please. My only request, or what I should say is our only request, is that you use your best judgement to determine what should be done with it."

"It sounds to me as if the two of you had your speeches rehearsed."

"We have both given this a lot of thought over the years, Reece. I have always tried to balance your father's wants and wishes with my own needs. At times that has been difficult for me to do."

"Mama . . . don't cry."

"I know. I shouldn't be crying. I've been waiting a long time for this day. I should be feeling relieved that all this deceit is finally over. I guess I've lived with it for so long the reality hasn't hit me yet."

"We only ask that you be careful with what has been kept secret for fifty years."

"I guess it would only be appropriate that I open this with you present."

"You can do as you wish, Reece. But as I recall, some things in there might need explaining from me. We wouldn't want to start a new conspiracy theory."

"No mama, we wouldn't."

"Perhaps I should leave,"

"And me too."

"No. Absolutely not. I feel . . . you both should share in this." Reece stood in front of the trunk for several seconds before he knelt down, inserted the key into the padlock, and turned it.

111

"It's so peaceful here, isn't it?"

"Yes . . . yes it is, Dora."

"This has been the best summer of my life."

"It sure has gone by quickly."

"Did I ever tell you my theory on why that is so?"

"Yes . . . yes you have, Dora."

"Sorry . . . it's the Alzheimer's."

"Since we've been up here I've seen a marked improvement in you. Don't you agree?"

"I thought I've been doing better over the past year. But, you're right. These past two months up here at the cabin . . . I feel free. Free to roam physically. And free to let my mind roam without thinking about . . . telling the truth, or telling a lie. As I said . . . the best summer of my life."

"And I've enjoyed Reece's visits."

"You two seemed to have bonded."

"It was difficult at first."

"Probably having something to do with sleeping with his mama."

"I'm sure it was. But he's seemed to have gotten over it."

"He must have. After all, he gave his blessing to let me move out of Loretto and move in with you. Another reason why we should have told him about our secrets long ago. Look at how much fun we've been having . . . you know, sexually."

"I thought our little trysts were always fun."

"The risk of getting caught does add a little excitement to it, doesn't it?"

"I think Reece knows how much we care for one another."

"I'm so glad you are getting to know him like I do."

"And what about you bonding with Rose."

"She's good for him."

"She is. They seem very happy together. Like you and me."

"They are handling things very responsibly, don't you think?"

"Yes . . . yes I do. But as Reece told me last time he was here, they still aren't done analyzing all the evidence that was in the trunk. The photos. The movie. As we asked, they are taking their time."

"Well, you better hope they give us more warning before they pop in on us next time."

"I think they will. They know we were down by the creek, naked. And, having sex."

"The having sex part is not what bothers me. It's the naked part."

"And why is that?"

"Well, actually not my nakedness, but yours."

"I'm listening."

"I would hate to have Reece see that scar on your side and ask you how you got it. I don't think it would take him long to figure out you got it in Dealey Plaza."

"You're probably right."

"Probably?"

"You are right. In fact, I'm surprised he hasn't figured it out yet."

"Would you like me to help . . . "

"No! Not you . . . or her either. Let him figure it out on his own."

"We should have told him."

"We both agreed it would be better to wait until we saw how he handled the other stuff. Don't forget . . . someone tried to kill me on

November . . . ”

“We think . . . ”

“Sage is dead.”

“You’re right. But he has handled it well.”

“Yes, he has.”

“We raised a good boy.”

“You raised a good boy.”

“You were there, in the background, the entire time.”

“I wish . . . ”

“Don’t. It’s the past.”

“You’re right. It’s the past.”

“But . . . what if he doesn’t figure it out?”

“Then we’ll tell him . . . eventually. Besides, if you keep slipping up and calling me Carl, he’s going to figure it out soon enough.”

“And what about the bullet? Isn’t that important evidence? Hard evidence?”

“Not really. I dug it up myself. But there is no proof of it. The chain of custody has been broken.”

“Where is it?”

“It’s in a safe place.”

“Do you mind telling me where? What if something happens to you?”

“There’s a fake bottom in the trunk. It’s hidden there.”

112

“This has been the best summer of my life.”

“Mine too.”

“How can the sex keep getting better and better?”

“Rosetta Stone, is that the only reason why this has been the best summer of your life?”

“No . . . but it sure has helped. Oh . . . and you don’t feel the same way, Dr. Landis?”

“Keep talking like that and I’ll show you how I feel right here on the beach.”

“Shouldn’t you be getting back to writing your book?”

“I got writers block. I thought I’d come out here and lay with you in the sun for a while.”

“So . . . me laying here topless had nothing to do with it?”

“I’ll take inspiration any way I can get it.”

“Answer me this, Dr. Landis. How come in the last two months we have been to six of the most beautiful resorts in the Caribbean, tucked back in a secluded bungalow, on a gorgeous white or pink sand beach, that also happens to be clothing optional?”

“That’s easy. First, I need the seclusion if I’m ever going to finish my book and get it published before the fiftieth anniversary of JFK’s death.

Second, I need beautiful scenery to motivate me. And third, I need a companion who will whip me back into shape if I start to slack off on my writing."

"So, are you saying that all I needed to do was lock you down in your playroom, walk around naked all day, carry a leather flogger, and that would have sufficed?"

"Damn . . . look at the money I would have saved!"

"Something tells me the plot wouldn't come out as well with the latter."

"Don't underestimate your talents, Ms. Stone."

"And what about Meeka?"

"Ah, yes. The fourth reason for staying away from Syracuse. I'm hoping she will get tired of stalking an empty house and find someone else to play with."

"Are you talking about me, or you?"

"You, of course."

"Thank you."

"For what?"

"For saving my life that night."

"So much for me coming home early and surprising you."

"Oh, I bet you were the surprised one."

"Surprised . . . that would be an understatement."

"Seriously, Reece. How's the book coming?"

"You tell me. You've been reading and editing every page I produce."

"I've told you. I think it's great. Although I'm a little biased. But . . . are you gonna finish in time?"

"It depends on how I end it."

"You don't know how you're gonna end it?"

"I have a few thoughts."

"A few thoughts? You've got a month left if you want to get it to the printer in time, and you have a few thoughts? That doesn't give me a comfortable feeling, Dr. Landis."

"I'm leaning toward the ending we talked about at dinner two nights ago."

"I thought that was a great one."

"You think they are all great ones."

"They are."

"Is that your unbiased opinion?"

"Very objective."

"You don't think he will be upset?"

"I think it will be a perfect way to let him know that you know."

"And I shouldn't verify my facts ahead of time?"

"Reece, the facial recognition software was ninety-nine percent confident. Sage is Carl Landis. Or should I say, Carl Landis is Sage. Sage is your father."

"And the scar?"

"You saw the computer enhanced photograph. It's definitely a scar. Although I still want to know how you knew they would be down at the creek, naked."

"I didn't. I mean. I thought they were down there, but not totally naked."

"They were naked. And doing other things besides wading in the creek. Sluts."

"Like son, like father and mother."

"I guess so."

"But . . . what about . . . someone tried to kill him that night. What if . . . "

"It's all circumstantial, Reece. And anyway, it was fifty years ago. Chances are . . . "

"Chances are? It's what he's feared all his life. It's why I didn't have a father to grow up with."

"At the time, I'm sure it was the right decision. No . . . looking at all the facts, it was the right decision. But . . . but, now it's over."

"Is fifty years long enough?"

"Reece, your father was wounded in Dealey Plaza on November 22, 1963 by a second gunman who shot at the president of the United States and missed. It's a great story. And a great ending for your novel."

"For fifty years only the conspiracy nuts believed that the blotch in the Moorman's Polaroid photograph was a gunman. Hard to believe the picture I took in Dealey Plaza that day with a thirty-five millimeter Pentax shows him clear as day, just as he took his shot."

"You must have flinched at the sound of that last shot, because that picture was the only one not of the motorcycles or the president in the limousine"

"Unfortunately, we still can't make out the face."

"But, isn't that why you decided to write a novel? Float the theory out there and see if someone finally comes forward?"

"If they do, hopefully you can work your magic with your computer to come up with a match."

"Are you going to confront him?"

"Yes . . . when we visit them next week."

"I think he wants to tell you, Reece."

"And if he does . . . "

"He's going to."

"I'm going to interview him about his time with Oswald in Japan. That needs to get into this book."

"It was probably another reason why they did what they did on the day of the assassination. He was in Dealey Plaza less than twenty feet from the president when he was assassinated. The police came to the house looking for him. The accident. And then, he probably found out the suspected assassin was someone he had spent time with in the past. Synergy at work. Any rational human being would have probably done the same thing. He had to disappear."

113

"Could I ask everyone to take your seat please, so we can get started again? We still have a long evening ahead of us."

The thirteen elderly men gathered their drinks – mostly expensive bourbons and cognacs – and cigars – mostly Cuban – and each took a seat in one of the high-backed leather chairs surrounding the twenty-one foot diameter mahogany table. There were thirteen to assure there would never be a tie vote. The men were considered elderly because no one was allowed to sit at the table unless they were at least sixty-five, although there was no written rule forbidding it. They were all men because that's the way it had always been. And the table was twenty-one feet in diameter to allow for five feet of space for each of them.

The group had no name which made it easier to deny it existed, and that you belonged to it. There were no by-laws, no written history, and no rules of order. In fact no notes were allowed to be taken during the meeting, nor was anything allowed to be written down after the meeting. No one else knew of the meeting, except for the thirteen, and even some of them upon leaving would question whether it really happened or not.

"I don't think those before us ever envisioned a digital world where everyone was instantly connected to everyone else. Seven billion people in the world and six billion of them have access to a cell phone. That's almost two billion more than have access to a toilet."

"What are you saying?"

"I'm saying . . . are we obsolete?"

"You mean . . . because we are all out of touch?"

"No . . . because of our inability to control things. Like we used to be able to. A lone uneducated protester with a cell phone anywhere in the world now has the power to change the course of human history. Create movements. Oust leaders. Topple governments. One person potentially has more power than we've ever had."

"Gentlemen . . . do not forget. Those before us struggled with similar disruptive threats we face today. The pen and paper, printing press, mass-media, radio, and television all threatened us in the past. Yet . . . we found a way to use each to our advantage. We will do the same with the instantly connected world. If a lone uneducated protester with no plan can do it, think what we should be able to accomplish."

"I agree. The way I see it, we are needed now more than ever. The fate of mankind cannot be left to chance."

"Very well put. End of philosophizing. Let's get back to business. Before dinner we were discussing the issue with the New York City Foundation."

"I know this is contrary with what we were just discussing, but in this case I say let it play out."

"I agree."

"It's been fifty years."

"Sometimes you can't put a time limit on these things."

"Do people still care about this?"

"Care . . . they're still talking about the Lincoln assassination. Of course they care. Especially when they smell a conspiracy."

"They should have never tried to cover it up. They should have let it play out. Two shooters. Neither one knowing of the other. There would have been so much pressure to draw a connection between the two, it would have overshadowed things for a hundred years. They blew it."

"Gentlemen . . . might I remind you. They is now us. We need to decide what to do."

"I say let this Landis character come out with his book. It will eventually fall on the conspiracy pile just like all of the other theories. Our predecessors did their job. We continue to do ours. It's time to move on to more pressing issues."

"I agree."

"All those in favor of letting this play out as is raise your hand."

Epilogue

November 22, 2013

"As I stated when I started my talk, fifty years ago today, ironically on a Friday very similar to this one, my innocence was taken from me. For years I searched for the truth about what really happened in Dealey Plaza that day. It took writing this book, a novel mind you, which is defined as a book of lies, to finally sort out and come to terms with the truth.

"Finally, I'd like to again thank the Rosamond Gifford Lecture Series for having me here tonight. And thank you, the audience, for coming. That said, who has the first question?"

Reece took a sip of water and looked up at the standing-room-only crowd that was packed into the Mulroy Civic Center in downtown Syracuse. He chose this venue, on the fiftieth anniversary of the assassination, as the one to debut his book about the new evidence uncovered regarding the JFK assassination. He pointed to a woman in the third row directly in front of him.

"Are you surprised that the book is on the *New York Times* best seller list after a few short weeks?"

"Surprised would be one way to put it, but probably thankful to you the readers for putting it there would be more appropriate."

"How were you able to complete the book in less than three months?"

"Although it took me less than three months to write the first draft, don't forget, I had been thinking about the topic for almost fifty years."

"You are exposing a new theory about the assassination. It is based on new evidence uncovered almost fifty years after the assassination. Why write about it in fiction?"

"That's a great question, one I thought about long and hard before I wrote my first word. There have been thousands of non-fiction books written about the JFK assassination that many believed were simply not true. The goal with fiction is to take a story that the reader knows is not true, and convince her that it is. To make her ask, 'There is no way it could have happened like that, could it?' This story . . . this story is so incredible that I felt the best way to make it believable was to write it as fiction. I present you with the same conflicting evidence I've encountered over the years and let you, the reader, come to your own conclusions."

"How much of it is based on fact?"

"In my opinion every author, even a fiction writer, to some extent bases what he writes about on both research and his own life experiences. In this case, my research was very much a part of my life experiences. So, much of what is stated in the book is based on actual fact, or hard evidence, albeit in some cases circumstantial, but none the less, factual."

"What about the trunk?" Someone yelled from the balcony. The rest of the auditorium went silent.

"Thc trunk was real."

"What about the sex?" Yelled someone else, but this time the audience erupted in laughter.

"The sex was obviously a fantasy." More laughter and applause. "Based on reality. Next question . . . ycs."

"If the trunk was rcal, what was really in it?"

"As was hinted to in the book, the actual camera held by me and the movie camera held by my father were in the trunk. The original pictures and negatives, and the actual original copy of the movie, were also in the trunk. That evidence provided the needed hard evidence to support the second shooter theory."

"Was your father really wounded in Dealey Plaza?"

"Yes . . . yes, he was."

"Was it your father or Sage Ventura who drove into town on the afternoon of the assassination?"

"The answer to that question is buried in the past."

"Was it an accident or was he deliberately run off the road?"

"There is nothing to suggest it wasn't an accident. Obviously, at the time, those involved thought it . . . well they thought differently. The subsequent fire was set after the fact to support the story that the photographic evidence from Dealey Plaza was also destroyed."

"How does it feel to know that someday you may be the last surviving eyewitness to the Kennedy assassination?"

"Ever since I was old enough to understand, I knew I was put in that place, at that time, for a reason. Those brief seconds in Dallas have . . . have haunted me, like they have haunted so many others, for fifty years. No matter what secrets continue to be uncovered, I suspect I will continue to be haunted by this for the rest of my life. Being the last witness will only be worth it if it leads to the truth."

"If you could go back to the morning of November twenty-second, would you do anything differently?"

Reece looked down at his mother, father, and Rose who were sitting directly in front of him in the first row. "Yes . . . yes, I would."

"What would that be?"

"The answer to that, my friend, will be in my next book."